The Genie's Heartwish

Heartwishes, Volume 2

Daisy Dexter Dobbs

Published by Department of Daydreams, LLC, 2022.

THE GENIE'S HEARTWISH

First edition. June 14, 2022.

Copyright © 2022 Daisy Dexter Dobbs.

ISBN: 978-1587850844

Written by Daisy Dexter Dobbs.

This book is joyously dedicated to my husband, Mike. Being married to him is like having my own personal genie. Mike's uncanny ability to keep me laughing, even when he's telling the same groan-worthy dad jokes repeatedly for decades, is the closest thing to magic I've experienced. A good bout of laughter is powerfully healing. It really is the best medicine, and Mike inherently seems to know that. If I had three genie wishes, one of them would be to ensure I never lose the ability to laugh, especially at myself. Want to know my secret for happiness? Combine one part laughter, one part soul-deep love, and one terrific guy like Mike, and you've created a jubilation elixir better than any genie could blink up. I'm truly one very fortunate woman.

ABOUT THIS BOOK

~<>~

In the musty basement of a historic mansion, thrift sale enthusiast Laila Malone rummages through estate sale castoffs and laughingly wonders if the ancient bottle she's just unearthed might be worth a fortune.

Uncorking it, she gasps as an imposing, saber-wielding genie whooshes out in a vapor. With sun-bronzed muscles, long dark hair and hypnotic eyes, he's devastatingly handsome, the epitome of her fantasies. And he claims he's here to give her pleasure? Well hell, if she has to lose her mind, this is exactly the hallucination she wants.

Five thousand years ago, Sumerian warrior Zakkar Tymon gallantly protected the virtue of a love struck virgin priestess, dooming him to an eternity of servitude to women. Reduced to being a slave to women's impulses, the bold, brave hero now exists solely to give women pleasure, act upon their every urge, and grant them three wishes before being sucked back into the cold, dark, empty abyss of the bottle.

Zak's newest possessor, Laila, is an opinionated female who spouts gibberish, speaks into a handheld box, instantly cooks food in a magic contrivance, and wears male garb rather than flowing dresses more befitting a woman. Her considerable potential stirs Zak's desire to grant the wide-eyed beauty all the pleasure she deserves.

Heartwishes, Book 2: Stubborn warrior hero with heart of gold, selfless devoted heroine, abundant humor, adorable dog, heartrending choices, snarky powerful goddess, fantasy, and a magnificent magical noble wish. This guaranteed HEA romcom can be read as a standalone but is better appreciated when read in order.

Chapter 1

Glassfloat Bay, Oregon: present day

~<>~

"EMPATHY AND SYMPATHY, people. That's key," Bunny Turner stated with conviction, rapping her pointer against the image on the screen. "If we want to keep clients coming back, we must convince them we know what they're going through." Her gaze roamed the crowd. The picture of sincerity, she tapped her fingers on her chest in the area where her heart would be—if she had one. "Let them know we've been there too. That we feel their pain."

Laila Malone knew what was coming next. Working for Tuned by Turner the last few years, she'd been through enough of her boss's corporate training seminars to be able to repeat the rarely varying sermon word for word.

And how do we make clients believe we've been tubby and can relate with their problems if it's not true? Laila silently mouthed along as Bunny spoke, resisting the temptation to roll her eyes and groan.

"With creative embellishment!" the room of weight loss counselors replied.

Nodding, Bunny offered a calculated smile. "While TBT offers a proven weight loss program incorporating diet, counseling and exercise along with our nutritious line of packaged foods, those aren't the things that keep our satisfied clients coming back each week, is it?"

"No," the counselors dutifully chorused.

"It's you." Bunny's voice was a reverent whisper while her benevolent smile bordered on heartfelt tears. "Without dedicated counselors, Tuned by Turner would be just another diet

1

program." Bunny's brown-eyed gaze swept the room of ninety men and women who had traveled to TBT's corporate hub in the small coastal town. "Let me hear it. What are we, people?"

"We're number one!" Hoots, hollers and clapping ensued as the troops rallied. Punching her fist high into the air, Bunny boasted a proud grin.

"At Tuned by Turner we turn tubbies into triumphs!" Bunny crowed.

While most overweight women don't like being called fat, Laila seriously doubted they found *tubby* any more endearing. With a surreptitious gaze around the room, she noted only a handful of the counselors were bigger than a size four.

She'd often heard her lean coworkers, most of whom had never been overweight by more than five pounds, openly ridiculing overweight clients behind their backs.

An eighty pound weight loss veteran, Laila had a strong sense of compassion for TBT's clients. She didn't need *creative embellishment* to understand what it was like to be the fattest woman in the room, to catch people snickering behind her back, to be heartbroken when a glimpse in the mirror revealed a reflection looking nothing like her imagined self.

She'd also learned losing weight wasn't necessarily a panacea. Shifting one's internal self-perception wasn't easy. Sometimes she'd catch her reflection in a store window, momentarily wondering who the slender, attractive blue-eyed brunette was staring back at her. Her default thinking still had her picturing herself as...tubby.

Still waiting for the profusion of changes guaranteed to come with weight loss, Laila felt cheated. The diet industry promised her life would transform after reaching her goal. Men were supposed to fall at her feet, dumbstruck by her leaner visage.

Although finding good men was challenging, Laila knew they were out there. Her fiancé, Tim McKevitt, had been a salt of the earth sort of guy. He lost his life three years ago, falling into an icy crevasse in Antarctica.

"Take me for example."

Bunny's commanding voice snapped Laila back to the present as the chic owner of TBT gestured to her pink-suited, model-thin frame.

"I convince clients that I can personally relate to diet and deprivation. They know I once battled a heartbreaking weight problem." She paused before adding, "It's true. I used to be nearly obese." Bunny validated her statement by puffing out her cheeks and positioning her arms to indicate a substantial belly. With a sensitive sniffle, she shuddered as she smoothed her TBT-pink fingernails along her beige-blonde hair, tucking a nonexistent stray lock into the bun at her nape.

"I ate my way all the way up to a size six back in college." A practiced speaker, Bunny allowed for a pregnant pause, slowly nodding as her gaze swept the room. "It took me more than a semester of living on coffee, lettuce, cigarettes, and sticking my fingers down my throat to get back into my size zeros."

Formerly a luxury car saleswoman, Bunny Turner had built a financial empire on her reputation as a fat guru. Disillusioned, Laila discovered early on that Bunny was cold, calculating and devoid of compassion. Especially when it came to TBT clients, people who'd struggled with the pain and complexities of living as a fat person in a thin world.

"Get ready," Laila's sister Maureen whispered near her ear. "Here comes the glorified bullshit."

Laila bit the inside of her cheek to keep from laughing at Reen's knowing remark. Her cute, sassy blonde sister was one of the only other people over the age of thirty in the room, and one of the only who'd lost a significant amount of weight.

Reen's fiancé had also died. Robert Brechler was an English professor. He and Reen purchased a house together, a fixer-upper, to move in after their wedding. They were happily making wedding plans until Bob fell off the roof while repairing the shingles. He and Tim died within weeks of each other.

Laila and Reen supported each other through their weight loss journeys, and the loss of their loves.

Emotional eating had the sisters packing on pounds due to stress, grief, and loneliness, along with poor eating habits. After losing weight, Laila and Reen applied for employment at Tuned by Turner, idealistic in their shared mission of helping people shed excess weight and live healthier, happier lives.

"Of course," Bunny continued, "it wouldn't be prudent for me to expound on how I actually lost the weight. I allow clients to believe I accomplished it by following TBT methods. It's essentially a helpful LWL. *Little white lie*," she clarified, hanging invisible quotes over the words with her fingers.

"That LWL doesn't hurt anyone because TBT is the best weight loss solution out there. Since we care, *really and truly care*," her expression was infused with soap opera dramatics, "about their health and wellbeing, we understand how LWLs can help clients achieve their goals. Right, counselors?"

The room exploded with shouts of "Right!" and booming applause while Laila and Reen slunk low in their chairs, exchanging dubious looks.

As the session closed, Bunny held aloft a navy blue canvas bag embroidered with the company's pink logo. "I'm giving each of you a TBT tote containing our ten newest foods. They're dynamite, people. Fabulous fat-burning gems."

Setting the bag on the table behind her, she drew out each *gem*, describing them in such a way that would make anyone unfamiliar with TBT's line of foods salivate. Those already familiar with the company's barely palatable edibles knew better.

Arms wide, in a universal embrace, Bunny told them, "During lunch you'll sample our tofu-based salad dressings, shelf-stable Saucy Chicken Cakes, and...are you ready?" Bunny looked as if she were about to announce she'd be serving gooey hot fudge sundaes. "Our brand new Berry-Lime Tapioca Tofu Pudding Cups!"

Again, rousing applause, while Laila and Reen engaged in inadvertent shudders.

"Our poor clients," Laila muttered beneath her breath.

"Your main focus this quarter, counselors, is to push TBT foods. Sell, sell, sell, people! Remember, our main revenue comes from our exclusive line of foods. And the more money TBT makes, the more money you make!"

"Sell, sell, sell, huh?" Reen whispered to Laila. "Heck, I can't even give those foods away they taste so bad."

"Makes you wonder who they use as taste testers," Laila whispered back.

With a confirming nod, Reen murmured, "My mind is screaming *Dutch baby!* Let's grab one at Griffin's Café after we get out of here."

Laila gave her sister a sideways glance. If she didn't watch herself under Reen's dastardly influence she'd start packing on the pounds again. "I'll split one with you."

"Bacon too? Seriously, what's a puffy pancake without bacon?" Reen gave a wicked conspirator's wink. "We deserve it. We've been soooo good. Um...unless you'd rather stick around and dig into tapioca tofu pudding cups instead."

Just the name was enough to make Laila wince. "Bacon it is. Just a strip. And only if we walk afterward."

"Deal."

At the end of the seminar, Laila and Reen claimed their embroidered totes packed full of inedible edibles before surreptitiously heading for the exit. They almost made it before Bunny's piercing voice seized them.

"Uh-oh..." Laila recalled the last time they'd tried to sneak out of a meeting only to have Bunny hook them into being on a panel to sample the newest foodstuffs. Laila had no appetite the rest of the day after ingesting all that gloppy, chemical-laden stuff that tried to pass for real food.

"Oh please God, please, please, please don't let her make us stay for lunch again," Reen muttered, crossing the fingers on both hands and closing her eyes.

In lieu of an invitation to dine on TBT *goodies*, Bunny handed each of them a sealed letter. After brief innocuous small talk, she turned on her stiletto heel, wiggling her miniscule butt as she headed for the unappetizing lunch spread.

"Let's get the hell out of here while we can." Reen snagged Laila's uniform jacket, hauling her to the door.

~<>~

"I haven't seen you two in here in weeks," Annalise Griffin, owner of the retro-themed café said, handing menus to Laila and Reen. "Great to see you back."

"Thanks, Annalise. It's been too long since we've treated ourselves to one of your Dutch baby pancakes," Reen said.

"How've you been doing?" Laila asked.

"Good. Crazy busy—and you won't hear me complaining about that." She grinned. "Lots of tourists lately. I need to add a couple more servers. My sister, Sabrina, is moving back home from Pennsylvania." Annalise's expression twisted. "She just filed for divorce and said she'll need a job so that'll work out great."

"Sorry about the divorce," Laila said. "I'm glad we'll finally get a chance to meet her though. She was already gone when we moved here from Chicago."

"You'll love her. She's a doll and so is my adorable little nephew, Harry."

"How's Hud doing," Reen asked, dropping her gaze to the tabletop and drawing invisible circles with her finger. "Is he around?"

"Nope. Hudson doesn't take time to eat." Annalise tsked. "I think my brother's even busier than I am. The guy never stops working. He and his crew are renovating the old library. You can imagine what a job that is. Hey, I've made some changes around here too. What do you think?"

"I was just checking it out. I love what you've done," Laila gestured across the room. "The corner area with the loveseat, coffee table and cushy-looking chairs looks so cozy and inviting."

"It's a big thumbs up from me," Reen agreed, making the sign.

"Thanks. I'm getting a lot of positive feedback from the customers. I got the furniture at the Maythorne Manor estate sale up on the hill. It's been going on the past few days. Have you two gone yet?"

"No." Laila gave a little bounce of excitement. "I had no idea."

"Thanks a lot, Annalise," Reen said with mock annoyance. "Now she's going to drag me all the way up to Beauregard Hill just so we can go to that sale."

Annalise laughed. "It's worth it, Reen. Aside from furniture, they're selling most everything else too. You're still knitting and crocheting, right?"

Laila laughed at that. Before Reen could answer, she said, "Are you kidding? The two things Reen will never give up are knitting and chocolate."

"I saw lots of yarn when I was there," Annalise told Reen. "Skeins in all different colors." Her eyebrows jiggled playfully.

Reen's eyes went wide. "Really?"

"You did agree to a walk," Laila reminded her sister, nailing her with her best guilt-producing look. "Can you think of a better way to burn off the bazillion calorie lunch we're about to order? Plus you know you can't ignore the lure of yarn."

Folding her arms across her chest, Reen sat back in her seat and grumbled. "I suppose."

Returning her attention to Annalise, Laila asked, "Did you spot any baking-related stuff, or ceramic salt and pepper shakers?" While she'd been trying to cut back on her packrat tendencies, she had a passion for collecting kitchen antiques.

"Yes and yes." Annalise smiled.

"Great. We'll be there all afternoon," Reen mumbled.

"Yarn," Laila reminded her.

"Have you heard anything lately from Delaney, or your mom and stepdad?" Annalise polished the gray marbleized 50s era chrome-trimmed Formica table as she spoke. She was one of the first people their sister, Delaney, met when she moved to Glassfloat Bay from Chicago.

"Delaney and Varik are due back from their honeymoon cruise anytime now, and Mom and Tore are still enjoying themselves at their cabin in Norway," Laila said.

"Last time I talked to Mom," Reen added, "she said they'd be back in another month or so."

"I've got to tell you, a vacation sounds good just about now." Annalise flashed a bright smile. "So you're here for Dutch babies? I've also got a killer pecan pie fresh baked this morning."

"Oh my God, Annalise," placing her hands over her ears, Reen laughed, "don't tell us that. We're just going to split the pancake."

"No need. I've got special kid-portion pans that make half-sized Dutch babies. I'll make one for each of you, along with plenty of fresh lemon wedges, lots of butter and powdered sugar."

"And a side of bacon for us to split," Reen added.

Laila groaned. "I think I gained five pounds just listening to that description."

"Oh puhleez. Look at you two." Stepping back, Annalise studied them. "You're practically skinny."

Laila nearly choked on her sip of water. "We need to come in here more often. I forgot what a great BS-er you are, Annalise."

"I'm not kidding. You look great. Sooo...eating that TBT diet food must be the secret? Or, um," she leaned down, elbowing Laila, "maybe it's staying away from their godawful food that did the trick."

Laila and Reen shared knowing smiles.

"Let's just say Reen and I do our best to follow TBT's guidelines," Laila replied diplomatically.

The 30-something café owner bent toward them, cupping her hand at the side of her mouth. "Tried their food myself once."

"You were on their program?" Reen said.

"Nope. I just had to give it a try after hearing from some of my customers how awful it was. I figured they must be exaggerating because nothing could taste *that* bad." She made an exaggerated eye roll. "I was wrong. You should talk to their management team, Laila. Strike a deal to have them include your amazing reduced calorie scones in their food line. They fly out of here each time you bring in a batch."

"That's what I keep telling her," Reen said, rapping the tabletop with her fingers.

"Thanks...but I highly doubt Bunny would be interested."

After jotting down their order, Annalise was off.

"See, I told you we look good," Reen said. "Even if we have gained a few pounds each, those threatening letters we got from corporate are ridiculous."

"Do not," Laila raised a cautionary finger, "mention those contemptible letters until after we leave. I'm already feeling guilty ordering a Dutch baby and bacon. If I'm going to eat it I want to enjoy it."

"Not a word." Reen made a locking motion over her lips. "Pecan pie."

"What?" Laila shot her a disbelieving look.

"Sorry," Reen shrugged, "that just sort of slipped out."

"Well don't let it slip out again because we are absolutely not having any pecan pie. Honestly, Maureen, you're such a bad influence!"

"We both know Annalise is right about TBT's food," Reen said as they waited for their order. "Just the thought of eating it makes me..." An involuntary shudder finished her sentence better than any words. "If TBT sold your healthy baked goods, Laila, the clients would be thrilled. Why not talk to Bunny about contracting you to provide your scones, muffins, and cookies?"

"Bunny?" Laila gave Reen a deliberate look. "That would mean she'd have to pay me something, Reen, and we're talking about—"

"Tightwad Turner." Reen sighed. "Say no more. Besides, she'd hate giving you the credit when the compliments started rolling in."

"Right. She's not our biggest fan," Laila reminded her. "Plus I'd be making the food out of my own kitchen and I doubt insurance would cover that. A business insurance policy would cost a small fortune."

"Well we heard that the Crowe sisters are planning to close their bakery and retire to Barcelona. Maybe you could buy—"

"Reen..." Laila closed her eyes in a long blink. "Caroline and Peggy Crowe are close to eighty. They've been talking about selling the bakery for the last ten years. I doubt they have any intention of retiring, much less moving all the way to Spain."

"Yeah, I guess," Reen agreed. "I wouldn't be surprised if they're still there baking when they're ninety."

"There's no way I could afford to buy Crowe's Coastside Bakery or any other bake shop, anyway. I can barely make ends meet as it is. Although..." she gazed off into the distance as a familiar daydream took hold, "I'd give anything to own that beautiful historic building with all its Victorian charm. It's in a prime location too, right on Ocean Charm Boulevard."

Once they were served, she salivated while spreading butter and squeezing lemon wedges all over her pancake. Reen was ahead of her, already spooning powdered sugar over her eggy pancake.

"An approved Tuned by Turner meal, I see," a familiar voice said, dripping with so much sarcasm Laila feared it would plop onto their Dutch babies.

Nothing good ever came from run-ins with Saffron Devington, their ice queen cousin. A glance at the woman's conservative navy skirted suit told her Saffron must be working. With her rich nutmeg-brown hair and deep blue eyes, the stunning woman always seemed to look like a mortician. The daughter of their late father's sister, Colleen Malone Devington, Saffron was a real estate agent.

"Stuff it, Saffy," Reen said, not bothering to look up at their cousin.

"These are kid-sized portions," Laila offered, hoping it made their calorific indulgence sound more acceptable while, at the same time, being angry at herself for feeling the need to make any explanations about what she ate.

"So, five thousand calories instead of ten thousand, hmm?" Folding her arms across her chest, Saffron sneered. "Keep this up and you'll be TBT clients instead of counselors." She poked her finger in Reen's direction. "And stop calling me Saffy. You know I hate that."

Reen looked up now. "Sorry, Saffy. Wanna bite?" She waved one of the thick strips of crisped bacon beneath her cousin's nose.

"You think you're so funny, don't you, Maureen?" Resting her hands on the edge of their table, Saffron leaned down. "I wonder what my good friend Bunny Turner would say if she knew her counselors were seen eating one of these artery cloggers at the local greasy spoon."

"What I want to know, Saf," Reen glared at her cousin, "is what you're doing eating lunch at a place so obviously beneath you."

With a quick look around, Saffron spoke discreetly. "Needless to say, it's my buyers' choice, not mine." Spotting a man and woman entering the diner, she straightened, turned on her heel and headed for the couple, greeting them with her syrupy saleswoman shtick.

"Saffy's just as much of a stick in the mud now as she was when she was ten," Laila noted before sinking her teeth into her first forkful of pancake and humming her delight.

"I guess that's what happens when you grow up in a rich, pretentious family," Reen said. "Weird how she and Lorraine, are so much alike and their brother, Red, is so opposite."

"Hard to believe Lorraine is even worse than Saffron," Laila said. "Poor Red. He's such a sweetheart. I can't even imagine having those two as my big sisters."

The troublemaking Saffron aside, their Dutch baby lunch was delicious. Laila made sure to leave a bite of the pancake on her plate along with an inch of bacon, just to prove to herself she could. Although the bacon called to her while she and Reen chatted, Laila remained unflinchingly strong.

Until...

Along with their check, Annalise brought a slim slice of pecan pie with two forks—on the house. "I don't want to sabotage your diets," she explained, "so I just brought a sliver for you to sample. Enjoy!"

"We're doomed." Reen stared at the nut-crusted slice.

"Talk about sugar overload... Laila eyed the tempting sweet. "Aw what the hell." She picked up her dessert fork, digging in to half the slice and enjoying every last calorific morsel.

Heading out of the restaurant, she confessed to Reen, "Our discussion about opening a bakery, as well as all the sugar we just ingested," she laughed, "got me thinking."

"Good."

"Picture it, Reen." She spread her hands through the air, willing her sister to see what Laila envisioned. "My own bake shop brimming with healthier versions of decadent treats...muffins, scones, cakes, cookies and breads for people counting calories, as well as those who are vegan or paleo, gluten-free, sugar-free, and for diabetics too. I could help people by making weight loss pleasant instead of a drudge."

"You could help people like..." Reen's expression twisted, "poor obese Bunny."

"A whopping size six." Laila groaned. "Can you believe her?"

"Last time I checked, I think one of my thighs was a size six." Glancing down, Reen smacked her leg.

They window shopped as they walked, with Laila tugging Reen away from the gloriously tempting windows of Crowe's Coastside Bakery. The aroma wafting from the bakery as a customer opened the door to enter was an absolute killer. It cemented them in place, mesmerized.

"Oh my God, Laila, look." Reen pointed at the sign in the window. "It's their final day of business. I can't believe it. I never thought they'd actually retire."

Sucking in a deep breath, Laila was stunned. "It's for sale. The bakery, all the equipment, and the whole building, including their fully furnished apartment. Wow..." She took a few steps back to take in the large storefront and the building in general. "Remember that time the Crowe sisters invited us to afternoon tea in their apartment upstairs?"

"Yeah, and we had to cancel because Bunny called one of her *critically important*," Reen made double air quotes, "impromptu meetings. Wish we could have seen it. I've heard their place is really impressive. I wonder how much they're asking."

"It's got to be a few million at least because of the location, all the kitchen equipment, the furnished apartment, and the historic importance of the building."

The door opened again and they were entranced by the fragrant marriage of butter, sugar and flour transformed into heavenly morsels. A minute longer and Laila knew she and Reen would be magically sucked inside.

"We have *got* to get out of here." She broke into a jog, distancing herself from the bakery, unsure if her increased pulse was due to excitement about the bakery, aggravation about the letters Bunny gave them, or the brisk jog. They'd opened their TBT letters as soon as they left the meeting, jaws dropping as they scanned the warning communiqués. Laila wanted to burn hers and mail the ashes to Bunny.

"What a bunch of crap." Laila slowed her pace as they walked up a tree-lined side street. "You and I have more satisfied clients than any other counselors."

"Because they know we've been there too."

"They relate to us better than someone who's never been bigger than a size two," Laila said. "I remember when I was at my biggest, dreaming about being slim again. That cute red dress I kept hanging at the front of my closet as a goal reminder was a size twelve."

"Mine was a fourteen." Reen's hazel eyes narrowed. "A twelve or fourteen to our fat-phobic coworkers is heifer size."

"The average TBT client doesn't care about being a size zero, she just wants to get down to whatever magic number makes her feel good about herself. Corporate wants us to..." Laila cocked her head. "What was it they said?"

Reen dug the letter out of her purse. "*Streamline your body in accordance with the lean, healthy TBT image.*" She huffed a humorless laugh as she jammed the offending missive back in her bag and resumed walking. "They want me to lose twenty-five pounds in the next six weeks. Hah! Ain't gonna happen." She stopped. "Ooh look, String Me Along is having a sale."

Laila tugged her sister away from the yarn shop's colorful window. "Nope, uh-uh. If we stop we'll be there all day and I'll have to find a crowbar to pry you out. Come on, we need to get to that estate sale before all the good stuff is gone." They started walking again.

"Okay, you're right," Reen admitted, picking up speed. "We'll have that butter-soaked Dutch baby burned off by the time we get back to my car."

"By walking just a couple of miles? In your dreams. To burn off the number of calories we consumed at lunch it would take—"

Reen clapped her hands over her ears. "La-la-la-la. I'm not listening. Don't burst my joyful little exercise bubble, no matter how unrealistic it may be. After all, walking a couple of miles is better than just sitting on my ass, isn't it?"

"Absolutely." Laila draped her arm over Reen's shoulder as they trudged along the sidewalk. "Corporate says I need to drop thirty pounds in six weeks." Laila fumed again at the idea. "It's not only absurd, it's unhealthy. Neither of us is meant to be rail thin."

"Exactly. And that's why God created pecan pie," Reen noted and they laughed together. "I wish we'd crossed those stupid no-more-than-five-percent-weight-gain clauses out of our employment contracts before we signed on with TBT."

Stopping in place, Laila stood bracing a fist against her hip, the burn of anger simmering through her veins. "Explain how the hell my measly seven pound weight gain somehow translates into TBT telling me I have to lose thirty."

"The same way my six translates to twenty-five. Jerks."

Growling, Laila started walking again.

"If you had your own bakery we'd make a fortune. I say *we* because you'd hire me and I'd help you build a scone empire so wildly successful, and with food so superior to TBT's, it would put them out of business." Reen snapped her fingers. "Just like that."

"Of course I'd hire you but I wouldn't want to put anyone out of business. Lots of money would be great but that's not why—"

"Yeah, yeah, I know," Reen cut her off with a flippant wave. "I've seen those big blue idealistic eyes of yours looking off into the distance with grandiose thoughts of selflessly helping thousands of unhappy people often enough to know your intentions are pure."

"Jeez." Laila scrunched her nose. "You make me sound like a sappy televangelist or phony infomercial actress."

"Ooh, infomercials. We'd *have* to do those."

Laila barked a laugh. "Can you imagine us trying to get through a script without cracking up? All it would take is one look at each other and—"

"Laila, if you don't start giving your bake shop idea positive energy and visualizing your success, it won't happen. Before we lost weight, you would have sworn that us walking, mostly uphill, and neither of us keeling over, would be impossible. But see? Nothing's impossible if you want it enough. Our dream came true because we *made* it come true. Now that's positive!"

"True," Laila agreed, "but losing weight isn't the same as making a fortune from thin air. I can chant and visualize until I'm blue in the face but it won't change the fact that I'll never have enough money to start my own business, much less buy Peggy and Caroline Crowe's bakery."

"All I'm saying is a positive attitude never hurts."

"Okay, I'm positive I need a fairy godmother, or a genie who can grant me three wishes." Laila grabbed Reen's sleeve and pointed to a sign for the estate sale at the corner.

Reen gazed up. Way up. "Good grief that walk's gonna be murder. It's times like this that I really miss Chicago's flat landscape." She gave Laila a purposeful look. "Plus that address is just a few doors away from Aunt Colleen and Uncle Walter's place." She shuddered. "I don't want to run into them or Lorraine at the sale."

Laila let out a pop of incredulous laughter. "Come on, Reen, do you honestly think any of the Devingtons would be caught dead shopping at an estate sale?"

Once she thought about what she said, Reen laughed too.

"Just think," Laila went on in her quest to convince her sister, "they might have dozens of skeins of yarn tucked away in the back of a closet. Rare yarn that's not available anywhere anymore," Laila encouraged, knowing just how to push the avid knitter's buttons. "Plus we'd burn off more calories than we ate."

With another glance at the top of Beauregard Hill, Reen uttered a dramatic growl. "Dammit, Laila, you know searching for yarn is second only to being a foodie on my list of vices." She looped her arm through Laila's. "Let's go."

Once they reached the address they stood on the sidewalk, out of breath and gaping in awe at the enormous Victorian mansion. The whimsical fretwork, gingerbread shingles, balustrades, spindles, turrets, and fanciful ornamentation was incredible to see up close.

"This place is huge." Laila stood mesmerized as her gaze washed over the impressive manor.

"And really old," Reen noted as they raced up the long concrete walk and stone steps.

A current of anticipation coursed through Laila's veins. There was something deliciously appealing about digging through people's castoffs and discovering fabulous goodies.

She couldn't help the rush of excitement that whispered, *Maybe this time you'll find a rare, priceless trinket that will change your life forever.*

Chapter 2

~<>~

IT WAS NEARLY a whole house sale, the estate sale's organizers explained as they handed out flyers and shopping bags. The kind of sale Laila and Reen loved most. While Reen might claim not to be as addicted to rummaging through other people's castoffs as Laila, Laila knew better. They could scrounge around the attic, closets, basement, garage and many of the rooms in between, giddy as they hunkered down on hands and knees, checking dark, cobwebbed nooks and crannies for treasures.

A brief paragraph about the house's history stated it had remained within the same family since it was built for Abigail Maythorne in 1859. The last owner, Franklin Maythorne, a retired attorney, had died. There were three known heirs, brothers, who were great-grandnephews of the original owner. Proceeds of the estate sale were going to the Abigail Maythorne Foundation.

After rifling through the kitchen, finding a few items to add to their shopping bags, they headed for the basement, carefully navigating the narrow, rickety wood steps that led to a dim, cavernous area, piled floor to ceiling with all manner of stuff.

Only a few others surveyed the dank basement. Apparently not many were eager to dig through the layers of dust, cobwebs, and whatever it was that reeked of mildew.

"Laila!" Reen practically screeched after an audible intake of breath. "Look!"

Taken by surprise, Laila turned to spot her sister looking like a dog who'd discovered a cattle boneyard, excitedly waving her hand toward a row of shelves piled high with skeins of yarn and all sorts of sewing goods.

"There, you see? What did I tell you?" Laila said, highly amused at her sister's unbridled enthusiasm. "Stick with me, kid and you'll go places." While Laila searched the basement's perimeter, Reen was busy filling bags with her needlework finds.

Ten minutes later, Reen was at her sister's side. "You were right, Laila. There's all kinds of stuff here that you can't find in stores anymore. I really hit the jackpot." With a supremely elated expression, she presented her bounty for Laila's inspection.

"Wow, Maureen, look at all you found!" She bent to examine the contents of one bag only to bolt upright with a horrified expression. "Oh, Reen, sweetie, you can't buy that old yarn."

"What?" Reen's eyes were bugged. "Yes I can. Why not?"

Laila winced, waving her hand over the bag Reen held out to her. "Did you get a whiff of that strong odor? It's mildew."

"No." Reen sniffed the bag. When her head popped back up it looked like she was about to cry. "No! That's so unfair. Maybe I can salvage some of it. Maybe it's not all moldy." She and Laila went through everything together and were able to save about a third of what Reen had collected.

They continued making their way around the basement, making several good finds and being forced to put some of them, like vintage books and magazines, back because of the mildew. Laila was fortunate to find a couple of century-old cookbooks that had escaped getting moldy.

"Ooh, these are nice, Laila." Reen rummaged through deep wood shelves holding vintage salt and pepper shakers. She cooed over a delft blue set of ceramic wooden shoe-shaped shakers. "You still collect salt and pepper shakers, right?"

"No. I sold most of them at my last garage sale." Intrigued with the vast assortment, Laila searched through them.

"Then how come you're still here looking instead of going off in search of something else?" Reen snickered.

"Oh...well I..." She laughed to herself. "Don't judge, Maureen. You never know when I might find the world's rarest salt and pepper shakers that would look perfect on a shelf in my cozy future bake shop. How's *that* for positive thinking?" She beamed a grin at her sister before getting down on her hands and knees to examine the lower shelves.

"You're preaching to the choir." Reen hunkered down next to Laila so she could dig through a bin of vinyl record albums on the floor.

Laila scooted a few feet to the right, coughing at the cloud of dust her movement created. "My uniform pants are going to look like I crawled through the mud." Her laughter stirred up more dust. "Which would probably be an improvement."

"A perfect excuse to burn them, and the godawful jacket that goes along with them."

Laila glanced at her hideous TBT uniform. "They make us look twenty pounds heavier."

"We look like cotton candy hawkers at a carnival." Reen barked a laugh. "Can you picture Saffron or Lorraine wearing this getup?"

"Ha!" The ludicrous thought tickled Laila. "Our fashion-conscious cousins wouldn't be caught dead in it."

The jackets for female counselors were peppermint pink with dime-sized navy polka dots. A sleeveless pink knit top and navy slacks or a skirt completed the ensemble. Male counselors wore navy jackets with pink polka dots over pink oxford shirts topping navy trousers.

"What on earth was Bunny thinking when she chose these ugly uniforms?"

"She claims they're distinctive," Laila said. "And unforgettable."

"She's spot on about that, especially here in Glassfloat Bay where getting dressed up means wearing your good jeans. If we were still living in Chicago we'd be laughed out of the city."

"You can say that again." Laila leaned forward, tucking her head under the deep shelf above and bracing her hand on the bottom shelf so she could get a better look. Without any warning, the rotted wood gave way. Her hand plunged through the soft, splintered surface while her cheek fell hard against the wood.

A strangled whoop and holler followed.

"Jeez! Laila, what happened?"

"The shelf's damp and mildewed. It must be rotten."

"Are you okay?" Reen stuck her head under the shelf. "Whew, it stinks down here. You'd better be careful you don't get mildew lung poisoning from breathing that in."

"Mildew lung..." Laila's eyes bugged. "Is that a thing?"

"I dunno. I guess you'll find out."

"Thanks, sis, that's a big help."

"You're welcome. Can you get your hand out?"

"I think so, but..."

"Yeah...? But what?" After a long moment of silence, Reen piped up again. "But what!?" she asked with more vehemence. "But you're stuck? But you're hand's resting on a dead rat? But your fingers got snapped off in a mousetrap? But you're passing out from flesh-eating toxic mold poisoning? For heaven's sake, *what*!?"

"Oh my God, Reen, you sound just like Mom." Laila laughed. "Stop using your mom voice on me, it's not helping. There's something under here and I'm trying to grab it."

"Something as in treasure something or as in huge nest of spiders something?"

"Like I'd be trying to grab a nest of spiders. It's hard. It feels like stone or marble."

"A gargantuan petrified spider!"

"Stop with the spider talk, you're creeping me out!" Laila was quiet a moment longer as her fingers stretched for the object.

"Holy mackerel, I knew it!" Gasping, Reen raised her head so fast it hit the shelf above her, rattling the ceramic salt and pepper shakers overhead.

"Knew what? Watch it, Maureen, or you'll have this old thing crashing down on us."

"You've found the world's most prized salt and pepper shaker set, hidden away by the house's owner before he died because of its enormous value."

"Don't make me laugh when I'm stuck down here on all fours with my face plastered against a moldy shelf." She snaked her hand in deeper, trying to get a good grasp. "It's too far to the right. I can't get a good grip. And it's heavy." The challenge spurred her on. By this time Laila didn't care what the hell it was under there, she *had* to have it.

"Laila."

"Maybe if we try to punch out more of the shelf I can get to it." Laila pounded on the rotted wood with her other hand to no avail. Apparently she'd found the only vulnerable spot.

"Laila."

"Come on, Reen, help me pound on it."

"Laila!"

"What? *What!*" she growled, frustration tingeing her voice.

Reen removed a set of ceramic cat salt and pepper shakers from the bottom shelf, setting them on the concrete floor before erupting with laughter.

"I'm scrounging around in this spider-infested hole struggling to unearth a possibly costly treasure to secure our financial future and you're laughing?"

Reen reached in the back of the shelf, looping two fingers in the small circular hole at the center and easily lifting the removable shelf, exposing the floor beneath.

"Oh," Laila said sheepishly. Withdrawing her hand from the rotted wood, she cringed as she brushed cobwebs and bug carcasses from her skin and hair. Returning her attention to the area beneath where the shelf sat a moment before, she zeroed in on the item she'd been trying to reach. The stone box was about the size of two thick paperback books stacked together.

"It looks really old," Laila noted.

"Maybe it's filled with rare gold coins." Reen watched as Laila grasped the box with both hands, carefully drawing it out of the grubby cavity. "Or diamonds."

"Look at the strange writing on the metal strips around the box." Laila blew a thick layer of dust from its surface. "Maybe it's an antiquity."

"It probably says made in Taiwan," Reen joked.

Laila fiddled with the latch. "I think it's stuck," she said an instant before the latch popped open on its own. Cradling the heavy box in her lap, Laila lifted the cover and gasped at the sight of the multi-colored glass bottle nestled in layers of what looked like silk.

"It's beautiful." Laila gingerly fingered the exquisite glasswork. "It looks like it's made of thousands of strands of glass. I've never seen anything like it."

"Neither have I," Reen agreed. "Maybe it's an antique perfume bottle. Whatever's inside is probably so old it smells like ass."

Laila laughed at that. With the stench of mildew from the timeworn basement assaulting her senses, she wouldn't be at all surprised if the contents smelled atrocious. "I'll wait until I get it home to examine it more closely."

"Good idea." Trailing her finger through the dust, Reen shuddered. "That way you can set it on something other than a basement floor crawling with ancient crud."

"Maybe we've finally found a real treasure." Laila couldn't help a shiver of excitement at the thought. Noticing a wave of bargain hunters descending the staircase, she closed the box, latching it and placing it in her bag.

"We've seen everything down here," she said to Reen. "C'mon, let's go back upstairs."

Twenty minutes later, as they were about to leave the last upstairs bedroom, Laila paused. It was as if something in the room called to her. Instinct led her to a Victorian writing desk where she spotted a faded photo.

"Find something else?" Reen asked as Laila fingered the photograph. "Ooh, damn, he was a hunk."

"What a gorgeous man," Laila breathed, gazing at the sepia image of a tall man with nearly shoulder-length dark hair, dressed in Victorian garb and standing behind an elderly woman seated at the same writing desk Laila now stood at.

"Look at those dark, piercing eyes. Like he's looking at me through the centuries. And that broad chest..." Laila felt a twinge of longing as she studied the striking man.

Reen seemed nearly as mesmerized by the photo as Laila. "With that longer hair maybe he was a Native American from one of the Oregon tribes."

Scrutinizing the photo, Laila said, "I think he looks more Mediterranean."

"Yeah, maybe Greek." Reen took the picture, turning it to the back. "Abigail Maythorne and unknown gentleman, 1859," she read aloud. "She's the original owner of the house."

"Interesting." Laila traced her finger over the man's arm to where his hand rested on Abigail's shoulder.

"He looks solemn and stern, while Abigail looks exceedingy pleased about something," Reen noted. "I think Miss Abby had herself a boy toy."

Laila took the photo back from Reen. "Imagine what he must have looked like shirtless."

"Or pants-less," Reen offered.

They exchanged a giggle belying their years as Laila stuffed the unframed photograph into her bag of treasures. "I have to have him."

Glancing up again to catch Reen's perceptive smirk, she smiled. "Okay so he's been dead for more than a hundred years. So what? I have an imagination, don't I?"

"And a vibrator too, I presume." Reen nudged Laila in the ribs as they headed for the checkout table.

Chapter 3

Sumer—Third Millennium BC

~<>~

IT WAS THE GENTLE hum of a woman's chant that stirred Zakkar Tymon from the oppressive fog of shadowed darkness. Calling upon his warrior's strength, he fought to rouse himself from the dream, the commanding trance that had imprisoned his awareness. His head was thick and heavy as he tried to shift position. The weight of his eyelids hindered him from opening them to scrutinize his surroundings.

How long had it been since he'd been trapped between worlds, drifting amid the living and the shades? The last thing Zakkar remembered was defending the mud-brick walls of the Sumerian cities against the siege of Sargon of Akkad's army. On the bloody banks of the Euphrates he ordered his men into phalanx formation, shouting the battle cry to protect and defend at all costs as he led them forward.

Wielding his great penetrating axe with its narrow blade and strong socket, Zakkar had just pierced the bronze plate armor of yet another Akkadian soldier when...

He struggled to remember what occurred next. There was the ever-present metallic tang of blood is his nostrils. Hacked bodies stacked all around him. The anguished cries and groans of dying men roaring in his ears...and then...

And then there came the pain. The searing sharpness of a sword slashing his back, his ribs, his shoulder.

By gods, he, the great Zakkar Tymon, had been felled!

Agonized by the realization, Zakkar once again found himself focusing on the soothing sounds of the woman's song.

Nay, there were no women on the battlefield to offer the comfort of a sweet melody or the tender warmth of a soft breast. It could only be—Zakkar's body tensed as the unsavory prospect of his own death assailed him. The alluring voice tempting him back from the abode of the dead no doubt belonged to Ereshkigal, goddess of the underworld.

Owing to his rank and reputation as the bravest, noblest and fiercest warrior throughout all of Mesopotamia, the dark queen had come personally to escort him through the seven gates of *Kurnugi*, the land of no return.

"O my mighty, magnificent Zakkar," the woman's voice said, interrupting his introspection. He felt the cool, bracing touch of a damp cloth dabbed against his face. "Under your fearsome radiance, your terrible glare and storm, the Akkadians turned their steps away from you and your men in mute dread."

"Ereshkigal?" he managed to speak, his voice sounding dry and raspy to his ears. "Is it you, come for me?"

"You awaken!" the woman said. "At last."

On her sharp intake of breath Zakkar's eyelids parted. His unsteady gaze was met by a softly lit room and an abundance of voluminous veils hanging around him. It was then that Zakkar understood he was flat on his back on a padded platform, a bed far softer than those to which he was accustomed.

"The gods be praised. Fear not, Zakkar, for it is only I, Sabit the priestess, who calls you back from the brink of the underworld."

He listened to her words, which only brought more questions to mind. Her voice and her countenance were familiar, but he could not remember from where or when. "Do I know you? Why am I here?"

Shushing him and forcing him to remain still as he struggled to sit up, Sabit hummed the same haunting melody Zakkar heard earlier. "You have been in my care for near half a lunar cycle." Her small hands roamed his thighs as she removed the large fur covering him. "We have come to know each other quite well as you lurched back and forth over the threshold of the living and the dead."

With considerable effort, Zakkar pulled himself up far enough to brace himself on his elbows. A glance left, right and ahead brought a series of food, beer and wine-laden altars into focus as well as precious gold, lapis, ornate mosaics, harps, pottery and decorated clay tablets. These sumptuous accouterments were found only in the dwellings of royalty, abodes of the upper class or in *ziggurats*, the towering temples to the gods.

His brow furrowed in confusion. "I am in a ziggurat?"

"The tallest in the city," Sabit answered proudly. "Because of your rank and extraordinary service to Sumer and the gods, Ibi-Utu deemed you should remain here for the duration of your mending." She smoothed her soft, cool hands over his body from the top of his head to his feet.

"Ibi-Utu?"

"He is *patesi* of this temple," Sabit explained, her fingers traversing the path of dark hair from his chest, down his belly to beneath the flax cloth covering his *gis*.

As she spoke, Zakkar remembered Ibi-Utu. Named for the sun god, Utu, he was the powerful and revered high priest.

"Do you remember what happened to you?" Sabit asked.

Zakkar glanced at his body and the new set of jagged marks zigzagging across his flesh, adding to the extensive assortment of previous battle scars. "I was felled from behind," he surmised.

"Yes, you were sorely wounded in battle. Most feared you were doomed to be whisked away to the nether regions in the arms of Ereshkigal but I saved you from that fate, Zakkar, my beloved." She combed her fingers through his hair and kissed his forehead.

She was a pretty young thing, if somewhat plain, boyish and certainly too young for his tastes. She wore the traditional gown baring one shoulder, which appeared bony. His gaze fell upon her breasts. Far less than a handful, they stood firm against the softly draping cloth of her garment. As Zakkar lifted his gaze he noticed her staring at him as if she wanted to devour him lick by lick.

If he wasn't feeling so vague at the moment he would have chuckled. He was used to women seducing him. His reputation as a skilled lover perhaps even exceeded his celebrated standing as a great leader and warrior. His rumored heritage as half god only added to his apparent appeal.

"My thoughts are hazy, Sabit." Zakkar tried to regain his senses. "You call me your beloved, and yet I don't recall the two of us ever..." He arched an eyebrow in question.

"Nay, you have not yet moored in my new moon crescent, Zakkar, but I wish nothing more than for you to take my chaste *sal-munuz* and make it yours forever. I have fallen in love with you."

Zakkar's thoughts reeled. This bold, lovestruck wisp of a woman, this seemingly naïve virgin priestess loved him? Wanted him to bed her? He felt his *gis* stir at the thought. Not because she was particularly alluring, but simply because she was there, available and evidently more than willing.

Moreover, it seemed to Zakkar it had been a near eternity since he'd...how had Sabit phrased it? Ah yes, since he'd *moored himself in a new moon crescent*. He clamped down on his tongue to keep from laughing at the lustful girl and her romantic, poetic terms.

"You said you were a priestess, Sabit?" he asked gently.

"Yes." She breathed a melodious sigh. "I am priestess of Nanna, the Moon God of Ur. He is my betrothed. Symbolically, of course," she added quickly. She locked her gaze on Zakkar's *gis* swelling beneath the cloth covering his groin, a look of anticipatory bliss across her features. "Now that you are awake and well, Zakkar, we can join."

To Zakkar's amazement, the young woman tore the bed covering from his body and straddled him. By gods, she was preparing to mount him!

"Sabit!" He tried holding her in place. It was then that he felt how much of his strength had yet to be restored, for he was near as weak as a lamb. "Sabit," he said more softly this time, "you must know it is against our laws for you to bed a mortal man once you are betrothed to a deity."

"But once I take my sacred oath I shall never have my hungry *sal-munuz* soothed. I must experience a proper bedding at least once in my life. And who better to do it than the brave warrior whose wounds I have tended—the man I have come to love?"

"You could be beheaded if it became known you seduced a man, Sabit." Little by little, memories of her benevolent and loving ministrations flooded his thoughts. She'd chanted to him, spoke incantations, fed him, dressed his wounds with herbs and poultices as he lay immobile, battling his way back from the clutches of eternal darkness.

"You have been good to me, Sabit. Kind, sweet and caring. You are far too lovely to lose your pretty head." Zakkar stroked her arm, patting it with brotherly affection.

"Oh, Zakkar, must I resort to tearful pleading, lamenting and wailing before you will agree to bed me?"

Zakkar groaned as his *gis* strained at her provocative words.

"I long to feel your mighty essence inside me," she continued. "Your powerful arms around me as, enraptured, we take wing to the stars together." Sabit leaned forward, clutching his biceps with one hand while resting a finger on his bottom lip and tugging down with the other. She smoothed the tip of her finger over his teeth, giving him a wistful smile.

"With your legendary strength, a tooth can even crush flint. Crush me, Zakkar. Pierce me. Let me bear your babe."

"My babe?" a startled Zakkar said.

Sabit's eyes grew wide. "How could the gods be angry if a priestess bedded one of their own?" she reasoned. "Are the stories not true that you have a mortal mother and were fathered by Enlil, the great god of air and storms?"

Zakkar closed his eyes for a moment, gathering his thoughts. Women oft sang praises and composed poems about his supposed yet unconfirmed, half god heritage and striking masculine beauty. They seemed to favor his long locks of dark-as-raven-wing hair, his firm jaw and bark-brown eyes. It was both a blessing and a curse to be so favored.

Sabit's eyes were still wide when he opened his eyes again. Her cheeks pink with expectancy.

"My mother has said it is so," he told her, "but—"

Before Zakkar could stop her, Sabit drew up her skirts and sank fully onto his engorged *gis*, yelling out in pain as the membrane in her virgin channel tore.

The sweet feel of her chaste tightness wholly clasping his *gis* was overshadowed not only by the shock of what Sabit had done but by the sound of rapid footsteps approaching the chamber in answer to her anguished cry. Gathering every measure of his strength, Zakkar switched their positions, fast withdrawing himself from her depths as he now kneeled astride her.

"Zakkar Tymon!" Ibi-Utu's thunderous voice rang out as he raced to the bed, eyeing in horror the lightly bloodied bit of cloth between Sabit's thighs. Soon three other priests had sped into the chamber, all staring with revulsion at the incriminating scene. "Is this how you repay me and my priestess for our healing care? What say you, man?"

"Nay, Ibi-Utu," Sabit cried. "It is not as you suspect. Zakkar is innocent. I am the one who—"

"Silence," Zakkar roared, interrupting the death sentence the foolish, callow girl was about to draw upon her head. He had led a good, mostly honorable life, had led many brave Sumerian men into battle in honor of their king and the mighty gods. While his heart spoke of breathing his last as a white-haired old man, blessed with a good wife and many grandchildren at his knee, as a warrior Zakkar never really expected he'd live that long.

Perhaps he was meant to die in this last, fierce battle against Sargon's army. Sweet, idealistic Sabit had given him life. It was only fair that he reciprocate. Having butchered many a warrior for Sumer, Death was his constant companion. But he couldn't imagine living with the knowledge that this young, naïve girl he'd unintentionally sullied had met a fearsome death simply because she was enamored of him. Nay, Sabit did not deserve to have her life cut short on his account.

"Do not try to protect me, Sabit," Zakkar soothed, gazing down into her terrified eyes. "I alone am responsible, Ibi-Utu. I-I awoke with a start from my long sleep between worlds and, in my clouded mind, somehow mistook the innocent young priestess for one of my consorts."

Ibi-Utu's gaze again fell upon the blood-spotted cloth. "You have ruined Sabit for her betrothed. Nanna, the Moon God of Ur demands his wives be virgins. She is no good to him now, nor to this sacred temple. Both of you must die."

Sabit gasped, a strangled cry escaping her lips as her hands flew to her throat.

"It is not Sabit's blood," Zakkar lied, unobtrusively digging his thumbnail into one of the still fresh scars at his side and slicing along the tender ridge. Once he felt the warm trickle of liquid he continued, "It is mine. You see?"

Rising from the bed and gesturing to his side, he held his bloody fingers out and away from his ribs. "The wound still oozes blood. You arrived just as I was about to thrust into her but her cry of terror brought me to my senses before I could enter her channel. Sabit is still pure."

"Is this true, Sabit?"

The petrified girl looked up at Zakkar, who did his best to give her a reassuring nod and smile. He saw the pain in her eyes, the deep sorrow, the longing, fear and dread. She turned her head to face the priest. "I-yes," she said, collapsing into tears. "Zakkar speaks the truth."

"Make peace with the gods, Zakkar. Your beheading will take place first thing in the morning." Ibi-Utu spun on his heel to leave.

"Patesi, spare his life, please!" Sabit cried out. "You must know it was not Zakkar in his right mind who came upon me in such a crazed manner. He was fevered and under the influence of the potent healing tonics we have forced him to swallow." Rising to her knees, gesturing with one hand outstretched to Zakkar and the other to Ibi-Utu, she pleaded to the high priest, "You know this man. You know his reputation. He has fought and won many wars for our people, our king, the gods, has he not?"

Arms crossed over his chest, Ibi-Utu remained in place, silent while digesting Sabit's beseeching words.

"Stories of queens, maidens and wives falling to Zakkar's feet, offering themselves unto him abound, Ibi-Utu, do they not?"

The priest frowned at Zakkar. "They do. But that does not mean he has the right—"

"It is clear," Sabit forged on, "the mighty warrior Zakkar Tymon can have his pick of the fairest and most succulent women of any land. Look upon me, Ibi-Utu." She swept a hand from her head downward as tears coursed down her face.

"Do you really believe a man of Zakkar's uncompromised beauty would have any reason to glance twice at a plain, unappealing girl like me when the temple and streets abound with dazzling, full-breasted, fair of face women only too willing to bed him at the mere crook of his finger?"

Until that moment, Zakkar had forgotten he still had a heart buried deep within his chest, but he was reminded of the fact now because he felt sure it clenched as he listened to Sabit's harsh depiction of herself.

It seemed as if a small eternity passed as the priest stood silently, gazing from Sabit to Zakkar and back again.

Finally, he spoke. "What you say is true, Sabit. I have followed Zakkar's exploits since he was a boy just entering Sumer's army and never was there a time when I did not believe him to act with honor. His past actions, however, do not excuse his present. The gods are clear on that. Our laws state directly that Zakkar must pay with his head for the intended ruin of a virgin priestess. Unless..."

Ibi-Utu's frown etched deeper still while Zakkar's heart pounded out a hasty beat as he awaited his fate at the hands of the pious high priest.

"Unless?" Sabit asked, a glimmer of hope lighting her eyes.

"Imprisonment," Ibi-Utu finally muttered. "For the rest of his days."

Both Zakkar and Sabit gasped. "By gods, I would rather die," Zakkar spat. Folding his arms over his chest he stood tall, bracing his still-weakened body against a pillar as he elevated his chin in a proud manner. "Just lop off my head and be done with it so I may accompany Ereshkigal to the underworld. I am ready to die."

"Nay, Zakkar, do not speak that way!" Sabit implored. "What about the incantation of service to womankind, patesi?" she suggested. "It is more deserving than death. More humane than watching a valiant warrior rot away in chains."

After an infinite amount of time, Ibi-Utu nodded. "A fair solution. It shall be so." He stepped to one of the altars, selecting a clay tablet inscribed in cuneiform.

"Nay!" Zakkar said, not even understanding what an incantation of service to womankind was. He had learned long ago to be wary of the spells, rituals and incantations of those in devout service to the ferocious and mighty gods.

"Do you have an appropriate vessel, Sabit?" the priest said, ignoring Zakkar's protest.

Sabit scanned the chamber, pointing to a small stone box secured with metal strappings atop one of the altars. "There, patesi. Inside there is a bottle of the finest spun glass brought as an offering by one of the city's wealthiest matrons. It was meant to hold perfumed oil or for use as a tear vase, but is still empty and should be a perfect vessel."

Ibi-Utu gestured to one of the lesser priests who immediately brought the box forward, opening the latch for Ibi-Utu's scrutiny.

"Yes, this will do," he agreed. "It has significant weight, appears strong and sufficiently protected to survive at least one lifetime." He looked at the altars already set with lambs for sacrifice, lard and roast meat, as well as dates, fine meal, dried fruit and a confection of honey and butter. Nodding to Sabit, he stated, "We can proceed. The goddess will be pleased."

Zakkar's mind whirled. How he wished he had both his strength and his full senses to help him comprehend what was happening. Stories from his childhood of men imprisoned in jars and bottles, trapped in the abomination of perpetual servitude, slowly surfaced. Surely this is not what the patesi had in mind?

As the high priest and his subordinates examined the clay tablet bearing the incantation, Sabit rose to stand at Zakkar's side.

"Fear not, brave and honorable one," she whispered. "I shall discern a way to free you from your servitude soon. I shall never forget that I owe you my life as well as my eternal gratitude, dearest

Zakkar." With that she crossed the room to join Ibi-Utu, who held his right hand aloft and began to read aloud from the tablet.

"O great Inanna, Queen of Heaven, goddess of love and war, I summon you. I am Ibi-Utu, he who withdraws the first fruits from the temple. He who has received divine powers from the most elevated dais. You are the great lady of the gods. Your terror is fearsome as it weighs on the land. No man anticipates your commands. The heavens fold themselves in your presence like a mourning garment. You are she who hastens like a north wind storm into the midst of the people. You are she who hears prayer and pleading."

He looked to Sabit and nodded. She took the tablet from him and continued.

Zakkar released the pillar when he felt the room shake. He tried to take a step forward but was frozen in place.

Drawing upon his warrior's courage, he steeled himself for whatever may come, for he would not cry out in fear. Never! Zakkar Tymon feared nothing and no one! Even to the gods and demons who toyed with the lives of mortals, he feared not. Given that he no longer had the power of speech, Zakkar repeated those words inside his head, fortifying himself as the incantation continued.

"Great Inanna, I, Sabit, priestess of Nanna, the Moon God of Ur, summon you to intern Zakkar Tanojin Lugalbanda Tymon, mighty warrior who has fought many battles in your name, into this sacred vessel." She motioned to the open box containing the bottle, which Ibi-Utu held aloft, bowing as he did so. "So that Zakkar Tymon may obliterate his transgressions to womankind by serving them for all eternity."

Eternity. The thought of ceaseless captivity rose in Zakkar's throat like the bitter tang of bile. Sabit's words seemed to drone on forever as she delineated Zakkar's verdict of indentured servitude.

"The language of his possessor will Zakkar Tymon speak and understand," Ibi-Utu added, as the lesser priests chanted in the background while lighting fragrant incense.

"The matter of pleasing his female possessors and satisfying their every urge shall be Zakkar's sacred duty," Sabit read.

"Within the period of six lunar cycles," Ibi-Utu, said, "will Zakkar grant his possessor three wishes."

As the priests chanted and Sabit and Ibi-Utu spoke the endless words of the incantation, Zakkar became aware of a pervading heaviness seeping into his being. Servitude to women. By gods, Zakkar, the great and mighty warrior, the sought after lover of queens and women of the greatest beauty and wealth would be reduced to no more than a slave to women's peculiar impulses, which, he knew, could shift with the mere blink of an eye.

Zakkar would have shuddered at the thought had he not still been frozen in place like a great pillar of salt. Truly, it was a foul fate worse than death to which he was being condemned. He only hoped Sabit would be true to her word and quickly discern a method for his liberation.

"O make it be, great and wondrous Inanna! Let it be so!" Ibi-Utu nearly roared as he pulled the stopper from the bottle, elevating the container high above his head.

The ethereal visage of a woman, as beautiful as she was fearsome, suddenly loomed over the proceedings.

The last thing Zakkar remembered seeing before feeling his body curl and contort into naught but a vaporous substance that voyaged through the air of the temple chamber and into the bottle, was the tortured expression of repentance mixed with gratitude on Sabit's tear-stained face.

Chapter 4

Glassfloat Bay, Oregon: present day

~<>~

"YOU SURE YOU CAN'T come in for a while?" Laila asked, getting out of Reen's car. "I'll make us some sugar-free cocoa and we can examine our treasures together."

"Sugar-free? Is that supposed to cancel out our five thousand calorie lunch?" Reen laughed. "I'd love to stay but I've got to get home and changed. I'm volunteering at the children's hospital for a couple of hours before we go to Nevan's pub tonight."

Laila didn't know where her sister found the energy to volunteer after such a long day. She'd never known anyone as dedicated to helping others as Reen.

"I'll see you this evening about six-thirty, okay?" Reen asked. "Nevan said tonight's classic film starts at seven so that should give us plenty of time to get to his pub and find a good table."

"Hey, he's our brother. It's his job to ensure we get the best table in the house," Laila teased. "I forgot...what's he showing tonight?"

"*The Quiet Man*, with John Wayne and Maureen O'Hara. That's one of my favorites."

"Mine too," Laila agreed. "Nevan had a great idea starting his movie nights at the pub. It's been bringing in a lot more business."

"Drake's going too. He said he'll pick us both up. He doesn't want to miss out on Nevan's Irish pork pie special tonight. He'll have his kids with him. He's dropping them off at his parents' place so they can babysit."

"Sounds good. I haven't seen Lilly and Kevin in a while. They're such cuties. I'll be ready at six-thirty. Hey, weren't you supposed to see some film playing at one of the university's auditoriums with Drake tonight?"

"That's tomorrow." Reen rolled her eyes skyward. "He's all enthused about some educational documentary about the dietary and cultivation habits of the Maya, Aztec and Inca civilizations."

"Oh." Failing at projecting an expression of enthusiasm, Laila said, "That sounds positively...stimulating."

"Yeah, I saw how your eyes glazed over before I even finished the film's description," Reen offered with a chuckle. "It sounds boring as hell but I told him that if I have to sit through his boring film, then he has to take me to Jigsaw Landing for ling cod fish and chips."

"Boring movie, fish fry..." Laila shrugged, "sounds like a perfect tradeoff to me."

"Fried food today and again tomorrow. How can I complain?"

"You and Drake have been seeing a lot of each other lately." Laila wiggled her eyebrows suggestively.

With an indifferent wave, Reen said, "We're just friends. He lives two doors away, he's good company, and I like his kids. Nothing more."

"You sure about that?"

"Positive. Just biding my time until Hud notices me." Reen's face lit up as she mirrored Laila's wiggly eyebrow expression.

"Huh...I thought I detected a note of interest when you were asking Annalise about him earlier."

Reen sighed. "Doesn't matter. Hudson doesn't know I'm alive anyway."

After they said their goodbyes, Laila carried her TBT tote full of unappetizing foodstuffs along with her bag of goodies from the estate sale up the steps and into her weather-beaten house. As with most of the wood-built coastal homes in the Pacific Northwest, it was hard keeping the siding looking fresh since it was often exposed to strong winds, damp air, bright sunlight, and saltwater corrosion.

Known by the Malones, as well as the townspeople, as *Bekka House*, the large, nearly century-old structure was left to Laila's family after her Norwegian grandmother, Rebekka Eriksen, died. The family voted to keep Bekka House rather than sell it, not only because they loved the house and its ideal location but also because the house was haunted—by a couple of friendly ghosts.

Since her grandmother's passing, family members as well as visitors to Bekka House had noticed the spicy fragrance of Bekka's *pepperkaker*, Norwegian ginger cookies. Sometimes there was also the faint, welcoming sound of Bekka's laughter throughout the house.

Before reaching the kitchen, Laila was greeted by a whirlwind of short black and tan fur on four legs.

"Friday! How's my favorite puppy?" Squatting, she nuzzled the dog, laughing as he licked her face in joyful greeting. A moment later the dog's muzzle pushed inside the TBT tote, investigating.

"Sorry, buddy." Standing, Laila lifted the bag beyond his reach. "Last time you got into my TBT stuff it made you sick." Friday was at her heels as she walked to a kitchen cabinet, drawing out a lidded plastic container. "You'd much rather have one of my homemade doggie biscuits, wouldn't you, boy?" She held one aloft and Friday offered an enthusiastic bark of agreement. "Of course you would," she said using baby talk. "It's much healthier and tastier."

Friday snatched the biscuit in his teeth, happily crunching away as Laila headed for the sliding glass door to let him out to do his business.

The son of Delaney's dog, Thursday, and Annalise Griffin's dog, Choo-Choo Laverne, Friday was an oversized mutt. It was the family joke that Thursday and his offspring were part German Shephard, part donkey.

After getting a packet of diet cocoa from the pantry, Laila returned to the kitchen where she eyed the reprimanding letter from TBT that had slipped out of her purse. Her eyes narrowed.

"Thirty pounds in six weeks. Unreasonable jerks."

She studied the small packet of low-calorie, sugar-free cocoa in her hand, her lip curling as she remembered the wet cardboard taste of the prepared drink. Long accustomed to soothing herself with food when she was upset, she was tempted to head back to the pantry, grab the bottle of Baileys, and the Kahlua, and douse the chaste diet cocoa with the sweet, syrupy liqueurs. Not because she was much of a drinker, but because...

Oh hell, she had no idea why.

Other than stubborn rebellion and a sudden overwhelming craving for sugar.

"Uh-uh, no you don't," Laila chastised herself as she microwaved water for the cocoa. She added it to the powder, ignoring the damp cardboard smell as she stirred, then took a seat at the table, mentally gluing herself to the chair and ignoring the lure of sugar just several feet away.

"You know slurping down liquid sugar won't help a damn thing, especially TBT's ridiculous thirty-pound edict," she said before tasting the insipid, watery concoction and pretending it was chocolatey heaven.

Withdrawing her special estate sale finds, she investigated for any indication of priceless rarity, pausing when she came to the photo of Abigail Maythorne and the darkly handsome young man. With a sip of pseudo-heavenly cocoa and a wistful sigh, she set the picture on edge, leaning it upright against the cute frog prince ceramic sugar bowl she'd found at the sale.

"Gotta keep you within drooling distance, handsome." She winked at the Adonis-like visage. Curious about the story behind the photo, her thoughts wandered as her finger traced the image's border. Was he really Abigail's lover? No, probably a family member. Or maybe a servant. Or the gardener.

That had her snickering. What women has a formal photo taken of herself with her gardener?

"Maybe he was a lawn boy with benefits," Laila muttered into her mug.

The cryptic stone box was at the bottom of the bag. The entire bag had cost her thirty-six dollars, with the stone box and bottle accounting for twelve of that.

Positioning the box in front of her, she studied it over the rim of her half-empty mug, surprised when the latch popped open of its own accord, just as it had at Maythorne Manor. Evidently the old clasp was too worn to function properly. She examined the curious writing, some engraved into the stone and some on the metal bands. It resembled Egyptian hieroglyphs.

Friday's paw tapping at the door snagged her attention. She didn't want her lovable but clumsy dog knocking over the fragile perfume bottle so Laila grabbed a new rawhide bone from the same cabinet that held the dog biscuits before letting him in.

"This is for you, my cute, klutzy canine." She used the bone to lure him into the family room around the corner. "Stay here and be a good boy while I inspect my treasures." Entranced with his new bone, Friday paid no attention when she returned to the kitchen.

Upon closer inspection, Laila noted the silk fabric cushioning the bottle was so delicate a harsh breath might shred the aged fibers. The perfume bottle appeared to be in excellent condition. Holding it in her hand, she found it sturdy, yet with an air of fragility due to the fine spun threads of glass making up the entire shape and the bottle's stopper.

After draining her mug, licking the last vestiges of chocolate from her lips, Laila mused, "Let's see if Reen was right and whatever's inside smells like ass." Grasping the stopper firmly, she pulled, twisting slightly.

It was like trying to open the lid on a jar of crystalized honey. She hesitated to use more force, fearing she'd crack the plug's delicate glass filaments.

"Come on, open for me..." she muttered, giving another cautious twist.

As soon as she'd spoken those words, the stopper drew out easily. The small bottle lay open in her left palm as she held the glass plug in her right hand. The kitchen table and floor vibrated, as did the light fixture above her head.

At her side once again, Friday barked accordingly.

"It's okay, Friday." Laila scratched behind his ears. "Just another mini earthquake," she assured the skittish dog. As a former Chicagoan, it had taken her a while to get used to Oregon's small, mostly innocuous quakes. Now she took them in stride.

As she brought the bottle to her nose, sniffing it, it shuddered in her hand.

Then the bottle grew warm.

"What the...?" Laila slipped it back into the box so it was propped up against the back. When the bottle visibly shook, she set its stopper on the table, scooting her chair back across the tile floor a couple of feet.

"Whoa, this is no earthquake."

A blue-gray vapor wafted out of the bottle.

"No...*no*!" Paralyzed with fear, Laila sat ramrod straight in her chair, gripping its seat as if afraid she'd be jettisoned out of it.

Her mouth went dry as the vaporous cloud twisted, screwing upward.

Unable to tear her gaze from the phenomenon, Laila croaked out, "Oh my God, this is so *not* happening!" Her breath came in ragged bursts as the curious mist emerging from the bottle journeyed to the kitchen floor where it hovered more than six feet high before morphing into a human shape.

"Holy—!"

Friday barked like mad as a tall, handsome man materialized before them. He was dressed like—

"A genie!" Laila shrieked. Leaping out of her chair and backing into the wall, she didn't know whether to scream, laugh, cry or pee in her pants. She wasn't sure, but maybe she did a little of each.

Chapter 5

~<>~

LAILA DREW THE DOG close, grasping his collar and comforting him as her heart hammered.

The silky, billowy sultan-style pants the genie wore were shimmering turquoise. A wide golden yellow sash of the same shiny material hugged his trim waist. His short black vest showcased a broad, bare chest. Embroidered around the edges with the same colors found in his pants and belt, the vest also had touches of deep red, which appeared to be tiny embedded rubies.

"I am at your command." The genie offered a dramatic bow as the deep accented rumble of his voice set Laila's insides aquiver.

Caught in a bizarre mix of curiosity, terror, and maybe a teensy bit of lust, she breathed, "This isn't real..."

"I assure you I am most definitely real. I exist only to give you pleasure. To act upon your every urge." Hands steepled together in front of his face, he made a slight bow.

Her eyes roamed his impeccable Greek-statue body. He was barefoot and wore no turban or headpiece. He was one incredible hunk of sun-bronzed muscles, long hair and dark, hypnotic eyes. The epitome of every fantasy she'd ever had.

And he said he was here to give her pleasure?

If she had to lose her mind, this was exactly the hallucination she'd want.

For a moment she wondered if she'd added the Kahlua and Baileys to her cocoa after all...and forgot about it. Yeah, that must be it. It would take a lot of that sugary stuff to get anyone intoxicated...but what other possible explanation could there be?

As he shifted position she noticed the imposing curved sword sheathed at his hip. When her gaze swung to his face, he was smiling at her and her breath caught.

"I am glad you finally resolved to unfasten the bottle, Laila."

Awestruck, she gawked at him before recapturing the power of speech.

"H-how do you know my name?" He did look awfully familiar. Nope, on second thought she doubted she'd run into any sexy as sin genies at the mall lately.

Still clutching Friday's collar, Laila sidestepped to the drawer where she kept the cooking utensils. The guy may be striking, but he was carrying a weapon big enough to make mincemeat out of her with a few swipes. She needed protection in case his idea of pleasure and hers were at odds.

"I was awoken from my slumber upon hearing my new possessor's words. I have heard your every word since you first set your delicate fingers on the box," he answered. "I also heard the other woman, Reen, call you by name. Though I could not see you, your compelling voice spoke to my loins."

"Your—" Laila's gaze fell to the bulge between his thighs as the genie gave her a lustful half smile before dropping his gaze to his crotch.

"Loins," he repeated, as if his meaning needed elucidation. "I was in the midst of envisioning you, imagining your womanly visage as my *gis* bloomed moments before you set me free."

"*Gis?*" Laila said absently, only to see his gaze drop a second time. *Oh...*

"I also know this magnificent animal is Friday." Bending at the waist, hands resting on his knees, he grinned at the dog. "Come, Friday."

"Friday, stay!" Laila commanded, keeping Friday at her knee. "Friday's my guard dog. A trained killer. One word from me and he'll shred you to bits."

The genie looked tickled. "I shall be most cautious then." Standing tall and still boasting a smile, he patted his thigh. "Friday, come."

"He won't listen to you," Laila told him. "He only obeys my—"

In the midst of her impassioned speech, her traitorous dog pranced out of her grip, wig-wagging his way over to the genie, rubbing against his satiny pant leg and looking up adoringly into the potential mincemeat-maker's face.

"You and I shall be good friends, Friday." He clapped Friday's backside and the tongue lolling dog picked up his rawhide bone and sat in a corner of the kitchen, gnawing his treasure without offering even a fleeting look at his mistress.

Stung by Friday's cruel betrayal, Laila frowned. "So much for depending on you for protection."

"He knows I mean you no harm," the genie claimed. His gaze roamed Laila from head to toe. "You are a beauty. Eyes the color of celestial blue stones, hair the color of barley ale, skin the color of alabaster." His head tilted. "Is it as soft as it appears?" He took a step forward.

Her hand shot up like a traffic cop's. "Stop!" Ignoring the shiver of delight at his comments, she sped to the drawer, searching for a butcher knife. She pulled out a plastic soup ladle. It was that, a pair of tongs or a rubber spatula. Everything else was in the dishwasher or sink and she'd have to move past him to get at them.

"Hold it right there," Laila cautioned, waving the ladle as he took another step toward her. "This ladle is far more deadly than it looks, buster."

"I am not Buster. I am Zakkar Tanojin Lugalbanda Tymon, great warrior of Sumer," he announced proudly. Stretching to his full height he looked every bit the magnificent warrior.

"Well that certainly is a mouthful but I don't care what your name is. What I care about is that you're standing in the middle of my kitchen with a giant sword and—"

"This is no mere sword. It is a saber!" His hand curled around its hilt as his expression revealed his surprise that she was evidently unschooled in standard-issue genie weaponry.

"You look soft and sweet, Laila, more inviting than fresh, thick honey. I can tell our physical joining will be most pleasurable for us both." He took a step toward her.

"Our what?!" She felt her face heat crimson. "Oh my God, I am *so* calling the police." That would have worked really well if she hadn't left her phone on the table.

She could scream at the top of her lungs and pray old Mrs. Willoughby next door might hear her and come toddling over, thrashing the genie into a stupor with her walker. Everyone else on the block would still be at work.

"You appear to be frightened."

"No kidding." Soup ladle in hand, she made her way across the kitchen, step by agonizing step as he watched her every move like a hawk scouting his prey. "It's not every day a genie pops out of a bottle, brandishing a gigantic sword and making lewd comments."

"I am *not* a genie." A ferocious scowl took hold. "As I explained, my weapon is no paltry sword, but a saber."

Whatever he called it, the deadly thing was big enough to slice her in half with one purposeful swing. Her thoughts whirling, Laila narrowed her gaze.

"Do I get any wishes?"

The genie nodded. "Three. Each of which must pertain to your self-interest and not be the cause of harm or misfortune to others."

"Uh-huh. So you materialized out of a bottle in a puff of smoke, you're wearing sultan pants, carry a saber, and you can grant me three wishes." Laila ticked each item off on her fingers. "A rose by any other name is still a genie."

"Your prattling is strange to my ears. It makes no sense, little one. As for my sultan pants, as you call them," looking down, he grasped the material, "my attire and the saber were given to me by a sultan's grateful daughter in Persia after I kept her body trembling with delight until she collapsed in rapture."

Sexy images floated across Laila's traitorous mind, convincing her she must have lost all her marbles to entertain such thoughts while fearing for her life.

"But if believing I am a genie provides you with serenity, then let it be so."

"Right now I'm anything but serene." A spontaneous shudder gripped her.

"There is no need to fear me. I am here to see to your pleasure, not to harm you. What kind of man would I be if I inflicted injury on a small, helpless woman?" His charismatic smile warmed her like hot buttered rum on a brisk winter night.

This genie definitely had a way with words. And gosh, he just wanted to pleasure her, that's all. God help her, she inadvertently batted her eyelashes.

"I am *not* helpless." She shook the ladle at him, struggling to maintain rational thought. "I'm well versed in all manner of self-defense, karate, judo, chai tea—"

"You mean tai chi. One of my possessors was proficient at it. Do you mean to slay me with your serving spoon or are you priming yourself to prepare food? My belly cries out in hunger." He patted his firm abs.

"Tai chi, right, that's what I meant to say. At first glance this may appear to be a simple spoon, but it's a lethal weapon in the hands of someone like me who's been trained in the art of self-defense. I could knock your block off with one swift, calculated tai chi move while rendering that *gis* of yours completely immobile, so watch out." She punctuated her warning with a figure eight wave of her ladle.

"Thank you for the good counsel. But tai chi is not a means of defense," the genie explained with a perceptive smirk.

Hell. It was just her luck to get a know-it-all genie.

He stepped closer and she stepped back. "Tai chi heals, calming the body, mind and spirit. It involves subtle moves I will teach you if you desire. After which I would be more than happy to pleasure you until you are rendered limp and sated."

He swaggered toward her, all muscle and sinew and sizzling hot sexuality, with moves smoother and more sensuous than any male stripper could hope to mimic.

Laila felt an unmistakable zing low in her belly. "The only thing I desire is for you to keep your distance," she claimed, not at all convincingly. "My husband and his fearsome motorcycle gang will be home any minute. They're huge. Monstrous. Deadly. You better get back into your bottle before they tear you apart, limb from limb."

"Battle!" The genie's eyes lit up. "It has been far too long since I have engaged in face to face combat." An anticipatory grin took hold, baring his perfect white teeth. "I will crush each of these monsters with one clutch of my mighty hand," he said, gazing at his hand and arm as he made a fist and flexed his biceps.

Watching him curl into position was like watching the magnificent ballet of a body builder in the heat of competition.

"Then I will pick my teeth with their little bird bones." He stood arms akimbo, looking proud, fierce, threatening, glorious and, oh Lord, how Laila was tempted to strip naked and sacrifice herself to the pleasuring talents of his well-muscled body.

Whoa! She had to keep her head. She might be in for a swift head-lopping with that saber if she wasn't careful. So any naked hanky-panky was a big no-no.

The TBT letter warning her to lose weight came to mind. Maybe she'd suffered a stress-induced brain malfunction after reading it. She had to be logical. Rational. The man came out of a bottle. Things like that only happened in fairytales and cartoons. And this guy was definitely no cartoon. He was flesh, bone and muscle all wrapped up in sultan pants.

"You said you're not a genie. So what are you?"

His dazzling smile presented yet another layer of attractiveness. "As you stated, I am the gorgeous man with the broad chest and dark, piercing eyes that seemed to be looking at you through the centuries."

Sucking in a sharp breath, Laila recalled the words she'd uttered when she'd spotted the sepia photograph at the estate sale. Curiosity and wonder overriding her better judgment, she edged toward the kitchen table and picked up the faded photo. She studied it before transferring her gaze to the genie.

"It-it's you! But the man in this photo has been dead for well over a hundred years. This picture was taken in—"

"1859." The genie stood so close Laila felt his warm breath on her ear. She hadn't even been aware that he'd moved. "As you can verify, Laila," he was only a whisper away now, "though I have been held captive these many years, I do not smell like ass."

No, he certainly didn't. He smelled of something spicy and exotic. Like sandalwood and patchouli incense.

"You heard that, huh?"

"Indeed. I am glad you kept the photo of me within drooling distance." His chiseled features broke into a knowing smile.

Good grief, he'd heard that too. She swallowed hard as mortification commingled with the blood in her veins. "You've been cooped up in that bottle since 1859?"

"Yes. The last time I walked the earth was for a period of two weeks when Abigail Maythorne was my possessor."

"Over a hundred fifty years ago..." The thought was inconceivable. "Things have changed a lot since then." Somewhere in the back of her mind she was vaguely aware she was chatting with a genie, which wasn't possible.

"I see that." He glanced around the kitchen. "I know I am still in the Oregon coastal town of Glassfloat Bay because of where you found me. It is a good place with much cleansing rain and verdant foliage." He continued to observe his surroundings. "This dwelling is far different than Abigail Maythorne's."

Laila scanned the kitchen. While there was nothing fancy or elegant about Bekka House, it was filled with love and coziness.

She followed the genie's gaze as he took in the kitschy collection of vintage kitchenware dotting the counters, several doggie-shaped cookie jars displayed high over the soffit, and pairs of novelty salt and pepper shakers filling empty spaces. In addition, there were a number of clear, softball-sized glass balls, called glass floats, found along the Oregon coast and collected by her late grandmother, Bekka. No one could call Laila a minimalist. Like her grandma, mom and sisters, Laila carried the family packrat gene.

"That's because Maythorne Manor is a mansion. My family's home is just a modest house."

Nodding, the genie smiled. "There is nothing wrong with a humble abode." He pointed to the ceiling fan, then made a sweeping gesture at the electric stovetop, blender, coffeemaker, toaster and the light switches. "These are?"

"Electrical appliances," Laila offered in brief explanation.

His head cocked in curiosity. "Electrical means?"

"It turns on with the flip of a switch." His clueless look had her wishing she'd paid more attention in history class. "There weren't any electric lights in 1859?"

"The term is not familiar."

"Like this." Laila flipped the switch for the light over the sink.

"So fast. So clean." The genie's eyebrows knitted and his voice was awed. "I see no traces of soot." He walked to the sink, gazing upward. "In 1859 lighting came from oil lamps and tallow candles. You must explain how electrical works."

"I wish I could." She'd need Google at her fingertips before attempting a feasible explanation. "Right now I'm still trying to wrap my head around the fact that I'm chitchatting with a genie who popped out of a bottle." Laila's eyes closed for a moment while she massaged her temples. She opened them to find him studying her.

This time when the genie's gaze swept her it wasn't as appreciative.

"Do all women of your time wear male garb?" He gestured to Laila's slacks.

Laila tried to remember the last time she'd worn a dress or skirt. She suddenly wished she was dressed all frilly and feminine. Like a helpless Southern belle, mint julep in hand. *Why, ah do declare! It's a genie, come to pleasure me until ah expire from bliss.*

"We often wear pants. Jeans, mostly. It's the custom."

"I do not like her tradition."

"Whose tradition?"

"This Jean you speak of." He frowned down at her, appraising her from head to toe. "This garish manner of dress does not suit you." He gestured to her polka dot jacket. "The jester-like spotted garment cut like a gentleman's waistcoat is unbecoming. Repugnant."

Nearly forgetting what she had on, Laila followed his gaze. "Gee, why don't you tell me how you really feel?"

One eye narrowed. "I just did."

"Thanks a bunch."

"You are most welcome."

Not sure whether to laugh or cry, she explained, "I have to wear this uniform for work, my job." Divesting herself of the horrid jacket, she tossed it onto the kitchen counter before planting her fists on her hips and slanting him a steely-eyed glare.

"I can't believe I'm allowing a genie turned fashion critic to criticize me. Why should I defend myself? You're not even real."

"I am flesh and blood." He clapped his chest. "I hunger. I thirst. I bleed. I lust. I am indeed real, Laila. As for my notions regarding your vestments, I am merely being honest."

"Uh-huh, well maybe you can be a little less honest in the future."

"I have offended you. My apologies." He offered a slight bow. "I am forever bound to speak the truth. It was not my intention to dampen your spirits. I only meant that I find this curious custom of your time, for women to make themselves up as male jesters, to be...unfortunate."

Laila's shoulders slumped.

"When you spoke of me before opening the bottle," he gestured to the photograph, "I could feel the sensation of lust emanating from you as you gazed upon my virile image."

"Oh for heaven's sake. You could not. That wasn't lust, Mr. Egotistical. It was—"

"You are mistaken. I am not Mr. Egotistical. As I already told you, I am Zakkar Tanojin Lugalbanda Tymon."

"Fine. It wasn't lust, Mr. Tymon, it was just—"

"Call me by my given name. Zakkar." He inclined his head, a curious expression across his handsome features. "I have a question about the words you and your sister spoke as you gazed at the photograph. What is this vibrator Reen spoke of?"

"Oh..." Laila giggled like a schoolgirl. She couldn't help it.

"To vibrate is to tremble, to pulse, is this not so?"

"Uh...yes." There was no way in hell she was going to describe it for him. "A vibrator is an apparatus. A modern tool. It's far too technical for me to explain," she said as she peered up into those mesmerizing eyes with the killer set of long lashes hooding them.

"I'm glad you find me gorgeous. I am not surprised. Most women do. It pleases me you were trying to picture me shirtless. I am certain you are not disappointed." He flexed his pecs and she was tempted to swoon. "You will enjoy watching me shed all my clothing to pose before you. Pant-less, I believe was the term Reen used."

Oh good grief...

"Nothing like being a wee bit egotistical." She did her best to sound unaffected and nonchalant while the prickle of thousands of nerve endings stood at rapt attention throughout her pleasure-deprived body.

"Egotistical...again you use this term. It means confident?"

Her shoulder lifted in a shrug. "You could say that."

The genie elevated his chin and puffed out his chest, which was a case of pure overkill. Lord knew the man didn't need to draw any more attention to his meticulously defined body.

"And why should I not be confident? Centuries of experience with females of many different lands and times confirm that my hard battle-scarred warrior's body is what women crave."

"Well it's not what I crave."

Liar, liar. Pants on fire.

She clamped her fingers on his arm to push him away, a restraining action about as effective as trying to bend a crowbar. Lured by the solid feel of his flesh, she found herself overcome with the impulse to explore every inch of his body. Her attempt to conceal a whimper failed miserably.

"We shall see." He ran his hands up and down Laila's arms and she felt her resolve thawing. "Let me prove it to you, little one." He increased the pressure on her arms, yanking her flush against his body. "Allow me to soothe the burning hunger I see in your beautiful, wide blue eyes."

Laila strived to make some witty, cavalier remark. A glib line to make him believe she thought he had rocks in his head. But it was all she could do just to breathe, being held in the arms of a sensuous, half-naked savage straight from the cover of a romance novel. All that was missing was the wind blowing in their hair, with her wearing a bosom-baring dress for him to tear away.

The involuntary moan spilling from Laila's throat gave her away.

"Your desire for me is nothing shameful. I share the same hunger for you. I have not held a well-rounded woman like you in my arms for centuries. I long to gaze upon your nakedness." His hands curved around her waist, his thumbs just beneath her breasts, and she swallowed hard. "To torture you ever so sweetly with my mouth."

If he kept talking that way her body would ignite. Dislodging his hands, she stepped out of his grasp, looking up at him, trying to think rationally.

"I am at your command. You are my possessor. You only need to ask, to express your desires. With your consent, I will keep you quaking with bliss the whole night. I am hard, strong, and expertly skilled at providing pleasure in ways you cannot begin to imagine."

As she processed his promising words, the jet-haired genie drew her close again, slanting his mouth over hers, seeking entrance with his probing tongue. Her knees buckled and the genie held her tight, supporting her as he kissed her senseless.

To Laila's mortification, she yearned for him to take her. Right there in the kitchen of her grandma's house. They could simply sweep everything off the table and—

"Allow yourself to imagine, lovely Laila, how I can make you feel once we are divested of clothing and naked in your bed."

Oh, I am...I am...

"Do you not want my hands on you? My mouth on you?"

I do...I do...

"Do not deny yourself the pleasure of my highly skilled services."

Blink.

His highly skilled services...

As if doused with ice water, the fire inside dwindled to a smolder.

If Laila didn't put a stop to this now, she'd be nothing more than another notch in the belt of his voluminous sultan pants.

"You called me your possessor," she said with reluctance, drawing out of his warm embrace and already missing the feel of him. She spoke to his collarbone, knowing she'd lose her nerve if she gazed up into his hypnotic brown eyes. "Does that mean you have to do whatever I tell you to do?"

"Yes. It is my duty to fulfill your every desire. To service you in any way I am able."

Laila expelled the deep breath she wasn't aware she'd been holding. "Duty," she repeated as her shoulders sagged. "And service. That's what I thought."

While she might be starved for male affection and hot sex with a gorgeous guy, Laila still wanted a man to be attracted to her simply because he was. Period. Not because it was his duty to pretend he found her appealing.

She stepped a good two feet away, looking him direct in the eyes. "I don't want to carry this any further."

"But, Laila—"

Her hand rose between them. "I'm the one in charge. I give the commands and you obey," she said in a no-nonsense manner. "Right?"

A combined look of defeat, torment and anger crossed the genie's features so quickly Laila almost missed the shift in expression. In an instant he composed himself, steeling his features as he tightened the muscle in his jaw, making his emotions unreadable.

"I am your slave and you are my master...yes."

He looked so wounded she was tempted to pull him into a hug. Thwarting her impulse, she remained in place.

"Genie, I—"

"I have a name, Laila. It is Zakkar. I would ask once again that you use it, unless, of course, the idea displeases you." He regarded her with a flat, cold stare.

"Zakkar," Laila repeated the name. Her smile was met by his same guarded expression.

Her phone rang with Reen's ringtone.

With the seeming speed of light, Zakkar's hand was on his saber, drawing it partially from its sheath as the musical tone chimed again. "What is this malevolence? This witchcraft?"

"Whoa, hold on a minute, Conan."

"Zakkar."

"Right. It's just Reen." Laila wanted to snatch her phone from the table before Zakkar could turn it into mulch, but feared her arm might get hacked off in the process.

"Reen?" Once he finished speaking, another musical tone indicating voicemail played. He turned to Laila, one eyebrow raised in question.

"It's just my phone." Laila made a swift grab for it and held it aloft. "See?"

"This shrill object with its own light source is your sister, Reen? He eyed her with another quizzical expression. "Advancements have truly come that far?" It rang again and Zakkar spouted something in a foreign language as he gazed menacingly at it.

Laila held her hand up in what she hoped was a calming gesture. "There's no reason to start slicing, dicing and chopping. Reen's not actually inside. It's not magic. It's just technology. Part of the skill and knowledge of our time."

"Technology," he repeated.

"Yes. Remember how you felt the first time you saw your own image captured in that photograph?" He nodded. "You probably thought that was black magic too, right?"

"I am still not convinced otherwise."

Laila decided this wasn't a good time to show him how she could capture his image with her phone's camera. "This object is just a speaking device. There's nothing to be afraid of. It's not going to hurt you."

Zakkar looked downright appalled. "Afraid?" he thundered, reseating his saber. "I fear nothing! I only sought to protect you from harm."

"Right. Well, thank you for saving me from the fearsome phone, Zakkar. I appreciate it." Once again she felt the overwhelming urge to hug him.

His eyebrow shot up again. "You are mocking me, if I am not mistaken."

"Maybe just a teensy bit."

"I thirst to understand how technology works, to take this phone apart and study the internal mechanisms."

Laila blinked. Sultan pants and saber or not, her genie was clearly a typical man. And she sure as hell wasn't about to let him dismantle her phone.

"I don't have all the answers. It'll be Google to the rescue," she muttered beneath her breath.

"Who is this Google you appeal to for rescue? I guarantee I am stronger." His arms crossed over his chest while his expression bared great pride.

"It's..." She realized it was ludicrous to attempt to explain about computers and being online in a few sentences. Especially to someone who'd just stepped out of 1859.

"A beast? A dragon? An all-knowing wizard?"

"Yes, that's a good one. It's like an all-knowing wizard. I'll show you later." She smiled, trying to picture him seated at a computer. "For now, sit," she instructed, patting the seat of a kitchen chair. "I'll see what I have in the fridge to eat."

"Food would be most appreciated," Zakkar said as he sat. "My belly aches with hunger."

She opened the refrigerator. As he glimpsed the first shaft of light radiating from the inside, Zakkar leapt to his feet, clearly primed to protect her from the formidable refrigerator beast.

Chapter 6

~<>~

ZAKKAR CALMED WHEN an army of glowing armor-clad fiends failed to emerge from the lighted belly of the refrigerator.

Casually withdrawing salad fixings from the vegetable bin, Laila engaged in idle conversation with the brawny, half-naked barbarian sitting at her table. It was all quite surreal. His size and presence riveted her attention as he strode to the refrigerator and opened the door to inspect the unfamiliar object. Chin elevated, he flashed Laila a confident smile.

"You see? I am not afraid," he stated boldly.

The man was stunning. He moved like a panther, sleek, graceful and deadly. Taking in a deep breath, she caught his enticing scent as he walked by and the surge of desire she felt made her tremble.

"You have an entire market housed inside this chilled, illuminated box," Zakkar marveled. "You must be wealthy beyond imagination."

She mentally calculated how many days were left before her credit card bill, car payment, and utilities were due. "Actually, everyone has a refrigerator."

She couldn't recall ever being in such close proximity to a man like this, much less making him a salad as she stood at her kitchen counter, trying to be blasé and pretend her mind wasn't concocting sexy scenarios as she julienned a cucumber.

She opened the freezer, scanning the contents for something other than frozen diet dinners. Zakkar stood next to her, placing his hand on the freezer's icy contents.

"It is like the frozen tundra of Mongolia captured in your abode."

Opening two boxes of reduced calorie lasagna, she paused and looked up at him. "You've been there?"

"Hundreds of years ago. One of my possessors belonged to a fierce nomadic tribe. I will never forget the brutal cold of Mongolia's barren plains."

An image of Zakkar wrapped in furs and animal skins permeated Laila's brain. She would have loved being his body pillow on those frigid nights.

"And here you have its coldness isolated in a metal box," he went on, snapping her wayward thoughts back to the present. He watched as Laila placed the food in the microwave. "What is that?"

"A microwave. It heats the food."

"I see no evidence of wood or fire." Zakkar examined the appliance. "How does the heat source get into the small box?"

Laila eyed the microwave and shrugged. "I have no idea. It cooks with microwaves—and don't ask because I have no clue what they are."

"I understand." Zakkar gave a knowing nod. "You are only a female so you have not been taught these aspects of technology."

Leaning against the counter, Laila crossed her arms over her chest, eyeing him. "It has nothing to do with my gender, Macho Man. The average man has no idea what microwaves are either."

"What is the meaning of macho man? Is it a reverent form of address?"

"Hardly." Laila snickered. "It means pigheaded."

He ambled back to the kitchen table and sat in the chair, arms folded across the broad expanse of his chest. "Since I clearly do not have the head of a hog, your words indicate there has been a shift in male and female roles since I last walked the earth. Or perhaps it is merely you, Laila, who shows a lack of respect for your superiors."

Her jaw dropped. "My *what*?"

"The men of your time." Her look of shocked disbelief didn't seem to faze Zakkar one iota. "Do they not still fight the battles, slay the animals for the dinner table, work and toil to provide shelter and protection for the fairer sex?"

"Things have changed, Zak."

"Zak?" Fury zigzagged across his features. "No man has dared butcher my given name before."

"One, I'm not a man, in case you haven't noticed. Two, *Zak* is more twenty-first century, so we'll go with that, okay? Anyway Zak" she went on without waiting for his answer, "men and women are equals now." She thought twice about that. "Okay, scratch that. But at least we're making progress."

"Equals." Zak relaxed his handsome features into a patronizing half smile. "I like you. You are humorous, Laila." He sniffed the air and pointed toward the small meal she'd removed from the microwave. "This small container holds an entire supper? It does not seem possible."

"Tell me about it." Laila gave a meager laugh. "Unfortunately, all I have in the house is diet food. I wasn't expecting a six-foot-tall genie for dinner."

Zak straightened in the chair. "I stand six feet and five and three-quarter inches."

Laila's lips curled into a devilish grin. Regardless of what time they lived in, size and every fraction of an inch were evidently vital statistics with men.

"Did you learn how tall you are when you got fitted for your sultan outfit?" She dragged her eyes from his crotch to his face.

"No, Abigail Maythorne had me measured for a suit of clothing during my time with her. The suit I am wearing in the photograph."

His time with Abigail. The woman looked somewhere between seventy and a hundred in that photo. Laila wondered if Zak and the old lady had slept together. The idea made her cringe. But if

Abigail was having him measured for clothes, they were probably close enough to be doing the horizontal mambo.

Pushing unsavory thoughts of Abigail and Zak aside, she asked, "How can you survive in the bottle all those years without eating?"

"It is similar to hibernation. I exist in a dreamlike state, half alive and half in *Kurnugi*, the land of no return."

Teeming with curiosity about this man and his strange past, she asked, "How did you end up in the bottle? Did you murder someone? Or...hurt a woman?" Of all the reasons for imprisonment she could imagine, she really didn't want to think she was entertaining a murderer or rapist.

"While I have slain countless men in battle, I have never taken a life merely for the sake of killing. And I would sooner hack off a limb than harm a woman, even though some of them can be treacherous."

Whether prudent or not, she believed him.

"I will tell you about my imprisonment later. It is not good dinner conversation." He gazed at her like she was a warm, inviting bowl of marionberry cobbler. "I hunger for more than just food, Laila. It has been a very long time. Centuries."

And she thought *she'd* been without sex for a long time. Laila's gaze drifted over Zak's torso. He was all man, big, hard, solid and oozing with testosterone.

And he wanted to pleasure her until she was boneless.

Just once in her life she'd love to do something wild and risky with a man who could pass as a Greek god.

After downing his salad, Zak shoveled in forkfuls of the meat-free lasagna, practically inhaling the paltry serving of diet food. He wasn't kidding when he said he was hungry.

"I don't have much of an appetite," she said. After taking two bites of her food she passed her portion to Zak. "I'd give you some garlic bread to go with it, but I rarely have bread in the house."

"Bread...*ninda*..." Zak nodded. "The staff of life, Abigail called it. You do not like it?"

"I love it but I'm a carb addict. One bite leads to another until I blow up like a beached whale." She puffed out her cheeks.

"I am familiar with addicts." Zak nodded. "Carbs are like opium?"

"Good analogy." Laila rolled her eyes and laughed.

"I remember the taste and smell of fresh bread from the oven. It is not something anyone should have to do without if they enjoy it."

"I agree." She uttered a monumental sigh. "Unfortunately it makes some of us fat because we can't stop eating it."

"Fat?" Zak gave her an incredulous look. "But you are close to scrawny. You have made a mistake to avoid bread. Adding some plumpness will assure you do not lose your alluring womanly form."

This outstanding, outspoken specimen of manhood thought she was just this side of scrawny? Laila was stunned. She longed to record this moment to replay over and over. Maybe to Bunny.

Drawing invisible circles on the placemat with her finger she said, "That's nice of you to say, but men today usually prefer skinny women with prominent collarbones, sharp hip bones and gaunt, sunken faces." She sucked in her cheeks.

Zak made a scoffing sound. "Then the men of your time are idiots," he stated flatly. "You have described a starving street urchin or prisoner of battle."

"You won't get much argument from me." Laila screwed her features. "But even my boss told me I need to lose thirty pounds. I'm afraid full-figured just doesn't cut it in the twenty-first century, Zak."

"The size of your body should be of no concern to your employer. It is improper for him to focus on your womanly curves. Perhaps he harbors lewd thoughts about you."

"I sincerely doubt that. My boss is a she. A skinny she."

"A female employer?" Clearly surprised, Zak studied Laila. "You are a governess? A maid, or laundress?"

"A weight loss counselor. I help people reach their weight goals and maintain them."

"I don't understand. You purposely encourage people to waste away?" He looked aghast, his eyebrows drawing together in a frown. "In every society and in every time period I have existed, the goal was to prevent people from becoming emaciated, not cause them to become so. This cannot be healthy."

Doing her best to digest the surreal information that Zak had existed for numerous lifetimes, Laila cleared the table, placing the dishes in the sink.

Looking over her shoulder, she asked, "How long have you been alive, Zak?"

"Alive?" His gaze went cold as he uttered a harsh sound of disdain. "I was in my third decade of life when I was placed in servitude. I would not call my existence since then living." Zak's chest expanded as he drew in a lengthy breath. "I have lost count of the passage of time. My incarceration in that foul bottle," he gestured toward the spun glass artifact with a jab of his jaw, "has spanned hundreds of centuries. I have walked the earth for brief periods more times than I can count." His hand plowed through his hair and he groaned.

Laila didn't know what to say. The man's pain and resentment must run terribly deep. She wondered again what he could have done to deserve such cruel, unforgiving punishment. Who or what would have the power to imprison a man in a bottle for centuries?

Eyeing Zak surreptitiously, she decided he looked fierce enough to battle hordes of warriors. But he didn't strike her as being inherently criminal or evil. Of course, she was no expert on criminology or murderous psychopaths. For all Laila knew, Zakkar

Tymon could casually lop off her head in the middle of dessert without so much as a blink of an eye.

"It sounds like you have some painful memories, Zak. If you decide you want to talk about them I'd be happy to listen." She opened the refrigerator, looking for something to serve for dessert. Out of fruit, the only sweet she had was the aerosol whipped cream she saved for guests.

About to close the fridge, she got an idea. Drawing out the can, Laila flashed a smile at her hunky visitor.

"Open your mouth." She held the aerosol can a few inches from his face.

One of his eyebrows dipped low. "Why?" he asked, his gaze dubious.

"Just do it. Trust me, you'll like it."

"I think I will not do this. Trusting women has only gotten me into trouble." Folding his arms across his chest, Zak clamped his lips tight.

"Oh, sorry. I didn't think warriors were such wimps." Laila did her best to look innocent.

"Wimps?"

"Babies. Sissies. Cowards," she elucidated. "Gutless, spineless—"

Zak's mouth popped wide open and Laila fought to swallow rising laughter. Men were so easy, no matter how long they've been around.

She watched his eyes widen as she pressed the nozzle, squirting a huge tuft of whipped cream into his mouth. Turning the nozzle on herself she repeated the process, coating her tongue with a sizeable ruffle.

It was obvious Zak enjoyed the treat.

"See? I told you. Tasty, hmm? And, look, you haven't turned into a horned toad or anything."

"How many cans of this do you have?" Zak took it from her, experimenting with the nozzle.

"One more."

"Good." He glanced at her with glittering eyes and a wolfish grin. "I will use it when I bed you, to decorate your succulent fleshscape before I feast on you."

Aghast, Laila was rendered speechless, standing there opening and closing her mouth like a fish out of water.

"You can get that whole bedding me idea out of your mind, Zak. It's not going to happen."

He closed his eyes, breathing deeply through his nose. "I can smell your passion. Your musk. Your desire for me." His eyes opened, narrowing between thick, dark lashes. Intense and determined, they raked over her.

"I mean it," she warned. Damn. It wasn't easy being stern when all she could think of was his hands all over her.

Zak rose to his feet and Laila had to look up, way up, to meet the gaze of the finely honed mass of muscularity. He took her hand in his, brushing her knuckles with a kiss.

"I am here for no other reason than to protect and pleasure you. I am your slave. Ask and I shall obey." The deep timbre of his voice sent shivers up her spine. "Give me your permission to please you. I promise, you will not regret it." He kissed the inside of her elbow and her knees went weak.

So what if it *was* just his duty? Did it really matter? Why couldn't she simply think of him as a fantasy come to life? A scrumptious male prostitute there to do her bidding? Gazing into his penetrating eyes, she swallowed a sigh.

"What kind of woman would I be," she said, rationality rudely intruding, "if I hopped into bed with you, a man I just met?"

"A happy woman?" Zak's rakish smile dazzled.

She couldn't avoid her pop of laughter because, damn, the guy was probably right. "I'm serious, Zak," she claimed, while every fiber of her being balked at her maddening sense of practicality.

"As am I. You mentioned your motorcycle husband." Zak looked left, right and under the table. "Where is he? I am not in the habit of bedding married women."

"Oh, that. I, um, may have exaggerated." Laila felt her face flush. "I'm not married. But I can't sleep around willy-nilly. It's not right."

He looked genuinely baffled. "Willy Nilly is your lover?"

Choking back a laugh she answered, "It's not a who, it's a...it means I shouldn't have casual sex with someone I just met. It's not moral or responsible."

He gifted her with a tender smile. "Even for the short time we have been acquainted, I know there is nothing about you that would bring shame or dishonor."

The last thing Laila expected was for her eyes to well with tears. It was so long since a man complimented her. She could easily bend his ear for the entire night with sob stories of how tough it had been. How she'd grieved poor Tim's tragic death.

She could cry buckets about how she'd waited so long before dating again only to find herself in an emotionally abusive relationship with a man she'd made the mistake of trusting. During their last date she caught the guy boffing their pizza waitress in the restaurant's ladies' room.

Laila drew in a calming breath, expelling it with a quiet whoosh. Returning Zak's smile, she said, "Thank you," while dabbing her teary eyes with her napkin. "That means a lot to me."

He leaned close, cupping the side of her face and gazing straight into her eyes. "You are an adult. Old enough to give yourself permission to be pleasured. I am here to grant you the bliss you deserve."

It sounded so logical. God he was persuasive. "You know all the right things to say, don't you?" She placed her hand over his.

"I have had many lifetimes to learn the right things to say and do." He flashed a smile. "I may not always succeed, but I do my best, especially when I find myself in the midst of a good soul who is beautiful inside and out." He kissed the inside of her wrist. "Like you."

Laila didn't know which was more incredible, having a genie in her kitchen, or having a conversation with a musclebound warrior who had a distinct sensitive side.

"Did you have sex with Abigail Maythorne?" Apparently bothering her more than she realized, the gnawing question popped out of her mouth.

"An honorable man does not discuss his sexual conquests. To do so could tarnish the reputation of the females he has bedded."

"It's not like Abigail has anything to worry about," Laila pointed out as kindly as possible. "She's been dead for well over a century." She took in a shuddering breath. "I-I need to know, Zak."

She'd made her decision. If he'd slept with Abigail, Laila would turn him down. She wasn't sure she could get over the *ick* factor, picturing him pleasuring a pruney, naked old lady. Not that she had anything against seniors having active sex lives, in fact she thought it was great but...nope. Uh-uh.

On the other hand, if he *hadn't* slept with Abigail, she'd consider all his sound, logical reasoning. And then jump his bones.

Or order him to jump hers.

Pausing in thought, Zak nodded. "I did not bed Abigail. It was not her wish. Although I would have gladly accommodated her if she so desired."

Laila's eyes widened in surprise. "She didn't want to sleep with you?" Old or not, Laila couldn't imagine any woman not wanting to have a beautiful man like Zak make love to her.

"We slept in the same bed together. It made Abigail feel safe. We did not have sex because she dearly loved her late husband and felt it would be a betrayal to that love. He was killed in 1843 during their covered wagon trek over the Oregon Trail from the eastern side of America. They were married less than a year before she was widowed."

"How sad. Was the wagon train attacked?"

"No, some of the men were cutting through heavy timber to clear a trail through the mountains. A tree fell on them." Laila winced at the thought. "Abigail said many more lost their lives when the wagons had to be disassembled and floated down the Columbia River. It was a perilous journey."

"I can't even imagine. That means she was alone for..." Laila mentally calculated, "about sixteen years. Was it during the cross-country trip that she found you?"

"No, it was at the side of the road here in Glassfloat Bay."

"How did you end up in Oregon?"

"I have no idea. My bottle prison has been discovered in many peculiar places. An Egyptian tomb, a Viking longboat, in a rolled rug in Persia, in a geisha's quarters in Japan. Once it was encased in ice with the remains of a man and woman in the Andes." He offered a shrug. "And once beneath rotted shelving in the basement of Maythorne Manor." A smile lit his face.

"I'm glad I found you there."

"As am I."

Laila reached for the faded photo, studying the kind-looking face of the old woman. "Abigail must have been elderly when they got married. She looks about eighty in this photograph."

"Abigail was fifty-one when she opened my bottle. She married August Maythorne when she was thirty-five."

"Fifty-one?" Focusing on the photo again, Laila felt a tug at her heart. "My God...poor Abigail."

"She was a strong pioneer woman, making her way alone in difficult, dangerous times. Life was hard for her. Abigail was good and kind. I believe the term would be *motherly*."

Laila was struck by Zak's compassion for the woman, the knowledge warming her heart. While her swarthy genie had a bold warrior's body and a chauvinistic mindset, he apparently had a heart of gold.

"It was my honor to serve her and grant her wishes."

"Can you tell me what they were?"

Zak leaned in so close, Laila thought he was going to kiss her. "Perhaps," he whispered against her ear, "after I make your body quiver and shudder beneath me, I will tell you."

Her breath caught. The man was a living, breathing aphrodisiac. Impossible to resist.

"No *perhaps*. I want your word."

His handsome face still nestled in her hair, Zak gave a deep, husky chuckle. "I promise."

If that was the only way she'd be able to learn about Abigail's three wishes, Laila would just have to make the monumental sacrifice.

"Okay," she said so softly she scarcely heard the word as it left her lips. "Let's do it."

Zak scooped Laila into his arms. With a glance over his shoulder, he addressed the dog. "Friday, stay!" Laila had little doubt her dog would obey his favorite new buddy.

Turning to gaze up at him, her face collided with Zak's chest—hot male flesh, hard bone and perfectly sculpted muscle.

His pectorals flexed.

She indulged in one of those prolonged, melodic sighs heroines of old movies made when the hero gathered her in his arms, carrying her up the stairs and behind closed doors.

"Where?" Zak asked.

"My bedroom." Laila pointed upstairs. "Leave the saber in the kitchen."

"No. A warrior is never without his weapon," Zak countered. "I must keep it at my side to protect you."

Images of Zak's handsome features taking on a fierce demeanor, his sweat-glistened chest heaving as he braved the unknown, his saber slashing to defend Laila from the dreaded cell phone and refrigerator, made her feel like the heroine in one of those movies.

"Wait." The logical side of her brain interrupted her fantasies. "I don't suppose you have condoms, because I don't." It was a sorry truth to have to reveal. The last condom she had was so old it became brittle.

"Condoms?" Zak asked, not breaking his stride.

"You know. Rubbers. Prophylactics." Zak was silent. "Something to cover your *gis* so no sexually transmitted diseases are spread."

"Ah, you have a sexual disease," Zak noted, taking the information in stride.

"No! Of course not! I'm not the one who's slept with dozens of women."

"Hundreds," Zak corrected, and Laila groaned. "Which room is it?"

"There. The question is, do *you* have a disease? With all the places you and that busy appendage between your legs have been, your *gis* could be teeming with billions of nasty organisms."

Zak kicked the door of her bedroom fully open, tossing Laila on the bed. She landed with a surprised *oooph!*

"You need not worry about my *gis* being tainted. I am unable to transmit disease, unable to father children, and unable to die. These precautions were written into the incantation when I was imprisoned."

Zak removed his vest and Laila got the full effect of his muscular chest, as well as a series of long, ragged scars, which made her heart clench.

"Are all those scars from battles?"

"Yes, all prior to my incarceration. Any wounds I received since have healed without any trace of the injury. Again, it was part of the incantation."

"So, you can be hurt but not killed."

"Yes. No matter how close I come to death, I will always survive."

"That's good."

His expression grew dark. "It is a vile curse," Zak spat. "You cannot imagine what it is like to be hacked to—" He stopped abruptly, sucking in a deep breath, straightening his shoulders and elevating his chin. "My apologies. I am not here to complain or bore you to tears about my misfortunes."

"It's not boring." He was the most fascinating person she'd ever met. "Have you received many injuries since you were put in the bottle?"

"Many." He gave a curt nod. "I have come face to face with Ereshkigal more times than I care to remember, each time to be jolted back to...life." Zak's small laugh was humorless.

"Who is Ereshkigal?"

"Goddess of the underworld. Remove your manly trousers," he said without missing a beat.

Scooting to the edge of the bed, Laila complied, wishing she'd worn something other than her white cotton bra and panties. Granny panties of all things. If she'd known she'd be seduced by a hot genie this afternoon, she would have worn...

Her mind went blank. Sadly, she realized she didn't own any sexy lingerie.

As she kicked off her slacks, she heard Zak's intake of breath.

"This scant garment is all women wear beneath their trousers?" Pushing her back against the bank of pillows, he smoothed his hand over her industrial-style panties. "In 1859 this would have been scandalous."

He bent to plant a kiss on her thigh and Laila sighed. He'd just made her feel a whole lot better about her granny panties.

Zak's thumbs slid beneath the leg bands, toying with the stretchy material, snapping it against her skin. She guessed it was his first encounter with elastic.

"How you tempt me," he said as he explored. "I am eager to find what awaits beneath the rest of your garb. What is this raiment called?" Zak fingered her sleeveless pink sweater. "It is soft like the fur of a rabbit. Of this I approve. The color and suppleness are feminine."

"It's a sweater. A cashmere blend. Part of my uniform. I splurged on it instead of getting the acrylic one."

"I am familiar with the Kashmir civilization," Zak noted.

"You mean the goats?"

"Goats?" Once again he looked bewildered.

"I have a feeling we're talking about two different things. The yarn for my sweater came from cashmere goats raised here in Oregon. What cashmere are you talking about?"

"The area around India. I was there several hundred years ago."

"Did you see any goats there?"

"If I recall, yes."

"Well, there you go," she said matter-of-factly, spreading her hands, palms up.

After some contemplation, he asked, "Where do I go?"

Laila blinked.

"You're not going anywhere. It's just an expression."

Yanking her up and away from the pillows, Zak stripped the sweater from her so fast her hair stood on end from the static.

"Another revealing undergarment." His hands were all over her bra and a grin stretched across his face. "You have a body built to stop an army in its tracks."

He drew his saber from his side and Laila felt the blood drain from her veins. Before she had time to cry out, her bra fell from her shoulders.

"You sliced off my bra," she said, dazed and happy to still be breathing. "All you had to do was unhook it."

"I have no patience for complex fasteners when I yearn to see a woman naked." Zak peeled off her underwear. "Ahhhhh..."

That one, elongated expression of approval, combined with his killer smile, elicited a sigh of relief from Laila.

He cupped her breasts in his palms, curving his fingers around them as if measuring the weight. "You are a well-built woman with the luxuriant arcs and slopes of a goddess." Zak flipped her over as if she weighed no more than a pillow. She bounced, face-down on the mattress.

"As I had expected, your bottom is plump and curvy. Soft and pale." His fingers squeezed her cheeks, kneading and stroking. "Like bread dough."

He gave the most unusual compliments.

Before Laila could blink, Zak had flipped her over once more, pushing her shoulders until she fell against the bank of pillows again like a boneless rag doll.

His calloused fingers trailed a path over her flesh from her collarbone to her toes. "Beautiful...such lush, extravagant curves."

Zak's deep voice sent a thrill to her core.

"Do you mean that," she looked up at him through her lashes, "or are you duty-bound to flatter your possessors?"

Cupping her chin, Zak gave her a kiss so scorching it left her breathless.

"All I can do is speak the truth," he told her. "The incantation forbade me to lie. I speak to you purely as a man. Every word uttered of my own accord." After a lingering gaze, he captured her lips in another kiss, this one sweeter, more tender.

Bunching the voluminous fabric of his sultan pants in her fists, she melted into him, locked in his inviting kiss.

Zak unfastened the saber from his side, leaning the scabbard against the nightstand. Laila watched him unwind the long sash of fabric at his waist before removing his pants.

Standing tall and proud before her, he studied Laila's gaze. She hadn't intended to stare but everything about this man's physicality was beautiful, as if he'd been painstakingly sculpted by one of the masters.

"I see you are not displeased at seeing me pant-less. I knew it would be so."

He might be annoyingly cocky, but he was right.

Joining her in bed, Zak embraced Laila while whispering in another language. She had no idea what he said but the sound was romantic perfection. Wrapping her arms around him, she tracked the scars on his back with her fingertips. There were so many, the feel of each bringing tears to her eyes. What pain he must have endured. She didn't even want to consider the agony of all the wounds that had disappeared since his imprisonment.

A long, tremulous groan rumbled from deep within Zak's chest. "So very long," he whispered, "since I have felt a woman's delicate touch on my flesh." His fingers sifted through her hair as Laila continued to explore.

His gaze was fixed, heated, famished. "I am pleased you are the woman who will break my prolonged abstention."

"Sex," she said absently, almost as if she'd forgotten why they were in her bed. "I usually don't even kiss on the first date."

He looked mystified. "Kissing dates is a sexual ritual of your time?"

She considered it a moment. "I suppose you could say that."

"Odd. Do you eat them afterward?"

"My dates?" Laila's jaw fell slack. "Of course not, I'm not a cannibal. You...you're not either, are you?" It would explain why he liked his women on the plump side.

"You cannot be serious." Zak practically spat his indignation at her question. "I am not a savage."

"I have a feeling," she said, scooting to an upright position, grabbing a pillow in front of her, "we're talking about two different things again."

"I speak of the fruits of the date palm tree." He looked reminiscent. "A sweet, succulent pleasure I have not enjoyed in too long." His eyebrow arched. "But I would not find kissing them to be sexual."

"I wouldn't either. The kind of date I'm talking about is when a man comes to call and you go out to see a movie together," Laila explained. "That kind of date."

"Movie?" Obviously confused, Zak slanted his head.

"Yeah, it's..." Nope. No way would she try to explain a motion picture. "Anyway, there is no date eating involved. At the end of the evening the date drives you home, says goodnight and gives you a kiss."

"It makes no sense."

She'd planned to respond but he'd enchanted her with his magical touch. "That feels so good. You've got great hands."

"I know," he acknowledged with his customary bravado. He brought his finger to his lips. "Shhhh...just permit yourself to relax. Release your unease to the heavens. Be assured that our joining will be nothing but pleasurable for you. Fear not. I will not ask you to kiss my date."

He said it with such seriousness and sincerity that Laila bit the inside of her cheek to keep from laughing.

"I was making jest," he explained.

"Oh. I wasn't sure."

Zak took the pillow she clutched, placed it behind her and eased her to a reclining position. He kneaded her feet, legs, arms and each finger until Laila felt like a tranquil noodle.

"You feel soothed?"

"Very." Wiggling her fingers in invitation, she smiled up at him, feeling thoroughly relaxed and decidedly lustful. "Come on, Aladdin. It's time to play open sesame."

"I am not sure what that means." Zak grinned down at her. "But I like the way it sounds."

It wasn't long before Laila found herself in the throes of rapture, fully relishing the intimate act of lovemaking with her handsome, considerate genie.

Chapter 7

~<>~

"YOU HAVE GOOD lungs. I am not enamored of weak, lilting flowers. I prefer my women bold and feisty."

Laila couldn't believe she'd been so vociferous while they'd made love. But then, she'd never experienced such extraordinary sensations before. Thanks to Zak, she was ruined for anyone else. But she didn't care. She'd happily remain celibate the rest of her life in exchange for this one, wondrous experience.

Making love with Zakkar Tymon was like the part in *The Wizard of Oz* when the screen first blooms from black and white to color.

Reclining on his side, Zak propped his head on his hand. "Something you said while I pleasured you makes me curious."

"Tell me," Laila whispered, looking up at a man so exquisite he'd make Hollywood casting directors drool.

"What made you cry out to a religious icon of the people of India?"

Laila frowned. "What are you talking about?"

"*Holy cow,*" Zak said. "You invoked a sacred cow at least thrice."

Taking his face in her hands, she gazed at him. "Oh Zak, you make me laugh. And swoon and sigh and call out in pleasure."

"I am indeed a man of many talents."

"I can attest to that." She gave a throaty chuckle. "Holy cow is an expression of surprise. There's nothing religious about it."

He studied her face until the intensity of his scrutiny made her squirm.

"Your eyes are the color of lapis lazuli. They hold me spellbound."

Her lips parted but she didn't say anything. She was embarrassed to confess she had no idea what lapis lazuli was.

"It is a celestial blue stone," he said, as if realizing her predicament, "prized by priests and royalty going back to my original time on the earth. It's an opulent gem with golden points of light that sparkle like stars."

At the sound of the doorbell chiming, Zak stiffened, Laila's eyes grew wide, and Friday galloped into the bedroom, alerting them with a series of barks.

The muscles in his jaw tensing, Zak snapped to attention, hopping out of bed so fast Laila could barely keep up with his movement. He grabbed the handle of his saber and she heard the screech of metal against metal as it slid from its sheath.

"It's just the doorbell," Laila explained. "A visitor at the door." She glanced at the digital clock on her nightstand. Six-thirty. "Probably somebody selling home repairs or—"

Gasping aloud, she scrambled to her knees. "Oh my God, the kids are here!"

"Baby goats?" Zak looked dumfounded. "From Kashmir? They visit you?"

"No! It's Reen."

"You make my mind a jumble." His fingers spread across his head. "Your sister Reen is a talking goat?"

Gaping at him, Laila didn't know whether to laugh or cry. "For heaven's sake, no. Things haven't changed *that* much, Zak. I mean, this isn't Oz, you know. It's still Oregon."

"Oz?"

"Yeah, you know, Dorothy and the wizard," her hands flailed as she explained, "the tin man and the wicked—" He was giving her that absent look again. "Baum must have written those stories after 1859." She sighed. "Kids are human children. It's slang."

The bell rang again and Friday zoomed out of the bedroom and down the stairs, barking at the front door.

"Oh hell. Reen and Drake are here to pick me up for movie night at my brother's pub. Drake will have his twins, Lilly and Kevin, with him," Laila babbled absently. "He's dropping them off at his parents. What am I going to do? I can't believe I forgot about them coming."

"It is because you were in the hands of a skilled lover, being pleasured beyond your wildest expectations," Zak offered with a confident smile.

Set to argue with the swaggering genie, Laila couldn't refute what he'd said. She'd totally zoned out about going out tonight because she was busy being sublimely bedded by a character straight out of a fairytale.

The doorbell rang again, followed by knocking and the voices of Drake's children calling out, "Miss Laila, Miss Laila!"

"Ohmigod." Laila gulped, her mind racing as she looked at the naked barbarian next to her bed, saber securely gripped. He'd scare the bejeezus out of those poor kids, not to mention Drake and Reen.

"Listen, Zak, this is important." Tossing her hands into the air, she tsked at Friday's continued barking. "Friday! Shush!" Turning back to Zak, she clasped his upper arms, pinning him with a meaningful gaze. "You have to stay here while I go down to answer the door," she instructed. Snagging her bathrobe from the hook behind the bedroom closet door, she shrugged it on, yanking the belt tight.

"Don't make a sound. I'll tell them I came down with the flu and can't go out. Stay here and keep quiet. I'll be back soon."

Shoving her feet into her fluffy, pink bunny-head slippers, she took a deep breath and called out, "Be right there!" punctuating her statement with loud, faux coughs. Before heading for the front door, she looked back up at Zak, standing at the top of the stairs in all his naked glory. "Put your clothes back on."

"But I thought we would—"

"That's an order." Laila scurried into the living room to answer the door.

She pulled it open. With one look at her, Reen's face was full of concern.

"Aw, honey, are you okay?" First thing Reen did was clap a hand to Laila's forehead, as if Laila was her child instead of her sister. "Your face is all flushed and you feel hot. Did you take your temperature?"

"No, I—"

Glancing at Laila's tousled hair, she added, "Poor thing, you're a mess."

"I-I was just going to call you, Reen. It's the flu. Came on all of a sudden." Laila coughed again. "I'm sorry. I can't go with you after all." She looked down to where the five-year-olds had each clamped themselves on one of her legs after greeting Friday. Laila yanked the robe tighter. "You'd better take the kids and go. I'd hate for them to get sick too."

Patting the twins on their heads, she looked up at Reen and Drake again. "I feel terrible that I forgot to call."

"Don't worry about it," Reen said. "You just take care of yourself. We'll do it another— Holy mackerel!" she blurted, her eyes bugging and her jaw hanging.

"Whoa," Drake followed, his eyes just as wide as he gawked.

"Aladdin, Aladdin!" the kids shouted, bouncing up and down in place.

Uh-oh.

She turned to find Zak standing at the foot of the stairs, fully dressed with his saber sheathed at his side. Fists firmly planted at his hips, he looked fierce, foreboding and sexy as hell.

Yanking on the sleeve of Laila's robe, Reen slanted her a look of disbelief. "Who *is* that?"

"Oh good, you see him too." Laila uttered a sigh of relief.

Reen looked at her like she was crazy. "Huh?"

"He's a friend." Laila shrugged. "Sort of."

Looking Zak up and down as he strode into the living room, Reen absently wound a blonde curl around her finger. And then she smiled. "Laila, you've been holding out on me."

"It's not what it looks like..." she cleared her throat, "exactly." Stepping aside, she ushered them into the house. "Come on in, we've got lots to talk about."

Leaning close, Laila whispered in Reen's ear. "He's a genie. He came out of the old perfume bottle I got at the estate sale. In a big blue puff of smoke." She gestured with her hands.

"He *what*!?" Reen screeched. "Are you insane?"

"What? What's going on?" Drake's eyes darted from the women to Zak and back again. "Is something wrong?"

"No." Patting the air with her hands in a calming gesture, Laila assured them, "Everything is fine. Nothing to worry about."

"I like your outfit, Aladdin," Lilly said. "It's better than the cartoon one."

"Cartoon?"

Laila gave a dismissive wave. "I'll explain later, Zak."

"So you are Drake's little goats." Zak squatted to greet the youngsters eye to eye. "I have heard good things about you."

"Miss Reen and Daddy are on a date," Lilly said.

"Ahhh, I see...this is the kind of date that involves neither cannibalism nor eating fruit." Zak boasted a proud grin meant for Laila who realized he still hadn't figured the date thing out.

"You must not touch," Zak cautioned when the little boy's curious fingers reached out to touch the saber's sheath. "It is not a toy."

Laila was surprised to see Zak so at ease with children. Her heart warmed as she saw the genuine smile he gave them and the tender, paternal way in which he treated them.

"Are you Aladdin?" Lilly asked, fingering the rubies glimmering on Zak's vest.

"Sure he is," Kevin said. "Look at him."

"Who is this Aladdin? I have heard Laila speak of him as well." Glancing back at Laila, Zak smiled. "Open sesame," he said, and she about died on the spot when she heard Reen giggle.

"A genie!" Kevin and Lilly chorused, jumping in place and clapping.

Zak's laughter at the children's excitement was an authentic sound of mirth, rendered sexy by his rich, accented baritone.

"Do you like genies?"

"Yes!" The kids were as animated as if they'd just eaten a bowlful of sugar.

"Then you may indeed consider me a genie." Laila noticed he answered without lying, while still telling the children what they wanted to hear. "I come from an ancient land called Sumer."

"Sumer?" Drake frowned, crossing his arms over his chest.

Zak rose to his full height, walking to where Reen and Drake stood.

"You are Laila's sister," Zak said, taking her hand and kissing it. "She has great fondness for you, Reen."

Reen's girlish giggle was a sound Laila had never heard her sister utter before.

Drake straightened to his full five-feet eleven-inches, elevating his chin and swallowing the lump that seemed lodged in his throat as he looked up to make eye contact with Zak.

"Professor Drake Slattery," he said, extending his hand.

"Professor..." Zak cocked his head, as if organizing his thoughts. "A teacher. A worthy, admirable trade. I am Zakkar Tanojin Lugalbanda Tymon, warrior and leader of armies." He clasped Drake's arm just beneath the elbow, heartily clapping his free hand against Drake's shoulder in way of greeting. "Laila has chosen to butcher my name to Zak." He shot her an accusatory look.

"Grab a seat on the couch, you two," Laila told Reen and Drake. "Zak, you can sit there." She gestured to the large, overstuffed armchair in one corner.

Once seated, Drake eyed Zak with suspicion. "Your accent isn't familiar, though it seems to have a Mediterranean inflection. You said you come from Sumer?"

"Yes."

"That's what I thought." Drake nailed him with an *Aha, I've got you now!* expression. "That's impossible. Sumer hasn't been in existence for thousands of years."

"That is so," Zak confirmed with a nod. "I am surprised you know of it. Most people do not."

"Drake's a professor of ancient history and classical archaeology," Laila explained.

"He's practically a genius." Reen patted Drake's arm.

"Abigail Maythorne's husband, August, was a professor," Zak said. "She told me many stories of his experiences teaching in the East of America before they journeyed across the Overland Trail passage."

Drake's gaze narrowed with further skepticism before glancing to Reen and Laila. "Is this guy an actor or something?"

"Maythorne?" Reen squeaked. "As in the house with the estate sale?"

"That would be the one," Laila confirmed. "Remember the old photo I bought?" Reen nodded and Laila thumbed at Zak.

"The boy toy? No...*no!*" Eyes wide in sudden recognition, Reen grabbed Laila's arm. "Oh dear God. I need to sit down."

Laila laughed. "You already are."

"Good, because I was about to faint."

"What are you two talking about?" Drake asked. "Who is this guy?"

Raising her finger, Laila said, "I'll tell you everything in a minute." She turned to the children. "Come with me, kids, I have paper and crayons. Let's see which of you can draw the best picture of a genie and an Arabian castle. The winner gets a prize!"

The children followed Laila to the kitchen where she set them up with drawing supplies—after she placed Zak's bottle on the top shelf inside one of the cabinets.

Then she headed back to the living room to explain to her sister and Drake that they'd been entertaining an honest to goodness genie in her absence.

~<>~

"And that's it," Laila finished after detailing how Zak appeared. "The whole story." Flopping against the back of her chair, she sucked in a deep breath, expelling it in a whoosh.

Drake turned to Reen, mumbling something too soft for Laila to hear. She figured he was probably suggesting Laila had lost her marbles and needed to see a shrink.

"I know what you're thinking, Drake. I'm *not* crazy. After all, you and Reen see him too. So do the kids."

Drake sat forward, resting his elbows on his knees and giving her one of those calm, patronizing smiles Laila imagined he used on his students. "Yes, but you're the only one who claims to have seen him stream out of a bottle in a vaporous cloud," he pointed out, all logic and rationality.

"Laila displays no symptoms of one who is mad," Zak said. "I detect no lunacy."

"Thank you, Zak." Laila sat up straight, elevating her chin and directing a nod of thanks toward him.

"She does not foam at the mouth," Zak continued, "tear out clumps of her hair or rend her garments. Her eyes are not wild and unfocused, and she does not spout gibberish. And she has already confirmed she is free of sexually transmitted disease."

"Oh God." Laila sank low in her seat, covering her eyes. "Just take me now."

Eyeing the man comfortably sprawled in the chair across the room, Reen turned her attention to Laila, her gaze landing on her sister's terrycloth bathrobe.

"Something tells me we haven't heard the whole story yet." Reen's devilish smile told Laila exactly what her sister was thinking.

"Be right back." Laila sped upstairs to her bedroom where she slipped on underwear, a pair of jeans, and her sleeveless pink uniform sweater. Gazing at herself in the full length mirror, she smoothed her messy hair and wiped the makeup smudges beneath her eyes. Hopefully she looked more like a sane woman and less like a lust-driven harlot.

"He could be a magician who's hypnotized her into believing he's a genie," Laila heard Drake say to Reen as Laila returned to the living room. "Or maybe he drugged her."

Zak lifted his hands in defense. "I do not delve into the dark realms of magic. I did not tell Laila I am a genie. She came upon that false conclusion of her own accord."

"Because he wears Aladdin pants and I get three wishes," Laila explained with a shrug. "It's a natural assumption."

"Wishes?" Reen's hand flew to her chest. "Did you make them already?"

"We didn't get to the wishes part yet. We've been..." Laila glanced at Zak, who had one of those sexy we-share-a-special-secret expressions. Laila swallowed hard. "We've been busy talking about other stuff."

"Talking." Reen looked from Laila to Zak and smiled. "Uh-huh. Methinks the dry spell is over." She snickered.

Laila's swore she could feel her cheeks burn from pink to crimson.

"He's a scammer," Drake claimed.

"He's not, Drake. I swear, he came out of a bottle in a puff of smoke. I'll show you the bottle."

As Laila left the room, she heard Zak say, "I like you, Drake. You are a good man. It is good you are doubtful and seek to protect the women from perceived harm. I assure you, I do not pose a threat to any of you. I am here to serve and protect only. You have my oath."

"He sounds sincere," Reen offered. "Kind of like a cop."

"Or a cunning criminal," Drake noted.

"This is it." Laila returned, depositing the stone box with the metal strappings on the coffee table in front of Drake. "And here's the 1859 photo of Abigail Maythorne. Look at the guy standing behind her."

Drake lifted the photo, studying it closely. While he examined it, Reen turned to Laila, who had taken a seat next to her.

Folding her arms across her chest, it seemed Reen had a difficult time swallowing back laughter. "Laila Jane Malone, you are such a slut."

"I-I..." Laila felt her cheeks turn a guilty shade of crimson again.

"This is hilarious. You did exactly what we always tease Delaney about." Reen laughed.

With a sharp intake of breath, Laila's eyes widened. "I am *so* not like Delaney," she protested, recalling their sister's story about the first night Delaney and Varik met. Fresh from the mountains of Norway, he showed up on her doorstep in full Viking regalia, speaking badly broken English.

Under the mistaken assumption Varik was a high-class male escort sent to her by her late grandmother's estate—a sort of parting gift, so to speak—bedroom escapades ensued. Delaney still blushed peppermint pink whenever Laila and Reen teased her about the monumental misunderstanding.

"Maureen Malone, don't you dare breathe a word of this to Mom or Delaney."

Clasping Laila's arm, Reen winked. "You know better than that. My lips are sealed." She twisted an invisible lock over her lips.

"This photo's obviously been manipulated," Drake said, snapping their attention back to the moment as he looked from the sepia photograph to Zak and back again.

"For heaven's sake, Drake." Laila leaned over, jabbing a finger at the photo. "It's not photoshopped. It's the same man."

Drake picked up the ancient box. After scrutinizing every nook and cranny of the stone, the metal, the silk lining and the spun glass bottle inside, he looked up, an expression of amazement on his face.

"These are either the most clever reproductions I've ever seen, or rare antiquities." He traced his finger over the hieroglyphic-like symbols. "Do you have any idea what this is?" he asked, not really directing the question to anyone in particular.

"Some sort of Greek or Egyptian writing?" Laila said.

"Ancient Chinese?" Reen offered.

"No," Drake shook his head, "if I'm not mistaken it's—"

"Cuneiform," Zak said.

Gazing up in wonder, Drake said, "Yes. How did you know?"

"My people, the Sumerians, invented it."

"*Your* people? That's impossible," Drake said. "Cuneiform is the world's first written language. The last known cuneiform inscription was about 75 AD."

Zak rose from his chair and went to Drake's side. "May I?" He extended his hand toward the box. Drake turned it over to him with some reluctance. "It is a lamentation," Zak stated as he studied the pictograms. Tracing his finger along the metal strap, he read aloud,

"'She made her fly like a swallow from the window. My life was consumed...' It appears to speak of a child being taken by Ereshkigal, goddess of the underworld."

Drake fell back against the sofa cushions, aghast. He turned to Reen and Laila. "Incredible." After gathering his thoughts, he looked up at Zak, who had set the box on the table. "And the bottle, you know what that is?"

"Spun glass bottles such as this were owned by the wealthy. Their purpose was to hold perfumed oil or for use as a tear vase. Because of the lamentation, I suspect this vessel was used for tears."

Drake slapped his knee. "Well, I'll be damned."

Leaning toward Drake, Zak pressed a finger to the man's chest. "*Ummia*," he said. Then he touched his own chest. "*Amelu.*"

"My God, that sounds like—"

"Sumerian," Zak confirmed with a slow nod, maintaining direct eye contact with Drake.

"What did he say?" Reen asked excitedly.

"As near as I can decipher," Drake answered, "he called me teacher and himself soldier."

"It is close enough." Zak nodded.

"How do you know Sumerian?" Laila asked Drake.

"One of the umpteen degrees he has is in ancient languages," Reen offered when it was evident Drake's mind was totally focused on the swell of new information. "The man's a walking encyclopedia. Sometimes I think he's faster than Google."

"But the Sumerian language hasn't been spoken since before the time of Moses," Drake pointed out to Zak.

"Who?" Zak asked in all sincerity.

A stunned silence captured the room.

Closing his eyes, Drake ran his fingers through his hair. Looking back at Zak, his concentrated gaze was pregnant with questions.

"There was an ancient king of Uruk," he finally said, "who became legendary. Can you tell me why?"

"You speak of Gilgamesh, the son of Lugalbanda and father of Urlugal." Zak gave a knowing nod. "He was said to be two-thirds god and one-third human. The Sumerian people wrote a great epic telling of his exploits."

All eyes were on Drake as he silently digested the information.

"Are you okay, Drake?" Reen asked. "You look white as a sheet."

"Sonuvabitch," Drake muttered. "I think this guy's for real. I don't know how it's possible. It defies all logic, all science, but I believe it."

"That's what I've been trying to tell you," Laila said, finally feeling a reprieve from her frustration.

Drake held the bottle gingerly in his hands. "I have to know more."

"Where was Sumer?" Reen asked Zak.

"South of Akkad, between the Tigris and Euphrates rivers," he answered.

"In what's now known as the Middle East," Drake elaborated. "Sumer was part of Mesopotamia."

"All done, Miss Laila!" Kevin and Lilly ran into the living room, waving their drawings.

The kids crawled up on the sofa, competing for space on Laila's lap.

"They're wonderful," Laila said, studying their pictures. Alive with color, they showcased the unrestrained creativity of young children. "How will I ever choose a winner?"

"Great job, kids." Reen mussed the children's hair. "You're both such talented artists."

"Look, Daddy." Lilly waved her drawing under Drake's nose.

Drake looked from the scrawled drawings to his daughter. "Your perspective is off because you made your genie bigger than the castle," he noted, studying the crayon depictions as if he were surveying a college student's thesis. "And the sun is disproportionate to the foreground. The proper prospective would be—"

"What your dad means with all those big words is that he loves your beautiful drawing," Reen cut in. "Isn't that right, Drake?"

Drake gave Reen's knee an appreciative pat. "Miss Reen is right. That's exactly what I was trying to say. Great job, Lilly."

Zak removed the saber and its sheath from his hip positioning them atop a tall bookshelf. He came to the side of the couch on which Laila sat, squatting to peruse the children's drawings. "Such wondrous artwork. It seems we have two winners. One for the best castle and one for the best genie."

"Perfect!" Laila was amazed at Zak's acumen with children. Rising to her feet, she told them, "I'll be right back with your prizes, a new book for each of you."

"Yay!"

Laila returned in time to hear Zak tell the children that not everyone in Sumer was lucky enough to learn to read and write. Only certain children selected by the gods were called to be scribes. Most of them were male. Females became wives, mothers, or priestesses who served the gods in tall mud-brick, temples where people brought offerings and sacrifices to the gods.

"Amazing..." Drake muttered. "You know your ancient history as if you were there."

Zak flashed a white-toothed grin. "Indeed."

"Were you a scribe?"

"No, a professional soldier. My father was a scribe. In secret, he and my mother taught me, my brothers, and sisters, to read and write."

"My mind is racing with questions," Drake said. "How long will you be here?"

"For six lunar cycles, or until Laila makes her final wish and I have completed my servitude to her, whichever comes first."

"Then what?" Reen asked.

"I return to the bottle to await my next possessor."

"Were you a criminal?" Drake asked. "Did someone cast a spell on you because you broke a law?"

"I have never committed a crime. It was not a spell but an incantation spoken by a priest and priestess to place me in eternal service to womankind. I was falsely interned, defending the honor of a young priestess."

"Who was the incantation directed to?"

"Inanna," Zak answered Drake. "Queen of Heaven, goddess of—"

"Love and war," Drake finished with a grim nod. "She was believed to be extremely powerful."

"As I can confirm." Arching an eyebrow, Zak folded his arms across his chest.

"What was happening in your time before you were imprisoned?" Drake asked.

Zak had a faraway look in his eyes. "On the banks of the Euphrates, with my troops I defended the walls of the Sumerian cities against the siege of Sargon of Akkad's army."

"Sargon...Akkad..." Drake sat still and silent, apparently in deep thought. A look of astonishment crossing his features, he said, "But that had to be..." His gazed was fixed on Zak. "That was the third millennium BC. You've been in captivity for—"

"Five thousand years," Laila whispered, swiping at the fat set of tears spilling down her cheeks. She felt sure her heart would break at the sad, implausible revelation.

"You said eternal," Reen noted. "There's no way for you to get out of this incantation? That seems unnecessarily cruel."

With a resigned sigh, Zak gave an indifferent shrug. "I thought at one time there might be a way. The priestess, Sabit, promised to find a way to free me but..." His words trailed off as his eyes narrowed and a scowl marred his handsome features.

"She was the one whose honor you defended?" Laila asked.

"Yes."

"What happened?" Reen asked.

Zak looked at the children and back to the adults. "It is not an appropriate discussion in the presence of the little goats. I will tell you another time, if I see you again."

"Well, of course you're going to see us again. You'll be here for six months," Reen said.

Drake nudged her with his elbow. "Unless Laila makes her wishes before that," he reminded Reen.

"Oh..."

"You'll see Zak again," Laila assured. "I guarantee it." She planned to keep him here until the last possible moment.

"Holy mackerel," Reen said, "this is all so incredible."

"Does this sacred fish reference mean you are you a fish worshipper, or is this phrase similar to the sacred cow saying?"

Reen's expression screwed. "I hope you can translate, Laila, because I'm lost...unless he's talking about my worshipful love of lobster with drawn butter."

Laila explained that Zak comes out of the bottle able to speak and understand his possessor's language, minus slang and colloquialisms like holy mackerel, holy cow, gee whiz, etcetera.

"Well holy Toledo," Reen replied, watching Zak's clueless expression. "Sorry. I couldn't resist. So what's on your agenda for tomorrow, I mean besides..." Her eyebrows wiggled.

"Maureen." Drake's expression was half teasing, half scolding. Reen merely grinned in response.

"First on the agenda," Laila shifted her weight to one hip, giving Zak a head to toe appraisal, "is taking Zak shopping for clothes."

"Gee, I kind of like what he's wearing now," Reen teased.

"Uh, excuse me...did I suddenly become invisible?" Drake joked.

Reen and Laila exchanged a conspirator's smile.

"Come on, kids, time to go to grandma and grandpa's," Drake told his yawning children. His stomach growled noisily and he laughed. Patting his abdomen, he added, "As fascinating as this is, I'm not missing out on Nevan's pork pie special tonight. Ready Reen?"

"Sure." Turning to her sister, Reen squeezed Laila's hands. "Keep me posted." Laila nodded.

Once they left, Friday joined Laila and Zak at the window as they watched the kids being strapped into their car seats.

"Reen and Drake are husband and wife?"

"No, they're just good friends. Nothing romantic going on."

"I am not so sure. I observed the looks of longing he gave her."

"Hmm...interesting. I thought there might be something between them too but Reen insists she's interested in someone else."

A moment later, Zak stiffened, eyes wide as Drake backed out of the driveway. He was clearly astonished, but thankfully not to the point of drawing his saber.

"A horseless chariot? Surely this is magic."

"It's called a car, an automobile. It operates using a gas engine with lots of horsepower and—" Laila held her hand up as Zak's mouth opened to speak. "Just add it to the expanding list of things you'll learn about over the next six months."

Zak's responding smile didn't reach his eyes. "I will not be here that long."

"Yes you will."

"I will not. No woman has ever waited more than fourteen days to make her wishes."

"Two weeks?" Laila felt the sting of tears behind her eyes. "You've never been outside the bottle for more than two weeks at a time?"

Friday chose that moment to whimper, almost as if he understood.

"No. My time with Abigail was the longest." He smoothed his thumb over the single tear escaping Laila's eye. "There is no reason to weep. It is simply my destiny. I hold no animosity toward any of my possessors for making their wishes quickly. I would most likely do the same if I were in their situation."

He held Laila at arm's length, locking gazes with her. "Know that I will bear no ill feeling toward you either when you make your third wish and I return to the bottle."

"Oh, Zak," she whispered against his chest, "I wish I could—"

With an audible gasp, Laila's hand shielded her mouth and she yanked out of his embrace. "I have to be careful. I don't want to squander my wishes on something mindless because of a slip of the tongue."

"True."

They sat next to each other on the couch with Friday positioned at their feet. The room was silent except for the sound of Friday licking Zak's toes.

"Okay," Laila said after giving it serious thought, "ignore anything I say using the words *I wish* unless you specifically hear me say it exactly like this, *for my first official wish, I wish*," she hung invisible quotes as she spoke the phrase, "and so on, until the third wish is made. That'll be my official command so we prevent any mistakes."

"I understand." He mirrored her quotes gesture. "What does this mean? Will it be part of your command?"

"It's just air quotes." She could tell by his expression he was puzzled. "Yes, I'll make sure to use that gesture when I make an official wish," she confirmed, deciding the quotes would act as an extra safeguard.

"The thought of accidentally returning you to that bottle because I was stupid enough to say *gee, I wish I had a Snickers* is horrifying. So if you hear me randomly wishing I had some chocolate or ice cream, ignore it, okay?"

Zak chuckled, a pleasant sound that rumbled up from deep in his chest. "You are a very special woman." He drew her to him, smoothing her hair as she rested her head on his chest, listening to his heartbeat. "I will enjoy my time with you, however long or short it may be."

"Six months," she reiterated.

When he stood, scooping her up into his arms, she gave a surprised little yelp. "What are you doing?"

One look into his heated gaze told her all she needed to know.

Chapter 8

~<>~

"ARE THERE NO more lights to turn on?" Zak asked. "I love this electricity. I must learn how light bulbs work."

Click.

On. Off. On. Off. On...

Laila looked around her bedroom as Zak went from lamp to lamp, repeatedly flicking the light switches. She'd never seen the bedroom lit so bright at night. He'd insisted she also turn on the lights from the master bathroom for additional illumination.

She wasn't all that thrilled about him eyeing her naked body highlighted in stark clarity.

"I have lots of candles," she offered. "Pretty, scented ones. Wouldn't you prefer a dimmer, more subdued, romantic ambience?"

"No." His eyes flashed and she caught a glimpse of something resembling dread. "I like the light. After spending an eternity in the cold darkness of the bottle, this glowing brightness is a wealth of warm, golden treasure. If it is permissible, can we have all the electric lights on, as well as the candles?"

"Of course." She'd forgotten about him being bottled up for so long. Naturally he'd want to be surrounded by light now. Lighting a match and holding it against the first candlewick, Laila sighed. She'd just have to bite the bullet, trying not to cringe when Zak zeroed in on her well-lit imperfections.

Once she'd lit the last of the candles, she smiled. "This is all the lighting I have for this room. Except for the little flashlight tucked in my nightstand drawer in case the electricity goes out in the middle of the night."

"What is this flash of light?"

"A battery-operated device, mostly for emergencies. It doesn't require a cord to be plugged into the wall."

"Show me." Zak looked like a little boy hearing about dinosaurs for the first time.

Laila dug the flashlight out of her drawer, demonstrating how to turn it on and off.

"I must study this fascinating object."

She was having a marvelous time rediscovering modern technology through Zak's eyes. Everyday items she never gave a second thought to now seemed almost magical when she imagined what the world must have been like before their invention.

Zak touched the circle of glass covering the concentrated beam. "There is no fire, no burning or blistering of skin." Testing it further, he pressed the lit flashlight to his arms, chest, abs, and his face. Laila vowed never to clean the surface of her flashlight again.

A moment later, Zak's hands were on her, stripping away her clothes.

"You will put your *teslug* footwear back on." He handed Laila her bunny slippers.

"*Teslug?*"

"Small young animal."

Laila laughed. "So my bunny slippers turn you on, hmm?"

Zak stilled, a clueless look across his chiseled features as the gears turned inside his head. "Turn me on? Like electric lights? Is such a thing possible? Can we do it? Now?"

"Not literally. If something is a turn-on, it makes you feel especially desirous. Lustful."

Zak's lips eased into a grin. "Everything about you turns me on, Laila. The furry pink faces you wear on your feet amuse me. I have never seen anything quite so full of nonsense."

Wrapping a hand around one of the posts of her four-poster bed, he gave an affirmative nod. "These will do well for support." He glanced around the room, opening and closing her nightstand drawers, then he looked under the bed.

"What are you looking for?"

"Chains, leather straps, something with which to bind your soft flesh."

Her mouth formed a big silent O.

"Sorry, my bedroom isn't equipped for bondage," she quipped, totally unfamiliar with anything even remotely related to BDSM. "Maybe we can stop at Chains-R-Us when we go out to buy you clothes tomorrow."

Accepting her glib remark as truth, Zak nodded. "Excellent I will enjoy inspecting the chain merchant's wares." He stripped out of his genie garments and joined her on the bed, primed and ready for action.

"Zak, I'm not that experienced. What I'm familiar with falls into the category of ordinary vanilla stuff."

"Vanilla? Explain this food reference."

"Standard sex without any bells or whistles."

"Ahh, then you will add bells and whistles to the list of items we must procure."

Laila decided not to bother explaining further. "Sure," she replied, doing her best to avoid laughing. "I was just kidding about Chains-R-Us," she admitted. "There is no such store."

The look he gave her had her feeling guilty. "You were being mischievous, taking advantage of my lack of knowledge of your time."

It sounded so nasty and juvenile when he put it like that. "Sorry."

He shrugged it off. "I am not offended." His hands skimmed from her ankles to her shoulders, his thumbs kneading along the way. "Our times and worlds may be astoundingly different, but I find it hard to believe the craving for sexual satisfaction has dimmed. Are there no markets offering items designed for increasing intimate pleasure?"

"Sure, there are sex shops, places that offer sex toys, weird outfits and fetish stuff. But I've never been in one."

"You will take me to one tomorrow."

"No way." Laila felt her face heat. "I'd die of embarrassment if someone I know saw me."

"Why? They would know you are a woman unafraid to explore her blossoming sexuality. A woman who has an experienced lover at her side."

Sinking her teeth into her bottom lip, she glanced up at him. "That's exactly what I'm afraid of."

He paused, taking her hands in his as he gave her a solemn look. "Fearing life wastes precious time, little one. Embrace the gift of life. Enjoy it while you have it." A gentle kiss punctuated his thoughtful words. "I will make my flash of light inspection now," Zak happily announced without skipping a beat. Tugging, he shifted Laila into the ideal position.

"I will use this to explore your *mug*."

Laila's face fell. "You want to examine my coffee cup?"

Zak frowned. "Your words make little sense."

"That makes two of us."

"Yes, there are two of us," Zak confirmed, cocking his head in question. Laila cocked hers in return.

"Do you want me to get a mug?"

"It is already here."

"Zak..." He was making her crazy.

"I speak of your delicate *murub*," he explained, a gleam in his eye as his gaze dropped to her crotch. "I wish to inspect it with the flash of light. Understand?"

Laila's mouth fell open.

"Place pillows beneath your bottom so I have a clear view of your intimate flesh."

Laila hesitated. "I feel like I'm getting ready to be examined by my gynecologist."

"Your guy who?"

"Gyne—my doctor. You know, like a medicine man. The one who checks out my... intimate flesh to make sure it's healthy."

One dark eyebrow arrowed down. "I have no thought of medicine when I look at you, Laila. I am certain my touch, my gaze, my warm breath on your flesh, will in no way be similar to visiting your guy doctor."

"Oh..."

"Position yourself so we may proceed."

She really wasn't ready for this. She could probably command him not to do it but...

~<>~

Twenty blissful minutes later, a satisfied sigh escaped her lips. The beautifully romantic words falling from his lips, the loving way he explored, the warmth of his gaze as he studied her—it all made her heart quicken.

Laila was in the midst of sighing when she heard the distinct click of the flashlight. She saw light flash on. *Off. On. Off. On...*and then Zak was knocking it with the palm of his hand.

"The light dims," he noted with dismay.

"The battery's dying."

Zak shifted his gaze from the dimming flashlight to her face, treating her to an adoring smile. "How beautiful you are. I have enjoyed pleasuring you as your essence journeyed on *lil* to *an*."

Her eyelids intuitively fluttered shut. "Lil and Ann?" She opened her eyes, smiling up at her genie.

"In Sumerian, *lil* is the wind, the air—a breath, spirit, the atmosphere. *An* is what you would call heaven."

"Heaven. I can't think of anything more appropriate." Laila wove her fingers into the dark curtain of hair spilling onto his bronzed shoulders. "You definitely transported me to a different realm."

Reclining on his side next to her, he bent his elbow, resting his head on his fist. He looked so at ease, so natural, as if this was exactly where he belonged.

"You remind me of the air on a spring morning," he told her in that lyrical way he spoke. "Lively and full of life. Spirited and impudent as well as intelligent. There is one thing about you that I especially prize."

Laila's thoughts whirred, wondering what lovely praise he was about to bestow next.

"You make me laugh," he said, surprising her. He kissed her forehead and each cheek. "It is a great gift."

"It is?"

"Truly. Being in the bottle is oblivion. I exist with nothing but my own thoughts. It is so freeing to laugh, to enjoy the laughter of others. It heals inside and out." His hand swept from his throat to his belly. "You have done this for me."

If it was anatomically possible for a heart to flip-flop inside one's chest, she'd just experienced it.

"Thank you, Zak. I wish I could so eloquently express how much I'm enjoying our time together."

"I was not always skilled at speaking. I have gained the ability over centuries as I walked the earth with people of different cultures, locations and times. I have learned much."

The places Zak had been, the things he'd experienced. It was mindboggling.

"I learned actions are more important than words." He gave her an intuitive smile. "Your actions have been most illuminating. My past possessors gave thought only to their own gratification, never to mine, a truth I came to accept long ago. Once they understood I was there to grant their wishes and pleasure them, I was naught but a human contrivance. Merely a means to fulfill their desires."

A shot of anger jetted through her veins. "That's so cold. So selfish."

"I am still amazed you have not asked about your wishes. It is the first such occurrence."

"I have six months, right?"

"Yes, but are you not curious about a gift with the power to alter your life?"

"Very much." Smoothing her fingers across his shoulder, she couldn't imagine any woman being so materialistic she'd want to have this incredible man disappear from her life so quickly. "But we've got plenty of time for wishes." Laila had gone this long without wealth. Spending six months with Zak rivaled any riches.

"It sounds like some of your possessors treated you like a wish-granting love slave instead of a man with feelings."

"Often. I am a slave with a duty to perform. That is why it has moved me so for you to treat me like a lover. Like a man, Laila, instead of one to grovel at your feet and carry out your commands. For the first time since my imprisonment, you made me feel as though I were master rather than slave." His fist thumped twice over his heart. "Never," he shook his head back and forth, "not for the rest of eternity, shall I forget your generous heart."

Laila's eyes filled with tears that spilled onto Zak's chest. Frowning, he brushed the tears from her cheeks and lifted her chin to look in her eyes. "My confession was meant to make you feel joy not sadness. It pains me to see you weep."

How could she find the words to explain how her heart broke for him for the eons of inhumane treatment he'd suffered at the hands of callous, unfeeling ingrates? How could she explain how she yearned to cocoon him, keep him safe so the cruel forces that had imprisoned him could never find him again?

Grabbing a tissue from the box on her nightstand, she dabbed her eyes and nose. "I just think it stinks, that's all." If she tried to say anything more meaningful she'd start crying buckets.

"It smells like ass?" Zak asked, a teasing gleam in his eye and a devilish grin across his sensuous lips.

Laila couldn't help smiling. "Exactly," she agreed, leaning against him. "It smells like ass."

He cupped her face in his hands, studying her a long moment before they shared a kiss that felt downright magical.

Chapter 9

~<>~

ZAKKAR TYMON STOOD behind Laila, nibbling on her nape as she selected a pair of mugs from the cabinet. It was a wonderful way to start the day.

He sniffed the air as the coffeemaker hissed. "I like this aroma," he said before licking the outer shell of her ear and making her sigh.

"If you don't stop that," she chastised, reluctantly extricating herself from his embrace, "we'll never get to the mall. The coffee will be ready in a couple of minutes. You've never tasted it? Didn't Abigail drink coffee?"

"No. She drank tea."

"Oh right, she and her husband were originally from England."

"I grew to enjoy the taste of strong tea with cream and sugar."

"I think you'll like this. It's a rich, strong blend from Griffin's Café." Too bad she didn't have a couple of the almond cherry scones she regularly baked for the café, or some bacon and eggs to serve instead of TBT cereal.

Laila eyed Zak and smiled, mindful not to give in to a rising giggle. The way she had the poor man dressed was abominable but necessary. Taking him shopping would be a hoot.

The few fat clothes she'd saved came in handy. The powder blue sweatshirt adorned with huge pink cabbage rose appliqués and the super stretchy denim jeans with the elastic waist weren't exactly ideal adornment for a pillar of simmering testosterone. But it was either that, an old bridesmaid dress, or her tropical orange-floral muumuu.

She'd donated her favorite fat clothes to charity. The few she kept were examples of *this is what you'll look like if you ever get fat again* outfits hidden in the back of her closet as hideous reminders of her highest weight.

The sleeves of her sweatshirt ended at Zak's elbows. The legs of the stretchy jeans hugged just below his knees. He looked like a gargantuan drag queen gone terribly wrong. But she certainly couldn't take him out of the house wearing his genie garb.

Laila glanced at his big feet overhanging her flip-flops and winced. He came out of his bottle barefoot. The man needed some sort of shoes. Since she didn't have any gunboats handy, these would have to suffice.

As soon as they got to Glassfloat Bay Mall she'd get him into some manly clothes and shoes. Appraising his imposing stature again, she bit her lip, wondering if the average men's store carried triple-tall, extra-buff sizes.

The bell on her coffeemaker dinged, capturing their attention. "I'll start you off with it black to see if you like it that way first."

Zak sipped and one eye narrowed. "Good, bold, but not as flavorsome as it smells."

"Here," she ripped open a packet of sugar, adding it along with a packet of powdered creamer, "try it now."

After one sip his eyes closed and he offered a satisfied "Ahhh..." He sat back, sniffing and sipping, like a happy consumer in a coffee commercial. "Excellent."

"The cereal's made by Tuned by Turner, the company I work for." She poured a stream of almond milk over the cereal. Yummy Bran Nuggets was one of the few foods TBT offered that Laila found halfway palatable.

Zak outright shuddered at the taste. From the skewed look on his face, she thought he might spit the mouthful back into the bowl. But his table manners were too refined. Managing to swallow with another small shudder, he took the box from the table, studying the images of lip-licking people happily hiking spoonsful of cereal to their mouths.

"Yummy Nuggets indeed. With today's technology, why would people choose to ingest twigs, chaff and wood shavings for their morning repast?"

Laila laughed at that. "It does seem that way, doesn't it?" She'd have to take him to the store to pick up bacon and eggs, and to replenish her scone-baking ingredients so she could make a batch for him.

"I do not mean to seem ungrateful for the sustenance you provide, but..." His lip curled into a sneer.

"You don't need to say another word." She cleared the table. "After we get you some clothes I'll take you out for a delicious lunch." She grabbed her purse and keys. Zak grabbed his saber, affixing it to his hip.

"Uh...no, the saber stays here. Strolling around the mall with weapons is definitely frowned upon."

He looked at her aghast. "You cannot mean it, Laila. A warrior without his weapon is but a target inviting slaughter. How will I protect you should the need arise?"

Reaching up to stroke his rough jaw and the already healing nicks from her razor, she gave the cabbage rose-wearing genie a onceover and smiled. "My dear genie, you've got fists like ham hocks and the rest of you is muscle layered on muscle." She squeezed his biceps and he instinctively curled his arm to make a muscle.

She gave an involuntary sigh. "See? A definite case of overkill. You're stronger and more fearsome than any man deserves to be, with or without a saber."

He grabbed her to his chest, crushing her to him. "Your eyes darken with passion when you feel my strength. Why go to the markets when we can stay here and make love all day?"

Why indeed. His suggestion sounded a hell of a lot better than running errands.

The rational side of her brain kicked in.

Laila pressed her hands against his chest. Intending to push him away, she relished the feel of him beneath her fingers. She sucked in a deep breath and expelled it, reluctantly withdrawing from his embrace.

"There are several reasons, such as anyone I know stopping by. You need to look like an average guy." As if Zak could ever look average. Ha!

"Once you have transformed me into an average guy we can stay here making love all day, every day, yes?"

"No, naughty genie." Standing with hands on her hips, she asked, "Has anyone ever told you you're a very bad influence?"

"Most likely," he admitted with a mischievous smile.

"We need to get to the mall before it gets too crowded." The fewer people who saw him in that ridiculous outfit the better. "Ready for a ride in my horseless chariot?"

Zak's eyes widened and he gripped the edge of the kitchen counter. "You have a gas engine chariot like Drake's?"

"Mine's older and smaller but it works the same." Curving her finger in invitation, she headed for the door leading to the garage while giving Friday instruction to be good in her absence.

She was startled by the bold "Yes!" flying from Zak's lips as he rubbed his hands in anticipation. "I will relish driving this great metal monster on wheels!"

Laila stopped in her tracks. "Whoa, hold on, Evel Knievel. You're not driving. You don't know how. Your job is to be the pretty passenger."

"You will teach me." Zak's chin lifted while he stood fists planted against his hips, looking down at her. "Women should not operate chariots, whether horseless or not. It is a man's responsibility."

Laila opened her mouth and snapped it shut. No use arguing with her sexy chauvinist now, or they'd never get to the mall. She'd have to pull rank on him if he didn't give up the crazy notion of driving. Rolling her eyes, she grabbed his sleeve, marching him to the garage.

After the challenging task of stuffing the oversized genie into her compact car, the drive to the mall wasn't what she'd expected. She'd been prepared for a harrowing ride with Zak's shocked gasps and demands for explanations, but he was strangely silent as he watched all manner of trucks, motorcycles, motorhomes, and bicycles speed by.

"You okay? You've been awfully quiet."

"I am in a state of wonder." His head shook back and forth slowly. "How greatly the world has changed in the last century. It is…" His brow furrowed as Zak searched for the right word.

"Overwhelming," Laila offered, imagining what a shock the modern world must be to him.

"Indeed. My brain is burdened with more than I can conceive. Never have I witnessed a time with so many fantastical changes."

Without thinking, Laila turned on the radio. He turned to her, eyes wide, as music blared and singers sang.

"Like the phone?" he asked.

"Not exactly. It's a radio." After showing him how to switch stations by pushing the buttons, Zak zipped between jazz, rock, classical, country, rap and talk radio. When the news came on he listened intently, answering the newscasters wherever he deemed appropriate. And he argued with the meteorologist about weather conditions.

It was when Zak asked the announcers questions, awaiting answers, that Laila decided she deserved a gold medal for holding back peals of laughter. She did her best to explain what a radio was and how it worked, but technical explanations simply weren't her forte.

It was good to see him become more animated, until...

"Laila! *Laila!*"

She almost had a heart attack. "What? *What!*" Keeping her wits about her, she breathed deep and focused on staying in her lane.

Gripping the dashboard, Zak craned his neck, crying out, "Great Enlil, god of air, what *is* that great white bird in the sky?!" Gasping, he shoved his head out the open car window to get a better look.

"It's okay. It's an airplane, another modern mode of transportation."

"No. *No!*" He slapped the dashboard. "People are enclosed in the winged vehicle? How can that be? How can something so colossal take flight?"

"Maybe Drake can explain because I sure as hell can't. Will you *please* sit still?"

Hanging on to him by the elasticized waistband of her stretchy fat jeans as she drove, Laila was scared to death Zak might kill himself by jumping out of the moving car to explore the magical aspects of his new world.

Or to wage war on other drivers.

Honk...honk...honnnnnnkkkkkk!!!!

The insistent honking, followed by a pissed off male driver, shouting *Fuck you!* and giving Laila the finger as he sped past her seized Zak's attention.

"What is the meaning of this man's brash tirade?" he demanded as the other guy continued yelling a colorful array of curse words at Laila.

"It's because I've been driving beneath the speed limit for safety," she explained. "The other driver is in a hurry and doesn't like it. Just ignore him."

"Ignore him!?" Zak's eyebrows furrowed and her heart about stopped when his warmonger genes kicked in. Focused on revenge, he cried, "Catch up to the offending driver. I will teach this uncouth wrongdoer a lesson in how to properly treat a lady." He looked left, right, and practically climbed into the back seat. "By gods, where is my saber!"

"At home where it belongs."

"You see? I told you I needed my weapon!" Zak growled something in Sumerian.

When he hung out the open window, shaking his fist and spewing what she imagined were vile Sumerian curses at the other driver, Laila yanked on him, screaming, "For God's sake, will you *please* sit down and stop acting like a bloodthirsty warmonger!"

"But I *am* a bloodthirsty warmonger!"

Laila's shoulders slumped.

Thankfully, the other driver was finally so far ahead of them they could barely see him...or hear him. Laila sent up a silent prayer of gratitude that Zak didn't have the saber with him.

"Explain the meaning of the other driver's oft repeated chant, spoken as if it were an oath."

Inclining her head in confusion, she turned to him. "What are you talking about?"

"Fuck you!"

Her eyes popping wide, she said, "Excuse me?"

"Time after time the driver shouted *fuck you* with great vehemence. What is this *fuck you*?"

"Oh..." Though she tried her best, it became increasingly difficult for Laila to explain how the term and its numerous variations could have such distinctly different meanings. Zak was confounded that the same words were used as a curse and also sometimes spoken during a sexy, passionate moment.

When they finally arrived at the mall, she parked in the lot, breathing a sigh of relief. She had to get Zak into a clothing store fast before the giant of a man dressed like a female with atrocious fashion sense attracted too much attention.

Too late.

They hadn't taken ten steps before she heard a wolf whistle followed by a singsong *Well hello!* Laila had no doubt the whistle was meant for Zak.

"Hey there," an attractive guy with pineapple yellow hair addressed Zak after he and two other guys approached from behind.

The threesome, one wearing an orange sweater and another with tight lime green pants, probably assumed they were going to the same party as the cabbage-rosed genie.

None of them seemed to notice Laila.

"Isn't he delicious?" Pineapple guy openly flirted while Zak slanted him a curious look. "Where have you been all my life, sweetheart?"

"I have been—"

"Traveling around the world," Laila cut in.

"Well I know where you're traveling to today," orange sweater guy said.

Zak's eyes lit up. "Ahh, you are a seer? I have known many."

"I'll bet you have." The man in lime pants gave Zak a slow appraisal. "You here for the fest?"

"I am not familiar with it," Zak answered.

"Listen to that deep voice. He sounds foreign," pineapple guy said to his buddies, only briefly shifting his gaze from Zak. "The Gay Film Festival," he explained.

"Are we attending this happiness festival?" Zak asked Laila.

"Nope." She tugged him so they could move on, but it was like trying to move a block of granite.

"I regret I must decline your invitation," Zak said. "I am here to shop for typical male garb and to find chains and restraints."

Laila wished she could disappear into a crack in the asphalt.

"Sounds promising," lime pants guy said. "But you won't find any sex toys in the mall. Come by my place tonight and I'll show you my personal collection."

"Sorry, Zak's busy tonight...with me." Elevating her chin, she cleared her throat. "I'm his girlfriend."

The trio eyed her and Zak from head to toe. An exchange of knowing grins ensued.

"Of course you are, darling."

Laila's ego deflated at his incredulous tone and disbelieving expression.

"You are a merchant of pleasure supplies?" Zak asked. "I would like to inspect your wares."

Laila groaned.

"I'll show you mine if you show me yours," pineapple guy suggested.

"Oh Lord..." Laila tugged Zak's arm. "You don't understand, Zak. They're not merchants." She turned to the three men. "Look, it's not what you think, fellas. He's straight."

Orange sweater guy eyed Zak's ostentatious getup. "Right." The others snickered. "If you haven't come out of the closet yet, Zak, you shouldn't go around town looking like such a sweet thing. Go ahead," he thumbed in Laila's direction, "tell her you're gay."

"I did not come out of a closet. I came out of a bottle."

Laila gasped. "Zak!"

"Okay." The guy nodded approvingly. "I'm down with that."

"It is not necessary to tell Laila I am gay. She already knows of my elation."

"Oh boy," Laila muttered. "Look, guys, he's straight. He's just...he's from Bulgaria. Go ahead, Zak," she elbowed him, "tell them your full Bulgarian name."

"My name is Zakkar Tanojin Lugalbanda Tymon." He straightened, tall and proud. "You may call me Zakkar."

"See?" Laila said. "Bulgarian. You can tell from his accent. He just arrived and," she swallowed hard, "this is how straight men dress in Bulgaria. Right, Zak?"

"No." Zak gave her a curious look. "I told you, Laila, I have not been in Bulgaria since—"

A nervous giggle escaped as she slapped her hand against Zak's mouth, having forgotten his sworn obligation to tell the truth. She couldn't imagine going through life without being able to utter the occasional little white lie.

"He understands very little English," she claimed. The stern, surprised look in Zak's eyes was a no-nonsense signal that he sincerely disliked the idea of being muzzled.

As several other people passed by, Laila watched Zak checking out the jeans and khakis the men wore against the gay trio's clothing.

With his fingers splayed across his chest, Zak looked down at himself, clearly horrified. He pinned Laila with a none-too-happy glare. "These men think I am *assinnu*," he accused.

Laila didn't need an interpreter to figure out what he meant.

"You don't have to be shy with us," lime pants guy said, squeezing Zak's biceps for good measure.

"You assume incorrectly." Zak disposed of the man's hand from his arm. "I am not enamored of men."

"Well that's a pity," pineapple guy noted. Zak's eyes narrowed. "Toodles," the man said, giving Zak a wave of his fingers before looping arms with the other two and walking toward the mall entrance.

Zak's voice was solemn as he replied, "Toodles," and Laila burst out laughing.

Arms crossed over his broad cabbage rose covered chest, Zak stared Laila down. She could imagine from that one straightforward look how Zakkar Tymon commanded battalions of soldiers in his time.

"Laila...?" His tone was menacing as one eyebrow arched in question. "You did not tell me *gay* in your time means *assinnu*," he scolded.

"You didn't ask." Shrugging, she cracked a nervous smile.

"In Abigail's time the word gay meant—"

"Yes, yes, I know." She patted his arm. "Come on. We've got to get you out of these clothes and into something—"

"Into something a warrior would wear," he finished for her, scowl still firmly in place. "When I told you I felt like an ugly *munus* in this," Zak plucked the sweatshirt, holding it away from his chest, "you assured me this is appropriate male costume for your time."

Munus, she remembered, meant *woman*. Her eyes roved over him. "I might have exaggerated slightly, but I had no choice. I had to tell you that little fib to get you here for some acceptable clothes."

As she spoke, Zak eyed a handsome, buff guy strutting toward them wearing tight black jeans, a body-hugging black T-shirt and a black leather jacket. Devastatingly masculine, the guy was hot. Not as sexy as her genie, but a definite testosterone-oozing hottie.

"I like the look of this man."

"You mean, in an *assinnu* sort of way?" Laila's feeble attempt at levity was met with a warning glare. "Sorry. I couldn't resist."

"You will garb me in that manner," Zak stated. "Like a man who prefers to bed women instead of men."

Laila watched as the guy called out and ran to catch up with the three flamboyant guys who'd just left them, grabbing their asses as he wedged between two of the men.

Laila giggled.

Zak frowned.

"Come on, man who prefers to bed women. Let's go shopping." Laila tugged his hand. Zak followed, grumbling as he scuffed along the pavement on the too-small flip-flops.

She glanced up at him as they walked. "Are you bothered by the idea of gay people? You know, *assinnu*?"

"No. Why would I be?"

Laila shrugged. "I just wondered because of your reaction..."

"Several men under my command were *assinnu*. Shoulder to shoulder on the battlefield they fought just as fierce and bravely as any other men I have known. I am glad to share mutton and drink barley ale with them, but would not be pleased to find such a man waiting for me in my bedchamber."

That sounded perfectly reasonable to Laila.

As they entered the mall Zak asked her, "You told those men you were my girlfriend. This means?"

"I just said that to let them know you aren't gay," Laila explained. "A man's girlfriend is the woman he—"

"Ahhh, the woman he fucks," Zak said as they strode through the glass doors of the mall entrance, leaving Laila bug-eyed and slack-jawed.

"What?!"

"You were letting them know you and I are fuckers." He gave a knowing smile.

Slapping her hands over her face, Laila muttered, "Dear God, I cannot believe you just said the F-word. Twice."

"While I appreciate the praise, it is not necessary for you to address me as a god, Laila."

"Trust me, I wasn't praising you, Ego Boy. It's just an expression, like holy cow or holy mackerel."

"Yes, the saintly animals." He gave a thoughtful nod.

"You can't say the F-word in public, Zak. It isn't nice. It's considered very crude."

"But in the horseless chariot you explained the various meanings of the fuck word, did you not?"

"Yes but—"

"Was it not glorious when we fucked? I thought you enjoyed it immensely."

His words caught the attention of two elderly women who exchanged disapproving glances.

"Shhh! Oh, for heaven's sake, no. I mean yes. I mean—" Laila did her best to moderate her voice in the echoing mall. "I'll explain all about the F-word and girlfriends later, okay? Until then, please watch your language."

He looked skeptical. "You have a device that allows me to see it?"

"See what?" Her features scrunched in confusion.

"My language."

This would probably be a great time to introduce the magic of texting and things like Google Translate but that would have to wait.

"You're making me crazy, Zak. You can't take everything I say so literally."

"How then should I take it? And what should I do once it is taken? Help me to understand. I am doing my best."

She looked into the pair of dark eyes gazing down at her with such earnest and sighed. "For now, all you need to understand is that you shouldn't be using the F-word in public." Laila gazed left and right at all the moms with little kids in tow. "It's not proper." She pressed a finger to her lips in a quieting motion.

"Ahh..." he said just above a whisper, glancing at the children in the vicinity as understanding dawned in his gaze. "The F-word is not appropriate for the ears of little goats."

"Exactly." Laila knew she should correct Zak about the little goats thing, but it warmed her heart and made her smile each time he said it. English and Grammar 101 could come later.

The moms Laila spotted had more on their minds than just kids. Zakkar was a magnet, a veritable attraction. While he seemed fairly oblivious to the attention, the young women making goo-goo eyes at Zak brought out Laila's green-eyed monster.

Snagging Zak's sleeve, she whisked him into a department store where both males and females eyed her goofily garbed genie like he was a juicy prime steak.

"Oh good grief," she muttered beneath her breath.

"This means?"

"Nothing."

"But how can grief be good?"

Unable to keep from growling with frustration, Laila said, "It's not important. Too hard to explain. Just keep moving." Looping their arms, she hurried him along, away from the sea of adoring, inquisitive eyes.

Laila gazed at Zak after outfitting him in a pair of butt-hugging jeans and a long-sleeved black, button-down shirt, open at the neck and rolled at the sleeves of his bronzed, muscular arms. He looked delicious.

They waited in line at the store's checkout counter with Zak's new black leather jacket. The female clerk eyed him with undisguised lust. The way she said, 'Is there anything...*else* I can do for you?' with a look conveying her longing in no uncertain terms, made Laila want to smack the overactive hormonal smile right off her face.

"Do men and women always eyeball you like that?" she asked, a disgusted tone creeping into her voice as they left the store.

"Eyeball?"

Frustration gripping her again, Laila tsked. "Do they always look at you like they want to...you know..."

"Engage in sex with me?" Zak gave a nonchalant nod. "Usually. I cannot fault them. They are mesmerized by my perfect form."

He said it so matter-of-factly, so simply, Laila realized he wasn't being purposely arrogant. Zak was merely stating fact. She'd never encountered anyone with such self-assurance. She'd love to have his confidence.

"In my time others seduced me because of my reputation as a skilled lover," he gave Laila a pointed look, "to which you can now attest. At times that reputation even exceeded my celebrated standing as a great leader and warrior."

Silent for a moment, Laila visualized horny women throwing themselves at him throughout the ages. "Do the words modesty or humility have any meaning to you?"

"Yes but their meaning is not relevant in regard to my prowess."

"Or your astounding good looks," Laila said sarcastically as they neared the escalator.

"That is correct."

"Oh brother."

With a look of amusement, he reminded her, "I am most definitely not your brother."

She rolled her eyes. "Come on, we're taking a ride on the escalator." She motioned toward it, catching the uncertainty in Zak's expression as his gaze traveled up and down. The man had encountered a mindboggling amount of modern technology in a short time.

"Watch what everyone is doing," she instructed. He gave the escalator his rapt attention. "Just do what they did, and what I'm going to do. Do not put your hands on the stairs or the escalator will chew off your entire arm and half your face." She felt the need to embellish the truth in case he got too curious.

He nodded.

She got on the escalator, turning back to catch Zak's fascinated expression as he stepped on right after her. He was focused and silent for the short floor-to-floor excursion.

"Another transportation miracle," he pronounced, stepping off and looking back at where he'd just been. "I would like to do this again."

"We will, when we go back down before we leave the mall."

"Good. Returning to the subject of my pleasing looks, my rumored heritage as half-god has only added to my appeal."

Smacking a playful slap to his arm, Laila laughed.

"What is it you find humorous?"

Her gaze slid to him. "You were serious?"

"Certainly. It is said that my father is Enlil, he who guards the tablets of destiny."

"What are those?"

"The cuneiform tablets on which he writes the fate of everything on earth. Enlil is so powerful the other gods can't even look at him."

"If that's the case," Laila noted with a snicker, "how did he and your mother manage to get together?"

"It was Enlil's will that she gaze upon his brilliant, fearsome beauty as they copulated."

"How convenient."

"Those who lust after me cannot be held accountable. They cannot help themselves. Such was the case with Sabit, the young virgin priestess responsible for my captivity."

"So, you corrupted a sweet young virgin, hmm? Am I finally going to hear about that?"

"Not here." Zak's expression grew dark. "It stirs too much emotion within when I speak of what transpired. I will tell you soon."

"I look forward to hearing about it." She wanted to hear everything about the cruel, life-altering day he'd endured so many centuries ago. It was still difficult for her to believe such powerful, magical forces existed.

"Hungry?" she asked, breathing in a whiff of aromas drifting from the food court. "My brother's place, Nevan's Irish Pub, isn't too far from here. They've got great burgers and delicious pork pie if there's any left."

"What is a burger?"

"Sheer gastronomic heaven." Laila led him down another escalator to the mall entrance, eager to introduce him to some hearty, non-diet grub.

"Stop!" Zak commanded as they stepped off the escalator and walked a few yards.

Her breath catching, Laila came to an abrupt halt. "What's wrong?"

"We must shop here. For you, this time."

Laila looked at the broad expanse of window with the skinny, big-chested mannequins garbed in fancy bras and panties. My Silky Secrets, Glassfloat Bay's answer to Victoria's Secret. She swallowed hard. With her plentiful body she'd never had the nerve to set foot in one of their stores.

"No, Zak. I really don't think—"

"You think too much. Come. We will learn the mystery of her silky secrets." He grabbed her hand, striding inside.

"But you already made me buy new jeans, tops, skirts and dresses," she protested.

He'd clearly changed his mind about women wearing pants when he saw the difference between the way Laila looked in her baggy jeans versus the snug fit of the new jeans revealing every ripple and turn of her curves.

"Those are for others to see. The secrets," he motioned to the silky, satiny wisps throughout the store, "are for my eyes only."

Laila heard *may I help you?* chorusing around them as Zak surveyed his surroundings. Competing for his attention, the sales clerks selected pricey items for his perusal.

"I am a man who knows what he likes," Zak informed the handful of women licking their lips as they appraised him. "Your help will not be needed until it comes time to make payment. You may begone now." His words were uttered firmly but kindly as he easily dismissed the attentive females.

Clearly with regret, they left Zak alone, standing together to worship him from afar.

Zak eyed a smoky lavender bra and matching panties on display. A haunting smile took hold when he spotted the matching floor-length semi-sheer robe.

"The color of a Sumerian sky on a late summer's night." He fingered the fabric. "Your alabaster skin will look like the moon and stars against these garments. You will wear these for me, Laila."

His expressive words and the hungry look in his eyes convinced her it was a necessary purchase.

Before they were finished, he'd selected an assortment of sexy bras and panties. She'd be dead broke by the end of the day.

"What pleasure I will have peeling these from your lush body," he whispered in her ear as they left the store.

Clutching her bag of silken, lacy confections close, Laila smiled. "Just as long as you promise not to remove them with your saber."

Chapter 10

~<>~

TUCKED IN A BOOTH at her brother's dark wood-paneled pub, Laila heard her stomach growl. The last thing she should be thinking about, especially after purchasing skimpy little nothings from My Silky Secrets, was chowing down on a burger and fries. But introducing Zak to the best pub-style food in the Pacific Northwest was a special occasion.

"I like the look and feel of this gathering house," Zak noted, taking in the traditional pub decor. "The aroma here is most tantalizing." His chest expanded as he breathed in deeply. "My belly anticipates an enjoyable repast." He finished with a killer smile.

"You'll love it," Laila assured. "The food tastes even better than it smells."

While the service at Nevan's Irish pub-inspired eatery was always good, this was the first time a server approached so quickly at the height of the lunchtime rush. Two female servers stood drooling over Zak, arguing whose table it was. Once the table issue was resolved, Laila ordered Zak a bacon-cheddar burger with fries and onion rings from the American-fare side of the menu, adding a pint of Guinness along with a slice of Irish pork pie if they had any left after last night's film event.

It would be the best damn meal he'd had in over a century.

"You can take off the sunglasses now," she told him. She couldn't resist adding them to the tab as they shopped. He looked deliciously dangerous in them.

Zak removed the dark glasses and Laila heard a collective sigh. The server who'd lost her claim to the table stopped by to refill their already brimming water glasses, her hips gyrating as she moved.

The water pourer overfilled Laila's glass.

"Thanks," Laila said with a dismissive smile, snatching a handful of paper napkins from the tabletop dispenser to blot up the water, since the server seemed unaware the accident had even occurred. "I think we're okay on the water for now. We'll signal if we need more."

The server was too busy salivating to hear a word Laila said.

"Your service is appreciated," Zak said to the woman. "You may go now."

The young woman bowed, *she actually bowed*, and then she was off.

"Will you be okay here alone for a couple of minutes? I need to use the ladies' room, then check to see if my brother, Nevan, is in the back so I can introduce you."

Zak angled his head. "What do ladies do in this room?"

"It's the restroom. The bathroom. The toilet," she whispered, refraining from giggling as she remembered Zak's utter fascination with the amazing flushing box in her bathroom, flushing it repeatedly after Laila explained how to use it. Between that and his lengthy shower, she expected a whopping water bill.

"Fear not, little one. I will come to no harm during your absence."

Zakkar watched Laila walk away from the table, her bottom swaying back and forth with each step, though he could barely see the gentle movement through the baggy, shapeless breeches she wore today. He would relish watching her retreat once she wore her new...what was it she called them? Jeans.

He was amazed a woman could look so enticing in men's costume. As she posed for him in the store, his gaze was lured to the sturdy indigo fabric hugging her curves. It caressed her belly and the vee between her thighs, clasping the cheeks of her plump bottom like possessive hands. The image had his *gis* at attention.

As a warrior trained in mastering the art of control, he found it extraordinary for his manhood to respond in so unruly a fashion. It was as if Laila had enchanted him, bewitched him to the point that he hardened at the merest thought of her ripe body.

His newest possessor was an enigma. It was the first time he had encountered an owner so uninterested in hearing about her wishes. In the past he'd been all but tied down by his possessors, demanding he apprise them of the wish details as soon as he'd advised them of their gifts. Their eyes alight with greed, they first used his body to satisfy themselves. Then they scuttled from making one wish to another so swiftly Zakkar barely had time to register where and when he stood upon the earth before he was whisked back into the desolate bowels of the bottle for another small eternity.

Laila was gentle, funny, intelligent. Not only had she spent time teaching him about her world, feeding and clothing him and taking him for a wondrous ride in her horseless chariot, she'd also treated him with great consideration when they'd joined physically. She had bestowed the precious gift of allowing him to take charge, to feel like a real man again.

A satisfied smile took hold as he recalled her displays of jealousy. When women made suggestive overtures to him with their eyes and bodies, Laila strived to hide her unease, but Zakkar had made note of her discomfiture. It pleased him to know she was so covetous of him. Perhaps it meant that she cared for him to some extent.

Laila Malone was a woman he could envision making his own. Having her keep his house, warm his bed and bear him rosy-cheeked children.

His good temper curdled as Zakkar remembered it was not his destiny to settle down with a woman or father her brood. He was not permitted to partake in such simple pleasures. He was doomed to wander and sleep, not to experience life and love as a real man.

Laila made him feel more alive than he had in eons. Perhaps that wasn't a good thing. After knowing her, hearing the sweet ring of her laughter and seeing the warm gaze of what appeared to be genuine affection in her eyes, it would be difficult to return to his half-dead existence in the bottle. But return he must.

A hen-like clucking of voices assailed his ears. Aware of the women lurking nearby, eager for him to favor them with an appreciative nod or promising smile, Zakkar paid them no heed. It had less to do with the fact that he was allowed to engage in carnal union only with his possessor than the fact that he had grown weary of self-seeking women interested in him only as a walking *gis*.

While their bodies were appealing, the idea of bedding them was of more interest to his *gis* than his head. Or his heart.

Odd. He hadn't thought of his heart in ages. Why now?

"Because Laila has touched it," he muttered aloud.

Too many couplings with shallow, selfish women had left a bitter taste in his mouth. None of them, from queens to princesses to the most breathtaking of consorts, could compare with his Laila.

His Laila.

He gave a humorless chortle. She was not his. Quite the opposite, he was hers, to do with as she pleased. But she made it seem otherwise for him. He would be eternally grateful for that benevolence, keeping with him the memory of her kind heart and generosity of spirit.

"I'll meet you at the table in a minute, girls. Well, *hello* there."

Zakkar looked up at the sound of a female's seductive voice. An emaciated woman dressed all in pink and wearing too much paint on her face smiled down at him. With a quick gaze at her chest as she thrust it forward, he thought it peculiar that one so bony would have *uburs* as big as Laila's.

"Mind if I join you?" She slid into the booth seat opposite him without waiting for a reply.

"What do you want?" Zakkar asked, deciding he didn't care for this woman's aura or assuming attitude.

"Oh..." His purposefully brusque manner had clearly caught the woman off guard. "My name's Bunny Turner. I own Tuned by Turner, the weight loss centers." She gave him a gleaming merchant's smile, fully expecting, no doubt, for him to be suitably impressed.

The name was indeed familiar to him. Laila had spoken of the company and the woman who was her employer—the one insisting Laila become gaunt or forfeit her employment. His eyes narrowed. No, he did not like this woman who had caused Laila and Reen grief.

"You speak of the business requiring healthy, well-rounded people to starve until they become scrawny?"

A startled look etched across the woman's face, then she broke into cool, guarded laughter.

"Oh, I see. You're joking. Anyway, we're always looking for new faces and..." her eyes licked him, "new bodies, to use in our magazine and TV ads. You'd be perfect. Do you model?"

"I do not understand."

"Have you posed? For photographers."

Zakkar frowned. "I have posed for sculptors who have immortalized my likeness for others to admire."

"Mmm, I can certainly see why."

Her low, husky laugh did not reach her eyes as it did when Laila laughed.

"Interested? The pay is good. And..." she gave him that distinct lustful look again, "there could be some *very* special fringe benefits." One of her eyebrows arched. "If you know what I mean."

"Yes, I know. You wish for me to bed you," Zakkar said, not bothering to curb the sneer tainting his lips.

Her jaw sagged, but Bunny Turner regained her composure quickly. Unlike Laila, she was no innocent.

She focused her hungry brown eyes on his gaze. "We could each benefit from a mutually satisfying, discreet romp in the sheets."

"Such a romp is not possible," Zakkar advised her. "I belong to another."

"So do I." The woman's fingers reached across the table, walking up his forearm. "I won't tell if you won't."

Zakkar beamed a grin when he saw Laila returning to the table. Bunny's back was to her so she apparently mistook Zakkar's smile as a positive answer to her suggestion.

"Oh, good. I see that we can come to terms," Bunny cooed.

"Bunny..." Laila said when she reached the table seeing her employer seated in her place.

With a slow turn of her head, indicating irritation at being interrupted, Bunny gave Laila a disdainful perusal.

"Laila," she said with a bland, uninterested smile. "Nice to see you. I hope you're not planning to eat anything but a salad here." She wagged a chastising finger. "Remember, you've got a significant amount of weight to lose in the next few weeks." She puffed out her cheeks and patted her flat belly.

Zakkar watched as Laila's face reddened, his blood simmering in response. This woman enjoyed making Laila feel unattractive.

"We'll talk another time." Bunny dismissed her. "As you can see I'm tied up at the moment." She reached across the table, covering Zakkar's hand with her bony, bejeweled one in a possessive gesture.

As her gaze followed Bunny's hand, it was clear Laila felt intimidated by this bold boss of hers.

"Buh-bye, then." Bunny waved the fingers of her free hand before turning her attention to Zakkar.

"Um, actually," Laila's tone was timid, "you're sitting in my seat, Bunny."

Bunny's eyes grew impossibly wide. "Excuse me?"

"My seat," Laila repeated, gesturing to the booth with an apologetic smile. Zakkar wondered why she felt the need to feel contrite when it was the intrusive Bunny who had made the mistake.

Bunny's cool manner slipped as incredulity took over. "You know each other?"

Laila nodded. "He's...Zak is..."

"Laila is my girlfriend," Zakkar stated, his eyes on Laila as he took her hand, caressing it before bringing it to his lips and brushing a kiss across her knuckles. He was pleased to see the heated flush of humiliation dissipate from Laila's cheeks. The pleased and grateful smile replacing it was worth more than gold.

"Laila?" Bunny spoke the name as if she'd been struck by a bolt of lightning. She looked at Laila, aghast. "*He's* your boyfriend?"

"Yes." Laila gave him another beautiful smile, lifting his hand to her soft cheek for a brief touch.

"Did I not tell you I belonged to another?" he reminded Bunny.

The server, the official one as well as her competitor, brought their lunch and pints of Guinness to the table. She winked at Zakkar and left, whispering with the other server and giggling.

"I'm sorry, Bunny, but if you don't mind..." shrugging, Laila gestured to the food on the table.

"Oh...yes...of course." After removing her hand from Zakkar's and clearing her throat, Bunny slipped out of the booth and Laila sat in her place. With a disapproving glance at Laila's burger, she said, "Remember, you have six weeks to comply, Laila."

"Before you depart," Zakkar said, "know that Laila will not be living a life without *ninda*."

"What?"

Zakkar noticed that when Bunny frowned, only her lips moved. Her forehead was strangely smooth and still.

"Bread," he clarified. "And butter and sugar. She will not do without these pleasures to please the absurd directives of Tuned by Turner."

"I beg your pardon?" Bunny blustered.

"Zak!" Laila gasped. "Oh, he doesn't mean that, Bunny. Zak has trouble with his English, that's all. "Trust me, I'll get that thirty pounds off in time, don't worry."

Bunny eyed the table again and scoffed. It was the oily, false smile of a crafty snake. "Not eating like that, you won't. And beer too?" She tsked as she shook her head of stiff, oddly colored blonde-ish hair.

"You would allow yourself to become like a frail, undernourished bird to appease this woman?"

Laila's smile was tentative. "She's my boss, Zak," she said, just above a whisper. "I have no choice if I want to keep my job."

"Bingo." Bunny offered another unpleasant sneer. "I'll have you know," she said to Zakkar, "that Tuned by Turner is one of the most respected weight loss companies in the country, with branches nationwide."

"We had two similar places in my homeland where people became skeletal," Zakkar informed her. "They were called dungeons and prison camps."

With a stately sniff, Bunny said, "I won't dignify that with a response. I have to be going. I have friends waiting. Unlike you, Laila, I'm having the salad, sans dressing or croutons, in case you're interested." She shifted her gaze to Zakkar. "And regardless of your abominable attitude, my offer still stands. *All* of it."

"Offer?" Laila asked Zakkar.

"Your employer has suggested she and I engage in fornication," he explained. He had no reluctance mentioning the fact. After all, Bunny showed no hesitancy in bedding another woman's man.

"I did no such thing." Bunny's face twitched as she gasped. "I merely offered him an opportunity to model for TBT ads."

Zakkar noted Laila's lips curling into an amused smile.

"I'm sure you're mistaken, Zak," Laila said with a wink. "You see, Bunny is married. I'm sure she would never proposition you, no matter how appealing she finds you."

"Indeed." Zakkar understood at once the game Laila played. "Then I must not have heard your boss correctly. And it is a good thing. I would hate to embarrass her by rejecting her proposition because she is too scrawny for my tastes. I won't have to tell her that I like my women full and lush like you, Laila."

"Well, I...how rude!" Bunny huffed and puffed.

"By the gods!" Zakkar gave Laila a look of surprise and he could tell she was trying not to laugh. "Your boss is still here. I'm afraid I have misspoken." Inclining his head, Zakkar said to Bunny, "My apologies. Good day to you, Bunny Turner. Our food grows cold and my patience grows thin."

"Oh my God." Laila scraped her fingers through her hair once her boss marched off in a huff. "My ass is *so* fired."

Zakkar attempted to decipher yet another snippet of unfamiliar phrasing. "Am I correct in speculating you fear for a pet donkey that is in danger of being set aflame?"

Laila's responding laughter sounded strangled. "No, I mean I'm going to lose my job. All because of you!" she accused, jabbing a finger at him.

He watched her hands as she spoke. "Your hands are expressive. They are beautiful without being adorned with garish jewels such as those your boss wears in abundance." Grasping the pointing finger she offered, Zakkar caressed it along with her entire hand. "Bunny reminds me of Tsura, a gypsy woman who once possessed me."

"You're trying to make me forget why I'm angry with you."

"Is it working?" Offering his most inviting smile, he knew his mention of a former possessor would make Laila curious.

"No." She sat back, folding her arms beneath her breasts. "Was...was she beautiful?"

"Tsura?" Coughing out a laugh as he recalled the memorable woman, he told her, "No, she was mean and lurid. Her facial countenance was similar to Bunny's, except Bunny is not snaggletoothed with one eye gouged out. Also, Bunny does not smell of the fetid sheep grease Tsura utilized to keep her skin soft." His eyebrow hiked. "At least as far as I know. Perhaps if I accepted Bunny's invitation I might learn otherwise."

Sitting forward, she slapped Zakkar's hand. "You troublemaker." Her laughter spilled freely and her large almond eyes sparkled with amusement. "You said that on purpose to make me laugh when I'm this close" she held her thumb and forefinger together, "to losing my job because of you. You can just wipe that innocent look off your face, mister."

Offering a devilish smile, Zakkar sipped the beverage Laila called stout beer. "*Kash-gin*! Barley ale," he clarified. "Ahhh...dark, rich and strong. I have not tasted anything like this since..." He thought for a moment. "Not since I can remember." He downed most of the frosted mug in a few gulps. "I would like to partake in more of this."

"Whoa! Slow down. There's no way I can carry a drunken six-foot-whatever barbarian out of here on my own. Here." Laila shoved his plate toward him. "Eat. If you promise not to guzzle it, I'll give you the rest of my Guinness after you've finished half your food. It's too many calories for me anyway. Deal?"

"Yes, we have a pact," he agreed, bringing the thing called a burger to his lips. At the first bite of round bread containing meat and condiments, sparks of delight prickled in his belly. "This bacon-cheddar burger is better than any food I can remember." He glanced up. "Laila, this is so good it is almost holy."

"Tell me about it. Wait until you taste the fries and onion rings." She pointed to the golden strips and rings resting at the side of the burger.

He inspected the fried sticks and circles, sniffing a stick before placing it in his mouth. "Mmm," his eyes widened, 'delicious." He picked up another fried stick, studying it. "The sensation of salted crispness on the outside and the tender potato inside, all enhanced with a good amount of oil...it is entirely pleasing."

"You sound just like a commercial." Her eyes crinkled as she smiled. "Try an onion ring."

Zakkar did. "I have never sampled onion in this manner before, coated with a light, crisp, oil-infused veneer. These foodstuffs are delicious enough to be set on an altar for the gods."

"I agree completely. Unfortunately they're out of the pork pie. I'll have to bring you back for that the next time Nevan makes it. It's well-seasoned ground pork wrapped in a flaky pastry crust and cut into thick slices. It's just as good cold as it is hot. You'll love it. It's my brother Gard's favorite food."

"Is Nevan here? I would like to meet him."

"I'm afraid not. He's off now because he's working tonight."

"I like your brother's pub very much." Zak took another bite of his burger before asking, "Why does Bunny Turner not want people to eat and drink such delicious food? This is as different from the twig food you gave me this morning as the sun is from the moon."

"Because it's fattening." She gave her hamburger a guilty gaze, then set it back on her plate, pushing her food away.

"I do not like your boss. She does not have a good aura about her. It is clear she does not like you."

"No kidding." Laila offered a silly, twisted expression.

"She envies you."

"The only thing Bunny envies about me is that she thinks you're my boyfriend. Boy would she like to get her claws into you."

"She made that clear. I meant she envies you for your genuineness, your warmth and kindness. Spending that short time with her it is clear this deceptive woman does not possess those qualities."

Laila's face brightened with gladness. "Thank you, Zak." She touched his arm and he felt the insignificant gesture of affection right down to his *gis*. "But a woman that attractive isn't envious of someone like me."

"Attractive?" Zakkar spat a laugh. "She resembles a slithering snake," he gestured with his hand, "who tries to disguise her true nature with face paint and pink garb. You are more beautiful than she could ever hope to be, Laila." He watched her eyes glisten at his words. Fascinating how his speaking such a simple truth made her glow. How strange that she could not see this truth for herself.

She lowered her lashes. "I don't even know how to respond to such a lovely compliment."

"Then say nothing. Busy yourself instead by finishing your burger and fries. They are too enjoyable to discard. It makes me happy to see the expression of pleasure on your face as you eat. It is much like the look you have when we are naked together."

The sip of beer Laila took almost flew out of her mouth. She swallowed it, then coughed, choking. "Shhh! Keep your voice down. You can't talk about..." she glimpsed at the other diners, "about things like that when we're in a restaurant."

"Things like what?" he teased, loving the tinge of pink that crept up her neck to color her cheeks.

"You're playing dumb again, aren't you?"

Zakkar hid his smile by sinking his teeth into his burger and chewing. "Are we going to shop for pleasure restraints when we finish eating?" he asked, hoping for another embarrassed flush of color. As expected, Laila did not disappoint.

Her mouth full of fries, her eyes grew wide. Then she shushed him again. He was having more fun than he'd had in ages.

"Or will we be going to the food market to purchase clouds of cream to spray on our naked bodies tonight?"

Her face nearly as red as the ketchup, Laila swallowed her food and glared at him while shielding her face with her hand. "You're doing that on purpose." She leaned forward, whispering, "Trying to embarrass me."

He laughed at Laila's expression of discomfiture. "I cannot help it. It makes me smile to see you squirm so." He reached for one of her hands, grasping it tightly, smoothing his thumb over her knuckles and stroking her wrist.

"Thank you, Laila."

"For lunch?" Her voice was breathy, her cheeks tinged with a blush as she passed the rest of her beer to him.

"No...for you."

He relished the sound of her sweet sigh. For the first time since his long ago incarceration, Zakkar sent up a prayer of thanks to the gods for the unlikely circumstances that had brought him to Laila Malone.

Chapter 11

~<>~

"PARASOL COVE Ice Cream Parlor," Zak read the sign aloud, taking in his surroundings. "This is reminiscent of a place I visited with Abigail." Laila watched his chest expand as he filled his lungs. "The smell entices."

Inhaling deeply, Laila smiled at the inviting sweet chocolate fragrance. "It certainly does."

After spending twenty minutes walking off their lunch, she and Zak sat at a round, marble-topped table on wrought iron scrollwork chairs with red and white striped fabric seats. She loved the vintage feel of the place, patterned after old-fashioned soda fountains and housed in one of Glassfloat Bay's oldest buildings at the center of town. The long marble soda counter lined with stools and the black and white checkered floor tiles added a period touch.

Zak's eyebrows knitted. "What is that pervasive buzzing noise?"

Paying attention, Laila smiled. "That comforting sound you hear is the hum of malted milkshake mixers whirring in the background."

After placing their order, Zak said, "If ice cream is nearly as good as the pub food I will be most pleased."

"Wait until you sink your spoon into the sundae, it's to die for."

"I think not." Sitting with his back against the chair, he folded his arms across his chest. "I have already experienced more than my share of death. It does not merit repeating."

"You'll change your mind after a dish of butter pecan ice cream with a caramel ribbon and fudge brownie chunks, slathered with hot chocolate fudge and whipped cream. You'll think you've died and gone to heaven."

A low chuckle rumbled up from his chest.

Laila cocked her head. "What?"

"Your zealous descriptions of food amuse me. I think you are at your happiest when talking about chocolate."

"Talking about it makes me happy," her smile grew wide, "but eating it makes me happier."

Their sundaes were served, momentarily distracting Laila from their conversation. It had been more than a year since she'd allowed herself to indulge.

Snapping his fingers, Zak said, "You were not listening." An eyebrow arrowed up in accusatory fashion. "I am not used to being ignored in favor of edibles. Please attempt to pry your attention away from chocolate long enough to converse with me."

"Sorry. It's just been sooo long. Where were we?" She licked her lips as her gaze briefly slipped back to the waiting sundae and Zak sat back, giving a hearty laugh.

"Go on," he gestured with his hand, "attend to your ice cream, or it will melt under the heat of your impatient stare."

They each took a spoonful.

Laila wasn't disappointed with Zak's reaction. He grinned and his eyes shot wide in obvious surprise.

"Unlike anything I have tasted." He licked his lips. "Like creamy snow." He dug his spoon in for another hefty helping before declaring, "This may indeed be to suffer death for."

His comment snagged Laila's attention away from the ice cream. She covered her mouth and laughed. "You are so damned cute, Zak."

His expression twisting, he repeated, "Cute?" He looked positively wounded. Elevating his chin, he informed her, "Warriors are not cute. I, Zakkar Tanojin Lugalbanda Tymon, am virile, manly, powerful. Commanding and handsome."

"True. But you're still a cutie pie." Between the sundae and the gorgeous man sitting opposite her, it was hard to concentrate on the conversation.

"Well, well, Laila Malone. I haven't seen you in quite a while, dear."

Laila froze at the familiar sound of Miriam Schmidt's voice. The sixty-ish woman was the self-appointed unofficial town mayor. A busybody and gossip, she lived for getting the scoop on anything new so she could be the first one to spread the word. As nosy and intrusive as Miriam was though, Laila couldn't help liking her. She'd never been anything but kind and Laila knew the woman meant well.

"Mrs. Schmidt, so nice to see you again." Laila had learned long ago that the woman preferred to be called Mrs. Schmidt by everyone but her husband.

"I see you're taking a break from your diet today, hmm? Well there's certainly no harm in that...as long as you don't overdo." After shaking a chastising finger, she gurgled with laughter and patted Laila's hand. "I'm just teasing, dear. You deserve to treat yourself every so often."

Laila swallowed a sigh along with her mouthful of ice cream. Apparently there was no escaping eagle-eyed scrutiny when she strayed from her diet.

"I'm having a cheat day...something I do only once in a blue moon," she felt compelled to explain.

"Good for you, dear." Bending, Miriam covered the side of her mouth and said in a loud whisper, "Don't worry, I won't breathe a word to Bunny Turner." She winked, straightened, and her smile spread as she appraised Zak. "I see you have a new friend too."

"This is Zak. He's...an old college friend of my brother Gard."

"Happy to meet you Zak." Miriam extended her hand. "Is that short for Zachery?"

"No, Laila shortened my name from Zakkar Tanojin Lugalbanda Tymon to make it more appropriate for the twenty-first century."

That got a double eyebrow raise from Miriam.

Oh hell... Laila needed to take control of the conversation. In an effort to hastily swallow the sizeable spoonful of ice cream she'd shoveled in, she gulped, giving herself a thundering case of brain freeze.

"It is my pleasure to make your acquaintance, Mrs. Schmidt." Zak brought her hand to his lips and kissed it, eliciting a tuneful, girlish sigh from the older woman.

"What an intriguing foreign accent. Where are you from?"

"Greece," Laila quickly offered at the same time Zak said "Sumer."

"He means *somewhere*..." Laila said.

Miriam gave her a befuddled look. "Somewhere?"

"Eh..." Laila erupted in a nervous giggle. "Somewhere in Greece."

"Oh..." Miriam nodded as if she understood. "Where are you staying, young man? Moonstar Shores Cottages off Highway 101? I know Gard is still in Antarctica so you're not staying with him."

"No, I live with Laila."

Mrs. Schmidt's eyes popped open wide.

"No, no, no. He doesn't mean he's living with me." Laila burst forth with another volley of misplaced laughter. "He just means he's staying at Bekka House. Uh...in Gard's old room. Temporarily. Until we find someplace else for him to stay. Right Zak?"

"No, Laila, I mean—"

Clapping her hand over Zak's arm with a bit more force than she'd intended, Laila explained, "Zak has some trouble understanding English." Her fingers dug into Zak's forearm.

The last thing she needed was for Ms. Busybody to spread the word all over town that Laila was shacking up with some stranger.

She could just imagine if that got back to her overprotective mother. Astrid would be on a fast flight back from Norway, just like that.

"I see…and how long will you be staying here in Glassfloat Bay, Zak?"

"Until Laila makes her third—"

"Zak!" Laila's heart nearly leapt out of her throat. "He'll be here for six months."

"Hmm…" She was quiet just long enough to give Zak another appreciative appraisal. "And what about your sister? I hear she may have a new beau."

"Which sister?" Laila asked, still giving Zak the evil eye.

"Maureen. The buzz about town is that she's been socializing quite a bit with Professor Slattery."

"Oh, no, Reen and Drake are just good friends," Laila assured her, watching Miriam's expression sag from eager-to-get-a-scoop to disappointment in failing to snag a juicy new tidbit of gossip.

"Oh…" An instant later, her face radiating with renewed interest, she offered Laila and Zak an expectant smile. "Well then, getting back to you two—"

"Mrs. Schmidt, I've got your order ready to go," one of the ice cream parlor's employees said, holding out a bag large enough to contain a couple pints of ice cream. The timing of the employee's welcome intrusion couldn't have been better.

"Ooh, good. Thank you." Turning back to Laila and Zak she said, "I'd better get this home to Mr. Schmidt before it melts. We'll talk again, dear. Soon." She stressed the word with a pointed finger. "So nice to meet you, Zak."

As Mrs. Schmidt turned, heading out, Laila finally took a breath.

"Zak, you really need to listen to me and follow my lead when we're talking to people."

"Where will you be leading me?" He locked gazes with her. "To the Chains-R-Us market?"

"No, naughty genie. I meant away from prying eyes and ears." Zak's devil-may-care smile told her he was undeterred by her reprimanding look. "Chains-R-Us, indeed," she muttered beneath her breath. "Like most men, you have a one track mind. It's time for you to tell me how you ended up imprisoned in the bottle."

He swallowed another spoonful of his sundae. "Later today I will reveal all that happened. First, I want to hear about your lost fiancé. You briefly mentioned him earlier when we were in the car. What happened?"

"Tim," Laila said absently, her spoon halfway to her mouth. It stayed that way so long some of the hot fudge plopped onto the table.

"Tell me, little one, what happened to him?"

She mopped up the chocolate. "You're the one who's supposed to be spilling his guts." At his horrified expression, she clarified, "Sorry, that means telling your story."

"I will spill my guts after I hear about your life."

His response provoked her hint of laughter. "There's really not much to tell. My life is fairly boring." She glanced at Zak. Her genie. Her lover. "At least it was until yesterday."

"Tell me about Tim." He offered an encouraging smile.

"He was a good man. I met him through Gard. They were best friends and coworkers, glaciologists studying global warming and the melting icebergs in Antarctica. Gard named his dog, who's one of Friday's brothers, Tundra, because of—"

"The frozen tundra." Zak spoke the words without any fondness. "I remember it well." His brief shiver caught her eye.

"You were in Antarctica?"

"Briefly. A frozen, desolate land with few people."

"How long ago?"

"The early part of the whaling era there, about 1790. My possessor, Hester, was the wife of a British sealer."

"I think you mean sailor."

"No, sealers hunted the fur seals for their pelts. Hester's husband, Benjamin, fell into frigid water through a hole the crew made in the ice with a hand drill. They rescued him but he was close to death, fighting frostbite, hypothermia, then pneumonia. He was to have both legs amputated above the knees to help stall his demise, although the doctor admitted there was little possibility of saving him."

"How awful. You were there when he died?"

"He did not die. My possessor's first wish was that her husband would be whole and well again."

"You were able to do that?"

"Yes." Zak nodded with a faraway look in his eyes. "She made the wish as she watched the doctor walk toward Benjamin with a saw."

The extent of Zak's capabilities with wish granting was astounding.

"When the sick man suddenly rose to his feet from the cot, there was vexation among those who witnessed it. They feared witchcraft caused the instant healing."

"I'd be alarmed too. What happened to the couple?"

"They faced incarceration for the duration of their stay in Antarctica. Fearing for their lives, Hester was about to wish for everyone who knew of the miraculous curing to forget her husband had ever been injured."

"Sounds like a wise wish under the circumstances. Did it work?"

"I advised her against making the wish. It was unnecessary. The gods automatically resolve such problems. A moment after our discussion, we witnessed everyone's complete acceptance of Benjamin's unlikely healing."

"Wow."

"Indeed. Hester's second wish was for them to enjoy a long and happy life together. Her third wish was for enough money so Benjamin would never have to work again."

"All her wishes worked?"

"The wishes always work."

Laila could imagine how fascinating a book detailing centuries of the wishes of Zak's possessors would be. Of course, no one would believe it was nonfiction. "I'll bet they headed somewhere warm and sunny after that."

"I would suspect but I have no way of knowing." Zak shrugged. "Once the third wish was granted I was sucked back into the bottle."

Damn. She hated that dreaded reminder. She was silent until Zak spoke again.

"Did Tim lose his life in Antarctica?"

"Yes." She felt a familiar ache in her heart. "He fell into a crevasse while on a research expedition collecting snow and ice samples."

"I am sorry. Was your brother there when Tim died?"

Unexpected tears sprang to her eyes. Even after three years the memory still hit hard.

"Yes." With a shuddering breath, she continued, "Gard and the other two men in their party tried rescuing Tim using ropes and ice axes, but the crevasse swallowed Tim so fast nothing could be done."

"It must have been a terrible blow for Gard. I can relate to losing a comrade through failed rescue attempts."

"It still haunts him." Laila nodded. "He has nightmares about it. The other men told me Gard refused to give up, desperately trying to save Tim as Tim struggled to climb out of the crevasse." Laila grabbed a paper napkin from the metal holder on the table and blotted her eyes.

"Gard came close to losing his own life once Tim plunged down because Gard wouldn't release the rope. He finally had no choice because Tim was no longer on the other end." Laila fought to hold back tears.

"Gard returned home with badly torn hands, a broken arm, dislocated shoulder, three broken ribs and other injuries. At least, thank God, he made it home alive. It took him a long time to recover...physically. Emotionally, he hasn't been the same since the accident."

"Gard still works in Antarctica as a glaciologist," Zak said. It was more a statement than a question.

"He does, as well as working as a volunteer firefighter here in Glassfloat Bay when he's at home. How did you know?"

"Because I would do the same," Zak replied. "Your brother sounds like a good man."

"He is." Laila worried about Gard every day, dreading another life-altering phone call. "On top of the tragedy, Gard's fiancée dumped him for another guy when he was in the hospital, all black and blue and broken. Poor Gard. He deserves so much better."

"It is better she left him. Such a woman would have only caused your brother grief later if they had wed."

"I couldn't agree more." Laila nodded, surprised Zak was so perceptive.

"How many brothers and sisters do you have?"

"There are six of us. I have three sisters, Reen, Delaney, and Kady, and two brothers, Gard and Nevan."

His eyebrows rose. "A big family."

"Mmm-hmm. How about you?"

"I had two sisters and a brother." Zak asked about her family, including Grandma Bekka, who she'd mentioned a few times.

"I spent some time at the bidding of a Viking girl child with a sister named Rebekka," he told her.

"My brother-in-law, Varik, is descended from Vikings. When were you with them?"

He thought for a moment. "Late 700s or early 800s." Looking as though he was a million miles away in thought, he added, "It was a time and place quite foreign from today's world."

"My mom and stepdad will be back from their vacation in Norway in a month or so. I can picture you and Tore having long talks over pints of beer. I think you'd get along great."

"What is a stepdad?"

"Oh...my dad was a firefighter. He lost his life saving children in a school fire in Chicago when I was a child. Mom raised all of us on her own. She met Tore through Varik, they're cousins. They fell in love and were married recently. That makes Tore our stepfather. He's a wonderful man who treats Mom like gold, so we couldn't be happier."

Laila's phone rang. Hearing her mother's ringtone she stiffened. Talk about people being psychic.

"Sorry, Zak, I need to take this call. It's my mom."

"Of course."

"Hi Mom," she said in her cheeriest voice.

"Laila!" Astrid Malone said. "How are you, sweetie? Anything new since we last talked?"

Her overly cheerful question had an odd ring to it. Narrowing one eye, Laila asked, "Have you talked to Reen?" Reen would have hell to pay if she'd told their mom about Zak.

"No, why? Has something happened?"

Laila could hear the alarm in her mom's voice. "No, nothing. Everyone's fine."

"You sound...different," Astrid noted.

Laila's shoulders sagged. "Different? Nope. Everything is the same. Nothing's different." Her gaze snapped to the genie sitting across from her. "Except Reen and I got letters from TBT telling us we need to lose weight or lose our jobs."

"Good grief. What in the world is wrong with that woman?" Without a delay, Astrid added, "You're seeing someone, aren't you?"

"What?" Laila gasped, holding her phone at arm's length, half wondering if it was bugged. "No. I just told you, everything's the same."

"Mmm-hmm. What's his name? How did you meet him? I want all the details."

"You make me sound downright pathetic, Mom, like I've never had a boyfriend before. I'm in my thirties you know, not fifteen." Laila glanced at Zak to catch him eyeing her with amusement.

"Which is why it's even more important to have a good man in your life, sweetheart. No matter how old you are you'll always be my baby. So he's your boyfriend, hmm?"

Knowing from past experience it was fruitless to lie to her prying but well-meaning mother, Laila fessed up. "Okay, yes, I'm seeing someone. Satisfied?"

Laila's mind raced, wondering how much to say over the phone. Hearing your daughter is dating a genie probably wasn't the best news to divulge when your parents were nearly 5,000 miles from home.

"What kind of mother would I be if I wasn't concerned about my darling daughter? I love you and want you to be happy, that's all."

"I know. I love you too, Mom. And I am happy. I'd be even happier if you didn't worry about me so much." *Or meddle so much.* "I'm fine, honest."

"Okay."

Laila smiled, knowing that wouldn't be the end of it.

"Where did you meet him?"

In my kitchen when he floofed out of an ancient bottle in a puff of smoke and announced his sole purpose was to pleasure me.

"At an estate sale." It was true. Basically.

"What fun! I know how much you love sifting through other people's junk. You take after me that way. You never know where you might find the next treasure."

If her mom only knew. "You can say that again."

"So what's his name?"

"Zakkar. Zakkar Tymon." Damn...she should have said Tom or Joe or any ordinary name that wouldn't prompt more questions. "Zak for short."

"Zakkar. Interesting. Is he foreign?"

And the third degree was just getting started.

"Yes." Laila breathed another sigh. "Mediterranean."

"Is he here permanently or just visiting?"

"He's visiting for the next six months."

"Oh no."

"What?"

"You're heading for another broken heart."

Her mother didn't know the half of it.

"No I'm not," Laila lied, closing her eyes and willing away thoughts of Zak's inevitable departure. "We're just having fun, enjoying each other's company before he has to go back." She smiled as Zak took her hand, stroking his thumb over her knuckles.

"My poor Laila."

"Mom!" Laila cringed when patrons turned to glance at her. "Seriously," she said in a more discreet tone, "I'm fine. And I'm .." she looked into Zak's eyes and took a breath, "I'm fully prepared for when he has to leave." She was amazed her nose didn't grow six inches from that whopping fib.

"Really?"

"Really. Please stop worrying about me. I've never been happier."

"That's exactly what I'm worried about."

Aarrgghhhhh!

"I have to go. I love you, Mom. Give Tore my best. Try to stop worrying and enjoy the rest of your vacation."

"I will, Laila, sweetie. Love you."

Laila sat silent for a long moment after ending the call. She wouldn't be a bit surprised if her mother started packing immediately.

Chapter 12

~<>~

"I ADORE MY MOM," Laila told Zak as they walked to the car, "but she's a worrywart."

"She suffers from a skin condition?"

Laila gave a pop of unexpected laughter. "No, she suffers from an overprotective complex. She worries about me and my sisters and brothers too much."

"It is good she worries about her little goats."

Laila's smile quirked. "Her little goats are all adults."

"Be happy you have a mother who cares so deeply for you."

Laila felt like an ass for whining, and guilty for being annoyed with her mom. Zak hadn't seen his mother in thousands of years. He might not have had a chance to say goodbye before being bottled up for eternity.

"You're right. I'm very fortunate." She unlocked the car and they slipped into their seats. "I miss Mom and Tore when they're traveling."

"Do you know what would give me enormous satisfaction?" Zak's eyes studied each of her actions as she stuck the key in the ignition, started the car, and backed out of her parking space.

"Yes. And the answer is no, you may not drive."

"How did you know I wanted to drive?"

"Because you're a man," Laila said simply as she pulled out into traffic on Ocean Charm Boulevard.

"To ease my boundless disappointment you will take us to Chains-R-Us."

"I already told you, I was just joking about that shop," she told him, her gaze never veering from the road.

"The trio of *assinnu* men spoke of such a place."

"You want me to take you shopping for sex toys in a scandalous establishment where I'd die of embarrassment if anyone spotted me?"

"I suspect you will not die."

Laila heaved a weighty sigh. Maybe if she gave in to his shopping whim he'd quit bugging her about driving. "Okay...fine."

"Excellent!"

They soon arrived at Provocative Pleasures, their tawdry destination on the outskirts of town. Emblazoned across the front of the building, just beneath the name of the shop, a fluorescent mustard-yellow neon sign boldly flashed, *You Know You Want To.*

Oh dear God...

With a tension headache threatening, Laila's eyelids fluttered shut. Why hadn't she thought to bring a wig? A mask? A paper bag with cutout eyeholes to yank over her head?

She fought against the eerie feeling something awful might happen the instant she stepped over the store's threshold. Like she'd be their millionth customer. Flashing lights, blaring sirens, the media gleefully snapping her horrified expression, her video going viral.

"You are as still as a statue," Zak noted, standing outside her car door, hands on his knees as he bent to look at her. She didn't even realize he'd gotten out of the car. He opened her door, offering his hand. "Come, Laila. We will have fun."

She glanced up into his dark eyes and the long lashes fringing them as he hunched over the driver's side, peering down at her.

"Are you not eager to explore the inside of the sexual pleasure market?"

"Eager's not the word." Taking his hand, she exited the vehicle, knees knocking and heart thumping. She had no idea what to expect once inside. Maybe it would be decorated with inflated condoms, or strings of dildo lights, or sparkling pasties plastered all over. Maybe clerks were demonstrating the latest eight-speed vibrators. She shuddered at the thought...and not in a good way.

She felt the gentle tug of Zak's hand on hers.

A subdued *dingdong* heralded their arrival as he opened the shop's door. Once she'd taken a few steps inside and all was quiet, Laila let out the pent-up breath she'd been holding.

Then a bell went off and she let out a piercing yip.

"Are you ill?" Zak clamped her shoulders in a caring gesture. All she could do was shake her head *no* in response.

Primed for paparazzi, she stiffened. Then she heard the bell again.

Her shoulders slumped with relief when she realized it was just the phone in her purse making the racket. It was Reen. She answered, figuring Reen was on a coffee break at work and might need to talk to her about something TBT-related.

Nope.

"I got a call from Mom. She's worried about you."

"Oh hell. You didn't say anything about Zak being a genie, did you?"

"Don't be ridiculous. So..."

Before Laila had a chance to get more than a word in edgewise, she was getting the third-degree from her sister.

"You're not in bed together right now, are you?" Laila could tell Reen was cupping her hand over the mouthpiece. "Because that would really be awkward."

"Do you honestly think I'd be answering the phone if I was?"

"I hope to hell not. But you *are* out of practice." Reen snickered. "So what are you doing?"

"We're...uh, still shopping." Laila swallowed hard.

"Is this your sister, Reen, on the phone?" Zak asked. "Would it be permissible for me to speak to her?"

"Sure. Zak wants to say hi, Reen." She handed the phone to him. "You talk here and listen here," she explained.

"Hello, Reen, sister of Laila and date of Drake!" Zak's megaphone voice boomed and Laila shushed him. "Yes, it is I, Zakkar Tanojin Lugalbanda Tymon, better known in the twenty-first century as Zak, speaking to your spirit on the phone," he said, failing to modulate his voice. He grinned at Laila, giving her a thumbs-up sign. She couldn't help giggling.

"Can you see me, Reen? I cannot see you. You are invisible. I am completely unafraid to speak to your disembodied voice on the phone. Yes, okay. Buh-bye to you too, Reen."

With a mile-wide grin affixed to his face, he handed the phone back to Laila.

"You're going to bust a gut if you keep laughing like that," Laila whispered into the phone when she heard Reen guffawing on the other end. "Gotta go. We'll talk later. If mom calls you again just don't pick up, she has an uncanny way of dragging the truth out of us when we least expect it." She ended the call and stuffed the phone back in her purse.

"Hi there," a woman's voice called from the rear of the store, startling Laila. "I'm Dorothy. Just let me know if I can be of any help."

Following the source of the voice, Laila spotted a sweet-looking senior citizen. She was dressed normal, thank God, in loose black slacks and a pearl-gray sweater twin-set, topped by a double strand of pearls. Laila would have hightailed it out of there like a bat out of hell if she'd come face to face with a whip-yielding, leather bustier-wearing granny.

"Thank you. We will alert you should we need your knowledgeable assistance," Zak replied, striding into the store's depths and checking out all the kinky stuff openly splashed everywhere.

Laila's eyes widened as she scanned the curious inventory. There were umpteen types of vibrators, dildos, whips, cuffs, blindfolds and strange-looking paraphernalia she had no clue even existed.

"What is this, Dorothy?" Zak asked the nice old woman. Leila went to the area where Zak stood, groaning when she saw what he held.

The poor woman was probably on a fixed retirement income, working there to help make ends meet, maybe because no one else would hire her at her age. She'd probably be blushing from her roots to her toes trying to answer Zak's question.

"Shhh, you'll embarrass her," Laila whispered, tugging on his arm.

"It's a latex female sex doll," Dorothy explained, coming down the aisle with a lively smile. "With human hair, glass eyes and a realistic vagina. The vaginal material is soft and smooth enough not to chafe a penis during copulation." She turned the doll upside down to give Zak a bird's eye view of the doll's crotch. "They're quite popular. A vast improvement over the welded vinyl blow-up dolls, which often burst at the seams after just a few uses."

Stunned, Laila blinked.

"We get ours from France. They're top quality, with water-filled breasts and buttocks. This one comes with interchangeable openings for anus, vagina and mouth, complete with vibrating capabilities."

Laila didn't dare risk a glimpse at Zak.

"Our customers love them, although they're a bit of a pain to clean up. I recommend just taking her into the shower with you." Dorothy winked.

Laila felt as if she'd tumbled down the rabbit hole, ending up in the porn version of Wonderland.

"I know the inventory like the back of my hand." Dorothy's face crinkled with a smile. "I'm the original owner, for thirty years now."

"Why would I need this if I have Laila?" Zak frowned as he scrutinized the doll and its various orifices. He clearly wasn't trying to be a smartass or argumentative. He was simply eager to learn.

"You wouldn't." Dorothy gave Laila a friendly grin. "Not if you have a ready and willing partner available."

Returning her smile, Laila withered on the spot.

Zak looked from the doll to Laila. "I would like to see you in this garment." He gestured to the life-sized Barbie doll with the bright red puckered blowjob-ready lips.

Laila eyed the skimpy getup, consisting of black leather straps—she suspected there wasn't enough material to make a pair of leather gloves—shiny silver studs, and chains. "What garment?" she managed. "I sincerely doubt they carry things like that in my size."

"We carry a wide variety of sizes," Dorothy offered. "For both slave and master."

"Oh. I'm not a slave," Laila clarified, feeling warmth seep into her cheeks.

"I am the slave." His shoulders slumped, Zak's expression was dejected.

"Oh." Dorothy slanted a curious look. "My mistake. I'm usually not wrong about those things."

Laila crooked her finger, motioning for Zak to bend down. She whispered into his ear.

"Ahhhh." Zak nodded, his smile returning. "I misunderstood. Laila is the slave and I, Zakkar Tymon, am her master," he announced confidently.

"No!" Laila protested, turning to Dorothy. "He doesn't understand. Neither of us is slave or master."

"I understand very well," Zak countered, smiling at Dorothy. "Laila does not yet realize the joys of being bound as a naked pleasure slave. She is inexperienced and too timid to openly divulge her deepest sexual desires."

Oh God.

Oh God, oh God, oh God.

"Zak!" Mortified to her bone marrow, Laila felt her face heat tomato-soup-red. "Good grief, do you want a bullhorn?"

"What is that?" He glanced around. "Are they sold here as well?"

"It's something to help you announce my private fantasies to the entire north side of Glassfloat Bay."

His expression kinked. "You would like me to do this for you?"

"Oh for heaven's sake, no!" Rolling her eyes, Laila growled in frustration.

Offering a warm smile, Dorothy patted Laila's arm. "Bondage fantasies are nothing to be ashamed of, dear."

"But I don't have bon—"

"My husband and I have been master and slave for many years." Dorothy's smile was grandmotherly. "It can be immensely satisfying and pleasurable, whether it's a lifestyle or an occasional pursuit."

The woman's revelation fell under the category of *everything I definitely don't want to know about somebody's grandma.*

Imagining Dorothy in Big Latex Barbie's chained leather gear and doing God knows what with grandpa, Laila struggled not to gawk. She doubted her success when the woman chuckled.

"Yes, I know I look like the typical apple-pie-making grandma next door." She shrugged. "And I am. But I assure you, I know about every item we carry in the store." One eyebrow arched. "Personally."

Clamping her mouth shut, Laila clenched her teeth, determined not to let her jaw drop again.

"Ralph and I test every item before we allow them on the sales floor." She patted Laila's arm in a motherly gesture. "Nothing you could ask or tell me would make be blush or gasp in horror." She winked. "I promise."

Humming a peppy tune, Dorothy hunted through the packaged BDSM costumes on the shelves, plucking one and handing it to Laila. "A large should be just right for you, dear." She went back to her work, leaving Laila and Zak alone in the aisle.

Zak was still busy examining the multi-orificed doll.

Laila slapped his hand. "Will you please put that overgrown Barbie down?" she whispered. Zak readily complied, returning it to the stand where he'd found it.

"Ah, you have found the leather garment." A bright grin split his face.

Tossing the costume Dorothy had given her back on the shelf, Laila turned to Zak, narrowing her eyes. "There's no way in hell I'm wearing something like that, so you can just forget it."

"But—"

"Let's just get whatever it is you need and get out of here. I'll absolutely die if someone catches me in here with an armful of kinky stuff. And, please, *please*, don't ask Dorothy any more questions. If we can't figure it out ourselves, we're not buying it, okay?"

"Okay." Shopping basket looped over his arm, with the enthusiasm of a kid in a candy shop Zak made his way up and down the aisles, plunking item after kinky item into the container.

As Dorothy slid the packages over the scanner, Laila glimpsed the accumulation of unfamiliar playthings, cringing as she wondered why on earth she'd agreed to take Zak to a sex shop of all things.

"You decided against the BDSM costume?" Dorothy asked Laila.

"Um, yes...I remembered I, uh, already have one at home."

"You do?" An overly cheerful Zak piped up and Laila responded by nailing him with a steely glare.

"I thought we'd never get out of there," she said as Zak added the bag of adult goodies to the other packages in her car's trunk.

"We will go home to make use of them now," Zak stated.

"No," Laila countered with a resounding tsk. "We're going grocery shopping. And we're having a talk. It's time we got to know each other better." She got in the driver's side and slammed the door.

Decidedly cranky, she said, "I want to know who you are and how and why you ended up in a bottle."

Zak's smile was devilish as he hunkered his huge frame to fit in the seat. "I thought we were long past the introduction phase of our relationship."

She felt her cheeks flush. "We've only known each other for a day." It was hard to believe. It felt like they'd known each other forever.

"And one euphoric night." Zak's eyes twinkled when he looked at her, his gaze slipping to her mouth and lingering there. She licked her lips in response, having a devil of a time keeping her eyes on the road.

"You think you're irresistibly charming, don't you?"

"It's what *you* think that matters. And we both know you find me irresistible." She opened her mouth to protest, but Zak continued. "I find you just as irresistible." His hand curled around her thigh.

He knew exactly how to manipulate her.

Laila resisted the overwhelming urge to pull onto the shoulder of the road, hop on Zakkar and screw the living daylights out of him right there on Ocean Charm Boulevard.

She was losing it, rapidly morphing into a woman of dubious morals.

"Okay, no more stalling. You promised you'd tell me how you ended up in the bottle. If you don't, I promise that bag of sex toys goes right in the trash."

"All right, little one, I will spill my guts."

By the time they'd pulled into the grocery store's parking lot Zak had told her all the sordid details about what happened so many centuries ago. Tears slid down Laila's cheeks as his desperately sad story unfolded.

"Please don't cry." Zak thumbed away her tears. "It hurts my heart to see you weep for me, Laila."

If she hadn't been concentrating on driving, she'd be a red-eyed, snotty-nosed, blotchy-faced basket case after hearing his heartrending tale. Zak had virtually sacrificed himself to save the honor of a foolish young woman. Laila was sitting next to an honest to goodness hero, in the truest sense of the word. And that's just what she told him after putting the car in park and cutting the engine.

"I am no hero," Zak scoffed, his expression darkening. "I am but a man who was caught in circumstances beyond his control. Heroes prevail. I did not."

"That's the first time I've ever heard a shred of modesty pass your lips." Laila brushed a fingertip across his sensuous mouth. "You're a hero of the finest magnitude, Zak. A man who bravely defended a woman's honor to the—" She stopped short before *death* popped out of her mouth.

"Had I been given the option, I would have chosen death rather than becoming naught but a shade." Zak had clearly anticipated her unspoken words.

"Please don't say that." She leaned over, cupping his face in her hands, stroking his jaw. "If you had died, I never would have met you. You're the best thing to come into my life in a very long time, Zak."

She couldn't believe she was being so open with him.

Pinning her with the intensity of his gaze, Zak covered one of her hands with his. "You truly mean that, don't you?"

"With all my heart."

"And you are the best thing to come into my life in eons. You have restored vitality to my soul. Brought light and laughter back into my existence in ways you cannot imagine."

Knowing she'd given this wonderful man a sliver of joy in his bleak, endless existence made her heart swell.

"I can't understand why Sabit didn't keep her promise to find a way to free you from your servitude. She owed you so much after what you did for her."

Zak's broad shoulders shrugged. "I wondered the same for eras as I dwelt in the shadows. Perhaps Sabit feared for her life. Perchance she tried to petition but the great goddess Inanna turned a deaf ear. It is possible Sabit met with an untimely death and was unable to plead to the priests or the gods on my behalf. It matters not now. I gave up hope long ago that I will be set free."

What words of comfort could Laila possibly offer to soothe the gnawing ache deep in the core of Zak's ancient, heroic heart?

He must have seen the whirling mix of emotion in her eyes. "Make me a promise, my sweet Laila." His fingers smoothed through her hair. "During this brief time we have together, let us enjoy it fully. Do not weep for me or feel pity for my circumstances."

"But how can I—"

Zak placed his finger against her lips. "If you wish to make me happy, then promise to be happy yourself. Let me see you smile and laugh. Allow me to savor your expressions of wonder as you speak of chocolate, as well as your passion-filled gaze as we make love. Act as if we have endless time to spend together, rather than six lunar cycles. Can you do that for me?"

When she lowered her gaze, he kissed the top of her head.

"Will you give me those sweet memories to cherish, to lock away in my heart once I must return to the bottle?"

How could she agree when her heart was breaking? When she yearned to clutch onto him and never let go? How could she keep herself from dreading the moment he'd depart from her life as quickly as he came into it?

But agree she must. It wasn't fair to Zak for her to wear her emotions on her sleeve. If he could be brave after all he'd endured, so could she. The least she could do for this magnificent man was agree to a pretense of carefree happiness.

Zak's gaze grew intense, the soft smile across his lips flattening to a level line. "Promise me, Laila..."

Sucking in a deep breath, she exhaled with a wobbly hum. "I promise."

"Thank you." He kissed her hands, front and back, lingering at her wrists.

Silence embraced them for a few moments, allowing Laila to pull herself together. Conjuring her brightest smile, she cast tears and trepidation aside. Pulling down the visor she looked into the mirror, wiping away smudges of eye makeup and fiddling with her hair.

"So," she pretended her face was a happy emoticon as she turned to Zak, "are you ready to experience your first grocery store experience?"

"The giant food market with modern edibles and barley ale?" He clapped his knees. "Yes!"

Zak's delight over such a small everyday occurrence touched her heart.

"It will be a superb adventure!" he told her, opening the car door and exiting.

"Every moment with you is a superb adventure, my darling genie," she whispered for her ears only.

Chapter 13

~<>~

"THE PEOPLE OF my time would never believe this astonishing bounty," Zak said, taking in his surroundings. "Hunger would be eliminated. The yield here could feed an entire city for countless days." Planting his fists on his hips, Zakkar smiled. "It makes my heart glad to see the problem of hunger has finally been abolished."

Laila followed his gaze. A stranger to a modern supermarket could easily assume this was a time free of poverty and hunger. Like so many, Laila took the ready availability of food for granted.

She imagined dieting and body image issues didn't make the list of top ten things a Sumerian worried about...

Oh gods, blood is running in the streets, the enemy is fast approaching, but I dare not flee because my ass doth look gargantuan in this toga.

"I regret to say there's still plenty of hunger in the world, Zak. There are those with more than they can ever use, those with enough, and those who are always in need."

He nodded, looking thoughtful. "It is a pity this inequity still exists after so many centuries."

To maintain his warrior's physique with its absence of extraneous fat, he must have paired a healthy diet with plenty of rigorous activity. When she asked him, he told her their eating regimen included most things in moderation.

"We were hardworking people who rarely sat about doing nothing. It was rare to see rotund people in my time."

If Laila could master the art of moderation combined with exercise she'd never have to go on another diet and her closet would contain just one size instead of several.

"I'll bet the women of your time had no trouble keeping weight off with all the food preparation they did daily."

"True. They worked from before sunrise until time for slumber. Our food choices were limited to what we caught or harvested that day or to what the women found at the marketplace. There was no way to preserve foods, other than heavily salting them or steeping in turned wine. Instead of refrigeration we had fermented foods."

As they loaded the grocery bags into her already bloated car trunk, Laila's curiosity got the better of her.

"Did you have a wife or children?"

"No. I had planned to pursue those pleasures after I retired from soldiering. Being in my third decade, I was already growing too old for the vigorous life of a warrior. The constant sea of bloodied body parts had begun to lose its luster."

Laila nodded silently, unable to imagine something so heinous. The stark reality of all the butchery was too atrocious to fathom.

"Worse yet were the suffering half-dead men at my command, many limbless or with their bellies split open like ripe melons and their entrails spilling out on the ground."

A shudder vibrated through Laila. This was like those gruesome movies she refused to watch because they gave her nightmares. Zak had actually lived through it.

"I can still hear their distressed cries, pleading for merciful deaths at my hand." Zak stiffened for a moment as he bent over the trunk, brown paper bags in his arms. "Freeing them from their suffering was not a pleasant task. But it was my honorable obligation as their leader."

It was painfully clear Zak had seen and experienced carnage and atrocities Laila couldn't even begin to conceive.

"I'm sorry, Zak." She touched his arm. "It sounds like you led a difficult life even before you were locked away in the bottle."

He pointedly shook off whatever memories lingered as he closed the trunk and placed the last of the bags in the car's back seat. Turning to Laila, he smoothed the windblown hair from her face, tucking it behind her ears as he gazed into her eyes. She watched the troubled lines in his face ease as his expression shifted from grave to a charming smile.

She took a mental snapshot of the picture-perfect moment to keep tucked away in her heart.

"My life was good, Laila. As a warrior I had achieved a coveted rank of stature, as well as respect, both in and outside of Sumer. Battle was harsh and grueling but with victory came satisfaction and the knowledge that my actions had prevented untold violence by the Akkadians or other invading armies against my people."

They slipped inside the car, well *she* slipped in while Zak fought to scrunch and fold himself, and she started the engine.

"What I most regret is not having a family. A devoted wife in my bed and a passel of children at my knee. Were you planning to have babies with Tim?"

"Yes..." She filled her lungs, the breath escaping in a trembly sigh. "We both loved children."

"I am truly sorry."

As she buckled herself in, Laila's smile was wistful. "Hopefully I'll get the chance to have a baby before my biological clock runs out." In anticipation of his question, she added, "Which means, before I get too old."

"You would make a fine mother. I could tell by your manner with Lilly and Kevin."

Her thoughts were miles away. "I think Tim and I would have made good parents."

"You loved him very much," Zak said.

"Tim was very dear to me." Laila smiled. "We were good friends for years after Gard introduced us. Getting married seemed like the next logical step in our relationship. We'd planned to be married after he returned from Antarctica."

He covered her hand with his, smoothing his thumb over her fingers. "I deeply regret your sorrow."

"Thank you."

"Have you given thought to your three wishes yet? Your wishes can provide wealth and riches...ensuring a comfortable life for you and your loved ones."

"Some." While the idea of making life-changing wishes was thrilling, it was also a huge responsibility. "I want to make sure I give my wishes plenty of consideration."

Of all the things in the world to wish for, what three would be the most important?

The end to hunger, poverty and homelessness?

World peace?

The obliteration of cancer, AIDS, childhood diseases, Alzheimer's and...

What if she could just wish for everyone in the world to be healed and always remain healthy and well-fed? But then, if no one ever got sick and died, there'd be a monumental population explosion.

She'd like to have enough money to be financially secure for the rest of her life, but it would be selfish to limit the wish to just that. She'd want to include wealth and riches for everyone she cared about.

She could wish for an end to obesity and an end to low self-esteem so everyone could feel good about themselves.

Happiness. Now that was something to consider. A wish to abolish depression and for everyone to be contented and joyful all the time.

"I could radically change the world by uttering a few words. How do I make such a difficult decision, Zak? How do I decide what would be the best for everyone? With all your experience granting wishes, you must have some excellent ideas."

"Fascinating. It is a question no one has asked me before."

"Really?" Apparently all his other owners were sharp-minded and decisive. Although she doubted any of them had ever wished for the things she'd been thinking about. If they had, there'd be no more war, hunger, illness, unhappiness...

"What did most of the women wish for?"

Zak didn't hesitate. "Gold, wealth, lavish dwellings, majestic lifestyles, clothing, jewels, things of that nature."

"For the world?"

"For themselves. The wishes are conditional, Laila. They must pertain to the possessor's self-interest and not be the cause of harm or misfortune to others. This means you cannot make wishes that affect everyone else." He reached over to cup her chin. "Knowing you, I imagine you have been thinking of noble wishes like peace for mankind, the end to illness and suffering, righteous ideals of that nature."

She took her eyes off the road long enough to spare him a quick glance. His tender smile warmed her.

"Pretty much," she admitted.

"I regret these things are not within my power to grant. Your wishes must be for you alone. You must decide on three things that would make you happy personally."

Hope swelled in Laila's heart. "Could I wish for the reversal of the deaths of Tim, and Reen's fiancé, Bob?"

She felt Zak's hand caressing her shoulder. "I regret I am unable to restore life to those who have passed on to *Kurnugi*. There is good reason why it is called the land of no return."

As Laila pulled into her driveway, she gazed at Zak for a long moment. "What about you, Zak?"

"I do not understand. What about me?"

"Can I wish you out of the bottle forever? Can I wish that you could stay here with me?" She felt the color rise in her cheeks when she caught the peculiar expression on Zak's face. Maybe he'd feel as trapped staying with her as he did in that bottle.

"You wouldn't have to stay with me, necessarily," she clarified. "You could go wherever you wanted and be with anyone you wanted." She swallowed the knot in her throat.

"How you amaze me, Laila. Again, no one has ever asked this of me." Zak's broad chest expanded as he took in a deep, slow breath. His smile was wistful. "No, the incantation specified this would not be possible. But I cherish your sweet, unselfish thought." He leaned over, capturing her lips in a kiss.

This kiss was different from his others. It spoke of emotion, gratitude and so much more.

She reached up to the visor for the garage door opener while Zak deepened the kiss.

"The ice cream," she muttered, pulling back from him, which was damn hard. "It's going to melt."

"Let it," he said simply, dragging her against him, his hands traveling her body.

Her breath became ragged. Her heart rhythm erratic.

"The neighbors...they're going to talk."

"Let them."

Zak's fingers zigzagged beneath her sweater.

Amidst moans of pleasure, Laila sank down in the seat until she could barely see over the dashboard. Clutching the gearshift, she shifted into drive and gave the car enough gas to creep into the garage...

...and bang into the metal shelves full of stuff just in front of the wall.

As car-related stuff mingled with treasures from garage sales, cascading with clatters, clangs and thuds over the hood of her car, Laila managed to turn off the engine and close the garage door.

"You're exquisite," Zak breathed against her ear. His already deep voice was huskier still. "You intoxicate me. You stir my loins until I am consumed with lustful thoughts."

The ice cream was still frozen but Laila melted into a puddle.

Passion fogging her brain, she seized her genie.

"Oh the hell with the damn ice cream."

Chapter 14

~<>~

"I AM TOO BIG for this tiny chariot." Zak struggled to position himself. "I am unable to maneuver myself in this confined space. My *gis* cannot reach your *gal-la*."

Busy fumbling with both his jeans and hers, she didn't need clarification.

Zak's head thumped against the car's roof as his long legs clunked against the steering wheel, gearshift and dashboard while he tried to turn. It seemed his heavy breathing had more to do with exasperation than lust.

"By all that is holy," he growled in frustration, "we need to depart this miniature chariot before every muscle in my body is permanently twisted." Zak snarled as his elbow slipped and his face slammed into the glovebox. The pungent sound of cursing in another language permeated the car.

Having tried in vain to get it on in the front seat of her car, they were a jumbled mass of limbs.

Laila's face was wedged between Zak's knee and the gearshift. "This is obviously a sign."

"Of?" Still grousing, he struggled to disentangle from the human coil they'd created.

"That we're not a couple of teenagers," Laila slipped her head beneath his knee to get free, "and shouldn't be behaving like hormonal high schoolers."

Zak stopped scrambling long enough to ask, "You mean you do not want to make love?" He looked like a lost puppy.

"Of course I do. But later...after dinner. As adults, we should be more in control of our impulses."

"Why?"

"Because that's what adults are supposed to do." She hated having to be logical when she yearned to stay locked away in her bedroom, wrapped in his firm embrace for the next six months.

Locking gazes with her, Zak breathed a sigh of resignation. "As you wish."

She'd never seen pouting look so adorable on anyone but a child.

After another round of struggling, they finally made their way out of the car.

Wiping perspiration from his brow, Zak glared at the compact car with undisguised contempt. He kicked the front tire with his new shoes. Twice.

"I have not struggled so in ages."

Once inside the house they loaded the first round of bags onto the kitchen counter. Her gaze falling on the black TBT tote bag tucked away in the corner of a cabinet had her thoughts shifting to her job and she groaned.

"Something is amiss?"

"What am I going to do with you when I go to work Monday morning?"

"To the business where you labor for the strongly unlikeable Bunny Turner?"

"That would be the place." Laila rubbed her arms against the sudden chill. "I can't leave you here alone, and I certainly can't take you with me." She could imagine the commotion if she showed up at TBT with the gorgeous ancient warrior in tow. On the plus side, one glimpse of Zak would get the dieters' minds off food. She nibbled her thumbnail as she considered her options.

"You will stay here with me," Zak stated. "We will start with a brisk morning walk outdoors, have bread, cheese and wine for lunch, then spend the rest of the day pleasuring each other in bed."

"As tempting as that sounds, I don't want to give Bunny any more ammunition to fire me." Laila hated it when her logical side intruded. "Especially since she's already green with envy because she thinks you're my boyfriend and you turned down her," she shuddered, "*offer.*"

"It would please me greatly to be your boyfriend, Laila." His lips curved into a smile.

The sexy timbre of his voice had a shiver rippling through her from head to toe. The idea of being able to officially introduce the handsome genie as her boyfriend had her head and heart reeling.

"I'd like that very much, Zak."

"Good. Now we eat, yes? My belly is in dire need of provisions." With fingers spread, his hand clapped over his abs. "We will discuss Monday later."

The day had flown by and she hadn't even realized it was time for dinner. It was a rare occurrence for Laila to forget about eating.

"I'll fix something as soon as I go freshen up, and put the frozen and refrigerated foods away."

"While you are in the room of flushing water—"

"Bathroom," she reminded him.

"Bathroom. Zak nodded. "I will let Friday out to relieve himself before I finish unburdening the trunk of your chariot."

"Sounds good." Laila could definitely get used to having a burly guy around to unburden her trunk. Her spirits were so high she could almost float on air. Being this happy and content was unnerving. When things got too perfect she feared the rug might be yanked out from under her.

That's exactly what would happen in six months.

If she didn't protect her heart, Laila knew it would shatter once she lost him. While she'd loved Tim, her feelings for Zak were different. She'd never felt this sense of connection with a man before. The grief she'd experienced at Tim's passing was intense. The grief at losing Zak could destroy her. Blinking away the abrupt rise of tears, she shook the gloomy deliberations from her mind.

"I rescued the frozen cream," Zak announced proudly when she returned to the kitchen. "I deposited it in the great metal box's ice chamber for safekeeping." He motioned toward the freezer.

"Wonderful! Ice cream soup doesn't hold the same appeal." Laila glanced at the kitchen counter. "Wow, you already put most of the cold things away. I'm impressed."

His shoulders lifted in a casual shrug. "I learn quickly. I have also filled Friday's bowl with his food and replenished his water."

Laila microwaved a couple potatoes and cooked a bag of frozen sweet corn to pair with the rotisserie chicken. She salivated while slathering crusty bread with real butter and licked her lips as she scooped dollops of sour cream and a sprinkling of chives atop their buttery baked potatoes.

A bottle of earthy Oregon pinot noir rounded out their meal. With the sun setting, she lit a few candles, pleased at the way the gentle glow of the flickering tapers enhanced the overall mood. Soft jazz background music added to the ambiance.

"I like these yellow beads." Zak polished off the pile of corn on his plate. "Like pearls of steeped grain. The fowl is favorable as well." Eating the last of his potato, he noted, "It is most surprising this is the same foodstuff as that of the fries at the pub. A versatile food fit for the gods."

"You won't get any argument from me on that subject."

Reaching beneath the table, Zak petted Friday's head as the dog nudged him, circled in place, and settled at his feet. "I feel like a king," he boasted. "With a bounty of victuals at my table and my precious queen across from me." Gazing at her with a slow smile, he amended, "No, not my queen, my girlfriend."

Beaming in response, Laila glanced up at him through her lashes, noticing how the golden cast of the flames enhanced his masculine beauty. With the candlelight flickering, she could envision the way Zakkar Tymon must have looked centuries ago, partaking in a meal amid the torchlight with his army comrades after a hard day of battle.

This man thousands of years her senior sat across from her now, dining on grocery store rotisserie chicken instead of goat roasted over a crackling flame beneath the stars of the ancient sky. Each time she was reminded of the implausible reality that he was from a distant time, she was filled with a new sense of wonder.

If it was this difficult for her to fathom, Laila could only imagine how hard it was for Zak to face random snippets of time over the centuries, each vastly different from the last. Just when he was getting used to his surroundings, learning about the people, their culture, habits and advances, he was wrenched out of his new life, catapulted back to the inert existence of the bottle.

He didn't eat like an uncivilized man. His table manners were close to impeccable. Laila wondered if Abigail Maythorne might have tutored him in that area. Still, the feeling of urgency was palpable. Each time she'd seen Zak eat, she noticed how quickly he consumed the food. Almost as if he were afraid it would be snatched away before he had a chance to finish it.

Zak sipped from his wine. "A surprisingly smooth, fruit-like taste. The wine I imbibed in the past was more like vinegar. Most of it was stored in goatskin pouches."

Heaping second helpings of chicken, potatoes, and corn onto his plate, Laila wrinkled her nose. "That definitely would have affected the flavor." She refilled their wineglasses.

"In my time," Zak noted as he devoured a drumstick dwarfed by his large hand, "roast fowl was strong-tasting meat, tough and stringy, not mild and tender like this."

Laila enjoyed hearing tidbits of his past. "What would you eat with it?"

"A ration of barleycake with onion and cucumber, washed down with barley ale." He broke a chunk of rustic Italian bread and buttered it. "The bread we ate was nothing like this tender crumb with its pleasingly brittle crust," he told her once he'd swallowed. "And butter was not common at our tables."

"Did you enjoy being at Maythorne Manor? I fell in love with the period charm and character of that beautiful old house."

"Very much." Zak's smile reached his eyes, lighting his entire face. "I created that house for Abigail."

Once again he'd managed to amaze her. "Are you serious?"

"I am. Owning a grand house was one of her wishes. When she first became my possessor, she was living in poverty, uncertain where her next meal would come from. She carried a satchel with a pot, spoon, bowl, a few ragged garments and not much else. She had been forced to sell the rest of her belongings in exchange for food and shelter."

"That poor woman. No wonder she looked so old at fifty. Since Abigail found your bottle here in Oregon, I imagine your previous possessor must have been from here too." Laila cleared the plates from the table to give them some room, with Friday dancing around her feet as she walked, clearly waiting for any stray scraps to hit the floor.

Zak shook his head. "*Nein. Ich war in Deutschland.*" He grinned as Laila returned to the table with a wide-eyed expression. "I was in Germany," he translated, "for a brief time in the early 1800s. How the box journeyed to Oregon, I do not know."

"Probably early settlers coming to America," she surmised. "Do you remember all the languages you've learned over the centuries?"

"Some better than others. It depends on how long I spent in a location. Sometimes it was a matter of but a few hours before returning to the bottle."

Dear God...

"You give the term multilingual a whole new meaning." She kept her voice and comment lighthearted while wondering what it must be like to carry snippets of various time periods around inside your head.

"How did you build Abigail's house?" Reruns of *I Dream of Jeannie* came to mind. "Was it done with a blink of the eyes and, *boing*, there it is?" She made the accompanying gestures. "Or did it take a long time?" She sipped from her wine, thoroughly engrossed in their fascinating after dinner conversation.

"Over a period of days Abigail provided me with all the information about what she wanted inside and outside the house. The house appeared instantly once she made the wish."

"So one minute there was a blank space up on Beauregard Hill and another, *poof*," her arms waved in an explosive motion, "there was a huge Victorian mansion standing there. That must have been pretty shocking to the neighbors."

"Blink, boing, poof..." Zak laughed. "I do not understand these words or gestures in regard to granting wishes, but there were no neighbors to shock. Abigail's house was the first in the area. It was a time of vast wilderness. Glassfloat Bay was not as it is today."

"But what if someone was riding around in their horse and buggy and all of a sudden a house magically appears out of nowhere? How would that be explained?"

Zak tossed up his hands with a shrug. "I do not comprehend the workings. I know only that the wishes are granted seamlessly. What mechanism the gods use to achieve this, I cannot fathom."

Eating another forkful of potatoes, he closed his eyes, murmuring his satisfaction.

"Has there ever been a wish you couldn't grant?"

"Yes, a number of distinctly malevolent wishes that involved causing harm to others." His thoughts seemed far away for a moment. "As long as the wish is within the guidelines it can be granted. Some wishes, such as creating Abigail's Victorian house, require more preparation on my part than others."

"The house must have been very important to Abigail."

Zak gave a confirming nod. "She and her husband had planned to build it when they arrived here. Abigail carried August's detailed sketch of the house in her satchel, with measurements, a list of materials and building instructions. I studied the papers over a few days and went about building the house in my head. Once I could clearly envision every last detail, I processed the wish."

"Incredible."

"Even after all this time, I still find it so, yes."

"What were Abigail's other two wishes?"

"She asked to have all her possessions restored to her, including the belongings she was forced to sell to survive during her years alone here, the items lost along the Oregon Trail, things she had to leave behind in her home in Massachusetts, as well as in her ancestral home of England. She believed having items of sentimental value surrounding her would keep her happy until she joined her beloved husband in *Kurnugi*."

The sheer intricacy of the idea amazed Laila. "You were able to do that?"

"Over a period of a few days, yes."

"It must have caused some raised eyebrows when all of Abigail's belongings just started disappearing from all over and showing up in her house. And her third wish?"

"Ample wealth so she would never be hungry or homeless again and so she could live in the lifestyle she was accustomed to before journeying to Oregon. This wish was granted immediately."

The story of Abigail's life-changing wishes was mesmerizing. Trying to imagine how the woman's life transformed from abject scarcity to fruitful abundance with a mere snap of Zak's fingers made Laila's head swim.

Reaching across the table, she squeezed his hand, wondering what she would spend money on first if she were in Abigail's place. "Imagine her sense of security and happiness once you granted her wishes."

He covered her hand with his. "I would like to think she lived the remainder of her life in the happiness she deserved."

"We'll have to Google Abigail to find out what happened to her."

"If you say so, then we will Google." Zak chuckled at the unusual word.

Chapter 15

~<>~

"CAN I JUST TALK to you about my ideas before making an official wish?"

"Of course." Zakkar still couldn't get over the fact that Laila asked about using one of her valuable wishes to set him free. She was a remarkable woman, as rare as a fine gemstone.

Taking the wine with them, along with a plate of something called chocolate-dipped shortbread cookies, Laila led him into the family room where she asked Zakkar to build a fire in the fireplace

Zakkar's gaze fell on what looked like a metal evergreen tree in the corner, decorated with a variety of hanging objects. "Interesting..." he noted. "What is this silver object?"

"It's my sister Delaney's aluminum Christmas tree." Laila's face lit up as she smiled. "Her first husband didn't approve of Christmas decorations. After her divorce she found this vintage tree, it's from the 1950s or 60s, at the roadside, waiting to be picked up on garbage day. She dragged it home, cleaned and repaired it, and hasn't taken it down since." She gave a soft laugh. "She brought it with her all the way from Chicago. Delaney insists there's something magical about it."

He enjoyed listening to her stories and watching how animated she became.

She padded over to the tree. "Want to see something cool?" Laila plugged a cord into the wall and a round, lighted wheel of colors rotated, changing the color of the metal branches with each rotation.

Once the fireplace blaze was strong, they stood together for a short time, watching the golden flames crackle, while the silver tree shifted from blue to red, green, yellow and back again. He slipped his arm around her waist and she rested her head against him.

Laila took his hand, leading him to the sofa where they sat on the soft cushions, leaning into each other as they sipped wine. It was the perfect scenario—one Zakkar could easily envision them repeating for years to come.

But that wasn't to be.

"Maythorne Manor was so charming," she told him, her eyes sparkling with liveliness. "It has an almost enchanted feel. The sort of house I've always dreamed about. When I was younger I might have wished to own and live in that house."

"If you desire Maythorne Manor for your home I can make it so."

"No." Laila shook her head. "Now I realize I'd just be rambling around in a place far too big for me. I'd feel like I was living in the Taj Mahal."

"India." Zakkar's eyes closed briefly. "The Taj Mahal was magnificent. It was built by the emperor Shah Jahan, in memory of his wife and queen, Mumtaz Mahal."

"Your knowledge of history puts me to shame." Laila's eyes widened with wonder. "So you've seen it?"

"I was there as it was being built."

"Amazing...how long ago was that?" She reached for the table, bringing the shortbread cookies closer, offering them to Zakkar and taking one for herself. Sinking her teeth into the confection elicited a sigh from her as she chewed. How he enjoyed that look of delight across her face.

"Mmm...I'll probably be five pounds heavier in the morning after this dinner and dessert," she lamented with an expression of guilt, "but it was worth every calorific ounce."

Zakkar bit into a cookie, nodding his approval as he chewed. "You worry too much about weight gain." He gathered her close, loving the feel of her soft curves in his arms.

"I suppose you're right." Laila studied the cookie in her hand. "I do tend to be a little food and diet obsessed." She gave a tinkle of laughter before popping the rest of the cookie into her mouth. "Tell me more about the Taj Mahal." Pressing the tip of her finger into the cookie crumbs on the serving plate, she brought it to her lips and sucked.

"I was in India in the 1600s. The construction was nearly complete. The white marble structures glowed in the light of the full moon. My possessor was the wife of one of the builders."

Friday came sniffing around, making his desire for a cookie known.

"This is not good food for you, Friday," he said. With a defeated look, Friday skulked away.

"You said you wanted to ask me about your ideas for wishes," Zakkar reminded her.

"Well," she brushed the crumbs from her fingers onto her plate, "since I can't make sweeping goodwill wishes for the world, I'd like to make wishes for myself that will ultimately be of help to others. Is that okay?"

"It depends. What do you have in mind?"

"I'd like to own and be able to afford the upkeep of Crowe's Coastside Bakery and the building it's housed in. That would be my first wish. I understand that Peggy and Caroline Crowe, the sisters who are selling it, are moving to Barcelona, which means I'd be able to live upstairs. Their apartment is supposed to be stunning."

Zakkar slanted his head. "What is a bakery?"

Laila's face lit up as a smile captured her cheeks. "A place that makes everyone smile. A business where a variety of baked goods like cupcakes, scones, bread, cookies, cakes and pies are made and sold. The theme of my bakery would be providing healthier, reduced calorie versions of the more fattening originals. I've been supplying my friend Annalise Griffin, who owns Griffin's Café, with an assortment of scones the last couple of years and her customers love them."

"This sounds intriguing. I would like to sample these special scones."

"I'll make up a batch early tomorrow so we can have them with our coffee."

She wrapped herself around his arm, nestling close. "I figured I could just wish for millions of dollars, but that wouldn't guarantee me the Crowe sisters' bakery if it had already sold to someone else. And that building with its ideal location is what I really want. As for the millions," confidence radiated from her smile, "I'll make those on my own once I open my business."

Zakkar sensed his Laila could do just exactly that. "It is your intention to leave Bunny Turner's employ and establish your own business...this healthy bakery?"

"Absolutely." Laila nodded. "My second wish would be for my business to be successful so I can continue to provide nutritious, delicious foods for people who want to lose weight, or just eat better. Dieters need and deserve better food options. The foods from Tuned by Turner are practically inedible."

Recalling the twig cereal, Zakkar's expression soured. "I can attest to that."

"TBT's foods are loaded with chemicals, cheap ingredients and too much salt. Since they taste terrible, TBT's clients have trouble staying on the program. I want to help to make dieting more enjoyable rather than a drudge."

Her idea had merit. He couldn't understand the need for foods designed to help people lose weight at first but he was surprised by the number of stout men, women and children waddling about. They could benefit from physical activity and structured eating using more palatable foods, such as those Laila described.

"It is a good, sound wish," he said.

"I was hoping you'd think so. This way, people can have their cake and eat it too!" Laila's face brightened as she spoke that phrase, although the words didn't hold much meaning for him.

"What will you call your business?"

"I had a few ideas, like Kneady, or Fakery Bakery, but my favorite is The Great Pretender." Her voice bubbled with enthusiasm. "TGP for short." He detected a shiver of anticipation in her demeanor. She rubbed her arms. "Look—I'm getting goosebumps just thinking about it."

He was glad to see Laila so elated. "The Great Pretender...what does the name imply?" He threaded his fingers with hers, enjoying her obvious passion.

"My baked goods will be pretending to be something they're not—fattening indulgences. The Great Pretender will offer scrumptious but far healthier alternatives."

He kissed the top of her head, breathing in the sweet, floral scent of her hair. "Continue. I want to hear everything about your wishes and this pretender business you will start." He enjoyed listening to whatever it was that made Laila's pulse quicken its tempo as he noticed it had been doing since she began discussing her idealistic plans.

Splaying her fingers flat against his knee, Laila smiled up at him, seeming quite satisfied with her wish-making decisions.

"What do you think so far? Are my wishes doable?"

"Most definitely." His fingers closed around her hand still resting on his knee. While he was no seer, with her combination of intelligence, selflessness and passion, he could easily envision Laila experiencing great success with her plans. "I see no problem granting them upon your official command." His thumb stroked along her jawline. "And your third wish?"

Her shoulders hiked in a shrug. "I haven't decided yet. But I've got plenty of time." She squeezed his arm. "Six whole months."

Zakkar knew Laila had the best intentions. Because they were enjoying each other's company so much, she probably sincerely imagined she could wait that long before making her final wish. But he knew better. It would be unwise to get his hopes up. He'd long ago learned it was better to be fatalistic. After all, she would be the first woman in five thousand years to alter the pattern. No...history would no doubt repeat itself.

He gazed at her, sending silent thanks to the gods for whatever time Laila would be in his life. "Are you ready to make the first two wishes?"

"No, I want to sleep on them. In the morning I'll see if I want to make any changes."

"A wise decision." He tipped his wine glass toward her and sipped. Eyeing Laila, his slow gaze roved from her silky hair to her toes. Fully wrapping his arms around her as she leaned against him, he whispered Sumerian words of love in her ear.

His mind as ablaze as the fire in the hearth, he locked gazes with her, looking deep into her eyes. So deep he never wanted to surface.

"Zak...you look...is everything okay?" Searching his solemn features, she stroked his jaw.

"Perfect." He nuzzled her cheek. "I was committing you to memory...every beautiful inch of you, every flicker of color in your jewel-blue eyes. I want to remember every word you have spoken to me, every bright clatter of laughter that has spilled from your lips."

Laila's expression changed, twisted and he could tell she was about to weep.

"There is no reason for sadness." He brushed his lips across hers. "If I were to die this very moment, or be returned to the eternal imprisonment of the bottle, I would be the happiest man on earth. You have made it so for me."

He meant every word. He'd never spoken such words to a woman before, not in his thousands of years of existence.

Laila took his face in her hands, smiling up at him. Her expression was affectionate. He could almost think of it as full of love.

"I will always treasure your beautiful words, Zak. Thank you."

"It is I who thank you, Laila, for making my heart soar."

Before Laila had the opportunity to say another word, Zakkar kissed her as if he'd never get another chance.

Chapter 16

~<>~

THE CHIRPING OF BIRDS outside her window woke Laila the next morning. Snuggled against Zak's chest, she rested her head on his arm. He was flat on his back, one hand on his belly and his other arm wrapped around her, holding her close. The steady rise and fall of his chest, even pattern of his breathing and rhythmic beat of his heart lulled her into a state of supreme contentment.

She couldn't imagine a more ideal way to wake up on a Sunday morning. Or any other morning. It was the closest she'd get to heaven while still alive.

Not wanting to disturb him, or the sweet perfection of the moment, she didn't move a muscle, except for curling her lips into a smile of gratitude.

"You are awake," Zak said, his eyes still closed.

"How did you know?" She smoothed her fingers over his chest.

"I heard the change in your breathing."

"You're very observant."

"From years of training and preparation for battle." He opened his eyes and gazed at her. "Waking with you at my side would make it challenging to leave for battle."

Laila clutched him tight. "I'd never let you go."

The night before he'd told her how much she meant to him. She was tempted to tell him she loved him then, but feared she'd spoil the moment by revealing her innermost feelings. She didn't want to ruin the most treasured romantic relationship of her life. The last thing Laila wanted was for Zak to remember her as a needy, clingy woman he'd been stuck with for half a year.

186

They remained still together for a long while as she stroked across his collarbone and he caressed her arm from shoulder to fingertips. She easily pictured them together as a couple, as lovers, as man and wife all those centuries ago, wondering if he might be picturing them the same way.

"You will teach me to make coffee," he said, breaking the silence. "After which you will prepare real food for our breakfast."

Apparently Zak's thoughts were on sustenance rather than romance.

"Your wish is my command, oh great one."

Zak rolled onto his side, facing Laila. Elbow bent, he propped his head in his hand and looked down at her. He studied her before gifting her with a charming smile, a beautiful sight to see first thing in the morning. "You are teasing me."

"I can't help it." She mirrored his position, smiling back at him. "You make it so hard to resist."

"*You* are hard to resist." He had a devilish gleam in his eye. Grabbing her, he pulled her atop him.

Breakfast was clearly going to be delayed.

An hour later they'd both cleaned up and dressed. A batch of cherry almond scones was in the oven, and Friday had had his morning run in the yard. Zak wore one of the new black T-shirts she'd bought him, over a pair of jeans that hugged his muscular thighs and exceedingly fine ass.

At his insistence, Laila wore a pair of her new, figure-hugging jeans. Clearly pleased with her attire, he'd grab her butt at the most surprising times, like when she was in the middle of grinding coffee. The lid flew off the handheld grinder, spewing coffee grounds all over the kitchen.

The vacuum cleaner held Zak's interest as it sucked up the grounds. He insisted on operating the appliance, testing the hose on all manner of things, including her vee-neck sweater, the kitchen curtains, the roll of paper towels, and the stack of mail on the kitchen counter.

Friday was less enthusiastic, fearing the vacuum just as Zak had first feared her phone. That didn't stop Zak from chasing Friday with the hose.

She loved the way Bekka House was filled with fun and laughter; and a man so appealing she'd cornered the market on dreamy sighs.

After he'd sucked up her hair repeatedly, she finally got Zak to relinquish the vacuum, promising to let him examine the machine later.

As Laila demonstrated the particulars of making a good, robust cup of coffee, he watched intently, following her instructions and getting used to Friday dancing at his feet as he moved. Zak asked her to explain every little doohickey on the coffeemaker, disappointed when she admitted she had no idea where the instruction manual was. He wanted to learn every aspect of this modern marvel, how it was made and put together as well as how it operated.

If there'd been a screwdriver anywhere in sight, every appliance in her kitchen would be in pieces while her inquisitive genie examined their inner workings.

Zak puffed with pride as he poured steaming cups of coffee, reminding her of a rocket scientist who'd just discovered a previously undetected law of the universe.

His facial expressions and murmurs as he wolfed down mini-scones, scrambled eggs, thick bacon, and coffee told Laila he was thoroughly enjoying his breakfast.

"So this is the famous healthy Laila scone." Zak held up a half-eaten triangular scone, inspecting it as if it were a gleaming gem.

"Famous, hmm? I like that." She chuckled. "Maybe it will be one day. So go ahead, give me your honest opinion."

"I am bound to speak the truth," he reminded her. After another bite he said, "This bread-like morsel is most satisfying and delicious."

He plucked out a dried cherry and ate it, nodding his approval, then picked off a few of the flaked almonds topping the scone, depositing them on his tongue.

"It is just sweet enough, with a good taste of fruit and the slight crunch of nuts. The crumb is substantial, yet delicate. I rate it as...what is the descriptive food word you are so fond of? Scrumptious." He beamed a smile. "I have no doubt your customers will crave these scrumptious scones." He popped the rest of it in his mouth.

"Wow, that was quite the eloquent critique! I'm glad you like it, Zak. I make all sorts of flavors, chocolate chip, pumpkin, maple walnut, pecan salted caramel, and I'm always coming up with new ones. You can be my official taste tester."

"A task I gladly accept." He gobbled another mini-scone.

She'd never enjoyed Sunday morning breakfast more. And that was before she'd even had her first bite of food. Once she tasted it her eyelids fluttered shut. She'd almost forgotten how divine a plate of bacon, eggs and her homemade mini-scones could be. What a crime she'd deprived herself of this simple pleasure for so long. From now on she'd find a way to fit the enjoyable meal into her eating program on the weekends.

Glancing at Zak as he took his seat after pouring them both a second cup of coffee, Laila smiled. Having him at her breakfast table seemed so natural. She looked forward to him being there with her every morning.

"After breakfast I'll introduce you to TV. After that, the computer. It's going to be a day filled with so much new technology it'll make your head spin."

Frowning, his expression was cagey. "I trust you speak symbolically. I like my head just as it sits upon my shoulders."

Covering her mouth with her fingers, Laila chuckled. "Don't worry. We won't be recreating any scenes from *The Exorcist*."

"Exorcism?" Zak shot her a questioning look. "There are demons in TV?"

"Some critics think so." Oh, she was evil. She really shouldn't take advantage of his lack of knowledge and tease him so much. If only he didn't possess that huge adorability quotient making him so darned cute when he was baffled.

"We will be entering the demon realm?" Looking edgy, Zak sat straight, ready to pounce. "I must get my saber." He scooted his chair back from the table.

"Whoa!" Laila patted the air. "You're not going to need that gigantic sword of yours." She gave him a wicked smile. "Don't worry. I'll protect you from harm."

One of his eyebrows hiked while the other rode low, in a wary expression. Crossing his arms over his chest, he sat back in his chair. "Again you taunt me with humor."

"I know. I'm terrible," she readily admitted. "I can't help it. You're endearing when you're clueless."

"And last night, did you really expect me so naïve as to believe that man flew into space and landed on the moon?" Wagging his finger, Zak gave her reprimanding look. "The moon indeed." He rolled his eyes and laughed.

After seeing his expression of complete disbelief when she'd told him about moonwalk the night before, she'd decided to let it drop until he was more prepared for such startling news.

Zak sniffed the air after polishing off the last of his bacon. "What is that pleasing smell?"

A slow smile took hold as the familiar fragrance filled the kitchen.

"That gingery aroma is Grandma Bekka's *pepperkaker*. Norwegian ginger cookies. Wonderful, isn't it?" Laila took another deep sniff. "I think it means she likes you, Zak."

"I thought you said Bekka died a few years ago."

"She did." Laila nodded. If he had trouble believing man walked on the moon, he certainly wouldn't believe her ghost story.

"The house is haunted. Just a little," she added quickly. "By friendly ghosts." She watched for Zak's reaction to her peculiar revelation. Surprisingly, he took it all in stride.

"You're not scared, or shocked?" Maybe he thought Laila was crazy and didn't want to say so. She'd experienced that understandable reaction from people often enough when the unmistakable fragrance of ginger cookies suddenly permeated the air and she had to explain why.

"There is no reason to fear spirits." Zak shrugged. "I have encountered many in my time. But this is the first time one of them has baked cookies for me." An amused grin split his face.

"Unfortunately we don't get the actual cookies, just the scent. None of us has ever spotted Grandma, but sometimes we've heard the faint sound of her laughter. So you've really come across ghosts before?"

"It was unsettling at first," he nodded, "but I grew used to it after several encounters. It seems my state of being suspended between the world of the living and the dead," he made a balancing motion with his hands, "makes interaction with those who have parted this life easier."

"That's fascinating." It was also an unhappy reminder that for long stretches of time Zak was closer to death than life. "Were any of your ghost encounters frightening? Any evil or angry ghosts? Poltergeists?"

Her questions had Zak chuckling. "I have no chilling tales of bloodthirsty spirits. I would imagine their ghost demeanor probably matches their earthly character. Bekka is a friendly apparition. I can sense it in her presence. And I believe you're right." Zak's smile grew wide. "She likes me."

"Now?" Laila gasped, thrilled right down to her toes. "You can feel Grandma Bekka right now?"

"How like an excited child you are, Laila." Zak laughed. "Yes, her essence reminds me of a jovial grandparent. There is a man too. No..." Zak appeared lost in concentration. "It is two men actually. There are three spirits who haunt this house."

"Three? My family only knows of two, Bekka and Anders, Varik's grandfather. We often smell his—" Just as she was about to say *cherry pipe tobacco*, the aroma wafted across the room.

"His smoking tobacco," Zak confirmed. "I smell it." His head inclined and he was silent for a long moment, seeming to listen to something Laila couldn't hear. "And Jamie," he said finally. "Jamie Eriksen. Are you familiar with that name?" He laughed before Laila could answer. "If your eyes grew any wider, they would be as big as our breakfast plates."

"Holy cow, Zak." Delighted at the unexpected news, Laila slapped the kitchen table. "Jamie was Grandma Bekka's husband. My grandfather. He died in the war before my mom was born. Wait till I tell her about this!"

"Of which war do you speak?"

"The Second World War. It took place in the 1940s."

"I am not familiar with this war. I must learn of it." Again, Zak's head tilted to the side. "They are gone now. I sensed much love emanating from the ghostly trio. They watch over you and your family." As Zak finished speaking, the smell of ginger cookies and pipe tobacco dissipated.

"We like to think of them as our guardian angels. It was always cool that we had two ghosts, but three? That's the best news ever."

Over a second pot of coffee, Laila quizzed Zak about his past ghost adventures.

"I remember one pair of ghosts in particular," he said, a distant look in his eyes. "A few hundred years after my captivity I came into the possession of an Egyptian peasant named Farida. While outside cooking in the courtyard, she spotted my stone box half buried in the dirt not far from her mudbrick house. Lifespans were short then, so at the age of thirty, Farida was nearing the end of her days. She was a kind, hardworking woman who provided for her parents, brothers and sisters until they all died."

"She wasn't married?"

"No, Kafele, her beloved, was a member of the king's royal guard who died in service to the king ten years earlier when he was twenty-two."

Laila tsked. "So young..."

"Along with the king's servants, court officials, artisans, concubines, wives, and pets, Kafele was poisoned so he could accompany the king to the afterlife."

Horrified, Laila shuddered. "How awful."

"Gruesome." Zak nodded. "Such sacrifice was a common practice at the time but that changed with the end of Egypt's first dynasty. It was a hot summer night when Farida and I went up to her house's flat roof so she could make her three wishes before she slept."

Zak shifted his glance to Laila and smiled. "She knew she was dying and worried she wouldn't be able to find Kafele in the afterlife. As a peasant, she was not in the same social class as the king or his servants. She rightfully feared the dead king would forbid their reunion."

"That's heartbreaking."

"It was. Her first wish was for me to journey through the afterlife to locate Kafele and let him know she would soon be departing the living, and he should look for her."

"You could do that?"

"Well," Zak laughed, "I had no idea whether or not I could at that time. I was somewhat wary about staying in the underworld for too long and not being able to find my way out."

Laila couldn't even begin to imagine such a dilemma.

"Farida's second wish was for me to find the king and convince him to release Kafele from his sworn service. Her third wish was to be joined with her beloved Kafele after she died, for all eternity."

"Wow...incredible. So what happened? Were you able to—"

"I was. I remember this woman and her wishes well because they were among the most difficult I have ever had to grant. Time has little meaning when traveling among the shades so I don't know how long it took me to locate Kafele and the King. It seemed a small eternity. It was tense for a while but after a great deal of persuasion, the king finally permitted Kafele to leave him."

"Whew!" Laila blew out the breath she held.

"The king acknowledged that Kafele had always been loyal and trustworthy. He'd also saved the king's life on more than one occasion."

"And you got Farida and Kafele together?"

Zak had a distant look in his eyes as his thoughts traveled across the centuries. "As soon as I returned to the living and gave Farida the good news, she took my hands in hers, offered a heartfelt, teary smile as she thanked me, then closed her eyes and died peacefully."

Laila engaged in a long, tuneful sigh.

"Before being sucked back into the bottle I witnessed their happy reunion as Farida's spirit left her body and Kafele's spirit welcomed her into his waiting arms. Ahh, Laila," Zak closed his eyes and shook his head, "what a sight it was to see. During their embrace, both ghosts turned to thank me. In the next instant I was back in the bottle, feeling quite pleased and accomplished."

"Well I should say so! Zak, what you did was nothing short of amazing."

"I am in full agreement."

"I want to hear more of your ghost stories." She poured them each another cup of coffee.

The time she spent listening to his tales of ghostly apparitions over the centuries was utterly captivating. After they finished talking, Laila led Zak into the family room, having him sit on the sofa opposite the flat screen TV mounted over the fireplace.

Although not allowed on the furniture, Friday leapt on the couch, snuggling next to Zak and resting his head on Zak's lap, big soulful brown eyes looking from Zak to Laila and back again.

"That innocent look doesn't fool me, Friday." She shook a reprimanding finger. "You're spoiling my dog, Zak."

"Perhaps..." his knowing smile was playful, "but only for the short time I am here with you. He is a good dog and I will miss him." He massaged behind Friday's ears, getting a soft, contented bark in return.

Well hell, how could Laila possible argue with that?

"Remember listening to the radio in my car?" She chose to ignore the disobedient dog still blissfully lounging on the sofa.

"With all manner of music and conversation with disembodied people speaking to me of various topics? Yes!" A joyful spark of recall danced in Zak's eyes as he clapped his thighs. "I could spend hours engaging with the radio."

"Then you'll love TV," Laila assured. "Imagine radio, but with images too. Right there on that black space." She pointed.

"Photographs," his head cocked in question, "like the one of me and Abigail?"

"Except the people are in motion." She could almost see the gears turning inside Zak's head as he digested the information. "You'll see them in action as well as hear them talk."

"On this reflective black rectangle?" His gaze rested on the screen. "I cannot imagine it."

Laila sat at his right, one hand holding his and the other holding the remote. "Everything you're about to see is safe. Nothing can harm either of us. There is no magic, witchcraft or voodoo involved. It's simply modern technology."

"I understand. I have no fear of your technology." He rubbed his free hand along his jeans, looking enthused about learning something new. Still, she was relieved his saber was safely tucked away in the bedroom.

Pressing the power button on the remote, Laila watched Zak out of the corner of her eye as the screen came to life.

The muscle in Zak's jaw twitched. His posture stiffened, and he sat flat against the back of the seat, firmly gripping Friday's collar. Laila could tell he was doing his best not to appear startled.

"Lucy, you got some 'splainin' to do" was the first sound blip Zak heard as an *I Love Lucy* rerun came into view.

"They are so small," he whispered in her ear. "And their world is devoid of color. Are they demons? Or tiny beings trapped in the demon realm?"

"No, there's nothing demonic. It's just a TV show with real people that was filmed in black and white, before they had color."

"There was a time when your world had no color?" His eyes popped. "The gods must have been irate to cast such a ghostly pall upon the earth." He looked at his hands, turning them to and fro, then looked at the TV just as Fred and Ethel entered the scene. "I cannot imagine being drained of all color."

"No, Zak, what I mean is..." Nope, no way was she going to be able to explain this. "I'll have Drake explain black and white film versus color the next time you see him."

"Aw, but, Ricky, it's such an adorable little hat. Can't I keep it?"

His hands gripping his knees, Zak ventured a tentative, "Hello? I am Zakkar Tanojin Lugalbanda Tymon, also known as Zak. I am Laila's boyfriend."

Laila struggled to keep from laughing. As amusing as this might be for her, she had to remember how astonishing it must be for him. "They can't hear you, Zak."

"*Waaaaaaaaa.*" Lucy's face contorted as she dissolved into her fake crying.

"But they can!" He whipped his head toward Laila. "You see?" He pointed. "I have frightened the ghostly woman to tears."

She patted his knee. "No, it's okay. It's only part of the play they're performing."

"How do they all fit in there? Can they get out if they want to? Who put them in there?" He eyed the TV, leaning forward in his seat. "Do Lucy, Ricky, Fred and Ethel live inside this flat box? Do you own them? Must you provide them with food and clothing?"

Laila smiled at his rapid-fire questions, understanding how someone from a distant time might get those ideas. "No. Not to confuse you further, but the actors you see there are all dead now."

That tidbit of information had Zak's fingers digging into the seat cushions.

"Dead...we are glimpsing the land of *Kurnugi.* No wonder there is no color and all appears so bleak." He turned to Laila, his expression solemn. "This cannot be wise, Laila."

"It's not *Kurnugi,* I promise. Their likenesses are kept safe on film or videotape or something like that." She waved her hand. "The images you're watching originally happened decades ago."

His gaze glued to the TV, Zak shook his head. "I cannot fathom this. Do you watch the tiny foursome perform their play often?"

"It's one of the many different shows I enjoy watching. I'm going to show you something different now." She changed the channel.

"*That's right, it slices, dices and chops and yet the blades are safe enough to use right in the palm of your hand without injury! See?*"

Zak leaned forward, clearly fascinated by the exuberant man with the Australian accent hawking a handy-dandy kitchen gadget.

"It's an infomercial," Laila told him. "People selling wares."

"Is he dead too?"

"No, he's alive and well."

"Yes, it appears so because his world has color. And he lives in there? Can he see us or hear us? Listen," Zak said, growing silent as the guy on TV went on with his demonstration. "Laila, do you see how it cuts garden food and yet will not pierce human flesh? I must see this wondrous cutting tool he speaks of. Do you have one in the kitchen?"

"No, and remind me never to explain what a credit card is." She laughed and flipped to her favorite channel, Turner Classic Movies.

"The pellet with the poison's in the vessel with the pestle. The chalice from the palace has the brew that is true." It was *The Court Jester*, one of Laila's favorite Danny Kaye films.

"You can view the distant past," Zak noted as he eyed the lords, ladies, and the knights in shining armor. "I visited that time period, although I recall it being far more grisly and less joyful or colorful."

Laila pressed the remote again.

"...have mustered two or fewer first downs on twenty-two of those twenty-four drives. The only exceptions were back-to-back second-quarter possessions that resulted in a touchdown and a field goal in Sunday's twenty-ten win over..."

"Battle..." Clearly entranced, Zak's eyes glittered with interest. Mirroring his alertness, Friday sat at attention, his eyes glued to the TV. Laila aimed the remote and a second later the football game was history.

"Return to the men in conflict," Zak moved to the edge of his seat, "those wearing the strange armor battling to take possession of the oddly shaped ball. I wish to study their strategy."

"Football." She flipped back to it and sighed. "Typical man."

"May I use this tool?" Zak asked two minutes later, holding his hand out for the remote.

"Sure. All you have to do is—"

Flip...flip...flip...

"All righty then." In less than a minute, Zak had managed to find every sports game being aired.

"I'll just leave you to this for a while so I can catch up on some things, okay?"

Silence.

"Zak?"

"Hmmmm?" He sat as if in a daze, his eyes glued to the set as he flipped from one channel to another.

"I said, I'll just—"

"No! What is the matter with you?" Zak yelled at the TV and Friday added a woof. "Forty-two was there waiting. Why did you not pass the ball to him?" He gave Laila a speedy half-glance. "This number fifty-three is an idiot."

"Mmm-hmm." She patted his shoulder. "Have fun, I'll be back later." She figured a few hundred cable channels should keep him out of trouble for a while.

Laila headed for her computer. She Googled Sumer, and got several million results.

Reading accounts of Sargon of Akkad's army battling and finally conquering all of Sumer, Laila could imagine Zak's soldiers losing their motivation and fortitude without his leadership. If Zak hadn't been imprisoned, maybe the entire course of history would have been altered.

She frowned, wondering if he was aware that the ancient cities he and his troops fought so bravely to defend had fallen to the Akkadians, their mortal enemies. She decided not to mention it.

More searching turned up information about Inanna, Queen of Heaven, goddess of love and war, who Zak said the priest and priestess had summoned during their incantation to imprison him.

Next Laila found an article about ancient glassmaking. She learned the first glass bottles and jars were made in Sumer and other regions of Mesopotamia. The process was so extensive only royalty or the wealthy could afford them. The article stated glass bottles were often used as tear vases. Mourners shed their tears in the bottles, which were then sealed in the tomb so the deceased would see these tokens of grief when they reached the next world.

It was just like Zak's bottle. A quick search for some mention of the bottles being used to imprison men who'd fallen out of favor with priests or the gods proved fruitless. She'd have to look through the dozens of websites another time.

More than an hour had whisked by when it seemed she'd only been exploring for ten minutes. Once she and her football aficionado ate lunch she'd introduce him to the internet.

"Ham and Swiss on rye with potato chips," Zak said fifteen minutes later as he ate his sandwich, passing the occasional chip to Friday on the sly. "I like it. Did you know one ounce of Swiss cheese provides two hundred seventy five milligrams of calcium? That's more than a quarter of the one thousand milligrams of calcium recommended for adults."

Somewhat taken aback, Laila noted, "I see you're learning quickly from the TV commercials."

"Many wondrous things. I will coach you the next time we go to the market."

"Oh you will, huh?"

Zak nodded, clearly serious. "Did you know you don't have to give up absorbency to get the thin pads you want if you wear pads with wings?"

Laila burst out laughing, iced tea nearly spewing out her nose.

"Or that the brand of toothpaste you use is not the one most recommended by nine out of ten dentists because it does not fight germs and bacteria as well as Spark-o-White toothpaste?" He cocked his head. "What is a dentist?"

"A doctor who takes care of your teeth."

"And if you wear pads with wings, where do they transport you?"

"Not nearly far enough when it's that time of the month." She muffled a laugh. "Boy, you've retained a lot of information. It's like you have a photographic memory."

"What is that?"

"It's rare. Some people can look at something just once and remember it with accuracy, without having to look at it again."

"Yes, I have that," Zak said matter-of-factly as he took another bite of his sandwich.

Laila rolled her eyes. "No you don't."

"It is one of the reasons I was such a fine leader of men in my time." He swigged from his beer and smiled. "I remembered every battle plan I had ever mapped out without looking at it twice."

"You're not joking." Laila's head cocked.

"Go to the freezer."

Her features scrunched. "Why?"

"Take out the package of Mandarin Chicken and look at the ingredients."

Laila scooted her chair from the table and did as Zak asked. A moment later he'd recited every ingredient on the label. In order.

Her mouth agape, she looked from the package to Zak. "That's unbelievable."

One arm slung over the back of the chair, Zak sat in a confident slouch, his smile broad and smug. "I, Zakkar Tymon, am a man of many talents."

She wasn't about to argue.

Laila returned to the table. "Do you remember everything you read?"

"It is..." Zak pondered, "...selective." He tapped his temple. "I remember what I choose to recall and push the rest aside."

"Lots of men do the same thing." She laughed. "Gosh, if you lived in this time, Zak, you could be—"

He clasped her hand. "It matters not, little one. For I will not live in this time long enough to become any more than I already am."

She rested her hand atop his and smiled as her pinky brushed across his knuckles. "You're perfect just the way you are, Zak." Struggling against the tears that threatened, Laila forced a cheery smile as she took their plates to the sink. "Ready to learn about computers and the internet?"

"The football game resumes after halftime."

"Don't worry. There are plenty of football games on TV." Laila laughed quietly to herself as she rinsed the plates and put them in the dishwasher. Zak had become more like a modern man than he realized. She only hoped all she was exposing him to wouldn't make his dark, monotonous internment that much bleaker once he left her.

Shuddering at the thought of losing him, she dropped her wet glass on the floor. It shattered and, uttering a surprised gasp, she squatted to pick up the pieces, slicing her finger in the process.

"Oh hell..."

Zak raced to her side, taking her hand and examining the bleeding finger. "You have injured yourself." Acting on familiarity, he yanked the T-shirt from his jeans, grabbing the knife Laila had used to cut the bread and poking through the shirt. He tore off a strip of fabric, wrapping it around her finger.

She decided she'd wait to tell him he could have simply torn a paper towel from the holder instead of making a rag out of his new shirt. The last thing she wanted was to make him feel foolish when he was being chivalrous.

"I will tend to this mess, Laila. When I am finished, I will clean your wound and protect it with the all new anti-bacterial liquid bandage that is far superior to the old fashioned plastic strips."

Laila cried. She couldn't help it. He was so sweet and caring and gallant and funny. Even if he did have an inflated ego and hugely chauvinistic tendencies.

Zak cradled her hand. "Why do you cry? Is the pain severe?"

"No, not at all. I just—" She hiccupped a sob. "I just think you're wonderful, that's all." Once the waterworks started she had a hard time turning them off. All the thoughts about losing Zak and him being cooped up until some other woman found him and...

Some other woman.

She cried harder.

Laila waved her hand. "Don't pay any attention to me. I'm fine, really."

"Perhaps you are suffering from PMS, Laila. Symptoms may include but are not limited to bloating, anxiety, tearfulness, mood swings and—"

Laila's tears turned to laughter, just like that. "Come here, you great big wonderful genie." She held her arms open, so tempted to tell him she loved him.

Zak's eyebrow vaulted. "Mood swings, indeed," he noted, before embracing her. He kissed away her tears, smoothing wet strands of hair from her face. "Non-steroidal anti-inflammatory drugs such as ibuprofen are helpful for PMS-associated discomfort," he whispered against her ear, causing Laila to completely dissolve into laughter.

Then she started crying again.

And she wasn't even anywhere close to getting her period.

"Don't mind me, Zak." She dried her tears on the scrap of his torn T-shirt. "It's just a case of being overtired, then dealing with the stress of finding a genie in my kitchen two days ago. You know, everyday stuff like that."

"It is my fault. My presence has deprived you of sleep." Zak guided her back to the kitchen chair. "After spending so much time half-dead in the bottle, I crave the waking hours, choosing to sleep only when necessary." He tore the remainder of his shirt from his body, spread it on the floor, and picked up shards of glass, depositing them on the material.

She swallowed hard as she watched his muscles and tendons move like a fine-oiled machine. He was so sexy without even realizing it.

"That's okay. I've enjoyed every moment of our waking hours together, Zak. I've never had such fun."

"The same for me." He looked up from his task long enough to smile. "Being with you is like having the sun shine upon me, warming me, making me grateful to be...alive...for however short a period. It is the first time I have felt truly alive since I was locked away."

Laila started to cry again.

"Come." He extended his hand after cleaning the broken glass and depositing it in the trash. "We will tend to your finger, then you will show me the computer. We will Google together, yes?" He waggled his eyebrows and Laila realized he'd made an attempt at a bawdy joke.

"That's very cute," she said, in charge of her emotions again, at least for the moment. "You're catching on quickly."

Taking great care with her finger, Zak treated her small wound as if it were as serious as one received in battle, lecturing her about the lack of liquid bandages as he wound the beige plastic strip around her digit.

"You're going to see a lot of information on the computer." Laila dragged a second chair in front of her desk, signaling for Zak to sit. "With that photographic memory, you won't be in danger of going into overload or something, will you?"

"I will be selective."

Laila moved the mouse and the monitor's dark screen brightened. "A computer is kind of like having a brain inside a box. Not a human brain, it's a man-made manufactured one."

"A form of intelligence...like an oracle or a seer?"

Laila hedged. "It's more like a storehouse of knowledge gathered from people all over the world." She decided not to mention the one-on-one people connections of social media, leaving that explanation for another time.

"What does it know?"

"Just about everything." She clicked the mouse, taking them online. "The internet is like an entire library of books at your fingertips." She visited a few of her favorite websites as she spoke, watching Zak's captivated reaction as she made brief explanations, and his awe at all the *tiny TV shows*, which were the videos with automatic play.

Clasping his head, he admitted, "You were right, Laila. My head is spinning."

"Should we stop?"

"No, I must see more. Show me this Google you often mention."

"It's a search engine," Laila explained. "We type what we're searching for here, and—"

"The letters appear on the screen as your fingers strike the buttons!"

"Yup. This is my keyboard. It's used like a typewriter, except the words appear on the monitor's screen instead of on paper. Maybe Abigail had a typewriter...or maybe they weren't invented by 1859."

"I do not recall such a device." His finger hovered over the keyboard and he looked to Laila. "May I make some letters appear?"

"Sure. Type something and we'll Google it to see what information we find."

"I want to learn more about this genie entity you call me." He typed using his index finger.

Millions of entries popped up. She had Zak click on a link for the *I Dream of Jeannie* show from the 1960s. The familiar theme music played as the title flashed across a pink background. She chose a video clip from the first episode where, stranded on a desert island, astronaut Tony Nelson finds a genie in a bottle.

Zak watched with rapt attention as Tony pulled the stopper from the bottle. When he rubbed it to brush away the sand, out fumed a female genie.

"Like me!" Zak said in wonder.

Within forty minutes, hopping from site to site, they learned everything anyone ever wanted to know about genies, fact, fiction and speculation.

"Apparently some genies are born that way," Zak said, finishing an article, "but humans can also be transformed into them."

"So I was right. You *are* a genie!" Laila hugged his neck and kissed him.

"It appears so." Zak nodded slowly.

A seed of hope sprouted to life inside her. "We just have to find a way to undo the magic that got you into this mess and turn you back into a regular man."

Heaving a mighty sigh, his shoulders slumped. "I do not believe this is possible, with or without the Google. Those who imprisoned me are long since dead. There is no one left who remembers me or my fate."

"What about Inanna? If she's a goddess, she must be immortal, right?"

"I have appealed to the great and fearsome Inanna countless times. She turns a deaf ear to my pleas and lamentations. A goddess of her stature will not hear the petition of a lowly mortal unless that mortal is a holy man in her service."

"We'll see about that. We have six months to find a way to reach her and fix everything."

His arm draping over her shoulder, Zak drew Laila close. "I love your fierce, determined spirit. Thank you for being so concerned about my welfare." He kissed her...a gentle lip-brush of gratitude.

Stroking his jaw, Laila promised, "I'm going to do everything humanly possible to free you from your unjust imprisonment."

With the wealth of modern technology at her fingertips, there *had* to be a way to liberate Zak.

And if there was, she'd damn well find it.

Chapter 17

~<>~

MOVING THE CURSOR to the bottom of the page, Zak highlighted a short paragraph. The man was a fast learner. "Abigail Maythorne took in the homeless, fed them, taught them and helped them find jobs and shelter," he read. "She lived to be ninety-eight."

"Look at all she accomplished in her lifetime," Laila noted. "What a remarkable woman. See all the good you did?" Laila smacked a kiss on his cheek.

"Me?" His expression was one of genuine surprise. "I did nothing. It was all Abigail's doing."

"If you hadn't been there for Abigail when she needed rescuing, she wouldn't have been able to help all those people, Zak. By granting her wishes you helped countless people. And the foundation established in her name continues to help those in need."

"This makes my heart glad." Zak's smile evidenced a new sense of pride. "It proves my years of incarceration have not rendered me completely ineffective and powerless as a man."

Those few words broke Laila's heart. "You're a fine, strong, admirable man." She finger-combed his hair. "Think of all the frightening things you've faced each time you've emerged from the bottle. You never had any idea what to expect. But you faced each event with courage and bravery."

Laila loved the satisfied smile lighting his eyes. She trailed a fingertip along his jaw. "You're a remarkable man, Zak. I'm proud to know you."

His expression grew serious. "Your earnest words hold great meaning for me. In this time without end in the bottle, many centuries since I led the armies of Sumer, it has been difficult to remember I was once a man of worth."

It was a simple statement of fact, spoken without an ounce of self-pity. Not only had his life been cruelly ripped from him, his sense of importance, of counting for something, had been lost as well.

"You're *still* a man of worth. You don't need to lead men into battle to have value as a human being. You're a good man with a good heart. No one can ever take that away from you."

She watched his chest rise with a deep breath as he straightened in his chair. "Thank you," he said simply.

Laila felt tears threatening again.

"I've been looking at that computer monitor for so long my eyes are beginning to cross," she said, changing the subject before she started sniveling. "I could use a break. How about you?"

"Yes, my eyes are weary and my head spins from all I have learned." He rubbed his eyes and pinched the bridge of his nose. "But I have enjoyed this new experience, this vast pool of instant knowledge at the touch of a button."

Laila squeezed his hand, pleased she could add joy to his life simply by introducing him to something she'd come to take for granted. "You're an intelligent man thirsty for knowledge. I knew you'd appreciate the internet."

"I look forward to searching about the various times I have walked the earth." His gaze fell to the two large stacks of books on the floor against the wall. "I am curious. Why do your books sit in such a state where it makes them so difficult to access? I have noticed towers of books in other rooms as well."

"Oh...that's my fault. I love reading and keep adding books to my to-be-read pile. Unfortunately the rest of my family is the same way. There aren't enough bookcases to house all the Malone books." She laughed at the thought. "Which is pretty funny because, on top of all the print books, I also have my Kindle loaded with books as well." At his curious expression, she explained, "It's an electronic reader, like a tiny handheld library that holds hundreds of books. I'll show you later. You'll love it."

"I would like to examine this tiny library. Perhaps I will build you a bookcase," Zak announced.

"You could do that? That would be wonderful. One day this week we'll make a shopping trip to one of the big box warehouse stores to pick up whatever lumber, tools and supplies you need."

"Tools and lumber." He grinned. "I would like shopping at such a box." With another glance at the stacks of books, he added, "One bookcase will not be enough."

Laila mentally calculated all the books she had tucked away throughout the house. "I need an entire library."

He turned to her in his swivel chair, smiling as he caressed her face. He was silent for so long as he studied her it made her nervous. Slipping his fingers through her hair, he kissed her forehead, nose and lips.

"Gods, how I love you, Laila."

Mesmerized by his enchanting smile, she wondered if she'd heard Zak correctly. She could have sworn he'd just told her he loved her.

Laila brushed the lock of hair from his eyes, her fingers smoothing across the area just above his expressive eyebrows. *Gods, how I love you.* Did that mean he loved her like a friend...with benefits? Or did he mean he was *in love* with her?

Could he really have such strong feelings after knowing her such a short time? What if he'd been lulled into thinking he loved her because she was the only woman around. Or because he could only have sex with his possessor. Or because—

"Laila?" Zak snapped his fingers.

She blinked. "Hmm?"

"You have not heard anything I said. Is something wrong? Your expression looks..." he angled his head, "oddly pinched. Are you ill?"

She gazed into Zak's eyes as he waited for her answer. They looked the same as usual. There was no indication he'd suddenly realized she was the woman who completed him. The other half of his soul. The key to his heart. The salsa atop his enchilada.

He wasn't looking at her all gooey and doe-eyed, like he yearned to drop to one knee and propose. If he was really in love with her, wouldn't the look in his eyes be all foggy and romantic? Maybe those words just tumbled out of his mouth without him even realizing it. Words simply uttered in a moment of—

"Laila!"

Her eyes widened when he shook her and she focused on his face. The look she saw there was one of concern, not deep, abiding, *I want to spend every waking moment of my life with you* love.

"Perhaps all the Googling has affected your head." He tapped her skull.

His comment snapped her back to reality. "No...I'm okay..."

He studied her face. "I fear for your wellbeing. You are overtired and still in shock because of my sudden emergence from the bottle. Tonight you must have undisturbed rest. I will hold you in my arms as you sleep, without concern for my carnal desires to be appeased."

His sweet offer elicited a chuckle from her. "Don't you want to jump my bones?" she asked with a coy smile, finger-walking across his shoulders.

"If this means to make love to you, then, yes. I wish to jump your bones every time I look at you. But I am a man of honor and propriety. Such a man does not force himself upon the woman he loves when she is sorely in need of a full night's sleep."

Laila bolted straight up in her chair. "There!" She flailed a finger at him and her heart skipped a beat. "You said it again." She let out a joyful squeal, doing her best to avoid imitating a jumping bean.

He gaped at her as if she'd sprouted goat horns.

"Said what?"

"That you love me." He still had that strange look on his face, which had her doubting whether she'd heard him correctly. "That *is* what you said...isn't it?"

"Yes. So?" Zak shrugged, looking all hunky and handsome and blasé as hell. "It does not please you?"

"I—let me get some clarification first. When you say you love me, are you talking about the forever man-woman kind of love that makes people want to get married? Or do you mean you love me like a sister?"

Zak's lip curled in disgust. "What kind of man would bed his own sister?"

"Zakkar!"

"And you know I cannot marry you, Laila."

"Of course I know you can't marry me and you wouldn't sleep with your sister. I just want to know if you would if you could, that's all."

"Sleep with my sister?" He looked horrified.

"No!" Her frustrated tsk practically echoed off the walls.

"Of course I would marry you." He gave another nonchalant shrug. "Did I not tell you I love you?"

"How can you be so calm after telling me you're in love with me? Don't you even want to know if I love you back?"

He chuckled—actually chuckled at this single most important moment of her life.

"Of course you love me." Zak wrapped his arms around her, sifting her hair through his fingers and making her want to purr like a kitten. "Only a fool would not realize it." He trailed kisses from her temple to her throat and back up to her mouth, where he claimed her lips in a possessive kiss. "And I am no fool," he finished when their lips parted.

Tears rolled down Laila's cheeks.

Zak gave a frustrated sigh. "You confuse me. Why do you cry each time I try to say something to make you smile?"

"Because you're wonderful and I love you and I can't believe how lucky I am." She yanked him so close their bodies were nearly fused.

"Then I must say the words often. I love you," he whispered against her ear. "You are my moon, my stars, my sun. You are my everything, Laila."

Her heart leapt.

"*Ze ki angu.*"

"What does that mean?"

"That you are my beloved. In Sumerian, it is comparable to the words, I love you."

"Ohhhhh that's *very* nice." She practically melted right there in her chair. "*Ze ki angu*," she repeated.

"Ahhh..." Zak's eyes closed for a moment. "It has been eons since I heard my language spoken. The sound of those words spilling from your lips gives me great pleasure. If it were in my power, I would ask you to be my wife, to share my life, to bear my babes. Our own little goats. I love you, Laila, today, tomorrow and always." He rocked her back and forth gently as he spoke.

"Oh Zak..." she said on a sigh. "I love you so much it hurts."

"Yes, I know." He patted her back as she snuggled against him.

Laila's tears turned to laughter. "We have to work on that ego of yours."

"I think not. You love me the way I am. I am the perfect man for you."

"What are we going to do?" she asked, just above a whisper. "I mean, when you have to..."

"Shhh," he coaxed, smoothing her hair again, making her feel safe, loved and protected. "Rather than fixating on when we must part, we will create happy memories to last dozens of lifetimes." He held her at arm's length, smiling down at her. "Yes?"

"Yes." She nodded, grabbing a tissue and wiping the tears from her cheeks.

"Now no more tears. First we will watch TV together to learn about what miraculous products we must add to your market list. Then we will have dinner. After, you will rest and sleep while I watch over you. I will read your tiny handheld library until I fall into slumber myself."

"That sounds heavenly." Supremely happy, Laila yawned. "I do need to get some sleep because I have to be at work at—" She groaned. "Oh hell, I forgot all about work." She studied Zak's face as her thoughts raced. "If I leave you here alone tomorrow, do you promise you won't get into any trouble?"

"You disparage me with your unfounded fears," Zak scoffed, his pride wounded. "I, Zakkar Tymon, am a grown man. A leader of armies. I can care for myself without incident."

Laila didn't want to contemplate what could conceivably happen. "You can't leave the house. You can watch TV and use the computer until I get home. There's plenty of food in the house, so that's no problem."

"Are there more of your scones?" His eyebrow lifted.

"I'll bake up another batch tonight, just for you."

"Excellent. Why must you go to this job? Once your wishes are granted you will not need hostile Bunny Turner or her business. You will own your own successful company."

A thrill jetted through her at the thought. "I need to go through my office before I resign to gather all the special materials and recipes I created so I can take them home. Otherwise Bunny will confiscate them and use my ideas as her own. I need to get my things out of there before anyone finds out I'm quitting."

"I see."

"And I want to say goodbye to my clients. They're wonderful people who depend on me, who trust me. I don't want to just disappear from their lives without an explanation." She frowned at the painful twinge deep inside. "It's going to be tough leaving them. It'll be hard for them too. Like I'm abandoning them."

"Why not invite them to become customers at The Great Pretender?"

Laila smiled as the name of her future company spilled from his lips. "You remembered the name."

He clapped his chest, looking solemn. "I would never forget something of such great importance to you, Laila."

She sent up a silent prayer of thanks for this wonderful man. "You certainly are a keeper, Zak. One in a million."

He nodded in agreement. "Indeed I am."

"And don't forget modest." She tugged his head down to plant a kiss on his chin. "I'll explain to my clients that I'm leaving to open my own bake shop. I have to be careful. I don't want Bunny thinking I'm trying to harvest her clients so they'll purchase my baked goods instead of TBT's. That would be unethical."

"TBT will be losing an honorable counselor."

"Thanks. I'll turn in my resignation at the end of the day, giving a two-week notice. From past experience when others left the company, they'll probably tell me to leave right away. Then they'll have someone watch over me to make sure I don't take any company property with me."

"They are mistrustful." Zak nodded with understanding.

"Tomorrow when I get home I'll make the first two of my wishes." She nibbled her bottom lip. "You're positive they'll come true once I make them? There won't be any glitches?"

"No doubt whatsoever." He smoothed his thumb along her bottom lip before pressing a sweet kiss there.

Chapter 18

~<>~

MONDAY STARTED on a high note as Laila woke to the alluring aroma of fresh coffee, bacon, eggs and toast. Zak had prepared breakfast all by himself, which tickled her. His face alight with pride, he sat across from her.

"No eggs and bacon for you?" Laila asked.

"I already ate some scones. They were delicious."

"Wonderful. Did you cover the rest back up so they stay fresh?" Laila looked around the kitchen for the platter.

"No need. I finished them."

"All twelve?" Even she didn't have an appetite that big.

"Sorry, I could not help myself." He offered a sheepish grin along with his shrug.

"There's nothing to be sorry about." She gave him a smile, letting him know it was all right. "I'm glad you enjoyed them so much. Next time I'll make two dozen." She sipped from her coffee and her eyes went wide when she got a mouthful of grounds.

So what if the coffee was full of grounds because he'd forgotten to put in the filter? Who cared if the bacon was black, the eggs like rubber and the toast charred beyond recognition?

It was the caring gesture of the man who loved her and she cherished it.

"Are you enjoying the breakfast I made for you?"

"Oh...yes...very much. Everything is delicious, Zak. Thank you." She nibbled a burnt strip of bacon.

Sampling some of the food he'd cooked from her plate, Zak's eyes bugged. He took a sip of his coffee to wash it down. Horrorstruck, he whisked her cup and plate away, apologizing and insisting she mustn't eat the badly singed breakfast offering or muddy coffee.

She did her best to convince him how much she appreciated the gesture and that it's the thought that counts.

"I've got a nervous stomach about today anyway, so I didn't have much of an appetite," she told him truthfully.

Turned out she was right to be nervous.

Bunny was caustic and demeaning as both Laila and Reen tendered their resignations. Walking to their cars with their administrative-staff-inspected boxes of personal belongings, Reen paused, beaming the happiest ear to ear grin. "Have I told you how excited I am about working with you at The Great Pretender?"

"Only fifty times in the last five minutes," Laila teased. "I'm nervous, Reen," she admitted. "What if it doesn't work? What if there's a malfunction in the wishing mechanism? You'd be left without a job and I'd feel terrible."

Reen thought about it briefly. "Don't worry. If anything happens we'll find other jobs." With her arm clasped tight around Laila's shoulder, she confided, "Drake's been doing some archaeological detective work, trying to find a way to get Zak out of this hellish mess."

Laila's heart leapt. "That's wonderful! Any luck so far?"

"No, it's all been dead ends, but Drake's determined." She gave her sister a solid buddy squeeze. "Let's get back to your place so you can make your wishes."

Laila rested her head against Reen's, hugging her. "I just hope Bekka House is still standing. I've been biting my nails over leaving Zak alone there all morning."

A short while later, both cars pulled into Laila's driveway. She carried the box of the class materials she'd created, while Reen scooped up Laila's other box packed under the watchful eyes of TBT staff.

"No fire trucks or ambulances," Reen quipped. "And I don't smell smoke."

A quick scan had Laila breathing easy. "Looks like the place is intact. I don't know why I was worried. After all, he *is* an adult. What could happen?" She put her key in the door and opened it.

Laila and Reen stepped into the living room just in time to see Zak fly across the room backward, howling a noise Laila couldn't mimic if she tried. His hair was standing on end, like an ebony halo around his head.

"Holy shit! Zak!" Gaping, Laila dropped her box, letting it crash to the floor.

"Son of a bitch!" Reen shouted, letting go of the box she carried too.

Before either of them finished their astounded shrieks, Zak's body flew past them, crashing head first through the living room's picture window behind the couch.

"Oh my God!" Laila screamed as she scrambled out the front door to find Zak sprawled on the grass, spread eagle, bug-eyed, mouth open in a silent scream and huge shards of glass surrounding him. "Zak! *Zakkar!*"

"Oh, Laila, look at him." Reen squatted alongside Laila. "I-I think he's dead. His eyes are wide open but they're fixed in a lifeless stare." She gasped. "What the hell?! His body's smoking!" Looking up at Laila, she clarified, "And I don't mean in a sexy way."

"No! He said he can't die." Laila grabbed Zak's wrist to feel for a pulse. "Zak, look at me. Speak to me!" She turned to Reen, frantic. "I can't feel a pulse."

"I don't think he's breathing," Reen said, her hand just beneath his nose.

Laila sucked in a sharp breath. "Oh Reen, what are we going to do?"

"We need to call an ambulance. What the hell happened? How the hell could he just fly across the room like that?"

"I have no idea. Zakkar Tymon, listen to me." Laila held his hand in hers, slapping it. She was afraid to jostle any other part of him in case she made his injuries worse. "This is the voice of your possessor, Zakkar. I am Laila Jane Malone, your master, your owner, and I command you to breathe. Breathe, dammit! BREATHE! That's a direct order!"

Just as Reen was about to punch in 911, Zak's chest expanded with a mighty whoosh and his lungs filled with air.

"He's alive!" A warm gush of tears flowed down Laila's cheeks. "Oh, Zak, you're alive!"

Reen placed her hand over his forehead. "He might be alive but he looks like death warmed over."

"Say something, Zak," Laila urged. "Tell me what happened. Are you terribly hurt?" Zak mumbled something. "Did you hear what he said, Reen?"

"No. He sounds like the tin man in the *Wizard of Oz* when he was trying to say *oil can*." She slanted Laila a questioning look. "Do you think he's trying to ask for an oil can?"

"He's a flesh and blood genie, not a tin man." Laila tsked. "Come on, Zak," she urged. "Talk. Tell me what I should do."

Zak blinked. His eyeballs sort of jiggled, but he just kept staring straight up.

"Electricity," he said barely loud enough for them to hear.

"Holy shit, that's it," Reen said. "He electrocuted himself. That's why his hair was sticking straight out when he sailed past us."

"Holy shit," Zak attempted to repeat, his eyebrows squeezing together. "What is godly excrement?" He tried to lift his head but it fell back to the grass. "For eight hundred please, Alex." His eyelids fluttered closed again as if he'd passed out.

"What the hell is he talking about?" Reen asked.

Laila shrugged. "I have no idea. He must be delirious." She shook him gently. "Zak...are you okay?"

"Electrocution." His statement caught Laila off guard and she gasped as Zak's eyes popped open again, his eyeballs still jiggling as he attempted to focus on her. "What is capital punishment?"

Oh her poor handsome, wonderful genie. His brain was scrambled from whatever he'd done to himself.

"I suppose a powerful enough electrical shock could propel him through the air like that," she said to Reen. "I saw it on a science show once. Zak, is that what happened? Did you get an electric—"

"Silver paper." He turned his head with agonizing slowness, looking at the two women kneeling at his side. "Foil. I make experiment."

For the first time, Laila noticed the two-inch wide cuffs of aluminum foil coiled around each of his bare arms above the elbow and again at the wrist, as well as another pair around his ankles.

"What on earth did you do?"

"Examination of electrical outlet to see how it works. Metal foil made big shock."

"Typical man." Reen shook her head back and forth. "They're all a bunch of overgrown kids."

Sitting back on her heels, Laila growled in frustration. "Didn't I tell you not to get into any trouble while I was gone? Dammit, Zak, you could have killed yourself." She trembled from combined fear, relief and anger.

"No." He uttered a whisper of a chuckle, then winced. "Cannot die. Only feels like dying."

"Are you in a lot of pain?" Reen asked.

"Plenty."

The damn fool laughed again and pain engraved itself across his features.

"Now I understand meaning of conducting electricity," he said, his power of speech not yet back to normal. "Googled to learn about it."

Reen gave Laila a cockeyed look. "Did he say he Googled?"

"I showed him how." Laila gave a helpless shrug. "How was I supposed to know he'd do something stupid and practically fry himself?" She narrowed her eyes at him. "I'm very angry with you right now, Zakkar. The only thing keeping me from wringing your neck is the fact that you're in so much pain. I hope you learned a lesson from this."

"Learn you are pretty when angry." He gave her a loopy smile.

She couldn't help but smile in return. Then she leaned over him and kissed the corner of his mouth.

"Ow." He winced.

"Oh..." Her fingers flew to her lips. "I'm sorry."

"Not to worry, little one. I heal soon."

"Ohmigosh..." Laila's head bobbed to attention, turning left and right. "Where's Friday? Is he okay?"

"Friday okay, but he did not like experiments. Prefer to hide behind couch with bone."

"That's because you scared the bejeezus out of the poor dog," Reen noted with a snicker.

"What's all the ruckus?"

Laila looked up to see Mrs. Willoughby inching her way up the sidewalk with her walker.

"Ooh, Lord a'mighty. Is that poor boy okay?"

"Yes, Mrs. Willoughby," Laila answered. "He's...uh, he's the electrician I hired to fix an electrical problem. There was an accident but he's just fine now."

"Electrician, hmm? Guess they're workin' bare-chested and sleepin' over to get the job done nowadays." Her wrinkled old face cracked a smile and she winked. "I may be old but I've still got eyes."

Leaning closer, she spoke to Laila in a conspirator's tone, "Don't worry, sweetie, I'm not judging. I was young once too." She punctuated her sentence with another wink.

Laila could have died.

"Wow, you just turned twelve shades of pink, Laila," Reen helpfully observed.

"Thank you, Maureen."

"Your *electrician*," Mrs. Willoughby said the word with a roll of her yes, "seems accident prone. Flew right out the window, then down to the grass. Boom!" She elucidated with a sharp thwack of her walker against the concrete walk. "I was out front watering my rhododendrons and saw the whole thing. Thought he killed himself for sure."

"It's okay, Mrs. Willoughby," Laila said. "He's going to be fine."

"Anything I can do for the poor boy?" the old woman asked, her eyes roving over Zak's spread, half-naked body. "Like maybe some mouth-to-mouth?" She snickered. "It's been a while, but I think I could get the hang of it again."

"Why, Mrs. Willoughby!" Reen gushed laughter.

Clearing her throat, Laila smiled, doing her best not to give in to rising laughter. "No thanks, Mrs. Willoughby. Everything's under control."

"Electrician. Hah!" the old woman noted, toddling off with a *clack-thump, clack thump* as her walker connected with the ground. "Electricians never looked like that in my day."

"You never told me Mrs. Willoughby's a dirty old lady," Reen whispered, still laughing.

Laila grinned as she watched the old woman hobble back to her house, her step more spry than she'd seen it before. "I never had a clue."

Zak suddenly sat up. "I am better now."

Laila was shocked when she saw his back. "You're bleeding!" She carefully plucked small jagged shards of glass from his skin. "This is awful." She winced as she studied his torn back.

"He's bleeding profusely," Reen noted. "He needs to go to the emergency room."

"Come on, Zak," Laila said. "We need to get you into the car so we can get you to the hospital." She and Reen did their best to brace him so they could help him to his feet.

"No need. It will go away soon," Zak insisted, gently pushing them away. "It is only temporary agony. Did you know there are more ways than just a simple switch to turn on your coffeemaker?"

Still dazed by what had happened, Laila breathed a monumental sigh. "Oh good grief. Zak, what have you done?"

"By touching the correct wires together, I—"

Reen barked a laugh. "He probably blew up your coffeepot."

Shaking an outstretched finger at Reen, he smiled. "You make many jokes," he charged. "No, I did not blow up the coffeepot, I only took it apart to learn how it works. Then I made improvements."

"Aw jeez..." Laila's shoulders slumped. "I'm afraid to ask what else you did."

"Do not be afraid to ask. I have all the answers about the many excellent modifications I have made to improve your entire household, Laila." Zak beamed a grin and she groaned. "I have many other excellent ideas for modernizing Bekka House as well."

"Holy smokes. Look, Laila," an astonished Reen cried, waving a finger at his back. "The glass is falling off and the cuts are healing. They're just disappearing. He's not bleeding anymore. How the holy hell is that possible?"

"Holy smokes, holy cow, holy mackerel, holy Moses, holy Toledo, holy moly," Zak rattled off. An eyebrow arched, he scratched his head. "And apparently, holy hell and holy shit."

"Uh-oh. The poor guy's lost it," Reen muttered, half covering her mouth.

"Something must have short circuited," Laila agreed.

"What is an exclamation of surprise, astonishment, delight, or dismay, Alex?" Zak said, beaming a grin. "Let's make it a true daily double."

Laila and Reen exchanged bewildered looks.

"It sounds like he's talking about *Jeopardy*," Laila said.

"Watched *Jeopardy* marathon while conducting experiments," Zak confirmed. "Alex Trebek is the world's most intelligent man. I have learned much from this great teacher."

"You were watching a gameshow host," Reen explained.

"Yes, a true genius who knows the questions and answers about every imaginable subject," Zak stated with reverence. "Can it be arranged for me to meet this man?"

"Unfortunately," Laila informed him, "Alex is no longer living."

"What!?" Clearly distressed, Zak's eyes popped wide. "No, it cannot be. What a great loss to the world."

"Alex had many loyal fans who feel the same way," Laila draped her arm around his shoulder, resting her head against his, "but you'll always be able to watch him on the television." Noting once more how upset he was, she added, "You poor man. You've clearly been overstimulated in more ways than one. I'll get you some ibuprofen and make some tea and you can just rest until you feel better."

Zak jumped to his feet and stretched, startling both women. Watching all those muscles in his chest and arms ripple, flex and roll was a magnificent sight. If Mrs. Willoughby was peeking through her curtains, she was probably experiencing some unexpected rapid heartbeat activity, along with a hot flash or two.

"Come, I will show you the excellent improvements I have made to Bekka House." He wrapped his arms around Laila's and Reen's shoulders, leading them into the house.

Reen glanced at Laila and snickered. "Be afraid," she warned. "Be very afraid."

Laila couldn't begin to imagine what her curious genie had been up to. "Oh I am. Believe me."

"Whoa!" Reen said as the threesome stepped into the kitchen. "All you need is a disco light ball and you'll be all set."

"Magnificent, is it not?" Zak said with a proud grin.

"My God..." Laila's disbelieving gasp seemed to echo as she gazed at the walls, entirely papered with aluminum foil. Upon close inspection she found the foil had been stapled on in some places and glued in others. "Why did you do this, Zak?"

"To increase light. Google explains that in physics, this is known as the law of reflection. The silver foil also creates added insulation from both heat and cold. Metal foil is among the greatest inventions I have encountered in 5,000 years. It is not only for household purposes, it also makes cuff adornments. You see?" He held his arms out for inspection. "Did you know you can cut your roasting time almost in half for turkey by covering the fowl with a metal foil tent? And that the meat will be juicier? And that drinks will remain colder if the glasses are wrapped in foil?"

"You didn't..." Laila hoped aloud.

Zak stepped to one of the kitchen cabinets and opened it. Like a game show hostess, he smiled, gesturing to the water glasses, each of which had been cuffed with foil.

"You've been a busy boy," Reen noted. She leaned her face toward the wall and sniffed. "Um...what did you use to glue on the foil?"

"My solutions would make Alex Trebek proud. Mud did not work well. The foil loosened when it dried," Zak explained, and Laila wondered where he'd been digging for the dirt. "I discovered multiple uses for simple, everyday items around the house by Googling," he proudly announced. "I used toothpaste in some places. Once the tube was empty, I made paste from flour and water and used that."

Laila groaned.

"Peanut butter also makes good mortar. I ran out because I ate it from the knife as I worked. It is delicious."

Elbowing Laila, Reen laughed so hard tears ran down her cheeks. "Same thing we do." She took out her phone and started taking pictures.

"What are you doing?" Zak asked, as he watched the flash bouncing off the shiny wall.

"Taking photos." She glanced at Laila. "You haven't told him about that yet?"

"Not yet," Laila answered absently. "I can't believe you did all of this, Zak," she said on a sigh, afraid of what he might show her next. "I mean...I really can't"

"I knew you would be surprised and pleased." He looked quite happy with himself. "Did you know toothpaste makes an excellent substitute for plaster compound when covering nail holes? You will find no more unsightly nail holes in the walls of Bekka House."

Laila spread her fingers over her face and jaw. "Well, I'm just...tickled pink, Zak," she said with a deadpan expression. "I hardly know what to say."

"I have only done what Tim would have done for you if he had lived," Zak told her, and Laila thought it was about the sweetest damn thing she'd ever heard.

Openly admiring his handiwork, Zak marveled, "Such an ingenious time you live in. I enjoyed gaining knowledge of electricity. Your coffeemaker now operates by this wall switch," he gestured, "as well as the button on the pot. Here, let me show you." He reached for the wall switch and Laila grabbed his hand, stilling it.

"No!" she and Reen chorused as Laila moved his hand away, terrified he'd flip the switch, get zapped and go sailing through another window. "We can check it later." She did her best to make her smile sincere.

"I have also adjusted the wiring mechanisms on your other appliances to make them operate with greater ease and more efficiency."

"You didn't."

"Indeed I did."

"Well, that's great...really great."

"In other words," Reen offered, "he booby trapped the whole place. You'll never know when you might get jolted from here to eternity at the mere flip of a switch."

Zak's expression of pride was mixed with puzzlement. "Booby trap?"

"Never mind." Laila whapped her sister's arm.

"I would be happy to come to your abode, Reen, to make the same modifications if you have not already done so," Zak offered.

"Thanks, Handy Andy." Winking, Reen gave Zak a thumbs up sign. "I'll consider it."

"Good. It will be my pleasure to fix your dwelling, Reen." He planted his fists on his hips and smiled. "So, Laila...are you ready to make your wishes?"

"Yes." Laila sucked in a deep breath. "But let's do it in the living room." She had an eerie feeling something weird, like a lollapalooza of an electrical arc bouncing off her foiled walls, might happen. It wouldn't be good if her wishes came true and she wasn't around to enjoy them because she'd been fried to a crisp.

"As a word of caution," Zak offered as they left the kitchen, "you should avoid turning on any of the living room's music system components or speakers until I have finished my electrical modifications. That is what I was working on when I was suddenly transported through the air and out the window."

Laila looked at the ragged gash in the glass behind her and sighed. "I forgot about the window." She gazed around the room, noting stray wires poking out here and there. Her shoulders slumped as she watched wisps of smoke trailing up from her brother, Gard's, expensive receiver.

"Careful not to touch anything electrical," she advised Reen. "Okay, is everybody ready?" Laila briskly rubbed her hands together.

"Ready," Zak and Reen chorused.

They heard a whimper followed by a distinct doglike moan.

"Friday?" Laila peeked behind the sofa to find the dog cowering. "Aw, you poor thing. Come here, sweetie pie." Friday didn't budge. "It's okay now. You can come out," she coaxed, patting her knees. "Zak is done experimenting." Friday took a few tentative steps from behind his hiding place to join them, staying close to Laila and shivering beside her. It was the first time since Zak's appearance that the dog didn't rush to his side.

"Oh boy. Friday's got the heebie-jeebies," Reen said.

"He is not used to having a man in the house conducting important experiments," Zak stated, his arms neatly folded across his chest. "He will be fine soon. The more experiments I do the more used to them Friday will become."

"That's what I'm afraid of," Laila muttered, patting the hesitant dog. She sucked in a deep breath. "All righty, let's get down to the business of wish making." Filled with a mixture of excitement and apprehension, she rubbed her hands together, beaming a smile. "Here I go, Zak."

"Where...back to the kitchen?"

"He's a riot," Reen noted.

Her shoulders sagging again, Laila couldn't keep from tsking. "Nowhere, Zak. I'm getting ready to make my first wish."

"I am listening closely and fully prepared," he assured her.

"Okay then...for my first official wish, I wish to own and—"

Folding his arms across his chest, Zak turned his back to her.

Angling her head, Laila frowned. "What are you doing?"

Zak glanced over his shoulder. "Ignoring you, as instructed."

With mounting frustration, she growled, "What are you talking about?"

"You made me promise to ignore you unless you made this important sign," Zak said, hanging quotes in the air as he turned to face her again. "I thought you were testing me."

"Oh the air quotes. Right, I forgot. Okay, here we go."

"Where?"

Reen giggled.

Exasperated, Laila pinned them with a heated glare. "Shush dammit!" Reen, Zak and Friday were startled into silence. Taking a deep breath, Laila made sure to hang finger quotes before saying, "For my first official wish, I wish to own and be able to afford the upkeep of Crowe's Coastside Bakery and the building it's housed in."

She waited for Zak to clap his hands over his arms in a genie-esque gesture or wiggle his nose or maybe blink and nod, but he simply smiled.

"When does he go into his genie act," Reen whispered, clearly with the same genie-esque images in mind.

Laila watched him for a moment. "Aren't you going to do anything, Zak? You know, go boing, or something?"

"It is already done," he told her. "The wish has been granted. Crowe's Coastside Bakery is yours, little one."

"That's it? No boom or kabang or bolts of lightning or anything?" Reen sounded disappointed.

Zak laughed. "I am not like *I Dream of Jeannie* or other genies of fictional tales. The wish is voiced, channeled through me and granted. The process is that simple."

"Well that was rather anticlimactic," Reen muttered.

"So if we drive over to the bakery right now," Laila said, "I could just walk right in, tell them I'm the new owner, and nobody would question it?"

"I have no idea of the working mechanisms of the wishes, Laila. I can only tell you I am certain your wish was granted."

Reaching into her purse, Reen drew out her keys, looping them over a finger and jangling them. "So what the heck are we waiting for?" Her expectant smile was a mile wide.

Feeling a comparable smile take hold, Laila said, "Let's go."

"We will also take your car," Zak told Laila. "Because we will be spending the night in your new apartment."

"As much as I enjoy feasting my eyes on those aluminum foil-cuffed muscles of yours, big guy," Reen winked, "you might want to put on a shirt first."

"I need to throw a few things together too," Laila said.

"Do you want to make your second wish now?" Zak asked, as Laila headed upstairs to the bedroom.

"Not yet. If this one worked, I'll make wish number two from my very own second story apartment above my very own bakery." As she put together some clothing and toiletries, the thought tickled her. While she had the greatest faith in Zak, she couldn't fathom being the owner of the bakery and that fabulous historic Victorian brick building on Ocean Charm Boulevard.

As she left the bedroom, heading for the kitchen to gather dogfood and toys for Friday, Zak headed to the bedroom to change his clothes.

When Laila returned to the living room, Reen confided, "I like him, Laila. A lot. He's sweet, smart, funny, unpredictable and, jeez, such a hunk." She rolled her eyes. "I can see how much he cares about you." She pulled Laila into a hug. "I don't blame you for falling hard, honey."

Zak returned to the room, holding a large bag that appeared to be stuffed.

"What's all that?" Laila asked. "Your clothes?"

Zak turned the bag around, revealing the sex shop's Provocative Pleasures: *You Know You Want To* logo. "Some things we might need," he told her, his charming smile a flash of white. "I happened upon the bag you had mistakenly put in the recycling bin."

"Mistakenly my ass," Laila murmured beneath her breath. Feeling her cheeks color as Reen snickered away, Laila wordlessly turned on her heels and marched toward her car. "I'll have to call someone to board up that picture window," she said along the way.

"Thank you, I have enjoyed our meeting too," Zak said. "Yes, I will."

Stopping in her tracks, Laila turned around, her features scrunched in a puzzled expression. "What are you talking about, Zak?"

"He's probably still suffering from the aftershocks of being electrocuted." Reen twirled her finger at her temple.

"No, I was conversing with Rebekka."

Wide eyed, Laila and Reen chorused, "Grandma Bekka?"

"She talked to you?" Reen said in a loud whisper, glancing left and right.

"Indeed, and she appeared to me briefly," Zak said, "looking the same as in the photograph you showed me of her when she was quite young."

As Zak spoke, the warm, spicy fragrance of Bekka's *pepperkaker* wafted out of the house, surrounding them.

"Wow...I guess she did," Reen said, clearly amazed.

"Your grandmother expressed her pleasure at knowing me. She wishes you great happiness in your new home and business, Laila."

"Well I'll be darned," Reen muttered.

Bittersweet tears brimming, Laila smiled. "Thank you, Grandma. I'm going to miss you, Grandpa, and Anders." She blew a kiss into the air and headed for the car.

Chapter 19

~<>~

"I CALLED THE REAL estate number I found online," Laila told Reen as the sisters, Zak and Friday exited the cars. "They said their agents will meet us here in a few minutes."

"That fast?" Reen asked, surprised. "Good. I can't wait!" She rubbed her hands together.

"Don't get so excited. The number was for Wotring Realtors."

Reen grimaced. "The office just down the street?" She thumbed down the block.

"Yup." Groaning in unison, they exchanged wary glances. It was the high-end real estate office where their snooty cousin Saffron worked.

Laila absently petted Friday. "The receptionist said two agents are at the building now doing a showing for prospective buyers. She'll let them know we're coming."

"I hope to hell Saffy's not the listing agent," Reen said. "The car across the street looks like hers."

"She's the last person I want to see behind that door," Laila agreed, a sudden chill taking hold. "Especially if the wish didn't work."

"Wow." Reen gaped at the ornate Victorian brick building before them. "I forgot how huge and beautiful this place is. I've never really paid much attention to anything here but the food." She offered a guilty smile. "I can't believe you're actually going to live here. That apartment upstairs is amazing. Peggy and Caroline obviously put a lot of money and love into it."

Standing just outside her car at the curb, Laila was anchored to the spot, overwhelmed. The enthusiasm she'd experienced while making her wish drained away, leaving her with a serious case of doubt. Her gaze traveled up and down the historic building, resting on the Wotring Realtors sign prominently displayed in the bakery's window. How hadn't she noticed that before?

"There's no way in hell that I own this place."

"You own it," Zak assured. "Without doubt. I know it. I feel it here." He clutched his lean, firm belly.

"There's only one way to find out." Reen grabbed Laila's elbow and tugged.

"I'm so nervous." Her heart beating a rapid tattoo, Laila held tight to Friday's leash. "What if the real estate agent takes one look at me and laughs in my face when I tell her I'm the owner?" With a voluminous breath, she looped arms with her cohorts. "Let's do it." Together they marched up to the entrance. Laila wrapped her hand around the door handle and pushed. Then she pulled.

"It's locked," she murmured.

Cupping her hands to the window, Reen said, "I can see people in there. And the bakery cases are full of food." Reaching around her sister, she knocked on the wood and glass door while Zak rang the bell.

Before the door even opened the heavenly aroma of sugar, butter and flour imprinted themselves on Laila's senses. Closing her eyes, she breathed deep, knowing just inside that door were the sweet, memorable fragrances of Christmas, grandma's kitchen, birthdays, and love. On the other side of that door was her lifelong dream job of bringing lasting smiles to the faces of people who sampled her original recipe baked goods.

Lost in her meandering thoughts, her eyes popped wide when the door opened.

The chic, sophisticated, designer-label type who answered was more or less a Saffron clone, except she was a blonde while Saffron was a brunette. Laila felt the effects of the woman's icy onceover as she appraised her, expecting her worst fears were about to come true.

"Yes? May I help you with something?" After another sweeping assessment, she gestured with her hand, adding, "If you have a delivery, you'll need to use the back entrance." The model-thin woman's gaze floated to Reen, who got the ice treatment as well. When the woman's eyes settled on Zak, heat radiated and her demeanor changed.

And then she gasped.

"Oh good grief, he has a weapon!"

Shifting her gaze to Zak, Laila spied the scabbard affixed to his hip. "I told you to leave that thing in the car."

Zak's hand went to the handle of his saber. "I prefer to keep my saber at my side in the event of trouble," he explained, addressing his comment to Laila before giving the woman at the door a purposeful look.

The woman visibly shuddered, color draining from her face, as she uttered an unintelligible declaration of distress and slammed the door.

"Now see what you've done?" Reen chastised. "Take that damn thing off, Zakkar, and put it in the car before you get us all hauled off to jail."

"But—" Zak began.

"Do it!" Laila and Reen chorused in no-nonsense tones. Friday's bark added further exclamation.

"Honestly," Reen grumbled as the brooding genie marched back to the car. "Men and their toys."

Once Zak returned, frowning, weaponless and arms folded defiantly across his chest, Laila knocked on the door again.

"Go away or I'll call the police," the woman said through the door.

"It's okay," Laila assured. "The sword's in the car. Actually, it wasn't real," she lied, "just a toy. Zak is...um...he's an exotic dancer. It's part of his costume." It was a believable fib. With his physique, Zak certainly looked the part of a male stripper.

The door cracked open a few inches. "Perhaps you've mistaken the bakery for a strip club," the woman suggested acerbically as her gaze searched Zak.

"We're here because I'm, um..." Laila's eyes closed in a long blink. She swallowed hard, doing her best to drum up a believable sense of poise. "Because I'm—"

"Hungry?" the agent asked after giving Laila yet another judgy onceover. "Sorry, the bakery's out of business."

Elevating her chin, Laila forged ahead. "I'm Laila Malone, the new owner." It was sheer murder choking those words out while the urbane woman telegraphed an expression of downright incredulity.

"New owner of what?"

"This," Laila motioned with her hand, "the Crowe's Coastside Bakery building."

The door opened wide and the woman's eyebrow shot up while her mouth pinched. "Clearly you're mistaken," she said, as if speaking to an imbecile. "This historic structure and its contents is one of our premier properties. It's a multi-million dollar listing," she further clarified.

"I know. I'm the new owner," Laila said again in a tiny voice bereft of any confidence or belief in her own statement.

"I'm afraid you're mistaken." The real estate agent's shoulders straightened and her chin shot up several notches higher than Laila's. "An offer to purchase was accepted by the Crowe sisters early this morning, just before they boarded their flight to Barcelona." She gestured toward a well-dressed middle-aged couple browsing the large interior space.

Laila's whole demeanor drooped.

"Now, if you and your horse," the agent shot a glance at Friday, whose head leaned in question, "will excuse me..."

After dismissing them, she gave Zak a final longing onceover before shutting the door and locking it.

Laila turned to Reen and Zak, determined not to cry.

"The wish didn't work." Heaving a monumental exhale, she continued, "That's okay. Don't feel bad, Zak." She rested her hand on his arm, smiling up at him. "It just wasn't meant to be."

Scowling, Zak banged his fist on the door.

"Zak, don't." Laila tried tugging him away, which was like trying to haul a refrigerator. "She'll only humiliate us more. It's okay, really." She smoothed her hand along his back. "I love Bekka House and...and all the special modifications you made. Honestly, I don't want you to feel bad because the wish didn't work."

His glower deepening, Zak pounded on the door again and Laila cringed when the real estate agent yanked it open, looking none too pleased.

"Is there something else?" She glared at them, her words freezing in midair as they left her over-plumped lips.

"Monica, what in the world is going on? Mr. and Mrs. Stephenson are wondering what all the commotion is about." Saffron Devington appeared at the agent's side, pulling the door open wider, obviously stunned when she spotted her cousins.

"Laila...Maureen? For heaven's sake, what are you doing here?" Leaning close, Saffron whispered, "If you're looking for a cookie fix you'll have to go elsewhere. Crowe's is closed. My associate and I are in the middle of closing a major sale."

"You know them?" Monica asked.

"Regrettably," Saffron said with a sigh, motioning toward them. "They're my cousins."

"Hey, Saffy." Reen gave a finger wave. "So you're the listing agent, hmm?"

"Monica and I are the co-listing agents, yes," she said proudly. "And those are our buyers." She motioned toward the older couple.

"Perfect," Laila muttered. "Just perfect." It was humiliation on top of humiliation.

"Your cousin claims to be the new owner," Monica said, rolling her eyes.

Saffron shot Laila and Reen a disbelieving look, followed by a chuff of laughter. Once her gaze landed on Zak, her expression changed. "You mean him? He's not my cousin."

"Her." Monica pointed at Laila.

"Laila? Oh for heaven's sake, that's ridiculous. Look, we don't have time for silly games," Saffron advised them with little patience. "We're working. Go back to whatever drunken party you came from." With a shooing motion, she started closing the door.

"You have made an error," Zak stated with all the aplomb and self-assurance Laila lacked. "Laila Malone now owns the Crowe's Coastside Bakery building and all of its contents. Upon checking you will see I am correct." Friday backed him up with a companionable woof.

"I can assure you that *you*, sir, are the one who's made the error." Saffron's expression was caustic at best. "I know Laila Malone. There's no way in hell she's the owner of this building..." she gave Laila a disagreeable onceover, "or any other property."

"I already explained to them—" Monica raised her finger, indicating Saffron should wait. "Monica Sharp," she said, looking past them. Laila turned but saw no one there. "What do you mean? What kind of problem?" she said, and that's when Laila realized she had on a Bluetooth headset.

"What?!" Monica flinched at whatever the person on the other end said, then turned to look at the buyers. "If you'll excuse me," she said to Laila, Reen and Zak, closing the door. This time Zak caught it and pushed it open, following her into the bakery and gesturing for Laila and Reen to do the same.

"Get that animal of yours off these wood floors," the shuddering Saffron instructed Laila. "His nails will scratch them." Turning her back, she joined Monica, who was addressing the buyers.

"I'm sorry, Mr. and Mrs. Stephenson," Monica said, "it seems your earnest money funds failed to transfer. Your purchase contract for the Crowe property has been voided."

At the news, Saffron gasped, her hand flying to the locket at her throat.

"That's preposterous. Impossible," the short, bespectacled man blustered. "It was done by electronic transfer this morning at my attorney's office."

"Monica Sharp," the agent said again, answering a new call. Her face blanched. "No. You're absolutely certain?" Her stunned gaze shot to Laila, then to Saffron. "One hundred percent positive?" Her fingers flew to her temples and she sucked in a deep breath as she listened. "All right, yes, I'll take care of it."

Ending the call, Monica turned to Saffron, whispering something in her ear.

"What? Laila? No...that's impossible," Saffron breathed, the color draining from her face. "It has to be a mistake."

"No mistake." Monica turned her attention to Laila. "Ms. Malone," she swallowed hard, "may I see some identification?"

Laila whipped out her wallet and displayed license, credit cards and her library card.

"Your offer to purchase has been accepted by Peggy and Caroline Crowe, Ms. Malone," Monica said, looking dazed and bewildered.

"They said to tell you they're absolutely delighted that you'll be the one taking over their bakery. Congratulations."

"I don't believe it," Saffron muttered, still dazed.

"Woohoo!" Leaping nearly a foot off the floor, Reen grabbed Laila by the shoulders and yelped, "Laila, you got it! This fabulous wonderland of baked goods is all yours!" Stretching her arms wide, she twirled, taking in all the bakery cases around them. "It's just like Hansel and Gretel, but without the witch." Her gaze shot to Saffron. "Well...almost."

Thrilled beyond belief, Laila scanned the bakery. *Her* bakery! She bit her tongue to keep from shouting *whoopee!* while Zak's arm snaked around her in a congratulatory hug.

"You can't do this!" Mr. Stephenson belted out. "My offer was accepted before theirs. I'll sue."

"Herbert..." his wife cautioned, yanking his arm.

"I rather doubt you'll be doing that, Mr. Stephenson." Monica sneered as if he were a fat maggot.

Laila found the abrupt change in her demeanor amusing.

There was a rap at the door and two men in gray business suits entered the bakery. They flipped open their wallets, displaying badges. "Herbert Stephenson?" Sneer still firmly in place, Monica instantly pointed to the couple. "You'll need to come with us to the station for questioning, sir," one of the detectives said.

Mr. Stephenson turned a sickly shade of green. "You're arresting me?"

"Not at this time. But I'd suggest you have your attorney meet you at Glassfloat Bay Police Headquarters. There's a little matter of drug money that needs to be resolved."

The icy gaze Monica Sharp had used to greet Laila earlier grew deathlike as she turned it on her former buyers. "It seems your assets in Grand Cayman have been frozen due to suspicion of illegal activity," she said, her lip curling in disdain.

"Son of a bitch, I knew this would happen," Mrs. Stephenson growled.

"Shut up, Edna," her husband warned, adjusting his sloping bowtie.

Monica plucked the keys to the Crowe building from Mr. Stephenson's fingers. A moment later, he, his wife and the detectives had departed. She took Saffron aside and spent the next few minutes talking to her before guiding her to a chair where Maureen and Laila's white as a sheet cousin took a seat, her head in her hand as she mumbled to herself.

Taking a moment to regroup, Monica patted her hair and cleared her throat. Turning to Laila, she issued a smile. Not one of those condescending smiles she'd projected earlier, it was more like a *let's do lunch and be best girlfriends now that I know you have big bucks* sort of smile.

"Ms. Malone." She extended her hand, and Laila worried Monica's Botoxed face would crack if her smile grew any wider. "I apologize for the unfortunate mix-up earlier. In my defense, it's been a rather stressful day."

She shook Laila's hand, then pressed the building's keys into Laila's open palm. "I understand all the paperwork is in order, so you're ready to move right in. The apartment is fully furnished and, might I add, quite magnificent." Another million-dollar-smile beamed from her features. It was so bright Laila was tempted to shield her eyes.

"You mean all the mortgage papers have already been signed?" Laila asked, closing her fingers around the keys and clutching them hard enough to indent her skin. "Are they going to send me something telling me how much my monthly payments are and where to send them?"

Monica Sharp blinked. "Since you paid cash in full for the building and its entire contents, naturally there's no mortgage," she said.

"It's not possible," Saffron muttered from her chair, shaking her head. "No way..."

"Oh," addressing Laila, Monica tittered a chuckle, "I see. You're teasing me to get back at me for my momentary display of ignorance earlier." Her laugh sounded practiced. "I suppose I deserve it." Reaching out, she patted the top of Friday's head. "Nice doggy." Receiving a threatening growl in return, she snatched back her hand.

"You most certainly do deserve it," Reen scolded. "Your exceedingly rude treatment of my sister was inexcusable."

Monica blanched and Laila couldn't help feeling sorry for her. "That's okay, Reen. She didn't know."

"No, it is *not* okay. If it weren't for those dollar signs she sees when she looks at you now," Reen insisted, "she'd be treating you in the same shabby manner. Maybe Ms. Sharp, as well as our cousin, will learn not to be so judgmental when it comes to appearances in the future, hmm?" Reen leveled accusatory glares at Monica and Saffron.

"You're right, of course. There's no excuse for my unacceptable behavior," Monica readily agreed. She looked tempted to perform a practiced cry. The woman could give lessons in groveling. "I do hope you'll accept my profuse apologies and allow me to give the three of you..." her gaze lowered, "and your adorable dog, a tour of your new property."

"That will not be necessary." Zak stepped forward, scowling down at the agent. "You may go now. We will tour on our own."

"But you're not familiar with the property," Monica objected. "It's a vast structure with hidden rooms and I—"

"Begone, pretentious one," Zak commanded, directly pointing to the door.

Nonplussed, Monica Sharp slipped Laila one of her business cards and turned to her co-agent. "Saffron." Their cousin sat silent. "Saffron!" Monica called again and Saffron looked up. "It's time to go."

Before leaving the premises, Saffron stopped in front of Laila, cocking her head in question. "But how?"

"Magic." Laila winked.

"So long, Saffy." Reen gave another finger wave as the women gathered their gear.

Once they were alone, Laila punched the air, letting out a gleeful whoop.

"Did you see Saffy's face?" Hugging herself, Reen uttered a gleeful giggle. "She was floored. Flabbergasted. I've never seen her at a loss for words before. Damn, that was the best moment of my life!"

"She and Monica are going to make a fortune in commission from this sale," Laila reminded her.

"I know, but for right now please don't rain on my parade." Reen winked as she scampered behind one of the glass bakery cases displaying an assortment of fancy cookies. "Mmm," she plucked a cookie and bit into it, "chocolate with chocolate ganache filling and chocolate frosting. Yum!" Snagging another cookie, she took a nibble. "Ohmigod, this one's just as decadent...hazelnut chocolate." As she sank her teeth into a third cookie she said, "Ooh, and this one is—"

"Maureen Malone, shame on you!" Laila chastised as her sister chewed.

Cookie in midair, Reen slanted her sister a quizzical look. "For blowing my diet? Laila, this is time for major celebration." Waving the cookie, she added, "And what better to celebrate with than—"

"No, I mean for stealing. What if Peggy or Caroline Crowe walked in here and caught you eating up their inventory?"

Shooting a smirking glance to Zak, Reen told him, "She must me in shock."

Zak gave a perceptive nod.

Returning her attention to her sister, Reen reminded Laila, "The Crowe sisters are on a plane to Barcelona, remember? As for me being a despicable cookie thief..." Boasting a mile-wide smile, Reen opened her purse and handed Laila five dollars.

"What's this for?" Laila pushed the money back at her sister.

"To pay you for the cookies I stole. Because these are *your* cookies now, you big ninny." Throwing her hands into the air, Reen broke into full-fledged laughter. "Everything in here belongs to you!"

"Oh my gosh...holy cow, you're right!" Her fingers flying to her lips, Laila breathed in an exclamation. "I forgot! These are mine, all mine!" She couldn't suppress a giggle. "Reen, Zak," she nudged his arm, "feel free to eat to your heart's content. Later we'll box up the baked goods so we can bring some to Annalise at the café, some to the homeless shelter, and some," she pointed to Reen, "to the children's hospital."

Reen gave a thumbs up. "Perfect."

"Excellent sweets but too many of these," Zak said, licking frosting from his lip, "and I would soon be too rotund for my new britches." A few cookies in hand, he explored the retail space, studying the nooks and crannies. With an approving nod, he noted, "This old building has held up well. It seems to have been built in the same era as Maythorne Manor."

Finishing the last of his cookies, he brushed the crumbs from his hands. "Don't worry, Laila, I will inspect everything throughout the building for you and make any needed modifications." He smiled proudly.

"Oh...Zak..." Laila started, uncertain of how to say what she needed, for fear of hurting his feelings.

"Yes, little one?"

"Um...maybe we can just leave everything the way it is for now, hmm?"

"After all," Reen added, "the building has managed to last more than a century without foiling the walls and rigging the switches. It might be a good idea to leave it natural, don't you think?"

Zak looked dejected as Laila watched his broad shoulders slump. "You did not like the improvements I made to Bekka House."

"It's not that...it was well intentioned and I appreciate your effort," Laila assured him with a hug. "After you spend more time online learning about home improvement, I'm sure you'll be the envy of the block because of your fabulous handyman skills. But for now..." She finished her sentence with a hopeful smile.

Zak was silent a moment before returning her smile. "Do not look so sad. You have not permanently trampled my feelings. Come, we will explore everything about your new building."

The last thing Laila wanted to do was bruise Zak's ego further, so as soon as she got the chance she excused herself and stepped into one of the bathrooms in the back of the bakery so she was out of his hearing range.

Knowing she could depend on Annalise's brother, Hudson Griffin, Glassfloat Bay's resident handyman and general contractor, Laila called Hud, asking him to board up the living room window at Bekka House and see about replacing the glass. She also asked him to take a look inside the house to assess any electrical damage and see what could be done to restore the kitchen to its original non-aluminum-foiled state, giving him the go-ahead to contract out whatever work was needed.

After ending the call it felt strange as she walked through the bakery's enormous, fully equipped professional kitchen and the retail space to catch up to Reen and Zak. Almost as if she was trespassing. This wonderful place, this dream come true workplace, is where she'd be spending her days from now on, happily doing what she loved most. She wondered how long it would take her to become used to the idea.

With Friday in tow, they ventured up the staircase to Laila's new apartment. She couldn't wait to see it, especially after hearing so many positive things about the place.

Upon opening a broad set of double doors they entered a room that elicited an expression of awe from all of them. The unexpected space was an impressive library containing rich walnut paneling, hundreds of books, a pair of huge leather chairs with ottomans and a fireplace.

"So many books," Zak marveled. "Look, there are even several here about Mesopotamia." As he drew a thick book forward a concealed door in the shelving opened.

"It's just like in the movies!" Reen said, watching the secret door open. "Let's see where it leads."

"Wait, Maureen," Laila cautioned, "be caref—"

But her sister had already slipped into the passage. Exchanging glances, Laila and Zak shrugged before following her down a spiral staircase that took them to the huge, finished basement where they found a fully stocked wine cellar.

"Whoa...how cool is that!?" Reen said, checking out the expensive vintages.

"This is all so amazing!" Laila wrapped her arms around Zak and squeezed hard. "Thank you for making all of this possible, Zak." Getting on her tiptoes, she pulled his head down to plant little kisses all over his face.

He chuckled in response to her unbridled enthusiasm. "Although I cannot directly take credit for your wish being granted, it makes my heart swell to see you so joyful." He kissed the top of Laila's head before they located another set of stairs that led them into the bakery's kitchen area.

Returning to her apartment, Laila said, "You'd never suspect by the simple manner in which the Crowe sisters dressed that they lived like this…like millionaires." Her eyebrows knitted. "Shame on me. I'm as guilty as Saffron and Monica for judging a book by its cover."

"Wow, newsflash—Laila Malone isn't perfect." Reen gave her sister's arm a playful nudge. "There will be plenty of time to wallow in unnecessary guilt later." She looked up at Zak. "Laila does that so well."

"True. Especially when she eats chocolate." He cocked an eyebrow at Laila. "I have chastised her for it."

"Right now, Laila," Reen continued, "you need to give yourself permission to be happy and enjoy this fabulous place. It's beautiful and so big…like two apartments put together into one."

"I'll bet that's what they did during the renovations," Laila said. "I think this takes up the entire second floor of the building."

"And every bit of it belongs to you," Zak reminded her. "Come," he gestured to the bank of windows across the living room, "you must gaze upon your magnificent view."

Joining him, Laila sucked in an audible gasp. "The ocean! It's practically an unobstructed view. This just keeps getting better and better. Come on…" Grabbing Zak and Reen's hands, she dragged them into the next room. "I'm dying to see my new kitchen."

The apartment's gourmet kitchen was immense, grand and outfitted with state of the art appliances, quartz counter tops, a walk-in pantry and custom cabinets. It was everything Laila had ever dreamed of having in her own home.

She opened the door to what appeared to be a small refrigerator beneath the counter next to the huge refrigerator. Laila sucked in a breath when she spotted a row of champagne bottles lining the built-in wine rack. "It's the good stuff!" she said. "All pricey French labels." She closed the door.

"What the hell are you closing it for?" Reen asked "Let's break out the champagne and celebrate, girl!"

"I can't just take their champagne," Laila scoffed. "That wouldn't be right."

Rapping her knuckles against her sister's head, Reen said, "Hello?" in a singsong voice. "You still don't get it. It's not *their* champagne, Laila, it's *your* champagne. Right along with all those rows of bottles of expensive vintage wines downstairs in your fully stocked wine cellar. You bought everything inside as well as out, lock, stock and barrel. The whole shebang is yours, Laila, bought and paid for."

"The whole shebang," Zak confirmed.

Leaning her elbows on the counter, Laila massaged her temples where a tension headache began taking hold. "I know...I know you're right but..." she sighed, "I'm having a hard time wrapping my mind around it all. It all seems so unreal, like I'm living inside a dream, or a fairytale. I mean, a genie and three wishes and—"

"Okay, granted, it's weird and magical, but so what?" Reen groaned. "Will you puhleez stop analyzing and start enjoying?"

"Your sister is right," Zak said. "Life is too short and sweet not to enjoy the gift of every moment you are given. It can all be gone in the twinkling of an eye." He held Laila at arm's length, looking at her intently. "You must stop asking yourself questions that cannot be answered and start to relish your new life."

Laila listened, really listened. They were right. She'd been so busy manufacturing things to worry about that she was missing out on what should be the best most incredible time of her life.

"Thanks for the wake-up call." Laila smiled at them. "I needed it." Opening the wine refrigerator again, she retrieved a bottle of bubbly. "How about if we sip champagne as I make my second wish?"

"Great idea. I'll find the glasses," Reen said.

"Just imagine, I beat out a tweed-suited, bespectacled drug lord for this place." A peal of laughter rang from Laila. "Did you see the murderous looks those buyers gave me?"

"Yup. You're definitely on their shit list."

"Shit list..." Zak angled his head. "I am unable to fathom the meaning."

"Maybe it'll come up on *Jeopardy*," Reen teased and Zak nodded.

After unwrapping the wire cage on the bottle of Dom Perignon and twisting the cork, it popped with a satisfying celebratory noise. Laila poured the champagne into the weighty crystal stemware Reen found in a cupboard.

They sat at the kitchen table and Laila held her glass aloft. "As I sit here with my loved ones I—" Friday woofed. "Yes, that includes you, Friday." She chuckled, scratching him behind the ears. "I am instilled with loving warmth and a heart full of gratitude. A toast to us. Love, good health and happiness always."

"In the immortal words of Mr. Spock," Zak added, using the Vulcan salute, "Live long and prosper."

"Looks like you've got a TV addict on your hands," Reen teased Laila.

Once they'd each taken a sip, Laila looked across the table at Zak and smiled. "I'm ready for my second wish. Maybe this time you could do something a little flashy and dramatic, okay?" She wiggled her fingers in the air.

"You wish for me to emulate a fictional genie?"

Laila and Reen exchanged tickled glances. "That would be awesome," Laila told him.

Zak grinned. "I believe I can satisfy your whim." He motioned with his hand. "Proceed."

"For my second official wish," Laila remembered the air quotes this time, "I wish to establish The Great Pretender, a successful, thriving Bake shop, staffed with good, caring, knowledgeable people."

Zak rose to his feet, arms outstretched to the heavens, his palms up in a beckoning motion. "Oh hear me, great gods and goddesses," he roared, sending a chill zigzagging along Laila's spine. Clasping hands, she and Reen exchanged wide-eyed gapes while Friday hid beneath the table. "I, renowned warrior, Zakkar Tanojin Lugalbanda Tymon, beseech you to grant this worthy wish of the good, kind, fair and beautiful Laila Jane Malone."

Crossing his arms over his massive chest, he clapped his hands onto his arms, blinked, and nodded. Giving the women a sideways glance, he added a baritone, "Poof!" tossing his hands high into the air and making an arc. "As per your command, your wish has been granted, oh great master," Zak informed Laila with a sweeping bow.

Falling into laughter, Laila and Reen clapped.

"Better?" he asked.

"Perfect," Laila answered.

"You nailed it, Zak!" Reen agreed.

"What happens now?" Laila asked Zak.

"I do not know. We shall see."

"In the meantime, let's drink this big-bucks sparkly before it goes flat," Reen suggested.

Laila took a sip bigger than her first. The soft, velvety bubbles were unlike the harsh carbonation of the cheaper sparkling wines she was used to. "A girl could definitely get used to this."

"I'm tickled pink I'm your sister," Reen licked her lips, "because, Lord knows, somebody's got to help you drink up all this pricey wine."

"I have not supped champagne before," Zak noted after making short work of the liquid in his glass. "It is similar to barley ale, but more fruitlike, without the bitterness. I would enjoy this drink with a leg of mutton or a roasted goat's head."

Laila trembled in an involuntary shudder, while Reen's expression skewed. "You can forget about roasted head of anything, other than cauliflower," Laila told him. "You'll just have to sacrifice and make do with prime rib or filet mignon instead."

The doorbell rang. It was a grand, gracious, melodious tune, unlike any doorbell she'd heard before.

And it was all hers.

"Someone's at the door," she said absently.

"Well don't look at me to slip into a maid's uniform and answer it," Reen teased.

"No?" Laila rose from her chair and planted her hands on her hips. "Well heck, now I'm disappointed," she teased Reen before heading for the door. A quick glimpse at the kitchen clock told her it was after five o'clock. "Maybe it's some of the other shop owners welcoming me to the neighborhood."

"Or maybe it's Mr. Stephenson's drug cartel with a welcome to the neighborhood basket of hallucinogens," Reen called after her.

Using the intercom system Laila asked who was there.

"I'm here about the signage, ma'am," the man at the door outside the bakery said.

"Signage? You mean you're here to remove the for sale sign?"

"No ma'am. Can you come take a look so I can get your approval and signature?"

Zak and Reen followed Laila down the stairs where she unlocked the bakery's door. When the man at the door stepped aside, he gestured to his truck and the two men standing in front of it holding a huge sign.

Laila took one look and burst into tears.

Chapter 20

~<>~

"WHAT'S WRONG?" Reen scrambled to Laila's side.

"This man has caused you to cry?" Zak's strong, protective arm wrapped around Laila. "I will tear out his liver and feed it to him."

The poor man at her doorstep looked like he was going to pass out as Zak glared and snarled.

"No, look!" was all Laila was able to manage through her sobs as she pointed to the two men at the truck.

Reen and Zak turned to look at the elegant sign they held. It read *The Great Pretender*.

"It's my company. *My company*! Isn't it beautiful? It worked! My wish was granted!" Clapping her hands, Laila bounced in place like a rubber ball.

"I need your signature here, accepting delivery, ma'am," the man said with a cautionary glance at Zak. "We'll remove the old sign and install this one according to the specs on the order." He handed a pen to Laila.

As soon as she finished signing, a smaller truck pulled to the curb. Then another. And another.

During the next forty minutes, Laila met the representatives of a host of manufacturers, decorators, electricians, carpenters and other companies all on board to make The Great Pretender a reality. She was especially glad (almost as happy as Reen) to greet Hud Griffin, her new general contractor, who was understandably surprised as well as pleased to take on the task of renovating the bakery space to her exact specifications.

It was a dream team of first rate experts committed to fulfill her every whim—and it seemed they were all working overtime hours.

The last person at her door was Mr. Schmoll, a vice president from her bank. Handing her a slim portfolio, he introduced himself as the financial administrator for her newly established bake shop business as well as her personal accounts. He advised that, as per instructions, he'd taken care of the down payments for all of the professionals involved in completing her vision for The Great Pretender, and would manage the bill paying until all the work was finalized to Laila's satisfaction.

Laila could do little more than blink and gape, her mouth opening and closing like a fish.

"Your benefactor has sufficiently funded the account for purposes of the establishment and operation of your company," Mr. Schmoll explained. "A second account has been established for all your personal and household needs, Ms. Malone."

"My benefactor?"

"Yes." He selected a business card from his jacket's inner pocket and held it out to her. "Inanna of Sumer."

"Oh my God..."

Dead silent, Zak looked as stunned as Laila felt. When she clasped his arm she felt a tremor shimmer through him, or maybe the trembling sensation emanated from her.

Noticing the card was blank except for the name, Laila asked, "Is there any contact information?"

"No. Your benefactor stipulated strict confidentiality in regards to the release of any such information."

"Have you actually talked to Inanna?" Reen asked.

"No." The banker shook his head. "All correspondence has been through electronic means."

"Can you at least tell me if she has a phone number or an email address?" Laila pleaded.

"I'm sorry, Ms. Malone..."

After Mr. Schmoll left, Laila turned to Zak, smiling as she clasped his hands. "You know what this means, don't you? She's still out there, Zakkar. Inanna is still reachable. Once we find her we'll get her to free you, I know we will."

"I can't wait to tell Drake," Reen said excitedly, gathering her purse and car keys. "Now that we know Inanna still exists, he'll track her down. With all the university's resources and technology at his fingertips, it'll be a snap."

Zak's solemn expression telegraphed a distinct lack of enthusiasm. "Of course Inanna still exists. She is a goddess. Immortal. But she is elusive. Even if Drake locates her, she will not lower herself to answer the pleas of mere mortals."

"She hasn't encountered *these* mere mortals yet," Reen assured, thumbing herself and Laila. Friday added a supportive bark before giving Zak's hand a generous lick.

"Reen's right." Laila squeezed Zak's arm. "We won't take no for an answer."

"No, my love." Zak drew Laila close to his chest, smoothing his hand over her back. "You must not risk incensing Inanna. I briefly glimpsed her furious visage before I became a vapor. She is fierce. Powerful enough to smite you with a single breath. I could not bear to live with that memory for all eternity."

He wrapped an arm around Reen's shoulder, tugging her close as well. "Reen, my friend, you must not put yourself in harm's way for me. I ask for your solemn oath that you, Drake, and Laila will refrain from such perilous behavior."

"Okay, sure, you convinced me." Reen looked up into his dark gaze and sighed. "You have my solemn oath, Zak." She crossed her fingers, holding them behind her back and wiggling them for Laila to see. "Right, Laila?"

Laila smiled at her sister's childlike action, as well as her determination to help Zak. With one arm wrapped around Zak's waist, Laila crossed the fingers of that hand, waving them at Reen. "Absolutely. Solemn oath." She offered her most innocent smile as Friday licked her fingers.

Reen opened the door, stepping out onto the black and white mosaic tile entryway. "Wish I could stay longer but I need to finish a new batch of cute little animal-themed caps I'm knitting for the kids in the cancer ward. I'm volunteering at the hospital tomorrow morning."

"Before you go," Laila said, motioning for Reen to step back inside, "let's get those boxes of cookies packed up for the kids."

"Great! Thanks for remembering." Once they'd finished bringing the cookies to Reen's car, she waved. "Talk to you later, *Madame Bakery Owner.*" The last three words were loud enough for anyone in the vicinity to hear.

"Reen is like you," Zak told Laila as he watched Reen drive off. "A good woman with a big heart."

"I don't know what I'd do without her." Laila knew Reen would be filling Drake in about Inanna as soon as she got the opportunity. Hopefully the new information would aid the professor.

"Come," Zak clasped Laila's hand, "we will gather our things from your car, then make haste to your new bedroom suite." He paused, giving her the most beautiful heartfelt gaze. "Gods how I long to take you in my arms and never release you."

Laila drank in the perfection of the moment.

It didn't take long to bring the few belongings they'd taken from Bekka House into the building. Laila was nearly out of breath trying to keep up with Zak's pace.

"As I watched over you while you slept last night," he told her at the base of the staircase leading to her second floor apartment, "I burned with want." He started up the stairs, Laila in tow. "My loins raged with desire...with crushing need."

His deep commanding voice sent a warm thrill that coiled deep in her belly.

"How do you do that?" She hurried to keep up with his long strides as he climbed.

"What, little one?"

"Make my insides tremble with the mere utterance of a few words, all while I'm running up a flight of stairs."

He stopped on a stair and Laila crashed into him. It was like slamming into a boulder. She sucked in a deep breath, blowing it out with a whoosh. Zak flashed a confident smile as he stood angled toward her on the step above, his muscles standing out in touchable relief.

"The answer to your question is simple yet complex. While I could truthfully tell you it is because you are transfixed by my strong, hard body, which is evident, the real reason you tremble at my words is because you love me, as I love you. The power of love is mightier even than my saber."

Laila's lengthy responding sigh seemed to echo off the walls.

Lifting Laila into his arms, Zak took the rest of the stairs two at a time. Entering the master bedroom suite at the end of the long hallway, he kissed Laila before depositing her gently on the bed.

"We will celebrate the first night in your grand new dwelling with a bounty of love making."

Laila wrapped her arms around the delectable man hovering over her. "I can't think of a better way to celebrate my good fortune."

"No, I am the fortunate one. To celebrate, we will experiment with all the special implements from Provocative Pleasures."

"Oh...um...maybe not all of them." Laila chuckled. "Let's start slow and try out one or two of your, uh, special gadgets tonight."

"Your wish is my command." His loving gaze swept over her as his hands slid down her body, landing on her backside with a tender squeeze.

His face inches from hers, she heard his breath catch.

"Gods, little one, the things you do to me," he whispered. This kiss teemed with passion so intense, so possessive, it brought tears to her eyes. "Such a magnificent woman. *My* woman," he breathed.

"Yours alone," Laila whispered at his ear. "Forever, my darling genie." She wrapped her arms around his neck, clutching him close, never wanting to let him go.

Making love to Laila as if he'd never get the chance again, Zak whispered words of love to her in Sumerian.

"Your words are so beautiful." She rested her head on his shoulder once he'd shifted position.

"Beautiful words for a beautiful woman. Welcome to your new abode," he said against her ear, depositing a gentle kiss on her lobe. "I love you."

"I love you too," Laila told the incredible man who had become the other half of her soul.

Chapter 21

~<>~

THERE WAS A SOFT, steady pitter pat of rain during the night, serving as peaceful white noise as they slept, limbs tangled together. Laila awoke several times, pleased there was enough moonlight for her to glimpse the beating pulse in Zak's neck, to see his chest rise and fall with each breath. She loved feeling the warmth of his body next to her, to hear the gentle buzz of his snoring.

They were all confirmations that he was with her, alive and well and loving her as much as she loved him. She savored every moment they had left together.

Her thoughts drifted to her brand new status: a financially secure woman who owned the home of her dreams and the business of her heart. She knew it was real but it hadn't sunk in yet. She found herself reticent about getting out of bed to start the day because...well...what is it that well-heeled women do anyway? She really hadn't a clue. An unintentional sigh escaped her lips.

"Your mind is busy with thoughts of your new life," Zak said from behind her, kissing the nape of her neck and caressing her shoulder.

"That obvious, hmm?"

"It is understandable. I remember Abigail's similar quandary. She had no idea how to carry on after her first two wishes had been granted. She said she felt strangely unlike herself. It is the same for you?"

"Yes, I suppose that's it. I've never been wealthy before. I've always struggled financially." She turned to face Zak. "I'm still just me. Just plain Laila. What am I supposed to do? How do I act now that I have all this? It's all happened so fast. I-I guess I'm a little afraid I might do something wrong."

"First of all," Zak's hand traveled from her shoulder to her wrist and back in a calming motion, "you are not *just plain Laila*. There is nothing plain about you, my love. Once you are fully awake and start your day, things will fall into place as they did for Abigail. She adapted to her new role within a day or two."

Resisting the potent urge to pull the covers over her head and hide from her amazing new circumstances, Laila pulled herself to a sitting position and Zak followed, each of them yawning while they stretched.

The thought of being afraid to face the day because she was rich now filled her with amusement. How ridiculous could she possibly get? Here she'd been blessed with the gift of these two fabulous wishes and she was wasting precious time worrying because she no longer had money problems.

Aw, poor baby.

She used the pillow to muffle her inadvertent giggle.

Wrapping his hand around her arm, Zak asked, "You are all right?"

"Sometimes I crack myself up," she answered, swinging her legs over the side of the mattress and scooting to the edge.

"Please tell me this is merely a phrase and you are not in danger of cracking due to the stress of too much joy."

His sweet concern only had her laughing more. The bout of laughter felt good, like an all over relaxation massage, inside and out, helping her release the tension.

"Aside from feeling more than a little silly, I'm perfectly fine," Laila assured, leaning over to cup his chin and plant a kiss on his jaw. "I'm ready to start the day as the brand new non-plain Laila."

Raiding her new refrigerator and room-sized pantry in her spacious new kitchen, they enjoyed toasted English muffins topped with butter and orange marmalade, and a couple strips of thick-sliced bacon on the side. Rich coffee with real cream and sugar, and mimosas made with fresh-squeezed oranges and pricey champagne rounded out the first breakfast in their new home.

As time passed she felt herself growing more confident, her mind racing with all the wonderful, positive things she wanted to do.

After breakfast, Laila and Zak made a trip to Bekka House to gather what she'd need until movers could haul over the rest. The shattered living room picture window was boarded up so she knew Hudson Griffin had already been there.

While she packed items to take, Hud pulled up in his *Griffin of all Trades* company vehicle, complete with its griffin logo. They talked while Zak carried boxes to Laila's car. Hud told her he'd arranged to have a crew at Bekka House today and through the week to fix everything.

She suppressed a smile as a group of high school girls walked by, all flirty and giggly. Between Zak's and Hud's considerable charms and well-muscled physiques, it was no wonder the girls' hormones were on high alert. Like Zak, Hud barely seemed to notice the attention.

Gard was due back soon from his latest glaciologist job in Antarctica. Laila wanted to have Bekka House ready for him, free of any electrical hazards. She hoped he'd be back in time to meet Zak. She knew they'd hit it off well.

As Laila and Zak drove back to Ocean Charm Boulevard, she spotted her building and its new The Great Pretender sign over the doorway. She still couldn't believe she'd actually be living in this beautiful Victorian era brick building with her very own thriving bakery business on the premises.

"I think I'm going to like being rich, Zak," Laila said as they headed back to her car after carrying another load inside. "Do you realize how many people I can help?" She opened the car's trunk, breathing a sigh of relief to see it would be their last trip. She'd had more exercise packing and carrying boxes back and forth this morning than she'd had in months.

"I am not surprised to hear you focus on benevolence." His arms full, Zak leaned over to give her a peck on the cheek as they strolled up the sidewalk to her building with the last couple of boxes.

Once they'd climbed the steps and entered her apartment, Laila's phone rang with her mother's ringtone. She set the box down on the coffee table and dug in her purse for the phone.

"Hi, Mom, what's—" Before she had a chance to finish, Laila was hit with a barrage of questions. "I'm at home, why? What do you mean, no I'm not? I'm standing right here in the living room as we speak. No, of course not, why would I lie, Mom?"

Astrid Malone Thorkelson's next words had Laila succumbing to an all over shudder. "What!?" Drawing in an audible gasp, her anxious gaze flew to Zak. "When did you arrive? I thought you and Tore were going to be in Norway at least another month."

Laila's mind skyrocketed into panic mode. Her mother informed her that Laila's sister, Delaney, and her husband, Varik, just arrived home from their honeymoon on a different flight. The four of them left the airport together and were now parked outside Bekka House, which was having the front window replaced while a parade of construction workers were tramping in and out of the house.

"Your stepfather and I just talked to Hudson Griffin," her mother said.

Ohmigod...ohmigod...ohmigod...

"Hud told us there's a construction crew in the kitchen removing aluminum foil from the walls while electricians work on fixing all the outlets. *And*," Astrid added powerful emphasis to the word, "we had to hear from Hud that our daughter has moved. Laila Jane Malone, what in the hell is going on?"

Damn. Laila thought she'd have another month to come up with explanations about her new home and business and, she gulped, her new genie.

"Oh that..." A volley of nervous laughter bubbled forth. "Well, yeah, I did just sort of move. In fact, I'm still moving. Believe it or not I was just about to call you and Tore to tell you all about it." More nervous laughter, which wasn't helping any because if her mother had any doubt about Laila lying, she sure as hell knew it for sure now.

Astrid asked the next logical question, which Laila parroted back to her.

"To where?" Naturally Laila would have to come clean. She couldn't possibly keep her new address from her own parents...could she? "Um...no, money isn't so tight that I had to rent out Bekka House and move to an apartment, Mom." Laila nearly choked on the gush of ironic laughter threating to spill forth.

"When we talked the other day I told you I was fine. Remember?" Even to her own ears her declaration of assurance didn't sound convincing. "My new address?" Her heart thumped wildly. "You and Tore must be suffering from jetlag something awful right now. Delaney and Varik must be exhausted too. Why don't you all just relax today and get a good night's sleep and then tomorrow...or," she cleared her throat, "maybe the next day, we can get together and—"

Closing her eyes in a long blink, Laila listened to her mother's concerned harangue. She was worried something terrible had happened and Laila was afraid to tell her. She'd also called Reen only to have Reen tell her she couldn't say anything, other than not to worry because everything was fine.

"I'm not stalling," Laila lied. "My boyfriend?" Her gaze shifted to Zak again who was carrying books into the walnut paneled library. *Her* library. "Yes, we're living together but—" It had reached the point where Laila realized she could no longer hold her mom off. She relented and gave her mother her new address.

Rolling her eyes skyward, Laila prepared to face the rest of her mom's interrogation. Once Astrid realized her daughter was living in the historic building just steps from the ocean, she'd have a bazillion more questions.

Laila heard the four of them discussing the Ocean Charm Boulevard address, certain it must be wrong.

"Yes, Mom, I'm positive that's the address. No," Laila made a raspberry sound, "I'm not renting a room in a boarding house. I'm in the same building where the Crowe sisters had their bakery. No, my boyfriend doesn't own the building. I..." she swallowed hard, "I own it."

The other end was silent for so long Laila became alarmed. "Hello? Mom?" From what she could hear, they were all jabbering together. A moment later Astrid was back on the line. "No, Mom, Zak's not in the mob. No, he's not a drug dealer. A crooked politician? Seriously, Mom, where do you come up with this stuff?"

She plowed her hand through her hair as Astrid informed her they'd all be at the new address within the hour.

Shoulders slumped and feeling ten years older, Laila ended the call. Groaning, she looked up at Zak. "My mom and Tore are on the way here now with Delaney and Varik, my sister and brother-in-law. None of them know anything about you."

"Excellent! I am eager to meet them and get acquainted."

Before she could reply, her phone rang again. She wasn't surprised it was Reen.

"Mom and Tore are back in town," Reen blurted in a rush. "Delaney and Varik are with them. Mom's been trying to reach you and was worried when you didn't pick up. You'll never guess where they were when she called."

"I know. I just hung up with Mom. The four of them are on their way here. I didn't hear the phone earlier because we were moving boxes and I left my purse in the car's trunk until we got back here. Reen, what am I going to do? How am I ever going to explain..." she looked around, flapping her arms, "all this? Not to mention the fact that I'm shacking up with a genie."

"I'll call Drake to see if he's available and we'll come over."

"Thank you. Maybe they won't think I've lost my mind with you two here to back me up."

"This is our super-protective mom we're talking about, Laila. No matter who's there supporting you, this isn't gonna be easy. See you soon."

"Thanks for the encouraging words," Laila muttered to herself after ending the call.

"Your family will be so happy for you when they see your new home and business. Your mother will be free of worrywarting when she learns I am here to protect you."

A dozen possible scenarios of Zak and her parents meeting swept across Laila's mind. None of them positive.

"You can wipe that grin off your face, Zak, because the proverbial shit is about to hit the fan." Holding up her hand, Laila clarified, "That means you and I have a hell of a lot of explaining to do once everyone arrives." Looking her genie up and down, she sighed. "And I've got to do a massive amount of coaching before you open your mouth in front of them."

~<>~

"Whoa..." Drake craned his neck as he stepped over the threshold of Laila's new apartment. "You weren't kidding, Reen. This is like something out of Architectural Digest." He turned his awestruck expression toward Laila. "I'd say you most definitely have arrived!"

"I still can't believe it myself. Wait'll you see the whole place, Drake. It goes on forever. It's got secret passages, hidden rooms, and a wine cellar too—all in addition to my big, beautiful bakery downstairs." Laila paused, sucking in a deep breath. "But all that's gotta wait. Thank you guys *so* much for coming." She pulled them into a hug. "They'll all freak out when they see this place." Laila looked behind them. "Where are your kids, Drake?"

"I dropped them off at my mom's. Where's Zak?"

"In there." Laila absently pointed to the set of double doors off the vestibule.

"Her massive walnut-paneled library," Reen clarified with a lift of her eyebrow.

"Wow..."

Laila had never seen Drake gawk before.

"Zak's practicing. I gave him all sorts of instructions." She held up crossed fingers. "Here's hoping he remembers everything."

Zak exited the library, Friday prancing along at his heels. "It is good to see you, my friends!" He shook Drake's hand and patted Reen on the back. "Today is the day I meet the Thorkelsons and the Jenssens!"

"He's really excited," Laila said. "Drake, I'm depending on you to help convince them that Zak's the real deal."

"Once your brother-in-law hears about Zakkar's time with the Vikings," Drake said, "that should be a big help. Who better to know about such things than a professor of Scandinavian Studies, right?"

"I hope so." Laila nodded. "Reen, you need to help me work on Mom."

"Of course." Reen squeezed her hand. "Don't worry, everything's going to be fine. Now take a deep breath and try to relax, Laila. You look like you're about to jump out of your skin."

"That obvious, huh?" Laila asked.

"Do not worry," Zak told Reen and Drake with confidence. "I have been coached." Counting on his fingers, he said, "I will blend in. I will not attract attention to myself. I will not speak unless spoken to. I will watch Laila for warning signs as I speak, and do my best to interpret her eye signals."

He mimed some of the indicators Laila had shown him, such as one eye narrowed, both eyes narrowed, big wide eyes, and eyebrows arrowed down in anger.

"You see? I have learned them all."

Covering her mouth, Reen dissolved into giggles.

Drake couldn't keep from laughing either. "Welcome to the modern world, Zakkar. You've just had a crash course in The Look."

"It is not unfamiliar. The women of my time could turn men into pillars of salt with naught but a single threatening glance." He offered his rendition of The Look once again.

Squelching the urge to join the others in laughter, Laila said, "Come on guys, I need you to be serious. I need you to—"

The elaborate chime of her new doorbell sounded and Laila felt the blood drain from her veins.

"Oh boy. Oh boy, oh boy, oh boy..." Her mouth suddenly dry, she said, "Zak, you and Drake wait in the library until it's time to come out. Take Friday with you."

Wrapping an arm around Laila's shoulder as she walked with her to the intercom, Reen assured her sister, "It's going to be all right. Breathe, Laila. *Breathe!*"

Sucking in a fortifying breath, Laila nodded. At the intercom she greeted them and buzzed them in so they'd be coming directly up the alternate staircase rather than walking through the bakery to get to Laila's apartment.

As they reached the second floor, Laila stood at her threshold, doing her utmost to appear cheery. And normal.

"Mom! Tore! It's so great to see you!" She yanked them into hugs, clutching tight, but not half as tight as the death grip Astrid had as she clung to her daughter. "Really, really great. I missed you both."

"Laila, sweetheart, it's so good to hold you. I've been so worried." Her mom sounded as if Laila had just been rescued from a hostage crisis.

Once her mother's bear hug eased up enough to steal a breath, Laila said, "I wish you wouldn't worry so much, Mom. I told you I'm fine. I feel terrible that you flew home ahead of schedule because of me. You and Tore are supposed to be relaxing and enjoying your retirement."

"You're far more important to me than any vacation." Astrid smoothed her hand over Laila's face, finger-combing her hair like she was a toddler again. "A mother can tell when she's needed."

"But—"

"You know your mother." Tore gave a resigned smile. "There's no way she's not going to be here for her little girl if she thinks there might be the slightest hint of a problem."

She always felt better having Tore's calming influence around when her mom was seized by trauma mode. He usually knew how to bring Astrid back to a semi-unruffled state.

"*This* is your apartment?" her sister, Delaney, asked, clearly astounded as she stepped inside and looked around, absently accepting a hug from Reen. Varik came in right after her, looking as astonished as Laila would expect.

"No...it can't be," Astrid said. "This place would cost..." Her eyebrows knitted together. "You said you own it?" Her expression was beyond incredulous.

Laila had never seen her mother so dumbfounded. "I-I know it's a little hard to believe."

"A little?" Tore gave a low whistle as he took in the lavish surroundings. "My stepdaughter's living in a high end apartment across from the Pacific Ocean on Ocean Charm Boulevard. Did you win the lottery?"

"Not exactly." Laila's shoulder lifted into a shrug. "But close." Her nervous giggles sounded like machine gun fire. "I'll make us some coffee and tell you all about it."

"The floor is marble," a distracted Delaney noted as she scanned the sizeable foyer.

"Good Lord," Astrid clutched Tore's sleeve, "look at this place. Have you ever seen anything like it? Only in the movies," she answered her own question. "And, my God, that massive crystal chandelier..." Swinging her attention back to her daughter, she said, "Young lady, you've got a lot of explaining to do."

"Mom, Tore, welcome home!" Reen gave them a quick hug and kiss once Laila stepped aside. "See, Mom? I told you Laila was fine. Better than fine, actually."

Laila watched as her mom and Delaney leaned to the right while Tore and Varik leaned to the left of Reen, straining for a better look at Drake and Zak, who'd both just exited the library.

"Hello Drake and...?" Astrid said, her eyebrows arcing.

"Oh..." More rapid fire giggles. "Everybody, this is Zak, my, um, boyfriend." Laila watched as Zak looked to them, then back at Laila, then did it all over again. It finally dawned on her that she'd told Zak to keep quiet unless she gave him the high sign.

"Say hello, Zak," she said with a nod indicating permission, aware it probably sounded like he was her ventriloquist's dummy.

"Hello." He offered a charming smile and extended his hand first to Tore, then to Varik. "I am very glad to meet you, Mr. and Mrs. Thorkelson and Mr. and Mrs. Jenssen. I have heard many good things about you all," he said while Laila absently mouthed the words along with him as he spoke. So far so good. Thanks to Zak's astounding memory, he'd said exactly what Laila had instructed.

Extending a hand to Astrid, Zak said, "It is a pleasure to meet you, Mrs. Thorkelson. I hope you and Mr. Thorkelson had a good trip back home from Norway."

"None of that Mr. and Mrs. stuff," Laila's stepdad said. "Call us Tore and Astrid."

"And please, call us Delaney and Varik." Delaney motioned to herself and her new husband.

"Thank you." Zak bowed.

Everything was going according to plan, except for the unrehearsed little bow Zak tacked on. But no big deal.

Friday wiggled his way between Astrid and Tore, licking Tore's hand.

"*Fredag, se hvor stor du har vokst!*" Tore said in Norwegian. "*Du ser akkurat ut som din bestefar, Torsdag.*"

Leaning close to Zak, Drake elbowed him, whispering something and Zak nodded.

"Friday, look how big you've grown!" Zak said, translating Tore's words. "You look just like your father, Thursday."

Tore's eyebrows shot up in surprise. "You speak Norwegian?"

"Some." Zak nodded. "From the time I spent in Norway."

"Well, well, well." Tore and Varik beamed smiles.

Oh good. Breathing a little easier, Laila said, "Come into the dining room and sit down." As she led them into the grand room with its long, imposing carved table, sparkling crystal chandelier, walnut wainscoting, and beautiful built-ins with leaded glass doors, Laila watched their heads craning the same way she'd done when she first saw the interior of the magnificent apartment.

A reverent "Wow..." was chorused by the four visitors.

"Whose furniture is this?" Astrid smoothed her hand across the ornately carved dining room chair. "It looks like it costs a fortune."

"Oh, it's...it's mine." Laila's smile stretched impossibly wide as her head bobbed. "Zak, why don't you help me in the kitchen?" It was the best way to keep him from suffering the third degree and risk him saying something suspect.

"Of course. I'd be happy to," Zak answered, as they'd rehearsed. "Excuse me," he said to everyone before bowing again.

"Reen, dear," Astrid held a hand up urging Zak to stay put, "why don't you give your sister a hand instead? That way we can get to know Zak better."

"No!" Reen and Laila chorused before exchanging frazzled looks.

All eyes were on Laila and Reen as the skittish pair erupted into a round of staccato laughter.

"Go ahead." Drake nodded at them, the steady voice of encouragement. "It'll be fine."

Wringing her hands, Laila said, "But—"

"Don't worry," Tore assured. "I promise I won't let your mother subject Zak to water torture in your absence." His casual smile was reassuring.

The tawny glow of Zak's face blanched. "Water torture is common practice when meeting a girlfriend's parents?"

"Only if you have something to hide." Astrid pinned Zak with distrustful look.

With a stiff glance Laila's way, Zak said, "You neglected to mention this in your briefing, Laila."

Pinching the bridge of her nose, Laila murmured, "Great. Just great."

"Mom's just kidding," Reen assured.

"I see." Zak visibly relaxed. "Do not worry, Laila. Go make coffee. I remember my coaching." He gave a thumbs up and Laila felt like the air had been let out of her tires.

Varik covered his mouth, muffling laughter. "Sounds like Zak's a fast learner."

"So, Zak," Tore said, "how long ago were you in Norway?"

Zak looked thoughtful for a moment. "About twelve hundred years ago."

Tore's face fell.

Astrid gasped.

Varik and Delaney exchanged alarmed expressions.

And Laila gave Zak The Look.

Dragging the mega-stressed Laila by the elbow, Reen urged, "Come on. You may as well just let this happen naturally."

"But—" Releasing a reconciled sigh, Laila mumbled unintelligent garble as she followed her sister to the kitchen. "You really think it's okay to leave Zak in there without me? They probably think he's crazy. Maybe dangerous."

"It'll be fine." Reen stood in front of the ornate brass coffeemaker, ogling its many buttons and levers. "I've never seen anything like this. Looks like you need a barista degree to operate it."

"Zak and I used the little single-cup espresso maker this morning because we couldn't figure out how to work this behemoth." Laila trilled a lengthy sigh. "Reen, there's no way Mom's going to believe—"

"Laila, relax." Reen's hand glided up and down her sister's back in a calming motion. "Once Drake explains I'm sure Mom will deal with this really well. And you know Delaney, with her trusting nature, won't be any problem. Drake will convince Tore and Varik, they'll get caught up in their professor-speak, then, with Delaney's help, they'll all convince Mom." Reen brushed her hands together. "Piece of cake."

"You what?!" Astrid's screeching voice had no trouble reaching across the vast expanse between the dining room and kitchen.

Laila and Reen exchanged apprehensive grimaces.

A minute later, Astrid blurted, "He's what!?"

Laila's knees knocked. "I'd better go out there and—"

"Coffee," Reen reminded her. "With Kahlua, Baileys, and a shot of whiskey. We'll liquor them up good." She cracked a laugh and Laila joined her as they headed to the pantry, ready to engage in some creative mixology.

~<>~

Zakkar was proud of himself. He'd done a fine job following Laila's implicit instructions. As he had reminded Laila, he was unable to lie. She coached him not to offer any information unless he was asked. It was working out quite well.

"Five thousand years old?" Astrid gave him a dubious look after he'd answered her question. "That's the most ridiculous thing I ever heard. You're either insane or on drugs." Her eye narrowed. "Or both."

"There's no reason to jump to conclusions." Delaney patted her mother's hand.

Zakkar watched Astrid give her daughter the same foreboding look Laila had given him before heading for the kitchen.

He sat silent, just as Laila had instructed. It was difficult not to offer explanation until he was asked, but he was sure Laila knew best when it came to her family. So he simply smiled at Astrid's incorrect assumptions.

"Aren't you going to respond?" Astrid asked. "No explanation as to how a man supposedly thousands of years old suddenly becomes my daughter's boyfriend?"

"If you ask me a question I will gladly answer it," Zakkar said helpfully. It was clear he was winning the trust of her mother with each calm word he spoke.

Folding her arms across her chest, Astrid asked, "How did you meet my daughter?"

"It was when she opened the bottle in which I was imprisoned thousands of years ago."

Astrid's jaw dropped. Zakkar noted she seemed to do that a lot, much like Laila.

"You what?!" she yelped.

"Oh my God..." Delaney's head dropped to her hand.

He could see where Laila got her attractive looks. While Astrid's hair was blonde and Delaney's was black as coal, Laila's was more the color of walnuts. They all shared the same lapis blue eye color, except for Reen, whose eyes had a green hue.

Tore and Varik, who had Norwegian accents, had golden hair and their eyes were more of an ocean blue. They were tall, sturdy men who, Zakkar imagined, women would find handsome. Unlike Laila's mother, the men seemed to take things in stride.

"I know how it sounds," Drake told Astrid, "but Zakkar's telling the truth. He's not crazy or on drugs. The man is a bona fide genie."

"He's what!?"

"Calm down, Astrid." Tore patted his wife's back but she shrugged him off. "Let Drake and Zak tell us about it before you get all riled up."

"Riled up? Seriously, Tore?"

Astrid looked at her husband as if he'd transformed into The Dragon of Babylon, with a serpent's head, forelegs of a lion, hind legs of an eagle, and long wriggling serpentine tail. Without doubt, she'd just given Tore The Look.

"Professor Slattery and Laila's boyfriend are trying to convince us this guy is a genie. A *genie*, Tore!"

She turned to Zakkar with a narrow-eyed glare similar to an expression Laila had given him before. Clearly, the women of Laila's family made ample use of The Look.

"You want us to believe that you," Astrid twirled her hand in the air, "whirled up out of a bottle in a vaporous stream."

"Yes." Zakkar smiled, relieved Laila's mother was closer to understanding the situation. "Exactly."

"Wow..." Delaney muttered.

"Drake," Astrid said, to be met with Drake's shrug.

"Tore? Varik?" Astrid shifted her focus to her husband and son-in-law, who mirrored Drake.

"I don't know what to say," Tore admitted.

"While it sounds impossible," Varik said to Delaney, "you and I, of all people, should believe in the power of magic," lifting his wife's chin with his finger, Varik gazed into her eyes, "after what happened to us." Varik's other hand rested across the small bump of her belly. It appeared she was with child.

Looking down at her hand, Delaney nodded, twisting the ring on her finger. "Our heartwishes." She rested her hand over her husband's.

Zakkar's gaze settled on Delaney's ring. He noticed Varik wore one nearly identical. The lustrous stone at the center of each ring appeared to be matching, broken halves.

"I had a feeling the ring was meant for Laila next," Delaney said, almost as if talking to herself, "I just didn't know when. Grandma Bekka told me I'd know when the time was right to pass it on." She held her hand aloft, turning it back and forth, then turned to her husband. "Remember when I told you the stone was glowing the other day?" Varik nodded. "By this morning," Delaney smiled, "I knew...I felt it. It's time."

Varik leaned close, kissing his wife's cheek before cupping her chin and gazing into her eyes with a loving expression. "As long as you let your heart guide you, you can't go wrong. That's what our angels told us." Varik gazed at his own ring, "Remember?"

Her fair face a reflection of her husband's affectionate expression, Delaney gave a slow nod. Her smile reached her eyes as she said, "I remember, darling. I remember."

They exchanged a brief kiss which touched Zakkar's heart. It must have done the same for Astrid because he heard her sigh. Their love for each other was evident. How easily he could picture himself and Laila sharing the same depth of love together if circumstances were different.

He wondered if both couples at the table realized how fortunate they were to share such timeless devotion.

He liked Laila's family. Like Drake, these were good people. When the time came for him to return to the bottle he would be comforted in the knowledge that his beloved Laila would be surrounded by loved ones. They would help her through her time of grief.

"Tell me more." Tore's words transported Zakkar's thoughts back to the moment. "About your time in Norway."

"I want to hear this too," Varik said.

Astrid huffed a humorless laugh.

"It seems you picked up some of the language during your visit" Tore noted. "Were you there long?"

"A brief but memorable time."

"So...would you understand if I told you..." Tore held Zakkar's gaze as he uttered a warning in Norwegian.

"Tore!" Astrid, who spoke fluent Norwegian, reprimanded. His eyes still on Zakkar, Tore patted his wife's arm.

Zakkar couldn't help smiling. "Absolutely," he answered. Making direct eye contact with Tore, Zakkar translated. "You said, 'if you ever do anything to hurt Laila, Zakkar, I'll break every bone in your body.'"

Zakkar replied to Laila's stepfather in Norwegian.

"What did he say?" Delaney asked Varik.

"Exactly the answer he wanted to hear," Varik answered with a smile.

Maintaining eye contact with Zakkar, a slight smile settled at the corners of Tore's mouth. It was accompanied by an almost imperceptible nod of acceptance. "Zak told me, 'though I am not able to die, sir, should I ever harm even a hair on Laila's head I will hand you my saber to exact untold torture upon me.'"

"Honestly, is all that bloodthirsty bravado really necessary, gentlemen?" Astrid asked, clearly displeased.

"How utterly romantic." Delaney expelled a sigh.

"It is getting a little heated in here." Drake loosened his collar. "Ladies?" he called to the kitchen. "What the heck are you doing, roasting the beans? Is that coffee about ready yet?"

"Almost," Reen called back. "This fancy coffeemaker is complicated. I'm counting on you to hold it together until we get in there, Drake."

Zakkar noted Reen's reply failed to instill confidence in Drake whose complexion had paled.

"Why don't you tell them about your time among the Vikings?" Drake suggested. "Varik is Professor of Scandinavian Studies at Wisdom Harbor University." Addressing Varik and Tore, Drake said, "Trust me. You're going to find this fascinating."

"And that would be your visit to Norway twelve hundred years ago?" Tore asked Zakkar, tongue firmly in cheek.

Zakkar nodded. "It would."

A single eyebrow arched. "Mmm-hmm."

Zakkar felt the heat of the man's careful scrutiny.

"I want to hear this." Delaney scooted forward in her chair.

"Oh come on, wait a minute." After doing something with her phone, Astrid held it up, with the calculator facing out. "You're talking about the year 800?"

"Approximately," Zakkar offered with a smile. It was getting easier all the time.

With an obvious look of mistrust, Astrid shook her head from side to side. "I'm sorry, that's not possible." Clasping her husband's arm, she cautioned Tore, "Remember, anyone can do research about life in Viking times."

"We'll see. Drake believes him, honey, and he's no fool."

"I believe him too," Delaney offered, folding her hands on the table and giving Zakkar her rapt attention.

"Yes but you're so trusting you believe anybody about anything," Astrid told her daughter.

"She's got you there, sweetheart." Varik offered his wife a wink. Leaning forward with a look of frank curiosity, he rested his elbows on the table, giving Zakkar his undivided attention. "Go ahead, Zak. Convince us you were really there."

"Ridiculous," Astrid muttered, crossing her arms over her chest as a disbelieving smirk settled on her lips.

Zakkar understood. He had seen this very reaction hundreds of times before. He was also familiar with the expressions of astonishment when people finally accepted what he told them as truth. Closing his eyes, he focused on his long ago time with the Vikings.

"My possessor was Sigrid, a Viking girl of thirteen," Zakkar began. "She found my bottle amidst cargo on a longboat. She was about to be married to a man not of her choosing, selected by the family chief to be her husband."

Amid a flurry of questions from Varik and Tore over the next several minutes, Zakkar gave them a full account of daily life among the Vikings, including many lesser known particulars.

"Damn!" Sitting back against his seat, Varik slapped the tabletop, a look of astonishment across his features. "Damn!" he said again. "Everything he said is spot on."

"Of course it was," Delaney said flicking her wrist.

"Didn't I tell you?" Drake sat forward. "Ask him about any location or time period he's experienced and he can tell you things most scholars don't even know."

"I don't understand." Astrid rested her elbows on the table, folded hands supporting her chin. She was studying Zakkar with such intensity it felt as though she was trying to glimpse his very soul. "How could you possibly know all that?"

With a confident smile, Zakkar replied, "Because I was there."

"What happened to Sigrid?" Varik asked.

"The last of her wishes was for wealth because her family's circumstances and outlook for the future were so bleak, with little food and insufficient clothing."

Zakkar watched everyone's eyes grow wide. "Wishes?" they said in unison, their gazes alight with curiosity and surprise.

Enjoying their states of wonderment at this revelation, he explained, "Each possessor is allowed three wishes within a period of six lunar cycles."

Taking in his surroundings with renewed interest, Tore smiled at Astrid. "This property must have been one of Laila's wishes."

Astrid craned her neck, studying the dining room and its stately furnishings. "She's always loved this building with all its Victorian trim."

"Even Laila's dollhouse was Victorian style," Delaney reminded her mother.

"The more gingerbready the better, inside and out," Astrid recalled with a fond smile.

"Just like her mother." Tore grinned as he gazed at all the ornamentation in the room. "Astrid's never been a fan of minimalism. Most of our moving costs from Chicago came from her endless boxes of, ahem..." he hung air quotes, "*treasures*."

Astrid offered an agreeing smile. "Guilty as charged."

"I must take you on a tour of the house," Zakkar offered, feeling safer now, speaking without being asked a question first. "The bathrooms with their elaborate toilets are akin to throne rooms!"

"Really?" Tore, Varik and Drake chorused, riveted by Zakkar's further description of the lavish bathrooms.

"Bathrooms like throne rooms indeed." Astrid huffed a chuckle.

"That's men for you." Delaney shrugged.

Zakkar watched with relief as Astrid's expression transformed from one of antagonism to one of acceptance.

"I truly enjoyed your stories," Zakkar told Delaney honestly, remembering the *Delaney's Diary* book he'd read on Laila's Kindle the night he'd watched over her as she slept. He was surprised when Laila told him her sister had written the charming stories, and decided this was probably a good time to let Delaney know he'd read them.

She seemed puzzled. "My stories?"

"*Delaney's Diary*, the book with humorous stories about your experiences."

"Really?" Her hand rested at her throat as Delaney's expression of puzzlement transformed into one of delighted surprise. "You read one of my books?" Her full, down-to-earth smile reminded Zakkar of Laila's and he knew he'd made the right decision to mention he'd read the woman's book. Anything he could do to win over Laila's family would be a step in the right direction.

Varik chuckled.

Tsking at her husband, Delaney elevated her chin. "And just what are you snickering at?"

"I was counting up all the points Zak scored with that." Varik tossed Zakkar a wink, further confirming the wisdom of Zakkar's strategy to get on her family's good side.

"Reading it," Zakkar told her, "made me feel as if I knew all of your family."

"Why thank you, Zak." Delaney's cheeks took on a pink luster and her smile held steady. "The books are collections of my newspaper columns."

"My daughter has a wonderful way with words," Astrid said. "Of course, she's been known to embellish facts so keep that in mind when you read anything she's written about," she cleared her throat, "me, for instance." She offered a tentative smile.

"I'm so glad you enjoyed *Delaney's Diary*, Zak. There's nothing better than getting positive feedback from my readers."

With a broad smile directed at Zakkar, Varik licked the tip of his index finger and drew a vertical mark in the air. Delaney elbowed him in return.

A moment later, Laila and Reen came into the dining room carrying trays with coffee and cookies.

Zakkar was sure Laila would be pleased.

~<>~

"Soooo..." Laila set filled mugs in front of her mom and sister while Reen saw to the men. "How's everything going in here?"

Boasting a smile, Varik said, "I could talk to this guy for days."

"That's just how I feel," Tore agreed.

"He's a walking, talking fount of knowledge," Drake said.

Her posture relaxing, Laila took a seat at the table.

"I am almost as good as Google," Zak offered.

"Ooh, I almost forgot." Snapping her fingers, Laila popped up from her seat. "There's something I want you all to see." She went to the library, returning a few moments later with Zak's box and bottle, as well as the old photograph of him with Abigail. The four who hadn't seen the items before were suitably impressed. Amazed is more like it as they examined the artifacts.

"Mom?" Laila turned a hopeful glance at her mother.

"What can I say?" Astrid offered an apologetic shrug. "I'm sorry, Zak."

Looking uncertain, Zak asked, "But why?"

"For the way I treated you earlier. It's only because I was worried about Laila. I didn't believe you." She darted a repentant glance to Laila. "Or my daughter. But, as unbelievable as it seems, you, young man, appear to be the real deal."

Spotting the sincere smile her mother offered Zak, Laila breathed easier.

"Told you so." Delaney raised her hand.

"See Mom? I told you everything was fine." Regarding her mother over the rim of her mug, Laila smiled. Evidencing the effects of all the spiked coffee sipping she and Reen did in the kitchen, Laila hiccupped, then giggled. Reen followed a moment later.

Sniffing the contents of her mug, Astrid gave Laila a knowing look, which had Laila offering an expression of feigned innocence.

"Trying to get us loaded, hmm?"

"Maybe just a little," Laila admitted.

"You owe me no apology, Mrs. Thorkelson," Zak began. "I completely—"

"Call me Astrid. Please." She took a sip from her mug, making a satisfied murmur.

"Astrid." Zak's features relaxed. "I fully understand your concern for your daughter."

"Zak felt the presence of the ghosts at Bekka House," Laila said.

"That's no surprise," Delaney said. "Zak's seems very intuitive."

"He said Grandma Bekka briefly appeared to him, looking like she does in that photo we have of her when she was young," Laila went on. "He said she looked like an angel." She glanced at Zak and they exchanged smiles.

"Oh..." Delaney's eyes brimmed with tears and her hand flew to her heart. "You have no idea how happy that makes me. Grandma was so important to me."

"He felt the presence of your grandfather, too," Laila told Varik.

Looking alert, Varik's face lit with gladness at the mention of the man who raised him. "Grandpa Anders?"

"Yes." Her brother-in-law's delighted expression had Laila smiling. "And that's not all," she addressed her mother and Delaney. "Zak identified a third ghost as Grandma's husband, Jamie."

"The grandfather we never had a chance to meet," Reen said.

"My dad..." Astrid's smile was wistful. "Oh that makes me so happy."

Tore covered Astrid's hand with his. "They're watching over all of us," he said, leaning over to kiss her cheek.

"Before we go any further," Astrid said, "there's something I want to do." Getting up from the table, she went to the coffee table where she'd left her purse. "That old photo of Zak and Abigail reminded me."

Laila and her sisters shared a knowing smile.

"Here comes the Kodak," Reen said, pretending she had the camera in hand, taking a shot.

"Time for a Kodak moment," Delaney added, chuckling.

Astrid returned, small camera in hand. "Okay, now I want all of you to squeeze together so I can get some good shots of you all."

Laughing as she complied, Laila said, "Honestly, Mom, you need to get with the times and use your phone."

"Ha! Forget about it." Delaney gave a dismissive wave.

Astrid gave her camera a fond look. "This Kodak Instamatic is what your father and I used to take all our family photos while you grew up, remember?"

Glancing at each other, her smiling daughters nodded.

"How could we ever forget?" Reen said with affection.

"I don't know, maybe it's silly but..." Astrid studied the camera in her hands, "there's something special about this old camera...and about holding an actual photograph in your hands, then keeping it in an album. So you young people," she waved toward them with the back of her hand, "can all keep taking photos with your phone cameras. I'm sticking with my trusty vintage model."

"You have the ability to take photographs such as the one of Abigail and me?" Zak asked.

Nodding, Astrid proudly replied, "And mine are in color."

"May I request one of these to keep for myself?"

"Of course, Zak. You can have copies of all the photos I take today if you like." Astrid gave him a warm smile. "I want to get a few of just you and Laila together too. I think you'd like to have those especially."

"Very much. I would tuck them away in my clothing before returning to the bottle." Zak's loving gaze turned to Laila. "It would be most wonderful to keep an image of my beautiful Laila with me for all eternity."

With the exception of Astrid and Delaney's shallow gasps, the room was silent from the impact of Zak's compelling words. Breathing deep, Laila did her best not to start bawling like a baby. She didn't want upset Zak or to ruin this special day with an ugly cry.

After sipping from her second cup of coffee, Astrid broke the silence, saying, "I want to hear all about this apartment, that big The Great Pretender sign over the bakery and," she smiled at Laila, "our daughter's three wishes."

The group sat around the table for the next hour as Tore, Astrid, Delaney and Varik were filled in on what had happened since Laila and Reen's visit to the estate sale.

"Have you thought about what you're going to tell the townspeople when they ask about your new home and business?" Tore asked. "I doubt anyone in Glassfloat Bay's going to believe you made enough as a TBT weight loss counselor to be able to afford all this." He sported a wide grin.

"I hadn't thought of that," Astrid said. "I can just imagine all the questions. How will we ever explain it? We certainly can't tell people Laila found a genie."

"We can say Zakkar's a wealthy benefactor," Drake suggested.

"You mean like a pimp?" Reen joked between sips of spiked coffee.

"You can tell people I am the man Laila will marry. Her fiancé, from Sumer. Most people know nothing of the ancient place and most likely will not question it. You can say I come from a rich family who gave all of this to Laila as a wedding gift."

"That could work," Laila said.

"I like it," Astrid said. "I say we go with that."

"Once I must return to the bottle," Zak continued, matter-of-factly, "you can explain my absence and lack of a wedding by telling people I was killed in an accident on a journey home to visit my family."

Laila's heart seized.

By the loving look in Astrid's eyes, Laila had no doubt her mom knew exactly what was in Laila's heart concerning her eventual loss of Zak.

Astrid reached across the table for her daughter's hand, giving it a gentle squeeze.

Extending her hand, Delaney wiggled her fingers. "Give me your other hand, Laila." When she did, Delaney said, "This is yours now, little sister..." When she moved her hand away, her heartwish ring rested in Laila's palm. Happy tears in her eyes, Delaney looked to Varik, who tugged at his own ring, which wouldn't budge.

Feeling the weight of the ring in her hand, Laila said, "Thank you, Delaney, I really appreciate it...but I don't really need the heartwish stone ring." Holding her arms wide and glancing around, she said, "Look at the good fortune I've been given, and I still have a third wish to make. I think you should give the ring to someone who needs it more than I do." She held her hand open for Delaney to take it back.

"It doesn't work that way." Astrid closed Laila's fingers around Delaney's ring and gently squeezed her daughter's hand. "When the time is right, the ring's owner must pass it to the one person for whom it's next destined. In this case, Delaney knew that person is you. When the time comes you'll know who must receive it next. Put it on, Laila," Astrid said. "It should fit perfectly."

"Delaney's fingers are smaller than mine. It'll never fit."

"Go ahead, put it on." Nodding, Delaney gave a reassuring smile.

Laila did. It fit her finger perfectly, as if it were made for her. As soon as it was in place the stone glowed and an audible gasp rose around the table. Friday, who'd been sleeping at Zak's feet until now, perked up with a bark.

"Look, it's shimmering. It's just like..." Laila paused, gazing up at her family.

"Just like the heartwish story Grandma Bekka always told you when you were children." Astrid nodded. "The ring is exactly where it belongs now."

Laila remembered being fascinated by her grandmother's ring as a child. She'd begged her to let her try on her ring but Bekka claimed it wouldn't come off. Laila thought she was fibbing because Bekka was afraid she might lose or damage one of the rings.

When she was small, she loved hearing their magical story about messages from angels and the legend of the enchanted heartwish stones. By the age of twelve she'd dismissed the stories as childish fantasies.

After all, everyone knew there was no such thing as real magic in the world.

Her gaze shifting to Zakkar, her honest to goodness real life genie, she smiled. There was no way she could ever deny the existence of magic and enchantment again.

Chapter 22

~<>~

TIME PASSED QUICKLY as workers transformed the first floor of the building into Laila's precise vision of her perfect bake shop.

The professional, state of the art kitchen was convenient and enormous. The retail space housed glass-front cases, wood shelves, and refrigerated units. The work of local artists and craftspeople covered the walls. A cozy, inviting combination of café tables and chairs, as well as upholstered seating and coffee tables rounded out the space so her customers could linger over scones, coffee, and conversation. Finally, the room behind the kitchen included offices for Laila and her staff.

It was all picture-perfect and just as Laila had envisioned.

Three months after she'd taken possession of the former Crowe's Coastside Bakery building the work was completed. The rapidity in which it was finished was astounding. Of course, most construction projects weren't set in motion by a genie's magic.

Laila was thrilled with the final results of the renovation and The Great Pretender's warm, welcoming vibe.

According to a large panel of taste testers gathered from Glassfloat Bay's residents, her new line of reduced calorie scones, muffins, cookies, energy bars, granola and other foods were vastly superior to TBT's unappetizing fare. She'd also included gluten-free baked goods, and selections for diabetics, vegans, and those following paleo. Each variety received a big thumbs up for taste and overall satisfaction.

Everything was perfect—absolutely, positively, unquestionably faultless.

With one glaring exception.

In less than three months Laila would lose Zak. Forever.

Each time someone offered Laila congratulations on her upcoming nuptials, it tore a little hole in her heart.

Her relationship with Zak was an ideal coupling of mind, body and spirit. So much so, Laila couldn't imagine life without him. Supportive and successful in his efforts to keep Laila happy, he'd tried hard to keep her mind off their inevitable parting.

~<>~

On the day before The Great Pretender's grand opening, Laila was riding high on an energized wave of excitement.

Until the arrival of an unexpected visitor.

"Bunny!" she said, startled when she opened the bakery's front door. The last person she expected on her doorstep was the owner of Tuned by Turner, especially after Bunny's parting words when Laila had turned in her resignation.

"I knew from the beginning you wouldn't make it as a weight loss counselor," she'd told Laila with a smug smile the day she and Reen resigned. "Your need to consume chocolate supersedes any drive to succeed. I'm sure you wouldn't have met TBT's mandatory thirty pounds in six weeks deadline. You're far more suited for a job as a clerk in a bakery."

With a final, uppity sneer, she'd turned her back to Laila, returning to her work.

Laila wasn't surprised. Bunny Turner's stinging remarks were telling of her petty personality. Knowing she was losing her most popular counselor, she took pleasure in getting in a final jab, purposely designed to wound.

And now here she was, standing across Laila's threshold.

"Sorry, Bunny, we're not open for business yet. Come back tomorrow." She started closing the door only to have Bunny hold it open.

"Hello Laila." The air chilled considerably as the starchy woman strode into the entryway, uninvited. "I understand congratulations are in order." She surreptitiously craned her neck, scrutinizing The Great Pretender's welcoming décor while Laila couldn't help puffing with pride.

"Nice of you to come to wish me well," Laila said, fully aware Bunny hadn't offered her good wishes.

Any pretense of warmth was abandoned when Bunny turned sharply on her stiletto heel to face Laila.

"I'm here to warn you that if your company exploits any of Tuned by Turner's ideas, methods, recipes or materials, you'll be slapped with a lawsuit and your brand new little business will be shuttered before you can blink."

She uttered every word through an oily smile.

Laila smiled as she gathered her thoughts. "How kind of you to express your concern. But this is a bakery, Bunny, not a weight loss center. I assure you, the baked goods I've created for The Great Pretender are as far removed from Tuned by Turner's foods as possible."

Bunny gave Laila an icy once-over. "Apparently you've forgotten about your signed employment contract. Opening a competing business within three years of leaving TBT's employ is expressly prohibited."

"For heaven's sake, Bunny, I have no intention of competing with TBT. Besides, I'm afraid you're the one with a memory problem." Laila broke into a genuine smile.

"Hey, Laila," Reen said as she came into the front part of the bakery. With her head down, looking over some paperwork, she didn't see Bunny at first. "What should I do about the—"

"We have company, Reen," Laila interrupted, and Reen's head popped up, a look of disbelief etched across her features. Bunny had treated Reen to a similar, cutting farewell upon her resignation.

"Bunny...what are you doing here?"

"Warmth and people skills have never been your forte, Maureen," Bunny noted. "Which makes me immeasurably pleased you're working for Laila's company instead of mine. Although your term of employment here will be painfully short."

"Bunny's here to put the fear of God into me about opening a competing business," Laila explained. "Something about a clause in my contract." Her chuckling was an entirely joyful sound.

Bunny's nostrils flared, reminding Laila of a highly perturbed bull.

The woman bristled. "I doubt you'll be laughing when my team of attorneys—"

Jabbing a finger beneath Bunny's nose, Reen said, "Hold that thought, Bunny," before hurrying out of the area.

A delicious sense of victory coursed through Laila's veins. She knew exactly what Reen was up to.

Bunny made use of the few minutes Reen was absent by studying her surroundings. As much as the woman endeavored to hide it, Laila could tell Bunny was seriously impressed. Who wouldn't be? The Great Pretender was a masterpiece of functionality, organization and ambience.

"The mortgage and debt you've incurred must be staggering." Bunny gave a haughty sniff. She'd probably have a heart attack on the spot if Laila told her she owned TGP free and clear. But that wasn't any of Bunny's business.

"Pity you'll have to let it all go after you're shut down," Bunny added. "Perhaps I can assist by purchasing the property to convert it into a TBT food manufacturing facility, dear." She glanced around as if eyeing rotting sewage. "Although it would take a great deal of work to convert this to TBT standards."

"You can say that again," Laila agreed, swallowing the urge to guffaw. "Always thinking of others, aren't you, Bunny?" While she'd never excelled at bitchery, being in Bunny's callous presence made it much easier. "But your help won't be necessary...dear."

Reen bounced back into the room, Zak at her side. Bunny's posture turned fluid as she eyed the big hunk of male.

"Hello, Rabbit," Zak said without a trace of humor.

"Bunny," she cooed in correction.

"Same animal," Zak offered, straight-faced, while Laila stifled a snicker. "You have come to offer your congratulations on the eve of the opening of Laila's bake shop?"

"Actually, I've come on a matter of legal concern," Bunny said. "Regrettably—"

"Regrettably," Reen said, effectively cutting her off, "you neglected to reference Laila's customized TBT employment contract before showing up here, threatening her with the dissolution of her new business." She held a paper out to Bunny.

Eyes narrowed, Bunny glimpsed at the paper as if it were contaminated with flesh-eating bacteria.

"You'll note," Reen continued, "that the clause in question was struck from the contract, initialed by both you and Laila."

Bunny's expression turned foul. "Let me see that." Setting her purse on the marble countertop near the cash register, she snatched the contract from Reen. Her eyes widened as she studied the crossed out section. "This is ludicrous. Scratching that clause out and forging my initials, isn't going to save you from financial and personal ruin, Laila. You'll only embarrass yourself by opening tomorrow."

"The day you hired me," Laila reminded Bunny, "TBT was still a fledgling company, hungry for growth and eager to sign on counselors with people skills and a solid knowledge of TBT's diet program. When I saw the no-compete clause in the contract, I decided not to sign. Remember?"

Bunny's face was blank, noncommittal. But Laila caught the eye twitch.

"I told you then," Laila continued, "that it was my goal, my dream, to open my own bakery one day so I could offer dieters my unique line of reduced calorie baked goods. You laughed when I confessed that to you, Bunny. You said every former fat girl yearns to work in a candy shop or bakery. You assured me I'd forget my dream once I worked for you. In fact, you were so doggone certain, you crossed out that clause and initialed it. Does that ring a bell...dear?"

As realization dawned, Bunny's face drained of color. Laila relished the moment.

"When you get back to the office, take a look at my TBT employment contract too. Same strikeout." Reen offered a triumphant smile.

Bunny's cheeks pinked to match the color of her designer suit. "My people will be watching you and your business with an eagle eye," she threatened, wagging a cautionary finger beneath Laila's nose. "If there's the slightest indication you've stolen any of TBT's recipes, you'll rue—"

"Steal TBT's recipes? Seriously? Ha! That's downright hilarious, Bunny."

Ignoring Laila's remarks, Bunny continued, "You'll rue the day you left my employ to start up this sham of a business that's purposely designed to cut into TBT's food profits with your allegedly healthy muffins."

"Allegedly? All of my recipes have passed the strictest scientific testing standards for ingredients and nutritional information. The Great Pretender baked goods are so far removed from TBT's revolting, chemical-laden foods it isn't even funny."

"You won't even eat them yourself," Reen said. "Don't think we haven't noticed how you always manage to avoid tasting anything when you introduce new TBT foods to your counselors during those lunch meetings."

"I swear I'll ruin you if I start losing business because my clients are buying from your bakery instead of from my food list."

"If you offered palatable, quality food products to the people who trust you to help them lose weight," Zak said, "then you would not have to worry about losing customers. I have sampled your so called foods and they are unpleasant at best."

"Think about it, Zak," Bunny said, eyeing him with undisguised lust. "With your handsome face and buff body I could have your likeness as a TBT spokesman all over billboards and TV. What do you think Laila can do for you with her rinky-dink startup business, hmm? Nothing, that's what." Bunny's gaze narrowed as she turned her attention to Laila. "He must be gay," she groused, "or a gigolo. That's the only feasible explanation why a man with his looks would be interested in you."

"Enough! You are not a nice woman," Zak stated. "Your wicked presence casts a pall on Laila's home and business. You will depart now." Taking Bunny by the elbow, he ushered her to the door as Bunny toddled along on her stiletto heels.

"Mark my words—" she managed to say before Zak slammed the door in Bunny's face.

"Whew!" Reen shivered. "What a mega-bitch."

"I am not familiar with this term," Zak said, "but it sounds appropriate."

"I'm sure we haven't heard the last from her," Laila surmised. "I just hope she doesn't do anything to harm the success of The Great Pretender."

"That would not be possible," Zak assured. "You wished for your company to be successful." His smile was broad and reassuring. "It cannot be otherwise, no matter what Bunny attempts."

"I forgot about that." A relieved smile relaxed Laila's features. "That makes me feel a lot better."

Zak patted his six-pack abs. "My stomach speaks to me. I need food."

Laila laughed. "You're always hungry."

"There's plenty of stuff in the refrigerator in the back room to make a little picnic lunch for the three of us," Laila said. "We can eat outside on the patio. We need a break after our social call from the wicked witch of the Pacific Northwest."

The trio left the retail area and walked back to the kitchen.

~<>~

Damn. Half way to her car, Bunny realized she'd left her purse in the bakery. The last thing she wanted was to go back in there to face that smug Laila Malone and her self-satisfied cohorts. Well...except for that glorious specimen of manhood. What she wouldn't give for just one glorious sex-saturated night with that sexy hunk.

Expelling a sigh as the warmth of desire spread low in her belly, she retraced her steps until she stood facing the shop's front door. Her hand poised to ring the bell, she realized the door was slightly ajar. Maybe she could sneak in and retrieve her purse without them even knowing. She felt a migraine coming on and didn't need another unsavory confrontation.

Easing the door open, Bunny tiptoed to the marble counter. As she lifted her purse, voices from another room caught her attention.

Son of a bitch...they were talking about her!

Bunny looked around. There was no one in sight. She scooted closer to the back room to hear better...

"Did you see the way Bunny eyeballed Zak?" Reen asked. "She wanted to hump him right there in the lobby.

Laila laughed. "She's hot for him, all right."

"Most females have a lusty response to me," Zak said. Bunny had to stifle a moan at the delicious sound of his deep, accented voice. "This is what happens when you have a perfectly honed physique."

"He's far too modest," Reen joked.

"In serious need of a shot of self-esteem," Laila agreed.

"Thank God he's your genie and not Bunny's," Reen said. "Can you imagine how insufferable she'd be if she was Zak's owner? She'd keep him strapped to the bed twenty-four-seven to, um, service her needs."

Bunny's ears perked.

"Many of my possessors have done so," Zak said. "I remained restrained until they made their third wish and I returned to the bottle."

Bunny's jaw dropped.

"Tore and Drake think they've discovered some leads about Inanna," Laila said.

"Drake said it would help if they could borrow the box and bottle Zak was trapped in to examine them for clues," Reen said.

"I told you not to put yourselves in harm's way on my account," Zak said. "Drake and Tore must not proceed."

"Oh, yeah...I forgot," Reen said. "Thanks for the reminder."

"Um...Zak," Laila said, "why don't you go wait on the patio? We'll bring lunch out in a few minutes. There's beer in the fridge if you want one."

Bunny heard the sound of the refrigerator opening, then it sounded like a door opened and closed.

"So where'd you hide his bottle?" Reen said.

"Downstairs in the wine cellar," Laila answered. "On top of the old cabinet with the wine inventory book. It looks like a decorative piece designed to look old. Nobody would ever expect it's the real deal."

"Of course not." Reen laughed. "Who'd ever dream genies really exist? I'll scoot down there and put it in my purse before I go home so Drake and Tore can examine it."

"Great. Oh, Reen, I hate talking about the bottle. It's a sad reminder that I've got less than three months left before I lose Zak forever. He'll be imprisoned in that tiny bottle and I'll never get to see or hear him again...much less touch him. What am I going to do?"

"You can't give up hope, Laila. I'm sure we'll find a way to save Zak."

"God I hope you're right," Laila said. "Grab your plate and open the door. I'll get mine and Zak's."

After the sound of a door opening and closing, there was silence.

It took a while for Bunny to fully digest what she'd heard. Surely it couldn't be possible. The man couldn't be a genie.

Ludicrous. Preposterous.

And yet...

It would explain that magnificent man's attachment to Laila. The only reason Zak refused to sleep with Bunny when she propositioned him at the restaurant was because the poor man had no choice with Laila as his...what was it Zak called it? His possessor. Laila no doubt wouldn't allow him to sleep with other women.

Three months, they'd said. If Bunny had the bottle in her possession when Laila's time with Zak was over, she could have that god-like hunk of muscle in her bed, thrusting into her. The hell with her mealy-mouthed, limp-dicked, poor excuse for a husband. Bunny had been planning to ditch him anyway.

And what was that about three wishes? Good God, what she could do with those! The power, the wealth, the delicious satisfaction of revenge!

A burst of exultant laughter threatened to explode from Bunny's mouth.

Now all she had to do was to find the wine cellar...

Chapter 23

~<>~

"HEY, LAZYBONES, why are you calling me on your phone when you're right downstairs?" Laila asked, chuckling.

"Where did you say Zak's box was?" Reen asked.

"On the cabinet with the ledger book."

"I don't see it."

"You're probably looking at the wrong cabinet. It's the one with the worn green paint against the narrow brick wall just inside the entrance."

"The box isn't here, Laila."

"Sure it is. I'll be right down." Pocketing her phone, Laila headed down the stairs.

"See? I told you." Reen gestured to the cabinet.

A trickle of panic snaked up Laila's spine. "That's impossible. This is where I left it."

"Are you positive?"

"Absolutely." Laila checked inside the cabinet and behind it before she and Reen scoured the entire wine cellar. "What the hell could have happened to it?"

"Beats me. Lots of people have been through here the last couple of months, Laila. Maybe somebody got sticky fingers and swiped it."

Laila nibbled her bottom lip as she searched her memory. "It was here yesterday morning when I came down to get a bottle of pinot for dinner. I'm positive. Let's check with the staff. Maybe they saw someone come down here."

Ten minutes later Laila's bookkeeper, Charlene, confirmed, "Yes, I ran into your wine supplier as she was heading for the wine cellar."

"What wine supplier?" Reen asked.

"What did the woman say?" Laila asked. "What did she look like?"

"That she was your wine supplier and was here to check the inventory. She was chic, haute couture, wearing—"

"A pink suit," Reen ventured.

"Right," Charlene said. "And beige hair," she twirled a finger behind her head, "done up in a coil."

Laila and Reen exchanged horrified looks. "Bunny!" they cried.

Laila felt faint. "How could she have found out?"

"Did I do something wrong?" Charlene asked.

Laila sucked in a calming breath. "It's not your fault." She patted Charlene's arm. "You didn't know." She turned to Reen. "We need to put locks on the interior doors."

"Locks later." Reen yanked Laila up the stairs. "Right now we need to go hunting for a lowdown dirty skank."

~<>~

"It is unfortunate, little one, but nothing to grieve over."

"How can you say that, Zak?" Laila paced the bedroom, arms flailing as she spoke. "The woman stole your box and bottle! She tried to deny it when Reen and I confronted her, but instead of being outraged at the accusation, she just gave a smug *heh-heh-heh* laugh. She had guilt written all over her."

"Strange. Did she write the word on herself?"

Upset beyond the point of patience or humor, Laila tsked and rolled her eyes. "It's just a saying. If it weren't for that big bruiser bodyguard-slash-butler of hers we would have pushed past Bunny and searched the house. That woman is setting herself up to be your next possessor."

"If it were not her, then it would be someone else," Zak said with an impassive tone of acceptance.

Laila growled in frustration. "For heaven's sake, Zak, don't you understand? Bunny wants to have sex with you! Do you have any idea how I'll feel knowing you're in her bed doing God knows what every time she crooks her little finger?"

With realization dawning, Zak's features contorted, morphing into a scowl. "I'm sorry. I hadn't thought of your discomfort. It will indeed be difficult for both of us." Drawing her into a comforting hug, he said, "There is one advantage to having Bunny as my possessor. I will not be with her long. She will make use of her wishes rapidly, I have no doubt."

"This is terrible." Laila's hands plowed through her hair as she paced in small circles. "We have to get the box back."

Again, Zak wrapped his arms around her tense body, soothing her, smoothing one hand through her mussed hair and the other along her spine.

"Do not upset yourself so on the eve of your grand opening celebration. You must—"

"I don't care about tomorrow, Zak. All I care about is you." Tears flowed down her cheeks. "Please don't leave me, Zakkar. I'll die without you." She clutched him tight, wrapping her arms around him, pulling him close with all her strength.

"Shhh...you mustn't say such things, my love." He kissed the top of her head. "I promise to be here with you as long as I possibly can. Each moment of our time together will be filled with heartfelt love. My love is something Bunny can never steal from you, Laila. It is eternally yours. No matter who owns my body, you will always own my heart, my very soul."

"I don't deserve you." Laila sobbed harder. "All I've done is selfishly whine and complain when here you are on the verge of having to return to that bottle. Oh, Zak," she cried with a hiccupping sob, "you shouldn't be comforting me, I should be comforting you?"

Zak smoothed his thumbs over her cheeks, catching new tears. "No, you are not selfish, Laila," he said softly. "You must not be so hard on yourself."

Clutching his shirt, she looked up into his eyes. "You've worked so hard, done so much for me since you've been here. It isn't fair that you can't stay with me and enjoy the little slice of heaven we've created for ourselves. You'd be a perfect match for this time. You love the computer and electricity and all the other stuff you've learned about. You belong here, Zak. With me."

"That would be heaven. However, it is not within our power." He rocked Laila in his arms. "I will forever be grateful that I was able to spend this small measure of time with the woman of my heart. The memories we have fashioned will nourish my soul and illuminate the path of my dark journey ahead."

Laila rested her head against his chest, listening to his heartbeat, memorizing the luxuriant feel of being held in his arms. "Because of you, Zak, I've achieved my most important goals. I've had my deepest desires fulfilled. I've become so impossibly happy I have to pinch myself to make sure it isn't all a glorious dream." She looked up into his eyes again, sniffling. "Oh Zak, I love you so much I can barely stand it."

Zak wrenched her hard against him, almost wringing the wind out of Laila. His lips captured hers and he kissed her like never before. Her bones went rubbery, her stiff joints loosened, her cold sense of fear and indignation about rotten, sneaky Bunny Turner dissolved until Laila was nothing but a mindless gummy bear in his arms.

"Laila...my Laila," he gazed at her with love, "you are the only woman capable of possessing my heart...for all eternity."

Chapter 24

~<>~

"YOU ARE CRUEL and heartless," Zak accused. "If you truly love me as much as you profess, you would allow me this privilege."

Laila stood at the driver's side of her car, door open and ready to scoot in. She opened her mouth to protest, but when she looked up at him, her heart turned to jelly. In the nearly six months they'd been together, Zak had asked only one thing of her. And she'd refused.

Dammit, he was right. She *was* cruel and heartless.

"Okay. But, I warn you, Zak, you'd better do everything exactly as I tell you. No being obstinate and trying any fancy stuff. You could land us both in jail."

"Incarceration? Why?"

"One," she counted on her fingers, "you don't have a driver's license or permit. Two, you don't have a birth certificate. And wouldn't *that* be a sticky situation to try to explain to a judge? Three, if they don't deport you to...wherever, they'll probably keep you locked up in the psycho ward once they find out you think you're a five thousand year old genie."

A wounded look across his features, Zak clapped his chest. "But that is what I am. I do not tell false tales. I will assure them of that."

"Yeah, that'll work." She huffed a humorless laugh. "With that *I am bound to tell the truth* rule they imposed when they bottled you up, you'll get yourself, and me, in hot water. We have to avoid drawing the attention of any cops, got it?"

"Got it." The jovial *kid on Christmas morning* grin across his face was infectious.

Laila looked left and right. The grocery store's parking was still fairly empty at the early hour. She sucked in a deep breath, expelling it with a rush, then slipped into the car and turned on the ignition. Stepping out again, she said, "Get in. And make sure to put on your seatbelt."

Zak complied. It was a good thing Laila had purchased a bigger car. It was painful watching him pleat his massive frame like an accordion into her old compact model.

She sat in the passenger seat and buckled up. "Pay attention while I explain everything. The pedal on your right is the gas. It makes the car go. The pedal on the left is the brake. That makes it stop. The automatic gear shift—"

Zak shifted the car into drive, put his foot on the gas and took off.

"Whoa! What do you think you're doing?" Her hands slapped the seat on either side of her and her pounding heart nearly exploded. "Didn't you hear a word I said?"

"There is no need for worry," Zak assured. "I have watched you maneuver the car numerous times. I read detailed driving instructions online, complete with diagrams. If a woman can operate this vehicle, then a man surely can without any problem." He gave her a patronizing smile. "Relax, Laila. All will be well."

"Famous last words. You told me the same thing when I left you alone at Bekka House and you nearly blew it up with your electrical experiments, remember?"

"You exaggerate, Laila. I blew myself up, not the house. Do not be such a worry mort. I have learned much since then. I am in control."

"It's *worrywart*," she corrected, fidgeting nervously in her seat. "Watch where you're going. Stay in the parking lot. Don't go into the street. Keep your speed under ten miles an hour."

"I will drive us home," Zak responded. "It is not far."

"No!" Like a cartoon, Laila's eyes almost popped out on springs. "You most certainly will not!"

Zak pulled out of the parking lot onto the side street and Laila gasped.

"Ohmigod, ohmigod, ohmigod." Digging her fingers into his thigh she screeched, "Stop the car, Zakkar. Stop it this instant."

He patted her knee. "Your man is at the wheel," he reassured, stepping on the accelerator and picking up speed. "There is no need for angst, little one."

"There's a stop sign." Laila gestured frantically. "You have to stop there."

"Yes, I know." With a smug smile, Zak mashed his foot on the brake, nearly jettisoning the two of them through the windshield.

"Holy—! Are you trying to kill us?" Laila yelped. "The seatbelt nearly cut me in half."

"I-I am truly sorry, Laila." He looked befuddled. "I did not intend to hurt you. For some reason the car did not stop as smoothly as when you drive it."

"You have to ease the brake down, Zak, not slam it to the floorboards." Arms folded across her chest, she said, "You see? This is why I haven't let you drive before. Not only are you inexperienced, you're also pigheaded and stubborn and—"

"When I am back in the bottle all alone and without means of transportation, I will never forget that you let me drive your motorized chariot this day, Laila." His doe-eyed look thawed her insides. "Your kind gesture has given me abundant happiness."

Oh, poor Zak...he was right, he had such little time left here and—

Suddenly it hit her. Laila's eyes bugged and she gathered her wits. The man was playing on her sympathies. Laying a guilt trip on her! She glared at him. "That was totally unfair. Shame on you."

"Curious." Zak frowned. "According to the online relationship article, "Managing Your Woman," the guilt trip method should have been effective."

"Get out of the car."

"But—"

"Your driving lesson is over, Mr. Tymon. Get out." Laila unbuckled her seatbelt. As she was about to open the door, the car lurched, rolled across the small intersection before she could do anything about it, jumped the curb and rammed into a big blue and red United States Postal Service mailbox.

"What happened?" Zak's face was aghast. "I was about to exit the car and it drove itself like magic."

"Magic my ass! You didn't shift into park before you let your foot off the brake, Mr. I Am The Man And Can Do No Wrong." She was so angry steam could have vented from her ears.

"Yes, I remember that part of the instructions now." Zak put the car in park. "But you made me anxious, Laila. Your angry words and harsh tone distracted me."

"Oh, so it's my fault you screwed up? You could have killed someone, Zak. What if that was a child instead of a mailbox? Honestly, I could just wring your neck. Look at us. Now what are we supposed to do?"

She got out of the car to survey the damage, groaning when she eyed the sizeable dent in the property of the U.S.P.S.

Damn.

Zak got out and stood next to her. "The metal box and your car have both been damaged," he stated the obvious.

She just glared at him.

"Perhaps we should get back in the car and you should drive us home," Zak suggested, his big old macho persona taken down a peg or two.

"We can't just leave the scene of an accident." Laila wondered if running down a mailbox was in the same category as running into another car. No, of course not. Maybe they *could* leave. Sure, she'd just call the police department, explain what happened and—"

Whoop-whoop-flash-flash...

"Aw hell," Laila muttered as the police cruiser pulled up behind her car.

~<>~

"Yes, absolutely, Officer Hartinger," Astrid assured after hearing out the cop at Glassfloat Bay Police Headquarters. "I can vouch for both of them."

Laila's mom was the fourth call she'd made after calls to Reen, Drake, and Delaney had all gone to voicemail. Crossing her fingers, she hoped her mom kept her cool.

"I don't know, Mrs. Thorkelson." The cop eyed Zak and Laila skeptically. "There's something fishy going on. First your daughter tells me *she* was driving and he's her fiancé from Greece. She says he can't speak English. I ask him if that's right and the guy tells me, *in English*, no—*he* was at the wheel and he's a genie from someplace called Soon-air."

"Sumer," Zak corrected. The cop, Laila and Astrid scowled at him.

"What's going on?" the officer asked. "Is this guy an illegal alien?"

"No, I do not come from another planet. Merely another time. As I explained previously, I, Zakkar Tanojin Lugalbanda Tymon, am a genie."

Laila groaned. Astrid's eyebrow arrowed down and she shot Zak a warning look.

"I told you to keep quiet, Zak," Laila said. "Mom and I will handle this."

Turning to Astrid, Zak whispered, "The flames shooting from your daughter's eyes cause me to be unnerved."

With a quick glimpse at Laila, Astrid replied. "No doubt."

The cop narrowed his gaze. "If I hadn't administered a breathalyzer test myself I'd swear this guy was drunk." His gazed fixed on Zak. "Is he screwy or something?" he asked, almost in a whisper, twirling a finger at his temple.

"Yes!" Astrid readily affirmed. "Aside from having a difficult time with English, Zak is a bit...slow. I give you my word my husband and I will keep our eye on him until he gets his driver's license."

"I don't know. I think it might be better if I hold him for—"

"Your son, Ronnie, is in Professor Drake Slattery's ancient history class, isn't he?" Astrid broke in. Hartinger gave a confirming nod. "How's he doing?" She offered an innocent smile.

"He...well, Ronnie needs a passing grade in that class to keep from flunking out."

"Mmm, I see. Remember last year when your daughter, Trixie, was in the same position and my husband helped tutor her?"

"Oh yeah. If it wasn't for Professor Thorkelson," Officer Hartinger admitted, "Trixie would have failed."

"Well while you're seeing to the release of Mr. Tymon and my daughter, why don't I check with my husband to see when he can fit in time to give Ronnie some personal tutoring," Astrid offered, whipping out her cell phone. "Free of charge." She gave a bright smile. "Although he's retired, Tore is always happy to do what he can for our town's fine law enforcement officers and their families."

Breathing a sigh of relief, Laila was glad her mom was the one who answered her call.

"Hey, that would be great, Mrs. Thorkelson. Ronnie's a good kid. He just needs to get his priorities straight."

"Of course." She moved a few feet away while making her call.

Laila and Zak stood silent as they waited.

"All taken care of," Astrid said in a singsong voice as she walked back to Hartinger's desk. She handed him a card. "Here's my husband Tore's email address. Have your son contact him to make the arrangements for his tutoring."

"Thanks, I'll do that." Hartinger accepted the card with a smile, which quickly morphed into a frown when he eyed Zak again. "I don't want to see or hear anything about you getting behind the wheel without a driver's license again, mister, you got that? I'll be keeping my eye on you."

"I understand," Zak said with a confident smile. "You do not have to worry because I will soon be returning to my bottle—" Zak *oophed* when Laila elbowed him in the gut from one side and Astrid did the same from the other.

"No problem, officer," Laila assured. "You have my word that my fiancé will stay out of trouble from now on."

After narrowly escaping Zak being taken into custody, Laila thanked her mother profusely before they parted ways and she and Zak headed for The Great Pretender. Upon their arrival, Reen hauled them into her office to interrogate them. Drake had stopped by to pick up some scones for himself and his kids.

"I warned him not to say anything." Laila thumped Zak's chest. "But did the big know-it-all numbskull listen? No! He just kept going on and on," she made a jabbering gesture with her thumb and fingers, "burying himself deeper with each word." She gave them all the details.

"Oh jeez..." Drake muttered, covering his eyes with his hand.

"Uh-huh." Laila's head bobbed. "My mom finally had to tell Officer Hartinger that Zak had a few screws loose," she made a twirling gesture at her temple, "but that he was harmless. We were damn lucky the cop didn't throw us both in the slammer and throw away the key. If Mom hadn't vouched for Zak he'd be in a jail cell wearing an orange uniform right now. I swear to God," Laila growled, "I was ready to leave the big dope at the station, walk away and never look back."

"Holy mackerel, Laila." Reen blinked. "I haven't seen you this ticked off since...well, ever."

"Can you blame me? Do you have any idea what it's like to have a stubborn, macho barbarian underfoot constantly? That's it, I've had it. I can't deal with this anymore." In a huff, she opened the door to leave Reen's office, but Zak caught it, closing it again.

"Stay," he commanded. "You are too upset to leave now. It would not be good for your customers to see you in such an angry state."

Damn...he was right. That made her even angrier.

Laila turned away from everyone, folding her arms across her chest and scowling. She knew she was being unreasonable, childish, even, but she couldn't help it. Lately everything Zak did got under her skin.

"This isn't like you, Laila," Drake said.

"I believe Laila is suffering from referred anger," Zak noted. "That is why she has been so...I believe the word is *bitchy*, lately."

"Well thank you, Doctor Freud," Laila retorted.

"He's right," Reen said. "You've been awfully cranky lately."

"Pay her no heed, Reen," Zak advised. "I Googled this strange temper of Laila's and learned she lashes out in anger due to separation anxiety. The pain of losing me in a few days is too great for her conscious mind to cope with."

A dead-cold shiver snaked up Laila's spine. She did *not* want to hear this!

"I'm leaving. Unlike some of you, *I* have work to do." She moved to the door again, only to have Drake block it this time.

"You should listen to the man," Drake said in a no-nonsense tone.

"Using anger is a protective mechanism," Zak said. "It is easier for Laila to ignore her deep-seated fears by resorting to anger. Part of her brain believes this will make our inevitable parting easier."

"Stupid pop psychology," Laila grumbled. Why didn't Zak just go away and leave her alone? Why didn't they *all* just leave her alone!?

Reen and Drake exchanged sympathetic looks. "Sounds like you've hit the nail on the head, Zakkar," Drake said.

"I have been researching psychology websites in hopes of helping Laila cope through our approaching separation."

"I wish to hell I'd never shown you and your stupid photographic memory that damn computer," Laila snapped. "You've turned into an annoying egghead."

"Hey, I thought that was my title," Drake joked, clapping his chest.

"See how she tries to engage me in a battle of hurtful words?" Zak noted. "Her subconscious hopes I will berate her, making her anger fester until she believes she does not want me to stay. But I will not cooperate. I wish to leave Laila with only good memories of our time together."

Laila held her hands over her ears. She felt like singing *la-la-la-la-la*, drowning them all out. If they'd just buzz off she could get some work done, then maybe go to bed early. That's what she needed. Extra sleep. She'd been pushing herself too hard lately, burning the candle at both ends to make The Great Pretender the best bake shop on the planet.

Why couldn't they understand she was overtired and out of sorts and stop badgering her?

"Aw, honey." Reen drew Laila's stiff, unyielding body into a hug, whether Laila liked it or not. "Zak's right. I should have realized that's what's been going on. Talk to us, Laila," she encouraged. "We're here for you, hon."

"There's nothing to talk about." Shrugging out of Reen's grasp, Laila blasted the trio with a caustic glare.

"I'm sick to death of listening to Zak's psychobabble," she barked. "He doesn't know what the hell he's talking about. None of you do. Can't I simply be angry because Zak acted like a horse's ass? Why does it have to have anything to do with the fact that...that..." she sucked in a shuddering breath. "That he's leaving me in a few...a few..."

Her chin trembled and two fat tears escaped her eyes, coursing down her cheeks. Her body shook with a series of violent trembles.

"Oh God," she sobbed, dropping to her knees. "What am I going to do?" She buried her face in her hands, weeping her heart out.

Zak knelt at her side, enfolding her in his arms, soothing her as she cried.

"I can't lose you, Zak," she sobbed into his chest. "Without you life is meaningless. And I can't bear the thought of you trapped in that awful bottle. Oh God, Zak, what are we going to do?"

"It will be hard for us," Zak's voice was calm and soothing, "but you are bold, brave and strong."

"I'm not. I'm not brave at all." She sobbed even harder. "I'm not strong enough. I can't do this."

Holding her at arm's length, Zak locked his eyes on hers, as if he gazed clear to her soul.

"You are and you must," he insisted. "You will not be alone, my love, you have the support of your parents, sisters and brothers, and all the people in this town who care about you."

"We won't let you go through this alone," Drake promised, resting a hand on Laila's shoulder.

"We'll all be here for you," Reen said, clasping her other shoulder.

Zak shot a smile in their direction. "You will be so glad to see Gard when he returns from Antarctica, and your sister Kady when she comes home from her backpacking trip overseas," he reminded her. "And, Laila, you must not forget Friday. He needs you. He will not understand why I have suddenly abandoned him. The daily operations of The Great Pretender will also help to fill your thoughts while you grieve. You will survive this loss, my dearest Laila, and you will go on to live a productive, happy life."

"No...not without you, Zak. I can't." She clutched onto him for dear life, digging her fingers in his flesh. She would have crawled inside him if she could.

"If I had it in my power to make a wish for myself," Zak told her gently, "it would be that you find yourself a good man who will give you a houseful of adorable little goats and take care of you until you are old...the way I wish I could do for you. I would ask that you consider making that your final wish before I must depart."

By this time, Reen was crying and Drake snorted in a big manly sniffle.

"How could I think of being with another man after I've had you in my life?" Laila asked through her sobs. "No man could compare to you, Zak. I could never feel the same about anyone else."

"With the passage of time," he stroked her hair, "the ache of loss will ease and you will find enough room in your heart for another man to share your life."

"I don't really think you're a horse's ass, Zak. Or a numbskull. Or a dodo, or any of those other awful things I said."

"What about macho and stubborn?" Zak asked.

"Definitely." Laila laughed a little. "But those traits are part of what makes you the wonderful man I love—with all my heart. I'm sorry for all those terrible things I said."

"It is all right." Zak brought Laila's hand to his mouth, brushing his lips across her palm, and wrist, then kissing each fingertip.

Zak rose to his feet, bringing Laila up with him. "Better?"

Laila took a deep breath and smiled. "Better."

Poking Laila's shoulder, Reen said, "Time to stop bawling. Chocolate's the best damn medication on the planet." She drew two pieces of chocolate from the box she'd taken from a drawer in her desk, passing one to Laila who just looked at it.

"Even chocolate can't solve this dilemma, Reen."

"Take a bite," Zak encouraged. "Have you not told me yourself that chocolate is medicinal?"

"I'm not in the mood for chocolate."

Clapping a hand to her chest, Reen looked horrified. "In all our lives I've never heard you utter such sacrilege."

Laila answered with a lifeless shrug.

Reen placed a chocolate in her own mouth, closed her eyes and uttered a blissful moan. "Mmm...ooh...there's nothing like the sinfully rich taste of a European milk chocolate truffle sliding down the back of your throat. Come on, sit down and give it a try, Laila,' she encouraged, patting the chair seat. "Trust me, it'll help you turn off the waterworks."

"There's something very wrong with this picture." Laila smiled as she sat and snatched a tissue from the box on Reen's desk, dabbing her eyes. "Former weight loss counselors aren't supposed to try to convince people to eat chocolate to make them feel better."

"So sue me." Shrugging, Reen winked.

Laila stared silently at the chocolate her sister offered for a long moment.

"If you stare at it any longer the chocolate's going to melt," Reen said, wiggling her fingers.

"Okay...Zak's right. I can't have our customers seeing me blubbering all over the place." Laila bit into the chocolate, closing her eyes as she savored the truffle. "Mmm...so good. Thanks."

Reen soothed a hand up and down her sister's back. "Drake, why don't you and Zak take a walk along the shore or something and give Laila and me a little time alone so we can talk."

"Good idea." Drake patted Laila while Zak kissed her cheek before leaving Maureen's office.

Reen waited until they were out of earshot. "I didn't want Zak hearing this because he'd start protesting all over again, worrying about our safety." Clasping her sister's upper arms, she gave a bright smile. "Laila, we might have a break. Drake, Tore and Varik discovered another incantation on an old handwritten parchment as they dug through old files at the university."

"Really?" Laila's heart leapt. "That's wonderful!" She scooted to the edge of her seat. "Can we try it tonight?"

"We're all set to do it upstairs in your apartment at six o'clock." Reen nodded. "Mom and Tore will invite Zak to their place for dinner to get him out of the way. Delaney and Varik will be here to help me do the required chanting while Drake reads the incantation."

"Perfect. Maybe this will be the one, Reen. Maybe we'll actually be able to conjure Inanna."

"I hope to hell we do. Time's getting short." As soon as the words flew out of Reen's mouth, her eyes bugged. "Oh hell. I didn't mean to say that."

"It's okay." Laila gave a defeated sigh. "There's no escaping it, Reen. No use pretending it's not going to happen. Three days from now, *poof,*" her hand swirled up, "back into the bottle he goes...until Bunny releases him." The idea made her stomach roil.

"Unless we can prevent it. Drake's even made it an extra credit project for his students, without revealing the real reason of course. They're all busy researching ways to contact Inanna, just in case this incantation doesn't work. He's got a brainy bunch. They've already come up with some good leads."

They each ate another piece of chocolate while Laila's mind skirted over the day's events and the single bright shining spot in it all. Zak. No matter what she'd dished out, he not only put up with her, he nurtured her, put her concerns above his own. He gave of his heart and soul so completely it put her to shame.

Chapter 25

~<>~

BUNNY TURNER SAT on the edge of her bed, wearing a silk negligee. Slipping her hand between her breasts she withdrew a small key suspended from a fine gold chain. She bent to unlock the gilt-edged drawer of her nightstand and brought out the ancient stone box containing the spun glass bottle.

She patted her hair, taking a deep breath before opening the box and setting the small bottle in the palm of her hand.

"Genie, come forth," she commanded, pulling the stopper from the neck of the bottle. "It is I," she elevated her chin, "Bunny Turner, your new owner. Come forth and do my bidding."

It was the same regime she'd gone through every evening for the last month, knowing the time was near. She didn't like to think of appropriating the genie's bottle from the bakery's wine cellar as stealing. Not when that bitch Laila Malone had robbed her of her prestige and her standing in the weight loss community.

In three months, Laila Malone had catapulted her reduced calorie baked goods business to astounding heights. Thanks to word of mouth, TBT had lost nearly all of the sales for their baked goods to The Great Pretender. Sure, TBT's packaged foods might unpalatable but until bleeding heart Laila came along intent on helping all the fat asses out there who yearned for delicious diet food, TBT foods were the only option for Bunny's chunky clients. Thanks to Laila, Bunny's income had been slashed and she was in financial trouble.

No, it wasn't stealing when someone owed you something. And Laila owed her. Big time.

Bunny stared at the bottle for a long moment, waiting to see if Zak would waft out in a puff of smoke, but nothing happened.

"I'm getting impatient, my handsome genie. But I can wait. The time's getting close. As long as I have your bottle, you're mine—then I'll show you what a *real* woman has to offer."

Leaving the bottle open, in invitation as she liked to think of it, Bunny placed it back in its box atop her nightstand, where it would remain until she locked it up again in the morning.

~<>~

It was almost over. Laila's life-changing love affair, her beloved heart of hearts, her brave, wonderful, handsome genie...all of it was about to come to a dreadful end.

She glanced at the clock on her nightstand for the umpteenth time in the last five minutes. There were less than two hours left before the clock struck midnight. Before she would lose the man she so dearly loved in a cruel puff of smoke.

Laila wasn't sure why she was still breathing. The pain in her heart was almost too great to bear. Drake and his students had found several incantations which he, Reen and Laila, had solemnly recited to no avail. Inanna could not or would not be summoned.

With the time limitation hanging like a grim fog over them, neither Laila nor Zak mentioned his impending departure during dinner. They kept their conversation light, turning to words rich, sweet, decadent and full of love by the time they ate dessert.

Back in the bedroom Zak reached for Laila's hand, studying it as if it were a precious jewel. His fingers glided across hers as his expression grew serious.

"I must hold you in my arms again, loving you, satisfying you. I want to see those incredible lapis lazuli eyes of yours wide with wonder as I take you on *lil* to *an*...one last time. This is the memory I want tattooed on my heart."

One last time...his words echoed in Laila's head. *One last time*...

"I want that too." Enfolding Zak's hand with her fingers, she clutched it tight.

His open arms beckoned her and they made love. It was exquisite. Slow, intense, expressive. A loving experience she would never forget. After, they held each other close, speaking no words as their hearts did the speaking for them.

Zak broke the meditative silence by telling Laila, "I could make love to you for all eternity and never tire of it."

Eternity. *Eternity*...

"Oh Zakkar..." A sob caught in Laila's throat as she turned, wrapping her arms around his neck, burying her face in the hollow of his shoulder. The reminder that their time together was so fleeting tore at her soul.

"Shhh..." Lifting her head, he smoothed her hair and kissed the tears from her eyes. "We must focus on the joy, the pleasure we give each other. We will keep those memories with us always."

Gazing into Zak's eyes, Laila drew in a shuddering breath. "I'm trying not to cry. I'm trying so hard not to make this any more difficult."

"It is time for us to talk, little one."

"No." Laila clutched Zak's limbs, wishing she could melt into his flesh and become one with him.

"You still have a third wish to make."

"Not until the very last minute. I don't want to lose a single precious second with you, Zak. I just want to pretend that we can go on like this forever."

Threading her fingers through his hair, Laila strived to commit every nuance of him and their precious time together to memory. Everything from the sound of Zak's breathing and the beat of his heart, to his captivating voice and poetic words, to the sight of his beautiful body and expressive eyes, to the battle scars on his flesh, to every moment they had shared during the last six months. Everything.

She had to, because she'd never have the opportunity again. None of the joy they'd shared would happen again. None of the loving glances, the sweet touches, the delighted laughter. None of it. Ever.

"I cherish our time together, Zak. Every moment has been magic."

He held her firmly, whispering words of love in Sumerian, as their bodies all but fused. No matter what language he used, his sentiments came through loud and clear. Sentiments her heart echoed.

His hands molded her curves and angles. "Every part of your body, every fragment of your being...I love all of it. I worship and adore you." His kiss was excruciatingly sweet, tender, gentle. Another moment she committed to memory. "Let us share another bottle of champagne. We will say to each other all the heart-true words we feel before I must leave you."

Her heart heavy with acceptance and understanding, Laila nodded. She suspected that Zak hoped the champagne might help soothe her anxiety, to cloud and soften her thinking about their parting. But nothing could accomplish that. She'd be aware, focused and alert until that final tortuous second.

"I want to spend the last moments we have together in each other's arms."

"To the last second," Zak assured her.

They lit all the candles throughout the bedroom. Laila lit sticks of sandalwood and patchouli incense, the two fragrances she first connected with Zak when he poured forth from the bottle. She breathed in the wafting, aromatic smoke and sighed. They would forever be her favorite scents.

Zak opened the bottle of champagne, the finest vintage from their wine cellar. They'd saved the rare selection for just this moment, to savor the superb bubbly together as they shared the splendid memories they'd created.

Her breath caught when Zak went to the dresser, drawing out his genie garb, the turquoise sultan pants, golden-yellow belt sash and the short black embroidered vest, embedded with rubies. And there was his mighty saber and its sheath.

Laila's heart clutched as she watched him set out his clothing, seeing the muscle twitch in his jaw as he eyed the garments.

After putting on his pants and sash, he took the photos he'd placed in the drawer with his clothing and brought them to Laila so they could look through them together. Astrid had doubles made of all the pictures.

"This one of us together is my favorite." He ran the tip of his finger over Laila's visage. "Your beautiful smile is captured perfectly. Your eyes glisten like lapis lazuli and your cheeks are pink from the spiked coffee you drank. There is a sweet look of mischief about you here." He looked up from the picture at her and chuckled. "That is the Laila I will always remember."

"I like that one too. You look so handsome and happy." Laila remembered how pleased and proud Zak was that day after making her mother, Tore, Delaney and Varik believe his story.

"Happy because I am with the woman I love. This photograph I will keep closest to my heart. Each night before slumber I will gaze upon it, thinking of you as I send you my eternal love."

They'd made a pact with each other to do just that. It would be their own private way of connecting with each other's hearts. "I'll be doing the same with my copy of the photo," Laila promised him. "Every night, Zak. Always. For the rest of my life."

"These two photographs I shall keep with me also." He pointed to one her mother took the day she first met Zak. "I chose this because Friday is in the photograph as well." The other photo Zak selected was one Tore took so Astrid could be in the picture.

"My family," Zak said softly. "I will never forget the wonderful Malone clan who welcomed me into their hearts and homes."

He tucked the three photos into the inner pocket Laila had sewn into the lining of his vest. It was directly over Zak's heart, as he requested. Once he finished, he put the vest on.

Slipping into her lavender bra, panties and the matching floor-length semi-sheer robe, Laila remembered the day Zak selected them for her at My Silky Secrets. She'd never forget the look of longing in his eyes as he lifted the wispy items and noted, 'The color of a Sumerian sky on a late summer's night. Your alabaster skin will look like the moon and stars against these garments.' After dressing she slipped her copy of the photos into her bra, over her heart.

Once they were dressed, Zakkar Tanojin Lugalbanda Tymon stood before her. The grim, solemn line of his lips could in no way be mistaken for a smile. It was a look she hadn't seen across his handsome features before. It broke her heart to see it there.

"Come, my love." Zak extended his hand and attempted a smile. "Let us toast to our six months of bliss together."

Laila slipped her hand into his and they sat in the middle of the bed with its diaphanous cream-color curtains around them. Laila loved their bedroom. Just stepping into it made her think of Zak. The lushness of the space, with its abundance of embroidered pillows, satins and touches of gold, brought a sultan's palace to mind.

"I remember the first time you told me that you would wait the full six lunar cycles before making your last wish." His eyes crinkled at the corners as his smile grew.

"You didn't believe me." Laila nodded, remembering all too well how determined she'd been to keep him with her the full allotted time. "You had no idea of your worth, Zak. You didn't believe you were far more important than any pot of gold or treasure chest full of jewels."

"How could I? Never could I imagine meeting a woman as rare and special as my sweet, unselfish Laila." Zak handed her a flute of champagne. "My heart desires to speak to you, with a special toast." Taking a deep breath, Laila nodded.

Looping arms with her, to drink from their glasses continental style, Zak gazed deeply into her eyes.

"O Laila, my *ki-aga*, my beloved of the fair-spoken mouth, of the ever kind lapis eyes, of the body so wondrous to behold. *Munus*, woman, sweet as the date. Your precious caress is more savory than honey. Your interior is the place where the sun rises, endowed with abundance. Just as the light of the rising moon, my sweet beloved too, is clothed in enchantment. *Ze ki angu*, Laila...I love you. Forever."

Zak sipped from his glass as did she.

His heartfelt words and the intense, sincere look in his dark eyes moved her to tears. "That was beautiful. Like a lyrical poem."

"It is an ode my heart sings," Zak explained, clapping his hand on his chest and nodding. "Expressed in the way of my people, in the manner of my time. It is my way of telling you how much I treasure you."

"You're going to have me bawling like a baby." She swiped tears from her cheeks.

Zak cupped her chin, giving her a loving look she'd never forget. "It is important to me that you know the depth of my love. The six months I spent with you are the most fulfilling in my long existence. Never in my life, Laila, have I cared for another more than I care for my own life. Until now."

He leaned close and kissed her, tenderly at first, then with more passion. "I am a changed man because of your unselfish love. The gift you have given me of yourself is more precious than gold. I will cherish it for the rest of my days."

"I've never had a man speak to me from his heart like that, Zak. If you only knew how much your words mean to me. But even if you hadn't said them, I would have known. Your every deed, your every gesture, the way you look at me and the way you treat me—all of that shows me how much you love me. I feel so very blessed."

In between kisses and loving caresses, they spent the next moments sipping champagne and reminiscing about their extraordinary time together.

Laila caught Zak giving the clock on the nightstand a surreptitious glance. Her blood ran cold when she followed his gaze and noted the time. They had ten minutes left before midnight.

Dear God! Ten minutes!

"It is time, my beloved," Zak said, his expression bleak. "You must make your final wish now. It would break my heart if you did not make a third wish for yourself before I leave you. I hope you have considered my suggestion, Laila. It would give me great relief to know you will find happiness with a good man who will love you and treat you as you deserve. A fine man like your fiancé Tim, who was lost to you too early. Or a man with Drake's admirable qualities. Someone who will cherish and appreciate you."

Laila's tears flowed freely now.

"You must word your wish," Zak finished, "to ensure the good man who takes Tim's place and mine will remain with you throughout your entire life."

"Now it's my turn to tell you what my heart needs to say, Zak." Laila wrapped her arms around his neck, pulling him close for another kiss. "You are such a remarkable man. The man every woman dreams of having in her life, in her bed. A man who's strong, decisive and masterful, yet loving and romantic when the time is right."

"Your words warm my heart, Laila."

"Shhh," she pressed her fingertip to his lips. "There's so little time and I have so much to say. You've given of yourself more than anyone else I've ever known. You're the least selfish person I know, even to the point of encouraging me to wish for another man for myself. You've gladly romped with Drake's children each time they've pestered you to play *genie*—even when you wanted to escape and romp with me between the sheets." They both smiled at the recollection.

"You've won over my mom and stepdad, who love you as a son. You've taught yourself amazing new skills and abilities and have used them tirelessly to help me and others. You've worked your fingers to the bone, pouring your heart and soul into The Great Pretender, making yourself truly indispensable in the process."

Laila glanced at the clock and shivered. Zak held her closer.

A sparkle caught her eye. She glanced at her hand to see the heartwish stone glimmer. Zak saw it too. They gazed at the stone, then at each other. The metal surrounding the stone grew warm around her finger. Since she'd slipped the ring on the day her parents met Zak she hadn't been able to remove it. She'd had no idea why the ring was meant for her...until the day she made the decision about her third wish. There was no longer any doubt after that.

"Before I make this final wish, Zak, you need to know that you have changed my life forever. I was merely existing before you came into my life. In these six months with you, I've lived an entire lifetime. I love you with every fiber of my being, my darling. I love you more than life itself. Promise me you'll always remember that." Her tears flowed now.

"I will, my love." Zak kissed away her tears. "I feel the same for you."

"I know." She smiled. "The wish I make tonight comes from the depths of my heart and soul. Know that I've thought it out well, Zak. You must never, ever blame yourself for what I have chosen to do."

"Blame?" He gave her a curious look. "Laila...I do not understand."

Holding her hand against her heart as the heartwish stone on her finger shone bright, she said, "As I make this wish, my heart makes it as well. It is my truest, deepest heartwish. Take my hand, Zak. Hold it tight against your heart."

He wrapped his hand around her fingers, clearly startled to feel the heartwish ring's unmistakable warmth against his skin as he held her hand to his chest.

"Goodbye my dearest heart, my sweet, beloved genie." With a shuddering breath, Laila kissed his lips softly, tasting him for the last time.

"You so richly deserve life, my darling Zakkar." She smoothed her hand over his cheek. "You must go on living in this world and this new time and find yourself another woman. A woman who will love you as much as I do and who will bear your children." She smiled. "Your own little goats."

Clearly alarmed and confused, Zak shook her. "Laila, what—"

She held her finger to his lips again.

Remembering to hang invisible quotes before uttering her wish, she said, "For my third and final official wish, I wish to take Zakkar Tanojin Lugalbanda Tymon's place in servitude so he can be free forever more."

Zak's eyes widened. "Laila, no!" he roared.

But it was too late.

As soon as the words left her lips, Laila was gone.

Only her heartwish ring remained.

It was on his finger.

Chapter 26

~<>~

PAIN SUCH AS he'd never known tore through Zakkar as he clutched at empty air, the bedspread, sheets and the bed curtains.

"Laila! Come back." He rifled through the pillows, hurling them to the floor as he looked beneath them. "You do not understand the fate you have chosen. I cannot bear to think of you existing in the dark realm of oblivion."

Spreading his fingers he studied them, scowling, unable to fathom how the ring that fit Laila's small finger could possibly be affixed now on his broad finger. He twisted but it wouldn't budge. Holding the ringed hand against his heart, he choked back a soul-deep sob.

Jumping to his feet, Zakkar paced, raking his fingers through his hair, growling Sumerian oaths.

"Gods and goddesses," he cried out, looking to the heavens, "I beseech you, I implore you, let me take Laila's place. She has committed no wrong. It is I," he pounded his chest, "I, Zakkar Tymon, who should be incarcerated, not her! Return me to the bottle and set Laila free!"

The room was deadly silent.

"Hear me, Inanna. Hear my worthy plea! Imprison me, torture me, kill me, do whatever with me that pleases your cold, fearsome soul, but return Laila's life to her. Set her free, O great Inanna!"

Silence.

Zakkar's anguished cries had gone unheeded, and for the first time he could remember, tears flowed down his cheeks.

"Damn you, Laila!" he bellowed, his hands balled into fists. "Damn you for doing this to yourself—to me!"

Friday practically galloped into the bedroom. After sniffing the air and searching the room, he gazed up at Zakkar, his eyes wide. The anguished howl he emitted further broke Zakkar's heart.

"You know..." Zakkar said, getting to his knees. "You can sense her absence...that she will never return." He and Friday howled their mutual grief and Zakkar pulled the frightened dog close, hugging him and feeling Friday tremble beneath his touch. "I am sorry, Friday. It is all my fault."

Crazed and tortured with anguish, Zakkar felt entirely powerless. "Gods, Laila, my love, didn't you realize that my life here would have no meaning without you?" His voice caught on another sob as he rose to his feet again, snorting with anger. "There, you see what has become of me? You see how I weep like a babe?" He continued his wild pacing.

"This pain, Laila," he shouted upward, shaking his fist, "far exceeds any gash from a foe's saber. My insides are dying. My heart bleeds. My soul is crushed. See what you have done!"

Zakkar stood still, his shoulders slumped. "She cannot hear me," he muttered. "She exists in a void. No sensation, except eternal heart pain and grief." Remembering the utter desolation of the bottle, he held his fists to his eyes and roared out his rage.

He couldn't bear thinking of Laila trapped in that bleak, forbidding existence.

His chest heaved. His beloved had made the ultimate sacrifice for him. It was so like Laila to put his needs first. Why didn't he realize what she was about to do and stop her? He should have known. *He should have known!* He would have done something, *anything*, to keep her from making this lethal choice.

Zakkar glanced around the room, feeling at a total loss. "Look at me," he said, catching his reflection in the full length mirror.

"Warrior. Leader of armies. Hah! I am as helpless as a newborn calf."
He plowed his hand through his hair, snarling. "What do I do?
Where do I go? Who is there to help—"

He spotted Laila's purse on one of the chairs and grabbed it,
retrieving her phone. He hit the speed dial and a moment later heard
Reen's voice.

"Laila! Oh honey, Drake and I have been here together waiting
for your call. Are you all right? No, of course you're not. Do you want
us to come over? Oh, for heaven's sake, of course you do. We'll be
there in—"

"Reen, it is I, Zakkar."

"Zak!?" She made an audible gasp. "Oh my God, it's after
midnight and you're still here. You found a way to break the curse?
Oh this is so exciting! Let me talk to Laila."

"She is not here," he said through gritted teeth.

"She must be in the kitchen getting ice cream and chocolate to
celebrate, huh?" Reen laughed.

"Reen, stop babbling and listen to me. Your sister is gone. Her
final wish was to take my place in servitude so I could be free. As
soon as the wish left her lips she disappeared."

There was dead stillness on the other end of the line.

"Reen? Maureen, did you hear me?"

"My God...oh dear God...oh no...no..."

Zakkar heard the wrenching sounds of Reen's sobs, then Drake
came on the line.

"Zakkar? What's going on?"

Zakkar repeated what he'd told Reen.

"I do not know what to do, Drake. Can you help me? I must find
a way to contact Inanna."

"We'll be right over. Laila told Reen we'd be needed after she
made her final wish, so I left the kids with my parents overnight. I-I

had no idea she meant *you'd* be the one needing us. I'll bring the latest set of incantations with me."

"Latest set?"

"Right, I forgot, you don't know about that. We've all been doing our best to conjure Inanna behind your back for the last three months."

Zakkar smiled. "That is just like my Laila." Saying her name ripped a new gash in his shredded heart. "Come quickly, my friend."

He ended the call and looked down. Friday had jumped up onto his thighs, whimpering. Zakkar lowered his hand to pet the dog, trying to comfort him. But it was Friday who offered comfort with his generous licking of Zakkar's hand.

~<>~

Setting down her erotic romance novel, Bunny Turner yawned. She glanced at the clock. Just after midnight. As she reached over to turn off her bedside lamp, she thought she saw something out of the corner of her eye.

Sitting up in her bed, she blinked and then her jaw dropped as she watched a faintly lavender-hued vapor waft across the room. She would have been scared witless it she hadn't overheard the conversation about Zak being a genie.

Her gaze followed the vapor to the mouth of the ancient bottle as the fog was sucked inside, disappearing into its depths. The bottle's stopper rose from the box unaided, seating itself. Finally, the lid of the ancient box closed and latched.

"Sonuvabitch, this is it," Bunny breathed, elation spiking from every nerve ending. "I have my genie!" Slipping into her high-heeled, poof-topped satin slippers, she opened the box again, grabbed the bottle, fingers on the stopper. "I'll have him forgetting Laila Malone in less than thirty seconds. I'll demand he forget he ever met her." She laughed at that, the anticipated power already making her heady.

Wishes...she had to word them to be universal, with each wish encompassing numerous wants. She wanted to be the richest, most powerful woman in the world with more jewels, furs, palatial property, fancy cars and yachts—including a stable of gorgeous, muscled young men to be at her beck and call—than anyone else has ever had or ever will have.

For wish number two she'd exact revenge on every rotten bitch or bastard who'd ever done her wrong, choosing significantly harsh comeuppance for those who deserved it. She'd ensure Laila Malone would have her own special place in Hell for what she'd done.

Wish number three...perfect health, youth and beauty, accompanied by eternal life ought to do the trick.

Not one prone to giddiness, Bunny was surprised when the desire to giggle gripped her. She kept herself from doing anything so buffoonish, especially since Zak might be able to hear her through the bottle. No, girlish buffoonery was Laila's specialty.

She didn't know what excited her more, making the first wish or commanding Zak to make her quake with pleasure as he humped her, over and over and....

Bunny pulled out the stopper.

"Genie, come forth," she commanded. "I am Bunny Turner, your new owner. Come forth and do my bidding, genie."

Before the last words were out of her mouth, the lavender-hued vapor rose from the bottle. Bunny suppressed another wild impulse to giggle as she watched the smoky mist journey to the plush carpet where it stood...a lot shorter than she would have thought.

Slowly the vapor took form. Eyes wide, Bunny watched it morph into the shape of...

"Laila!" she screeched, taking a few steps back. "What the hell are you doing here? Where's Zak? Goddammit, where's my genie?"

"Oh God, it was awful in there." Laila shuddered, rubbing goose bumps from her arms. "Cold. Total blackness, profound loneliness..."

Bunny noted with irritation that Laila seemed to be talking more to herself than to Bunny.

"I was semi-conscious, in a sort of hypnotic sleep state, but I couldn't move or even see my hand in front of my face, if I'd been able to place it there." She rubbed her arms again. "Terrible."

Bunny folded her arms beneath her breasts. "Spare me the sob story, Laila. Where's my genie?"

Laila took in a deep breath, expelling it slowly. "I am at your command," she said, looking none too happy about it.

Her face was wet with tears. At least that's what Bunny surmised because Laila's eyes, nose and cheeks were red and blotchy.

"To give you pleasure," Laila continued unenthusiastically. "To act upon your every urge."

"Whoa! Wait a minute. I don't get it. *You're* the genie, not Zak? But I thought—"

"We traded places," Laila informed her. And for the first time since she'd wafted from the bottle, she grinned. "Surprise, Bunny!"

"Traded places. What are you talking about? How? Why on earth would you do something like that?"

Laila smiled. It was one of those pitying smiles Bunny detested. "You'd never understand, Bunny. Not in a million years. In any case, it looks like you won't be bedding Zak tonight. And I hope to God I'm not your type." Laila shuddered.

"Hardly." Bunny glared at her. "I still get my three wishes, don't I?"

"Yes. All of Zak's powers and the rules he operated by have transferred to me."

"How can you be sure?" Bunny's gaze narrowed. "I don't want to get skunked on this deal. I want my three goddamned wishes."

"It's a sense of knowing that I have inside," Laila replied, her hand over her abdomen. "Even though you're an unkind, selfish, money-grubbing phony, I'm still bound to grant your wishes." She gave a smug smile.

Bunny laughed.

"What's so funny?" Laila asked.

"Before you popped out of that bottle I was trying to decide whether I'd have sex with Zak or make a wish first. I guess that dilemma's been solved. Of course...I can always command you to bring him to me."

There was that self-satisfied grin of Laila's again. "Sorry. I have to obey your commands, but that doesn't include making people do things against their will."

"Oh, I doubt it would be against his will." Bunny shifted her position, thrusting out her breasts. "Not now that he's free of *you*."

"I wouldn't be too sure about that, Bunny."

Bunny scowled at her. "I want you to call me Master."

"That's the masculine form. Wouldn't you prefer Mistress?"

"Master has a more powerful ring to it."

Laila shrugged. "Master it is."

Bunny gave a sly grin. "Bark like a dog."

"Excuse me?"

"You heard me. I command you to bark like a dog."

Laila promptly obeyed, sounding like a sick Chihuahua.

"Now hop on one foot and caw like a crow."

"Bunny—"

"Master. No, wait...I changed my mind. I want you to call me Most Beautiful and Powerful Master. Let me hear you say it."

"Oh for chrissakes." Laila cawed while hopping on one foot. "Most Beautiful and Powerful Master."

"Excellent. Now say, *I'm a big fat disgusting pig*—and keep hopping."

"That's easy." Laila laughed. "You're a big fat disgusting pig."

"Not me, you fat bitch, *you*! Do it. I command you!"

Laila sighed and rolled her eyes. "I'm a big fat disgusting pig."

Bunny clapped her hands, finally letting out the giggle she'd been suppressing.

"Granted, it's not as much fun as screwing Zak, but this should keep me occupied for a while," Bunny said to the still hopping Laila. After watching Laila for a few minutes, she ordered, "That's enough hopping. Get into the bathroom." She gestured to the right. As soon as Laila turned, Bunny gave her a good swift kick in the ass.

"Hey!"

"Hey what?"

Laila groaned. "Hey, Most Beautiful and Powerful Master."

"You're my property. I can treat you any way I want, right?"

"Yes, Most Beautiful and Powerful Master," Laila mumbled.

They walked into the bathroom and Bunny opened a drawer. "Here's a toothbrush. There's a bucket and cleaners in that cabinet. Scrub every nook and cranny of this room, including the toilet."

"Oh brother..."

"That's enough of your insolence, genie." She slapped Laila across the face, loving her new sense of power. "Be quick about it. If the job doesn't meet my expectations, you'll be punished. Down on your hands and knees. I want to see that floor sparkle."

"Yes, Most Beautiful and Powerful Master." Laila took the toothbrush and went to work, her sheer lavender robe dragging on the floor behind her.

As she moved to take it off, Bunny stopped her.

"Leave it on. Striking robe...although it needs a few alterations befitting your new status." She opened another drawer, drew out a pair of scissors and cut off the bottom of Laila's garment until it was a jagged waist-high length.

Laila uttered a little gasp.

"Forcing you to use that tiny toothbrush makes me seem rather heartless, doesn't it?" Bunny mused. "We certainly can't have that now, can we?" She took the plastic bucket to the sink, filling it halfway with hot water. Then she poured in an ample dose of ammonia. Balling the long, sheer lavender remnant of Laila's robe, she stuffed it into the malodorous mixture.

"There you go. Now you've got something to use besides the toothbrush." She held the scissors aloft, clicking them open and closed as she tsked. "Look at the way that mop of hair hangs in your face when you bend over. That's not conducive to scrub work, is it? No problem. I can fix that in a jiffy and make you far more comfortable."

Laila whimpered as Bunny fisted a hunk of Laila's hair, clipping through it and rendering a mass of short, patchy chunks.

"Much better." Dropping the shiny brown locks on the floor, Bunny rubbed her hands briskly, whisking away any remnants of Laila's hair from her hands. Extending her bejeweled fingers, she wiggled them. "You may kiss my hand and offer your thanks for my kindness now, genie."

Laila looked up at Bunny for a moment before leaning in and kissing her fingers. "Thank you for your kindness Most Beautiful and Powerful Master," she said just above a whisper as one fat tear coursed down her red, swollen cheek.

Yes! This was turning out to be about the best damn day of Bunny Turner's life.

~<>~

"I opened this right after you called," a weepy Reen told Zakkar, shoving a large manila envelope beneath his nose. "Laila gave it to me sealed the other day, asking me to bring it over after she'd made her final wish."

Zakkar glared at the envelope, leaving it untouched.

"It includes legal paperwork transferring ownership of The Great Pretender and the building to Reen," Drake said, drawing the papers out. Along with several legal documents, there were individual envelopes addressed to Zakkar, to Laila's brothers and sisters, and to Astrid and Tore.

"Should we call my mom and Tore?" Reen asked, holding the envelope addressed to them. "They'll be devastated when they hear..." She paused as the tears flowed.

Zakkar watched as Reen worked to regain her composure. When she looked up at him and Drake, Zakkar saw the look of abject helplessness in her eyes...eyes that mirrored the way he felt.

"I'd wait," Drake suggested. "We can't give your parents tragic news like this over the phone. Besides, we're going to do everything possible to have Laila back with us before daylight." Squeezing Reen's hand, he offered a reassuring smile.

Zakkar found it near impossible to match Drake's sense of optimism. Leafing through the paperwork, he frowned, shaking his head back and forth as he read Laila's words. He couldn't believe how meticulous she was in her instructions, or how selfless. Every word was designed to assist those she loved, now as well as in the future.

"So well thought out," Zakkar noted. "How long, I wonder, had she been planning this."

"I don't know," Reen said. "All I know is that she loved you with all her heart." She sobbed quietly into a wad of tissues. "You brought her such great happiness, Zak."

In Zakkar's mind, he had only succeeded in bringing his beloved, her family and friends, grief and despair. He had no right to sit here with them as they grieved when it should be Laila sitting here instead.

"Your sister deserved so much better," he muttered. "If not for me, her radiant smile and kind heart would still be lighting this world."

Reen's hand covered his. "You're a good man, Zak. You can't blame yourself for this."

"I can and I will," he vowed, cursing himself in his native tongue. No well-meaning words would ever change or soothe the fact that Laila had sacrificed herself for him.

"You're wearing Laila's heartwish ring," Reen noted, her lip trembling as she skimmed her finger across the stone.

"She used it as she made her final wish. When she vanished, it appeared on my hand, although I cannot understand how it is possible with my thick fingers."

Reen turned to Drake, handing him the envelope addressed to her. "Please tell Zak what this says."

Nodding, Drake read over one of the documents in the envelope. "Laila says she would have made you and Reen equal partners, Zakkar, except you have no legal identity. You'd be considered an illegal immigrant. She stipulated that Reen share the assets with you."

"Laila didn't want you to be without money," Reen interjected, still weeping.

"Or a roof over your head," Drake added, glancing up from the paper to Zakkar.

Zakkar growled, sailing his own copy of the paper across the kitchen. "I do not want any of it. I do not want *anything* but Laila!" He paced back and forth, mumbling with each swift step.

"To get her back you need to calm down," Drake said. "Stop doing an imitation of a caged lion and focus on a way to summon Inanna."

"I have been trying to summon her for thousands of years!" Zakkar bellowed, throwing his hands into the air. "She turns a deaf ear to me. I am naught but a lowly cockroach to Inanna." He made a squishing motion with his fingers.

Zakkar felt a firm hand on his shoulder.

"That may be," Drake admitted, "but as far as Reen and I are concerned, you're a good friend and an even better man, Zakkar."

Aware Drake and Reen, people with loving hearts and good intentions, were reaching out to him, doing their best to help him, even in the midst of their own despair, Zakkar knew he needed to quiet his agitation...to think of them instead of only himself.

"Thank you, Drake." He reached for his shoulder, covering Drake's hand with his own. "It is the same for me. Forgive me, good friend. I have never felt so weak or inept. I have never experienced such intense feelings of loss. As a man used to solving a crisis with action, it is difficult for me to know how to handle this. I thought I feared nothing, but I was wrong. Leading mighty armies and slaying formidable foes has not prepared me for the sense of helplessness that now engulfs me."

"I understand, Zakkar. I do," Drake assured him. "But the three of us need to set aside our sorrow and concentrate on finding a way to bring Laila back."

Nodding, Zakkar agreed. "What can I do?"

"Let's start with how to communicate with Inanna," Drake suggested. "Have you ever used the incantation that the priest and priestess used when they summoned her?"

Zakkar stopped pacing and stood in silent contemplation. "No. I do not remember it." Feeling useless, he pounded his fist on the kitchen table with such force, everything on it bounced.

Drake braced his hands on Zakkar's shoulders, giving them a squeeze as he offered a reassuring smile. "Of course you do, man. You have a photographic memory. The incantation is hidden in that ancient brain of yours." He tapped Zakkar's temple. "You just need to retrieve it."

"So many thousands of years," Zakkar began. "I don't know if I can recall—"

"You've got to," Reen said, resting her hand on his arm. "If you ever hope to see my sister again."

"We can do this." Drake's voice was a pledge of assurance. "Damn it, Zakkar, I'm sure of it."

Zakkar straightened, his fingers pressing hard against the quartz counter. For the first time since Laila disappeared he felt the strength of resolve flowing through his veins instead of the numbing cold of dread.

"Yes." Zakkar sat at the head of the table. "I will say the words as I recall them, Drake, and you will type them in your laptop."

"I'm ready."

"Good. Reen, you must prepare offerings of food for Inanna. Before we attempt to summon her we must have an array of pleasing food and drink ready to entice and persuade."

"I can definitely do that." Reen nodded. "What should I make?"

"Traditional offerings consisted of roasted goat or mutton with bitter herbs, chick peas and lentils. A few ducks and pigeons and some fresh fried fish from the Mesopotamian rivers. A platter of figs, dates and fruit conserved in honey, pungent cheeses, stacks of barley-wheat cakes with good lard, and onion and cucumber. Also, some barley ale or wine."

Reen blinked.

Zakkar smiled at the look of dismay across Reen's features, realizing his suggestions were beyond her culinary aptitude. Since he'd come to appreciate modern foods such as chocolate, he felt certain they would appeal to the goddess as well.

"I believe Inanna would perceive the sweets from The Great Pretender to be of rare and precious quality, especially anything chocolate," he told Reen. "To that we should add champagne."

"Maybe a meat and cheese platter too," Reen suggested. "And I'll make crab cakes, everybody loves those."

"Excellent," Zak said.

Reen got to work, whipping serving plates, bowls and other items from cupboards. "With a bakery right downstairs, a top-notch wine cellar in the basement, and a kitchen this well-equipped, I'll have a feast fit for a goddess prepared in no time."

Zakkar smiled and turned to Drake. "Reen is kind and good. More than just a sister, she is a true and loyal friend to Laila."

"They're closer than this." Drake held up two entwined fingers, watching Reen scurry through the kitchen, carrying foods from the pantry and refrigerator. Moderating his voice for Zakkar's ears only, he added, "I don't even want to think about what would happen to Reen if we didn't get Laila back."

"It would be a dark shroud of grief over her heart. We will succeed in our mission, Drake. I feel it deep in here." Zakkar widened his fingers into a claw-like shape and clutched his abdomen.

As he did, the stone in the heartwish ring glowed and the metal around his finger grew warm. "Did you see that?"

Drake nodded. "That's a little unnerving." His gaze traveled from the ring to Zakkar's face. "There must be a reason the ring transferred to your finger after Laila disappeared."

With a sudden knowing deep inside, Zakkar said, "There is...I feel it. I must make my truest heartwish at the same time I utter the incantation." Optimism began to override his pessimism.

"When we formulate our incantation," Drake said, studying his notes, "we'll make use of the fact that you were fathered by Enlil." He paused until he found the written passage he was searching for. "The great god of air and storms, who guards the tablets of destiny." He glanced up at Zakkar. "That should give you somewhat of an advantage with Inanna."

"Depending on whether or not the deities are at odds or on friendly terms these days," Zakkar noted, recalling stories of mighty clashes between the gods and goddesses and the considerable havoc they wreaked during their conflicts.

Within an hour the apartment was redolent with tantalizing aromas of sweet treats and savory dishes, and Zakkar and Drake had constructed the outline for their incantation.

"All we need to do," Drake skimmed the document he'd created, "is substitute your name and position for the high priest, Ibi-Utu, as well as for Sabit, the priestess of Nanna, the Moon God of Ur."

"We must light candles and incense before reciting our plea." Zakkar felt edgier than he could remember. His head pounded, his mouth was dry, his palms sweaty and his heart felt as if it was on the verge of exploding.

In a short time the trio had prepared the dining room, making the setting as appealing as possible.

"It looks like Christmas," Reen noted, taking in the bounty of foodstuffs, fancy china, crystal flutes, and the candlelit décor. "Inanna won't be able to resist."

Zakkar's hands fisted at his sides, the muscle at his jaw twitched. Fine rivulets of sweat trickled from his hairline to his jaw. "We shall see," he said solemnly, turning the laptop toward him and scowling as he witnessed his hands shaking. "You have been of such great help to me," he told Drake and Reen. "I would not have been able to accomplish this on my own. If all goes well, I shall return to eternal confinement in the bottle and—"

He paused at Reen's stunned gasp. The poor distraught woman stood there, wringing her hands and looking as if she were about to burst into another fit of sobs.

"No, Zak..."

"Reen," he offered the best smile he could manage under the circumstances, "I would gladly suffer the loss of life and limb to save

Laila. There is no greater agony for me than to know she has taken my place. Once I return to the bottle, our Laila will walk among the living where she belongs."

Gripping her hand and Drake's, Zakkar told them sincerely, "Whatever happens, know that my heart will forever be full of gratitude for your valued friendship." His gaze settled firmly, solemnly on his friends. "But now you must go. It may not be safe and I will not allow you to risk your lives."

"Hell no!" Drake crossed his arms over his chest with defiance, giving Zakkar a menacing glare. "I'm not going anywhere. According to the ancient texts, chanters need to be present at any invocation of the gods." He turned to Reen and smiled. "I know how much you want to help, Reen, but you need to go home. Zakkar and I can manage this on our own. You need to keep yourself safe."

"Sorry," Reen protested, "but there's no way in hell I'm leaving. Zak needs both of us here to chant and give him support. You know I'm right. If you think I'm going to sit at home twiddling my thumbs as you two macho men try to bring my sister back all on your own, you're crazy." She drew in a deep, trembly breath.

Drake smiled at her. "There's no use arguing with you when you make up your mind." He tipped her chin with his knuckle. "We're ready when you are, Zakkar."

Deeply touched, Zakkar told them, "I am glad to have had the privilege of knowing you both. Thank you from the depths of my being. I pray the gods keep you safe."

Placing the heartwish ring against his heart, he closed his eyes, saying a silent prayer, his truest heartwish, sending his undying love to Laila. He took a few minutes silently reading the document they'd prepared from Drake's laptop, committing it to memory. Handing it back to Drake, Zakkar looked to the heavens, raising his arms, palms up, in the traditional prayer of entreaty stance.

"O great Inanna, Queen of Heaven, goddess of love and war, I summon you," he roared and the stone from the heartwish ring illuminated the ceiling. Drake and Reen chanted short praises of adoration to Inanna that Drake had discovered in his ancient texts.

"I am Zakkar Tanojin Lugalbanda Tymon, he who boldly led the armies of Sumer into battle, who fought many battles in your name. He who was fathered by Enlil, the great god of air and storms who guards the tablets of destiny. You are the great lady of the gods. Your terror is fearsome as it weighs on the land. No man anticipates your commands."

The crystal candelabra on the table vibrated. Reen and Drake exchanged glances, shuddering.

"The heavens fold themselves in your presence like a mourning garment," Zakkar continued, his voice resonating in the sizeable room. "You are she who hastens like a north wind storm into the midst of the people. You are she who hears prayer and pleading."

The flames on all of the candles flickered, then grew higher and brighter.

"I summon you, great Inanna to reverse a mighty wrong, an injustice of the greatest enormity..."

Zakkar continued his heartfelt plea as Reen and Drake kept chanting, while palpable signs of supernatural forces surrounded them.

Zakkar spoke the final words of the invocation. "O make it be, great and wondrous Inanna! Let it be so!"

The entire room rumbled, as if in the midst of a small earthquake. A boom of thunder resounded throughout the apartment and fine threads of white lightning cracked overhead.

Gasping, Reen clutched onto Drake, who held her tight.

The ethereal visage of a woman, as beautiful as she was fearsome, suddenly loomed over the proceedings.

It was the same formidable countenance Zakkar had seen five thousand years before, on the fateful night that had sealed his destiny.

Chapter 27

~<>~

"YOU INSIGNIFICANT PEASANTS, you inferior organisms, you worthless oddments of mediocrity!" Inanna boomed before she became fully visible. "Why have you deemed to summon me?"

Zakkar stood tall, chin elevated, as Reen and Drake slipped behind him.

"Great Inanna, it is I, Zakkar Tanojin Lugalbanda Tymon, he who boldly led the armies of Sumer into battle, who fought many battles in your name. He who—"

"Yes, yes, I know." Inanna yawned, waving her hand, indicating for him to stop. "I heard all of it during your rather lengthy incantation."

Inanna's torso shimmered into solidity and she went on, "How am I supposed to keep the cosmos functioning when I'm constantly being pulled this way and that? This had better be good, Zakkar Tymon." Closing her eyes, she sniffed the air.

"Do I smell chocolate?" She opened her eyes, nailing the threesome with a fierce glare.

"Brownies and an assortment of chocolate cookies, your majesty." Reen curtsied.

"They had better be for me and they'd better be delicious or there'll be *Kurnugi* to pay."

"Oh they are, your majesty." Reen engaged in another bow.

Inanna crooked her finger and Reen, her head lowered in reverence, passed the plate of chocolate goodies.

"Delectable," she said as she munched. "You may keep your head. And do stop all that groveling. Now, what's up?" She licked the chocolate crumbs from her fingers.

Inanna's entire body was discernible now, as was the lion on a diamond-studded golden leash beside her. When the beast let out a bloodcurdling roar, Reen and Drake jumped about a foot off the floor. Used to stories of the gods and their wild beast pets, Zakkar stood firm.

"Holy shit!" Reen cried.

"Contain your vulgar outbursts." Inanna tsked. "You'll frighten poor little Ninazu." Petting the lion, she made soothing baby talk to the animal. It closed its eyes and purred, rubbing its mane against her.

"She's wearing a business suit," Reen muttered in surprise, taking in the ultra-chic personage hovering in midair.

Inanna looked down at the sleek gray shantung silk suit hugging her perfect figure. "What? You expected a diaphanous gown? Why is it you brainless mortals expect your gods and goddesses to conduct daily business wearing gauzy scraps of material? This is the twenty-first century. Inanna doesn't do diaphanous unless she's in the bedroom. I *am* a liberated goddess, after all." She patted her blonde chignon.

"Great goddess, my name is Drake Slattery. I'm a professor of ancient history and classical archaeology at Wisdom Harbor University."

Offering a dismissive appraisal, Inanna said, "Well bully for you." She pointed at a chocolate chip cookie, which floated through the air to her fingers. "Since we're throwing around titles, I'm the Queen of Heaven, Goddess of Love and War. I'm one of the seven gods who decree the fates."

Inanna gave a sigh of satisfaction as she bit into the cookie. "Are those crab cakes?"

"Yes, ma'am, I—" Reen began.

"Good. Bring them to Ninazu. He's hungry."

Reen's eyes bugged. "You-you want me to get close to—"

Inanna snapped her fingers three times in rapid succession. "Hop to it, mortal. I've just given you a command."

Platter of her crab cakes in hand, Reen muttered, "Ohmigod, ohmigod," doing as Inanna asked, inching toward the huge golden lion. "Nice kitty," she said as soothingly as her quavering voice would allow.

Wincing, Zakkar prayed the creature preferred crab meat over human flesh.

Drake swallowed hard, breathing a sigh of relief as the lion tested the crab and nibbled at it. "Uh, Inanna, we've summoned you because—"

"Because it was time for me to return to my bottle," Zakkar blurted, unable to remain silent. "I was fully prepared to face the bleak, dark realm once again when, to my horror, the woman I love, my possessor, Laila Malone, made her final wish and asked to take my place in servitude so that I could be free of the bottle's cruel imprisonment forever more."

"Is that pecan fudge?" Inanna asked Reen, making Zakkar's insides boil with rage at her indifferent attitude.

"Yes, your highness." Reen started to curtsey, then stopped, remembering Inanna's chastisement. As Reen awkwardly stumbled in place, Inanna summoned a piece of fudge, popping it into her mouth and murmuring her satisfaction.

"Laila is kind, sweet and good," Zakkar continued. "She does not deserve to be trapped in the cold, dreary netherworld of the bottle, great Inanna. I have summoned you to plead for Laila's freedom. I beg of you, I beseech you, O great and compassionate goddess, let me exchange places with my beloved Laila so that she—"

"No!" Drake and Reen exclaimed in unison.

Ninazu roared, plainly scaring the *Kurnugi* out of Reen, who was close enough to feel his hot breath on her face because her hair blew sideways as the lion bellowed.

"We..." Drake cleared his throat, "we beg you to set them *both* free, great Inanna. Neither Laila nor Zakkar deserve to be trapped in that bottle for eternity. Zakkar was wrongly imprisoned in the first place. You see, he was only trying to—"

"Silence!" Eyes blazing, Inanna raised her hand in warning and a series of lightning bolts shot straight up from her fingers. "Enough blather from all of you!"

She sat at the head of the table, with the vast array of food Reen had set out at her fingertips. With a subtle nod, a bottle of rare red wine uncorked itself and poured into her wineglass. At the same time, her crystal flute filled with champagne, while a chosen assortment of olives, cheeses, fruits, crusty bread, honey and olive oil were magically portioned on a plate.

"As stated in your plea," Inanna shot a glance at Zakkar, "your sentence was set in place to obliterate your transgressions to womankind by serving them for all eternity. Tell me, Zakkar Tymor, why you believe you were wrongly condemned. And for heaven's sake, don't drag it out."

Zakkar sat to the right of Inanna, with Reen and Drake taking seats at the opposite end of the table, away from the fearsome goddess and her menacing pet.

Zakkar told Inanna the whole story, trying not to sully the priestess Sabit's name as he explained. Drake jumped in here and there, fortifying the details to help Inanna understand it was Sabit who had unwittingly brought this terrible sentence down on Zakkar's head.

Once they'd finished, Inanna sat back, tapping her lacquered red fingernails against the tabletop. To Zakkar, it seemed she sat like at for an eternity. He yearned for her to hurry, but wisely kept his mouth shut as Inanna ruminated.

"If what you say is true," Inanna finally said, "you are the victim of an atrocious injustice, Zakkar. Why did it take you so long to come forth and bring this excessive, unwarranted sentence to my attention?"

At a loss for words, Zakkar's mouth hung open.

"He's been trying to contact you for five thousand years," Reen said. "You never answered him."

"The incantations must have been faulty," Inanna speculated. She held out her hands, palms up. A state-of-the-art laptop appeared in her grasp. She set it on the table, busily clacking away at the keyboard.

"You work with computers?" Drake asked, amazed.

"Only when my abacus is on the fritz," Inanna answered sarcastically. "Be silent while I search the hall of ancient records. I'm also sending Enlil an instant message so he can check to see what's been inscribed on the tablets of destiny regarding Zakkar Tymon's fate."

A short while later, Inanna shook her head and tsked. "Look at this, page after page of lamentations, all on your behalf, Zakkar. It seems Sabit pleaded with one god after another to...well, here, let me read it verbatim. 'To free the brave, honorable warrior who took the blame for my foolish actions to save me from being beheaded. Through my fear, my sweet mouth became venomous and I condemned a worthy, honorable soul to a cold, dark fate.'"

Inanna fixed Zakkar with a solid stare. "The woman pleaded, lamented, wailed and tearfully confessed her sins and failings for the rest of her life, trying to undo the harm she'd done to you."

"What happened to Sabit?" Zakkar asked. "Did she remain a priestess?"

"After five years in service to her symbolic betrothed, Nanna, the Moon God of Ur," Inanna read, "Sabit left the *ziggurat*, married and had children. When her children had grown, she returned to the temple, once again pledging her service to Nanna. She was past sixty when she died."

"Why didn't anyone listen to her?" Reen asked.

"Who knows?" Inanna shrugged. "Maybe they thought she was love struck or loony. If she tried to reach me, I never knew about it. Hold it a minute...incoming from Enlil, and another from Ereshkigal, goddess of the underworld..."

Zakkar, Drake and Reen sat forward in their chairs, waiting for word from the deities.

"Ereshkigal reports that Sabit's soul is now at rest." She looked up at Zakkar. "Apparently you're innocent."

A cumbersome burden evaporated from Zakkar's soul.

"As for Enlil..." Inanna clicked the mouse. "Ah, okay, that seals it." She slapped her laptop shut. "You've been completely exonerated of any wrongdoing by your daddy, Zakkar. Enlil said the tablets indicate you're destined to live a long and fruitful life, full of love and happiness, etcetera, etcetera. As of this moment that decree has gone into effect. Your curse is broken."

"I am full of gratitude," Zakkar said, "but, Inanna, what about—"

"Well, I guess that's it. All's well that ends well." Inanna stood and smiled. "I regret it took a while to resolve this, Zakkar, but—"

"A while?" Reen said incredulously. "You call being trapped in a bottle for five thousand years and undergoing humiliation and torture and God knows what else *a while*?"

Pulling Reen close, Drake shushed her.

Her eyes blazing, Inanna aimed an outstretched finger at Reen. "I caution you, mouthy mortal. Do not overstep your bounds. I am not renowned for my patience and I have no qualms lopping off the heads of those who annoy me."

Drake held Reen tight. "She didn't mean anything, Inanna. She just cares a great deal about Zakkar. We all do."

"Very well. I'll be off then." Inanna raised her arm in the air, looking as though she was about to snap her fingers.

"Wait!" the other three chorused.

"What about Laila?" Zakkar hurried. "She is trapped in the bottle as we speak. I beg of you, great Inanna, free her. Return her to me for I cannot live without her in my life. I will be but a shadow among the living without my Laila."

Inanna's gaze shifted to the ring Zakkar wore as the stone glimmered again. One eyebrow arched as she muttered, "Odin's heartwish ring," surprising Zakkar. She let out a thunderous sigh and sat down. "Okay, bring me the bottle. I'll take care of it." She stretched out her hand, wiggling her fingers. "Hurry up, it's nearly time for Ninazu's nap." The lion yawned, punctuating Inanna's observation.

Reen, Drake and Zakkar exchanged dumbfounded glances.

"Bunny!" they cried.

"I forgot all about it until just this minute," Reen said.

"Do you think Bunny's opened the bottle yet?" Drake asked.

"I hope not," Zakkar said. "She is not a good woman. Her wishes would not be beneficial, except to herself. She could be mistreating Laila." He scowled at the thought of Laila suffering at Bunny's hands.

Inanna's frustrated sigh was monumental. "Would someone mind cluing me in?"

"We don't have the bottle. Laila's former employer, Bunny Turner, found out Zakkar was a genie and she stole it," Drake explained.

"Bunny is wicked," Zakkar added. "And envious. I fear for Laila's wellbeing."

"Laila's previous boss?" Inanna asked. "What kind of work?"

"Bunny owns Tuned by Turner," Reen offered. "A weight loss clinic. She has zero concern about her overweight clients. All she cares about is their money."

"I see." Inanna's smile looked a tad malevolent. "All right, be silent while I take care of this."

Inanna stood again, arms upstretched in the same manner as Zakkar's earlier when he summoned her. Her powerful voice reverberating, Inanna uttered what Zakkar recognized as a ruling in ancient Sumerian.

The air chilled. Thunder clapped. Lightning sparked.

And Ninazu roared.

~<>~

"I'm ready to make my wishes, genie," Bunny yelled from the bedroom. "Get your fat ass off the bathroom floor and get over here to do my bidding."

Laila rolled her eyes. She wanted nothing more than to take the bucket of ammonia water and douse Bunny's head. But as she'd sadly discovered, genies were at the express mercy of their possessors unable to fight back against cruelty or injustice.

"Yes, Most Beautiful and Powerful Master." Laila got to her feet, wincing as her spine cracked while she straightened her back.

She thought of Zak and the centuries he'd spent fulfilling the whims of his owners, some good women and some cruel, selfish ones like Bunny...or worse. It was a miracle he'd maintained his sanity after thousands of years.

But he was free now. The knowledge warmed her, bringing a smile to her lips. Laila knew Zak would be angry and grieving now, but that would pass in time and he'd find happiness with a good woman. Reen would set him up with someone. *Reen*...oh how Laila would miss all the laughter they shared.

"Move that lazy ass of yours," Bunny barked. As soon as Laila stood before her, Bunny burst out laughing. "That's a perfect look for you, Laila. Take a good long look at yourself in the full length mirror. Get an eyeful of the great and mighty owner of The Great Pretender."

Laila gazed at her reflection, breathing a sigh as she spotted raccoon eyes from smeared makeup, haphazardly chopped hair and less than half of her sheer lavender robe, raveling around her hips. "It doesn't matter," she muttered beneath her breath. Setting her beloved Zakkar free was worth any humiliation Bunny could throw at her.

"Tuned by Turner and I will be back on top again before the end of the day!" Bunny reveled in a sneer. "I'll make certain during my wishes that your baked goods taste so foul you'll lose all your customers—customers you stole from me."

Laila maintained her silence, unable to rip into Bunny the way she craved. With a weighty sigh of acquiescence, she imagined the dark, deadly quiet of the bottle might be a welcome retreat after spending this demeaning time with Bunny.

"For my first wish," Bunny began, and Laila held her breath, wondering what heinous, selfish wish she was about to grant for the woman. "I wish to be the richest most powerful woman in—" Bunny's eyes widened in horror as her clothing split at the seams. "What the—" She looked down, grabbing the tearing material at her midriff. "What's happening to me?"

"Bunny!" Laila cried. "You-you're getting fat!"

Growing chunkier by the second, Bunny glared at Laila. "You! You did this to me, you despicable bitch!"

Caught up in wonder, Laila whipped her head from side to side. "No, I swear, Bunny, this isn't my doing. I don't know what's happening."

"Where are you going?" Bunny screamed. "Laila!" She started to sob. The usually self-assured woman suddenly looked weak and pathetic. "Don't leave me like this, Laila. Please."

"It's okay, I'm not going anywhere." Laila reached her hand out to comfort Bunny, only to discover her fingers were growing transparent. In fact, so was the rest of her. "What's happening...?"

Laila gasped, watching her flesh grow fainter and wondering if this was the end for her, if she'd just fade away into thin air and cease to exist.

As she became a vapor, she glanced Bunny's way once more. The woman looked fifty pounds heavier.

"Come back!" Bunny cried, reaching for Laila, clutching at thin air. "What about my three wishes? Chocolate. Oh God, I need *chocolate*!"

Bunny's earsplitting wail for chocolate was the last thing Laila saw or heard before everything went black.

~<>~

Inanna's eyes flashed like newly ignited torches.

The entire building shook. Ninazu continued to roar. Inanna's demeanor was formidable to behold as she called out the ancient words.

When gray storm clouds appeared just beneath the dining room ceiling, Reen shuddered from head to toe and clung to Drake. Drake clung to Zakkar. Zakkar's fingers dug into the back of the mahogany chair so tightly he half expected them to bore through the heavy wood. His teeth were clenched so firmly he was amazed his jaw didn't fracture.

It was one thing to be a warrior in battle, equipped with his saber and facing a mortal enemy. It was quite another being at the mercy of a temperamental immortal who was, Zakkar hoped, bringing his beloved back from the oppressive curse of the bottle.

As Inanna's resounding voice thundered, the heartwish stone shimmered on Zakkar's finger once more. Then, in the blink of an eye, it disappeared. Incredulous, he wiggled his fingers, examining them. A quick glimpse at Drake and Reen's stunned expressions told him they'd witnessed the ring evaporate.

With a resounding declaration, Inanna spoke the final words, seizing their attention. An instant later Zakkar, Reen and Drake were mesmerized by a lavender-hued vapor emerging from the storm clouds. Floating down toward the floor the fog slowly took form.

"Laila!" Zakkar cried, breaking away from the others and running toward the materializing form. The instant she became solid, he grabbed her into his arms, holding tight, terrified she'd disappear again if he let go. "Oh my love, my sweet, sweet love," he murmured, covering her face with kisses. "You've returned to me."

"Zak? But how...what happened?"

"Laila!" Reen and Drake shouted, running to the embracing couple and making a cumbersome but welcoming four-way hug.

"Oh, Zak...you're crying." Laila brushed a tear from his cheek.

"It is without shame that I do, little one. The intensity of my love for you and the immense gladness in my heart at seeing you again has momentarily reduced me to a sniveling babe." Zakkar rocked her in his arms, whispering words of love.

"Um...hello? Remember me?" Inanna reminded them. "Shouldn't someone be groveling at my feet and giving me kudos about now?"

Zakkar released Laila and fell to his knees before Inanna, thanking and praising her in his native tongue.

"Yes," she smiled, "that's much better."

"You were able to conjure Inanna," Laila said in awe. "How?" All eyes were on Laila's hand as the heartwish stone twinkled on her finger. "It's back. I thought I lost it when I floofed into the bottle."

"It transported to my finger the instant you disappeared," Zakkar explained.

Slack jawed, Laila looked again at the ring, watching the glow diminish before shifting her stunned gaze to Zakkar.

By the gods it was bliss to look upon his darling Laila's visage once more.

"The ring seemed to speak to me, telling me to make the truest wish from my heart," he told her, clapping his hand against his chest. "And I did."

"That's exactly what happened to me." Looking at Inanna, Laila's expression was filled with thankfulness. "I don't have words to express the heartfelt depth of my gratitude. Thank you so much, Inanna."

Though Inanna was silent, Zakkar detected a faint smile across her lips as the goddess offered a nod of acknowledgement.

"I can't tell you how glad we are that you're back," Drake said. "Zakkar's been out of his mind with grief." He pulled Laila into a welcoming squeeze.

"Thanks, Drake. I'm thrilled and downright amazed I'm back too." Laila looked over his shoulder, her eyes widening when she spotted Ninazu. Right on cue, the big cat yawned. "There's a lion in my dining room."

"It's okay. I think." Wrapping her arms around Laila, Reen hugged her sister. "This is Inanna's pet, Ninazu. He's crazy about my crab cakes."

Out of nowhere came Friday's barking as the dog rounded the corner, galloping into the room, wheedling his way between the others so he could nuzzle his mistress. His butt wiggled back and forth as his tail wagged. Ninazu let out an ear-splitting roar and

Friday, taken aback at first, stood his ground and growled at the huge cat. It was obvious he'd let nothing stand in the way of welcoming Laila home.

To everyone's grateful surprise, Ninazu ignored Friday's bold outburst.

"Good dog. Brave boy." Zakkar patted Friday's flanks.

"Friday!" Laila leaned down to kiss his muzzle. "I missed you too, sweetie pie."

"We were terrified we'd lost you forever." Reen hugged Laila again before standing at arm's length, eyeing her sister and best friend. "Whoa...you look like hell. What happened?"

Laila's eyebrow arched. "Bunny Turner happened. That woman's one crazy, power-hungry bitch."

"What you did was the height of foolishness, young lady," Inanna chided. "It was idiocy to sacrifice yourself for your lover like that. You could have been trapped for eternity in that bottle, looking like a drowned rat."

"Inanna is right," Zakkar bellowed, shaking a chastising finger at Laila. He remembered the sick feeling of dread that enveloped him when she'd disappeared from his grasp after making her final wish. "You had me turned inside out with guilt, rage and anguish. Had I known what you were thinking, Laila, I would have—"

"On the other hand," Inanna sniffed and dabbed her eyes with a tissue that suddenly appeared in her hand, "it was incredibly romantic. As the goddess of love, I've always been a sucker for a good romance story."

"I'm sorry for causing you all such heartache," Laila said. "But I had no other choice. I love you far too much to send you back to that horrid bottle, Zakkar."

Zakkar kissed her fingers. "You are foolish but you are also the most loving, devoted, selfless woman I have ever had the good fortune to know."

"True love," Inanna sighed. "Perfectly matched souls, according to all our records."

"So we're both free? Forever?" Laila asked the goddess. "Zak can stay here with me? No more bottle or genie duties for either of us?"

"You're both free." Inanna gestured with her hand and the spun glass bottle and box appeared on the table before them. "From this moment forward, this vessel is nothing more than a rare antiquity. Hang on to it for a keepsake, sell it, or smash it to smithereens if you like."

"We will have a ceremony," Zakkar stated solemnly, sneering as he eyed the objects that had been his prison for so many centuries. "We will take turns wielding deathly blows to the box and bottle until they are reduced to naught but dust."

"That suits me," Laila agreed.

Zakkar gazed at his beloved, smoothing his fingers through her hair. It was only then that he noticed her sad, sorry state of disarray, as well as the swelling patch of purple near her eye. "Oh, little one, Reen is right...you look hellish. What did Bunny do to you?"

"Aside from the obvious?" She flipped her choppy hair and fingered her ragged robe. "It was pretty awful." She took in a deep breath. "But it's over now. I'm sure it can't begin to compare to what you've been through over the centuries, Zak." Laila rested her head against his chest and sighed.

The feel of his woman in his arms was more precious than gold. "I vow to make Bunny pay for causing you such anguish," Zakkar promised.

Laila looked to Inanna and the women shared a knowing smile. "Oh, I think Inanna's already taken care of that."

"Indeed," the goddess assured, puffing out her cheeks like a blowfish and patting her almost nonexistent belly. "Bunny will stay that way until she learns her lesson and redeems herself."

"Stay like what? What happened?" Reen asked.

"Bunny's fat," Laila said. "Practically obese."

"No!" Reen gasped. "Seriously?"

"Fifty pounds heavier and profoundly addicted to chocolate," Inanna confirmed. "She will have no memory of Zakkar being a genie, or of you being her genie, Laila. She will only remember she has been gaining weight lately due to hormonal problems and her uncontrollable chocolate binges. It's fitting retribution for the woman's petty cruelty, and lack of compassion for the very people she claims to want to help."

"Oh, that's sweet." Reen's gave a satisfied smile. "Talk about getting her just desserts."

"I disagree." Zakkar frowned, folding his arms across his chest. "Bunny deserves to be boiled in oil."

"Not in my kitchen." Laila smiled. "Trust me, as a fat-phobic woman Bunny will suffer more than enough struggling to lose that weight." Turning to Inanna, she asked, "What happens as far as Zakkar's identity? He'll need some sort of legal identification so he doesn't get deported."

With a wave of Inanna's hand, a leather-covered container, the size of a cigar box, appeared on the table. "This will provide all Zakkar Tymon needs. Birth certificate, college degrees, resumes, letters of recommendation, bank accounts, credit cards, etcetera."

"College degrees?" Zakkar hadn't expected that. "In what subject? I doubt I am qualified for anything other than leading armies."

"Don't be modest, dear boy." Inanna flicked her wrist. "Your records indicate you've been busy these last five thousand years, acquiring knowledge and skills far beyond what most mortals achieve in a lifetime. Whatever degree or document you desire will appear there when you need it. Simply open the box and ask for it."

"You could be an exercise physiologist," Laila offered, recalling the Sumerian fitness exercises he'd taught them to help keep fit.

"Or a professor of ancient studies," Drake said.

"Just so long as he's not an electrician," Reen quipped.

"Ah yes, I heard about that incident." Inanna rolled her eyes. They all chuckled, surprised she knew about it.

The soaring possibilities for his future as a twenty-first century man eased Zakkar's mind. He'd be able to fit into modern society easily, without having to worry about eluding legal authorities. "This is magnificent. With my own driver's license," he said with a satisfied smile, "I will be able to drive immediately!"

"Uh...no," Inanna said. "That you'll need to earn the traditional way."

"Thank goodness," Laila mumbled.

"I saw the report on your mailbox encounter." Inanna wagged a chastising finger at him. "You have a stubborn streak, just like your father."

"Another question, great goddess," Zakkar said.

Inanna glanced at Ninazu, who was sound asleep and purring. "As long as I'm out of here before his feeding time. He gets testy when he's hungry."

Friday whimpered at that, skulking from the room, to find a table to hide beneath, no doubt.

Zakkar pulled Laila close, wrapping an arm around her shoulder. "Will I be able to father Laila's babes?"

"Yes." Inanna offered a full smile. "Enlil's tablets show that Laila is destined to conceive on your wedding night."

"How wonderful!" Laila gasped. "Oh, Zak, we're going to be parents!"

"With our very own little goats." He lifted Laila off her feet, swinging her around.

"You'll be mortal again," Inanna reminded Zakkar, "so for heaven's sake, listen to Laila and don't go getting yourself into electrical hazards or car accidents. Not only can you be wounded, you can also die. Understood?"

"Understood. I will strive to be a good husband who listens to his wife's cautions."

"Ha!" Inanna shot Laila a glance. "Good luck with that." She looked at the foursome and smiled. "Be seated, all of you. I wish to bestow my blessings for long life and happiness for you, your families, and all of your offspring."

Standing at the head of the table, she directed the four of them to be seated close to her.

Tilting her head with a contemplative expression, Inanna gestured between Reen and Drake. "You two," she said. "You're not married or a couple."

"No, we're just friends," Reen offered, resting her hand atop Drake's.

"I see. The coming year will be most eventful and life changing for you both," Inanna told them. "Drake, your soul mate is a woman you have already met. And Maureen, your soul mate is—" With an elegant lift of her eyebrow, Inanna gave a low, throaty chuckle. "Well...that's interesting."

Drake and Reen exchanged curious glances. "What is?" they chorused.

"Some things are best left unexplained," she cryptically informed them with a dismissive wave of her hand.

The four of them listened with respect while Inanna conferred abundant blessings and sang a soulful chant to the gods, asking that they be kept safe and protected for all their days.

Inanna glanced to the side, a smile curling her lip. Zakkar turned to where she was looking to see Friday timidly peeking into the room.

"My blessings upon you as well, brave, foolhardy little dog."

After the four offered Inanna profuse thanks, the goddess and Ninazu departed in a blinding flash.

Zakkar propped his elbows on the table, his face falling into his hands. "Gods," he groaned, raking his fingers through his hair, "that was a lengthy and precarious ordeal. I feared we would not be victorious."

"I wonder what Inanna meant with all that mysterious talk about next year," Drake said.

"I'm crossing my fingers she saw a happily ever after vision of me and Hud Griffin." Reen's grin was infectious. "What do you hope for, Drake?"

Drake sat silent for a long moment, staring ahead. "A woman who loves me as much as I love her," he said finally.

"Ooh," Reen jiggled her eyebrows, "and who might that be?"

Drake's smile was wistful. "Like Inanna said, some things are best left unexplained."

Zakkar looked to his side, smiling at Laila. "At this moment, with the other half of my heart, my soul, sitting beside me, I am truly the happiest man—whether mortal or immortal—on earth." He leaned close, giving her a tender kiss. "You taste of ambrosia, little one. The thought of existing on this plane without another kiss from your sweet lips was agony."

"I've always believed in happy endings." Laila smoothed her fingers over his jaw.

Drake and Reen exchanged knowing glances. "I think it's time for us to go," he said. "We've been at this almost all night and I have to pick up Lilly and Kevin in the morning."

"I'm sure you two would like to be alone," Reen agreed with a wink.

Laila and Zakkar exchanged a few muffled words.

"Reen, Drake, stay and sup with us." Zakkar clapped his belly. "My stomach speaks to me, and Reen's luscious array of food and drink beckons. You can depart after we eat." He gave them his warmest smile. "I shall forever be in your debt. If you are ever in need of a friend or assistance of any kind, you will call me first."

"That goes double for me," Laila said. "Thank you for being there for Zak...for me. Without your help I'd still have my head in Bunny's toilet, scrubbing it with her toothbrush."

"She didn't..." After Laila's confirming nod, a narrow-eyed Reen added, "What a bitch."

Salivating, Zak looked at the lavish spread of sweets and savories before him and smiled. He had his woman, his love, at his side and his appetite had finally returned. He was ready to dig in and soothe his savage hunger.

As he reached for the plate of cheese and olives, it disappeared. One by one, each of the platters of food were zapped away. Not even the wines were spared, they vanished too.

"Best brownies I've ever had," Inanna's voice echoed from far away.

"Well I guess that's it." Laila shrugged. "No brownies for us."

"True. It looks like we have no choice but to retire," Zakkar said, stretching with an exaggerated yawn.

Reen elbowed Drake and they shared a laugh. "Okay, okay, we can take a hint. Goodnight you two lovebirds." After another round of hugs and loving farewells they were gone.

Laila smiled at Zakkar. "My beloved gen—" She stopped herself and smoothed her hand along his jaw. "My beloved Zakkar," she amended and he captured her lips in a kiss.

Zakkar swept Laila off her feet, carrying her to their bedroom.

With each step he whispered Sumerian odes of love and devotion in her ear, illuminating a score of deeply sensual attentions for his beloved.

Chapter 28

One Year Later

~<>~

THE RING ON LAILA'S FINGER grew warm for the first time since Inanna's visit. Something inside told her the time was nearing when she would pass the ring to someone else. The identity of that person was still a mystery.

As for her brother-in-law's matching heartwish ring, Varik told Laila he knew he was meant to pass his ring to Laila's brother, Gard soon. With all her brother had been through, Gard could certainly use a little magic in his life.

"Our little goats are finally asleep," Zak whispered, gently drawing the blanket over Abigail Maureen while Laila fussed over baby August Drake in his crib.

"The twins are little angels," Laila said. "Gus looks just like you. He's going to be a real lady killer when he grows up."

"And Abby has the hypnotic lapis lazuli eyes of her beautiful mother," Zak replied as they tiptoed out of the nursery.

The children were named after Abigail and August Maythorne, two good souls instrumental in Abigail getting to Oregon and discovering Zak's ancient box and bottle. The babies' middle names honored their parents' dearest friends.

Each time she gazed at her children Laila gave thanks. A year ago she'd expected to exist only in a void, intermittently serving a variety of possessors, while Zak made a life with another woman. She felt bountifully blessed.

The Great Pretender thrived in Glassfloat Bay, becoming a favorite spot among locals as well as tourists. Everyone marveled at Laila's scrumptious reduced calorie scones and the rest of her growing line of healthy baked goods.

Bunny Turner ultimately sold Tuned by Turner, using the proceeds from the sale to open Bunny's Chocolate Haven a block away from The Great Pretender, where she popped in a few times a week for coffee and a scone. Still plump, she seemed happier and more content, boasting a ready smile as she proudly displayed her designer chocolates.

Dear Zakkar insisted their good fortune was due to Laila being a special woman. He was fond of telling her that goodness begets goodness and that a kind heart is rewarded with bountiful gladness.

"Did you bring the champagne?" Laila asked as they entered their bedroom.

"Along with a box of chocolates." Zak showed her.

"It was nice of Bunny to give us a box of her premium truffle collection, wasn't it?"

"We will not be eating those." Zak scowled. "I disposed of them."

"You threw out a three-pound box of chocolates?" Laila gasped. "That's a mortal sin."

His eyebrow arched. "Remember the kindly old woman who offered the apple to Snow White?" he asked, having just read the classic fairytale to the twins. "She turned out to be an evil witch and the apple was poisoned."

"Hmm...you have a point there," Laila admitted.

He drew her close, nuzzling her neck. "We have much to celebrate tonight."

Laila's thoughts skimmed over the last eighteen months. "Just think...it's been a year and a half since you popped out of that bottle, scaring the living daylights out of me."

"The day my life began." Zak deposited a series of kisses along her nape.

"And mine," Laila agreed as Zak peeled off her clothing. "It's also the one year anniversary of the night we each gained our freedom from the bottle." They glanced at the dresser. Atop it, on a marble pedestal, sat a transparent, solid plastic cube. Suspended inside were fine powdered glass and stone particles, remnants of the ancient bottle and box they'd ceremoniously smashed.

On the wall over the dresser, Zak's genie outfit and saber were displayed in a shadowbox frame. Convincing Zak to retire his saber hadn't been easy. Laila assured him he could always break the glass and retrieve it should a lethal band of ninjas break into the house.

"There is another anniversary we will celebrate tonight," Zak said and Laila couldn't think of what that might be. "We must toast to me getting my driver's license ten months ago today." His grin was broad and proud.

"Ah...yes...of course. That one is a biggie."

"Indeed. I had to memorize a great deal of information to pass my test."

Zak tended to be a speed demon. Whether it was working out, running along the seashore, or driving his car, he loved going fast—something he could never enjoy during all those centuries bottled up. Whenever little Gus and Abby were in the car, however, he drove like a cautious little old lady on Sunday, so Laila couldn't complain...too much.

As he disrobed, her eyes traveled his body. "I hope our children share your thirst for knowledge, as well as your photographic memory."

"And I hope they embody the qualities of their beautiful mother. What I celebrate most of all is you." Zak kissed her tenderly. As he gazed into her eyes, love shining from the windows of his soul, he charmed her with an adoring smile.

Happy tears trickled from the corners of Laila's eyes. "To think I almost passed up the shelf of salt and pepper shakers." She wrapped her arms around his neck, bringing his lips to hers for another kiss.

"Do you feel it, my love?" he said, threading his fingers through her hair.

"What, darling?" With her fingers meshed around his neck, she locked gazes with him. She could stay that way forever, never letting him go.

"The powerful love we have for each other." He held her close.

"Absolutely," Laila answered her husband, indulging in a blissful sigh. "I wonder how much love and happiness one woman can experience before she expires from an overdose of joy."

Zak brushed a kiss across her lips. "We have the rest of our lives, all eternity together, to discover the answer, my love."

Laila's heart soared.

"The rest of our lives..." she whispered, winding her fingers through his hair while counting her many blessings. "Yes...yes, my darling genie."

~<>~

Turn the page for a sneak peak of **THE FIREFIGHTER'S HEARTWISH**, book 3 in the Heartwishes series, featuring Laila's brave firefighter brother, Gard, whose life is forever changed when he meets a sweet little boy and his beautiful mother!

ABOUT THE FIREFIGHTER'S HEARTWISH

Isolated for months in Antarctica, amid icebergs, glaciers, and his own dark thoughts, glaciologist and part-time firefighter Gard Malone returns home, grumpy and craving more solitude.

Gutted by the tragic accident that took the life of his best friend, Gard blames himself for failing to save him. Surrounded by well-intentioned friends and family determined to brighten his spirits, he just wants to be left alone.

Brooding over coffee at the café, he hears a young boy singing a Christmas carol about "Hark," his special angel. Little Harold's mistaken song lyrics force a smile from the stoic Gard, expanding as he spots his server, a stunning redhead with the same big blue eyes as Harry.

Thankful she found the courage to leave her sadistic husband and move across the country, back to her hometown, Sabrina Hanklen feels confident she and Harry are safe. Harry's stuttering and developmental delay are the direct result of his father's cruelty.

Working as a server in her sister's café, she's distracted by the ruggedly handsome customer responding to her son in a kind, patient manner. Sabrina can't help wondering what life would be like with a good man like Gard in their lives.

Unfortunately, her idyllic daydreams are shattered by the sudden arrival of the one person she never wants to see again.

Heartwishes, Book 3: A grumpy knight in shining armor, fiercely brave heroine mom, precious little boy, beloved dog, heavenly angel, drama, humor, and an incredible Christmas miracle. This guaranteed HEA contemporary romance can be read as a standalone but is better appreciated when read in order.

Content Warning: contains scenes of child and domestic abuse.

~<>~

Turn the page to read Chapter 1 of The Firefighter's Heartwish...

The Firefighter's Heartwish: Chapter 1

~<>~

"HANG ON, TIM. I've got you. I won't let go." Coiling the rope around one hand and arm, Gard Malone held the cord tight with both hands, determined not to let his closest friend fall to his death. "Wally's getting an extra rope so you can prusik up the second line."

"Can't do it, Gard. Feels like both legs and one of my arms are broken. Can't really move... back might be broken too. I'm hanging here like a damn, useless rag doll."

Hearing the extent of Tim's injuries, Gard shuddered. Tim was so far down the yawning crevasse Gard couldn't see him. He could barely even hear him.

"Can you see a ledge?"

"Nothing," Tim answered. "There's no support. Just a straight drop."

As experienced glaciologists, Gard and his crew knew the importance of avoiding falls. More importantly, they knew it was easier to stay out of Antarctica's crevasses than to rescue someone from one of the icy, yawning chasms.

Nonetheless, Tim McKevitt had plummeted deep into a crevasse. Hidden beneath a thin bridge of blown snow only a few inches thick, the fissure had been invisible and the bridge wouldn't support the weight of a man.

"Stay with me, buddy. We'll get you out of there," Gard promised. "Jack and Tom are on the way with more rescue gear."

Gard felt a hand on his shoulder. "Gard, the lip of the crevasse looks ready to collapse at any moment," their fellow glaciologist, Wally, warned him in a subdued voice not loud enough for Tim to hear. "Tim's too far down. It's too dangerous. We'll lose both of you."

"Damn it, Wally, I've got to save him. If we don't get him out of there soon hypothermia's going to set in." They'd radioed the other two members of the crew at the research station, apprising them of the dire situation. Gard prayed they got there in time to help haul Tim out because he didn't know how much longer he could hold Tim's weight.

"Jesus, look at your hands," Wally noted.

Friction from the rope had torn through Gard's two pairs of gloves, leaving him with bloodied hands. Gard could tell his shoulder was dislocated and he had other injuries, but tending to his own wounds would have to wait. If he eased up on his hold he'd lose Tim.

They'd all worn proper safety equipment, including crash helmets and full body harnesses, tied to heavy ropes as well as to each member of the trekking team which, in this case, amounted to only Gard and Tim. With a broken arm and rib due to an equipment accident, Wally wasn't able to assist in holding Tim's weight.

Tim's fall was stopped by the ropes before he reached the bottom of the crevasse. The problem with this cavity was its boundless depth and lack of ledges or footholds of any kind. Without Tim having a foothold, Gard held Tim's full dead weight as the man hung suspended.

There was only one thing Gard thought of that might help at this point. "Wally, you think you can help me build an anchor so I can transfer Tim's weight and rappel down?"

"Yeah, I think so. But you can't—"

"I'm going to anchor and rappel down, Tim," Gard called down the chasm.

"No!" Tim hollered. "Too dangerous. Listen, Gard, I'm—"

The horrific sound of Tim shouting out as he slid further down the icy crevasse, along with the snapping sound of cracking ice, chilled Gard to his marrow. Tim's deep cry of anguish grew more distant as he fell.

"Tim?" Dead silence. "Tim! Don't give up, man, I'm not going to let you die, you hear me? I'm going to get you out of there."

"It's no use. I'm done, Gard," Tim called from what seemed like miles away. "The rope was sliced on the last fall...not going to hold. Love you, buddy. Don't blame yourself. Tell Laila I love her and—"

The sound of Tim McKevitt falling deep into the abyss was bloodcurdling.

"Tim! Tim, hold on, I've got you!"

But Gard didn't have him. All he held in his torn hands now was a weightless length of rope...with no one attached at the other end.

"I've got you, Tim, I've got you!" Gard yelled, abruptly sitting, snapping to attention from his deep sleep and the same nightmare he'd had frequently for the last three years. Drenched in sweat, he raised his knees, resting his elbows on them as he cradled his head in his hands.

His mind still gauzy from sleep, he growled his anguish from the depth of his soul, blaming himself for being unable to save the life of his best friend and his sister's fiancé.

"Home...Glassfloat Bay..." Gard muttered to himself as a reminder. "I'm here...I'm here..."

Plowing his fingers through his hair, he expelled a deep breath, glancing at the pills on his nightstand, one bottle to control anxiety and the other for pain. He kept them there just in case. There were times he was tempted to pop a couple of pills, but he hated resorting to them. They didn't do much to ease his pain or anxiety anyway, unless he took the maximum dosage at least. He'd learned early on that the more he took, the more he needed to get the same effect.

For a guy who disliked polluting his body with something as innocuous as aspirin or ibuprofen, Gard knew prescription meds weren't the answer. Developing a dependency on pills would only create more problems.

His best buddy chose that moment to leap onto the bed, eagerly nuzzling Gard with his wet nose.

"Hey, Tundra, how's my boy? Happy to be back home and out of that bone chilling cold, I'll bet, huh?" He mussed the dog's short black and tan fur and patted his flanks. Tundra went everywhere with Gard, even on his assignments to Antarctica. This last job was a four month stint. They'd been home for a week now. Having Tundra at his side while he was healing from his injuries three years ago and climbing out of the depths of despair, had helped Gard every bit as much as the medication the hospital docs had pumped into him.

Gard's gaze slid to the digital alarm clock. It was five thirty. "Looks like you've decided it's a good time for our morning run." Tundra answered with a long lick up the side of Gard's face. The sizeable canine came from a long line of oversized mutts. It was the family joke that their dogs were part German Shephard, part donkey.

Catching a glimpse of himself in the bathroom mirror as he brushed his teeth, Gard made note of his shaggy appearance. His blond hair was well overdue for a cut and the scruffy stubble across his cheeks and chin made him look like a bum. If it were up to him he'd just let the hair and beard grow wild but then he'd be hounded by his mother who'd be convinced he looked like a bum because he was depressed. Maybe she was right. But the last thing he wanted was to do anything that might trigger her motherly scrutiny.

Once outside Bekka House, the family home, Gard jogged the half-mile to the ocean, his faithful dog keeping pace beside him. Along the way he noticed Bekka House was the only place without holiday lights twinkling against the pre-dawn indigo sky. He smiled, recalling how the people in town wasted no time getting fully into the holiday spirit. There was no escaping Christmas in Glassfloat Bay.

It was two days after Thanksgiving. In the past, the day after Thanksgiving marked the annual Malone family Christmas decorating frenzy. He and his entire family would pull out all stops to decorate every nook and cranny, inside and out, of the main family home as well as the homes of everyone else in the family. But yesterday he skipped it. All he'd wanted to do was hole up and pretend it was just like any other day of the year. He used to love Christmas but the holiday had lost its luster for him.

His sister, Laila, told him decorations started popping up at the mall right after Halloween this year. Santa had arrived the first week of November, complete with an elaborate setup including pricey photos with Santa as well as T-shirts and other products for sale.

"That's crazy," he said as he ran. "Next thing you know Santa will be sharing space with the Easter Bunny." The money-grubbing aggrandizement of what used to be a joyous, family-oriented time of year disgusted him.

Even so, he knew he needed to get some damn lights strung before his parents and siblings arrived en masse, wearing their godawful Christmas sweaters knitted by his yarn-happy sister Maureen, and gleefully encouraging him to get into the Christmas spirit. He could picture them all singing carols as his brother-in-law, Varik, strummed his guitar.

His mom, Astrid, would have her trusty, decades-old Kodak Instamatic camera in hand, snapping away to memorialize the family gathering just as she did each holiday...and pretty much any other time the opportunity for picture-taking arose. She vastly preferred *real photographs* you could touch and put in a photo album, to those from a phone.

They'd pass cups of eggnog, spiked cocoa, and hot mulled wine while making merry, threading popcorn, baking ginger cookies, and decorating the family house from top to bottom.

And every one of them would be focused on making Gard feel better.

God how he hated that.

As much as he loved his family, being around them all for Thanksgiving dinner two nights ago was tough. So many questions, so much concern, endless hugs and kisses and positive, encouraging words.

It felt overwhelming, smothering, invasive.

And then there was all the well-intentioned nudging about Gard finding a good woman for himself, along with a full roster of suggestions of all the single prospects in Glassfloat Bay as well as neighboring Wisdom Harbor. He wasn't interested. Not only was getting involved in another relationship not at the top of his list of priorities, it didn't even make the list. He was perfectly happy being a bachelor. Good old loyal Tundra was the only companion he needed.

The best part of Thanksgiving was seeing Laila so happy with her husband, Zak, and their baby twins, his niece and nephew, Abby and Gus. For the past three years it had been damned hard looking her in the face after he'd failed to save her fiancé. Of course, Laila would never blame him for what happened. Neither did anyone else he knew...but that didn't make it any easier for Gard, who still shouldered a weighty sense of responsibility and guilt for the loss of Tim's life.

Fortunately his sister, Kady, was supposed to be arriving from her overseas backpacking trip soon. That should help take the focus off Gard. His globetrotting little sister had left on her latest trip shortly after moving from Chicago to Glassfloat Bay so the family would be scrambling to show her the town. She'd be staying in one of the bedrooms at Bekka House but Kady usually kept pretty much to herself so Gard wouldn't have to worry too much about endless chitchat.

With each footfall, he watched the gentle morning waves roll in and out. Relaxing. Hypnotic. Meditative. A helluva lot better than trudging through the snow in his hometown of Chicago, or freezing his ass off in Antarctica.

"I've got to get my shit together and stop being the poster boy for the anguished," he decided.

Gard remembered a time when he was fully on board with all the Christmas jollity. He bought into the magic of it all, loved seeing the awed looks on kids' faces waiting in line to sit on Santa's lap. Heck, he was even Glassfloat Bay Mall's Santa the year before the Antarctica tragedy. Sure it was hot as hell under all the padding necessary to puff out his lean muscled frame but how could he mind when he saw the kids' joy and excitement?

Back then, the Christmas spirit boldly had Gard in its grip as he enjoyed being in charge of spicing and spiking the anticipated wassail and eggnog.

But now? Now he'd much rather escape into a good first-person shooter videogame than be bothered by all the frivolity.

"Jeez...I've turned into Scrooge. Or is it the Grinch? Probably both. Yeah, no doubt about it, I've become the Scrinch."

Focus...he needed to focus on the moment. It was one of the tips he'd learned from his sessions with the therapist. He'd resisted therapy, convinced it was for weaklings and losers who were looking for excuses; for somewhere or someone to place blame rather than accept responsibility for their own decisions. Once it became clear he wouldn't be able to get his well-meaning mother and stepfather off his back, Gard finally agreed to see a psychologist who worked as a counselor at Wisdom Harbor University.

He could admit today, albeit grudgingly, that his mom and stepdad were right. The twice a month therapy sessions, which were unlike anything he'd expected, had made a positive difference. He only wished he'd started them earlier.

Just let the anxiety go, like sand sifting through your fingers until it's all adrift in the wind, Dr. Rikard Svenningsen told him. Gard did just that, paying attention to the birth of a new day. There was nothing as majestic as dawn, when the sun climbed over the horizon, painting the sky with swashes of pink, gold and purple as it rose to greet the day...unless it was the magic of a Northwest Pacific coastline sunset.

Ever vigilant and well-trained by his mom and sisters, Gard kept his eyes open for glass floats, agates, and sand dollars as he leapt over driftwood logs on the way to the shore. He'd been lucky to find a host of objects for their collections on his early morning runs.

A moment later Tundra took off, happily chasing a pack of cawing seagulls cruising and diving in search of breakfast. Breathing the salty air as he watched his dog romp in the wet sand, Gard felt the last vestiges of his nightmare dissipate.

"Home...Glassfloat Bay. I'm here...I'm here..." Gard again muttered his helpful mantra, designed to help keep him in the here and now.

Running in the sand with the early morning breeze in his hair and the waves softly crashing along the shore made him feel alive. Cleansed. Even hopeful. Dwarfed by the rising sun, he smiled, remembering to give thanks for being alive and able to experience the magnificence of dawn.

"Yeah, this is far better medicine than any damn pills."

Ever his loyal pal, the returning Tundra agreed with a companionable bark.

~<>~

"You haven't heard a thing I've said."

"That's nice, dear."

"Varik!" Delaney Jenssen rapped her knuckles on the table, rattling the vintage Santa and Mrs. Claus ceramic salt and pepper shakers she'd recently found at a church rummage sale.

Her husband blinked, almost looking surprised that his wife sat across the kitchen table from him. "I'm sorry, hon, I guess I was distracted. Did you say something?"

"I was asking why you've been sitting there staring into space while twisting that ring on your finger for the last twenty minutes.

Your poached eggs must be ice cold by now. Sweetheart, is something wrong?"

"No. No, it's just that..." Varik gazed up at Delaney who was sipping her coffee. "Gard's been on my mind lately."

"My brother?" Delaney's shoulders slumped as she lowered her mug. "Me too." She worried her bottom lip while twisting her napkin. "I'm afraid he'll never be the same. All this time and he still blames himself for Tim's death."

"I know." Varik nodded, expelling a lengthy breath. "I worry about him too. He's been working so hard without a break for too long, no doubt to help keep his mind off the accident."

"If he's not out there in that frozen wasteland," Delaney said, "freezing his butt off for humanity, doing whatever the heck it is that's apparently so damned important for global warming, Gard's here risking his life as a firefighter, picking up anyone's shift who asks."

She looked up from wringing her hands. "I-I'm almost afraid my brother has a death wish the way he takes on one dangerous duty after another."

"Don't think like that, Delaney." Varik reached across the table, patting his wife's hand. "Your brother has problems but he's not that screwed up."

Delaney wasn't so sure. After failing to save the life of Laila's fiancé, Gard had been plagued with nightmares. That is, when he could sleep at all. The doctors said he was suffering from PTSD. During the treacherous rescue attempt, Gard nearly died himself, sustaining serious injuries in the process that kept him hospitalized for a small eternity.

"He'd probably be a lot further along if he hadn't been so stubborn about seeing a therapist," Delaney said.

"True, but at least he finally agreed to see Dr. Svenningsen. I think his appointments have made a big difference, don't you?"

"I do. Laila and Reen think so too." Delaney nodded. "Rikard's given Gard some excellent advice. I'm glad Tore recommended him—and thankful as all hell that Gard finally agreed to start seeing him. Seriously, that brother of mine can be so stubborn!"

"Just like his sister." Varik snickered while Delaney lifted an eyebrow. "When Tore told me Svenningsen counsels the professors as well as the students at WHU," Varik gave a thumbs up, "I knew he was the one. The fact that my colleague is a fellow Norwegian didn't hurt either."

"Naturally." Delaney gave him a knowing smile. She was thankful Gard thought the world of Tore Thorkelson, Varik's cousin and their mom's second husband.

Absently watching her vintage black cat wall clock with its moving eyes and swinging tail, her thoughts returned to that awful time more than three years ago.

To no one's surprise, Gard had gone above and beyond in his attempt to save Laila's fiancé. He came home with badly torn hands, a broken arm, dislocated shoulder, three broken ribs and injuries to his spine and legs. At least he'd made it home alive. It was during his hospitalization, when Gard was still in critical condition, that his fiancée, Joanne—just the thought of her made Delaney bristle—left him for another man, claiming she didn't feel strong enough to cope with Gard's multitude of physical or emotional wounds.

"You're thinking about Joanne again," Varik said, taking Delaney by surprise.

"How did you know?"

"You get that certain narrow-eyed look when she's on your mind." He chuckled. "It was three years ago. You need to let go, Delaney. How can you expect Gard to get over what happened if you can't?"

"I know, I know." Delaney sighed. "It's just that every time I think about how she was cheating on my brother when he was working so hard in Antarctica to make money for that monstrously expensive wedding she wanted..." She growled her annoyance. "And then that lame excuse she gave about being unfaithful because she hated being alone," she said, imitating Joanne's sorrowful voice, "ugh! I swear, Varik, I want to punch her lights out." Delaney's eyes narrowed again as she folded her arms across her chest. "Selfish little bitch."

"You won't get any argument from me." Varik rubbed his wife's arm. "Just remember it was far better for Gard to find out Joanne was a self-centered two-timer, *before* rather than after they were married."

"Amen. Talk about a nightmare." Delaney shuddered. "Can you imagine having her as our sister-in-law? The thought makes my skin crawl."

Varik rose from the table to dump out his cold coffee and pour himself and Delaney a fresh cup. "I've heard around town that Joanne's got her sights set on Hudson Griffin."

"What?" Delaney bristled. "Well I'm just going to have to have a talk with Hud to let him know what—"

"You'll do no such thing my little Vengeance Queen." Standing behind Delaney, Varik enveloped her in his arms, kissing the top of her head. "Hud and Gard are good friends. He knows what Joanne did. He's not about to forget what she put your brother through."

"Yes but men don't always think with their brains," she pointed out. "And don't bother denying it because we both know it's true."

"I wouldn't dream of denying it." He leaned further to give Delaney a kiss on the cheek while snaking his hand down the front of his wife's nightshirt. "In fact my second brain is contemplating the two of us going back to bed and—"

"There, you see?" Delaney slapped Varik's hand away. "Typical man." She tsked while pointing a chastising finger. "How you can shift from discussing poor Gard's PTSD to us making whoopee just like that," she snapped her fingers, "is beyond me. Women's brains don't work that way, so you can just forget about it, Romeo."

"What can I say? Guilty as charged." Varik's gentle laughter filled the kitchen's eating area. "Trust me," he gave her another kiss on the cheek as he whisked away Delaney's breakfast plate, "Joanne won't be getting her hooks into Hudson."

"I hope not."

"And your *poor brother*," he hung quotes around the phrase, "is a grown man who can take care of himself just fine without all his sisters incessantly mollycoddling him. Now finish your coffee and get dressed," Varik went on, ignoring his wife's indignant gasp. "We promised Laila we'd get over to her bakery this morning to help get the place decorated for Christmas."

"Christmas..." Delaney was silent for a long moment. "You know, we've barely seen Gard since he's been home. Did you see how quickly he snuck out after Thanksgiving dinner the other night? And he didn't participate in the annual family decorating festivities yesterday either. I think he's avoiding us." Varik muttered something beneath his breath. "What was that?"

"Nothing, dear."

"Gard can't keep this pace up, Varik. He needs some downtime...preferably with his family, to remind him of the closeness we share, the love we all have for him. Otherwise I worry something will happen to him, being as overtired as he must be. It's like he's daring the universe to stop him." Used to being optimistic and positive, Delaney hated hearing herself sound so fragile and negative.

"I promise, everything's going to be okay." Varik's voice brimmed with assurance.

"You're just saying that to make me feel better. I know you're just as worried as I am." Filled with hope mixed with melancholy, Delaney sighed.

"I wasn't just trying to placate you." Varik's smile was broad and genuine. "I meant it. Things are about to change for Gard."

Delaney slanted her head in question.

The sound of their baby girl's cry distracted them both.

"I'll get her," Varik said. He was back in a few minutes, cradling little Rebekka Anders Jenssen while gently nudging her chubby cheeks and making baby talk colored by his Norwegian accent.

Delaney smiled. Her husband adored their child and definitely had a way with the baby. He knew just what to do to calm her and stop her fussing. They'd named their daughter after Delaney's grandma, Bekka, and Varik's grandpa, Anders.

"What did you mean about things changing for Gard?" she asked. "You mean because Kady's due back from her trip and will be staying at Bekka House with him?"

"No..." After placing Rebekka in her bouncy seat, Varik sat at the table again, holding his hand aloft. Delaney saw it—the gentle radiance of the heartwish ring on her husband's finger.

"It-it's glowing. For Gard?" she asked.

Varik nodded. "I've known Gard was destined to be the next in line for a while now. I just didn't know when. When I woke up this morning I realized it's time. The knowing was there," he clutched his abdomen, "just like it happened for you when it was time to pass your ring to Laila."

"It's not going to be easy convincing him." Delaney screwed her expression. "He thinks the heartwish rings are...what was it he called it?"

"Supernatural woo-woo nonsense." Varik laughed.

"If he'd been home instead of Antarctica when Laila found her genie in that old perfume bottle, Gard would have—"

"Honey, listen to yourself." Varik gave Delaney's hand a gentle squeeze. "We lived through it, know it's a fact, and it even sounds preposterous to me. How the hell can we expect your level-headed facts and figures glaciologist brother to believe one of his sisters is married to a former genie? As far as Gard's concerned, we all just got carried away with the idea and romanticized a bunch of coincidences, accepting them as fact."

"But that's not true. Gard met Zak for himself, Varik. He heard all about his genie experience directly from Zak, not just from us. Plus he's seen that exquisite Victorian building Laila lives in now. How can his sister owning that place possibly be explained other than by magic? By Laila making one of her three wishes for the house?"

"Your brother is convinced Zak's an eccentric billionaire, that's how."

With her gaze solidly fixed on her husband's expression, Delaney finally broke into a smile, which expanded into a laugh. "Okay, yeah, I guess it does sound pretty farfetched. If only Gard had been here when it happened. If only he could have seen the magic for himself. If only—"

"Shoulda, woulda, coulda," Varik said. "It didn't work out that way. Once the ring works its magic for Gard, he'll be a believer too."

"You're right." Rising from the table, Delaney nodded, a thrill of anticipation coursing through her veins. "We'll invite him for dinner one night this week. I'll ask Mom and Tore to come too. Then you can pass the ring on to Gard. Oh I feel so much better already." She grabbed her phone from the kitchen counter. "Want me to text him?"

"Sure. Just make sure you don't mention anything about the magic heartwish ring, because I guarantee your brother will make an excuse not to come."

~<>~

And So, Dear Reader,

You've finished reading The Genie's Heartwish, a Daisy Dexter Dobbs book that (*fingers crossed and hopeful sigh*) you were sorry to see end. Meanwhile I, author DDD, am gleefully clacking away at my keyboard, writing yet another sensational, utterly phenomenal (*please don't burst my bubble*) book. I'd like to conclude our time together with a heartfelt THANK YOU for choosing to read this book, the 2nd in my Heartwishes series.

I hope this magical love story brightened your day, providing laughter along with a few tears. I did far more research for this book about Laila and Zak than any other I've written. It took me a small eternity to finish writing this genie story because of all the time I spent looking things up and getting sucked down one rabbit hole after another. I had to be sure I had all my facts about ancient Sumer, the earliest known civilization, and the Sumerians as accurate as possible.

Writing about a hero, a warrior, who unwittingly becomes a genie, was so rewarding. There was additional research involved as I wrote about each time period Zak visited over his thousands of years of captivity.

My characters often wake me in the middle of the night with ideas, suggestions, and criticism. My genie, Zak, was responsible for disturbing my sleep numerous times with grievances about his character—*a true warrior wouldn't do this; a Sumerian wouldn't say that; an alpha male would act this way instead*—but, come on, how can I complain when a gorgeous warrior pops into my dreams to school me? LOL

~<>~

If you enjoyed The Genie's Heartwish I'd be delighted if you left a positive review or rating on the site where you purchased it. (Not that I check daily for new reviews, or ever Google myself, or do anything else indicating I'm an insecure creative person craving validation. Nope, nothing like that.) Your review can be long, short, or just a star rating. Reviews help other readers find my books, and keep my stories from getting lost in a site's complicated algorithms. Plus, it gives me encouragement to keep on writing!

Speaking of other readers, you can help them find this book by recommending it to your friends, neighbors, relatives, coworkers, your dentist, doctor, mail carrier, all the strangers you meet in the grocery store, at the mall, the neighborhood pub, your favorite coffee shop, and, of course, everyone you know online. (I'm ready with additional suggestions if needed.)

Thanks again! Wishing you love, laughter, romance and happy reading!

—*Daisy Dexter Dobbs*

~<>~

DAISY DEXTER DOBBS BOOK LIST

SERIES

Heartwishes

Small town Contemporary Romance / Romantic Comedy (spice level: mild to medium)

Family legend says the magical heartwish ring was given to the matriarch of a Viking king by Odin, the most powerful of Norse gods. It must be held against the heart when making a sincere heartwish and will remain on the finger until it's time to pass it on. Though the mind may be cluttered and uncertain, the heart knows the right wish to make. Always trust your heart.

(Can be read as standalones but better appreciated when read in order so you can get to know all the characters and fall in love with the Malones!)

The Viking's Heartwish (Book 1: Delaney and Varik)
The Genie's Heartwish (Book 2: Laila and Zak)
The Firefighter's Heartwish (Book 3: Gard and Sabrina)
The Knitter's Heartwish (Book 4: Reen and Drake)
The Nymph's Heartwish (Book 5: Nevan and Aladee)
The Psychic's Heartwish (Book 6: Kady and Rylan)
The Daughter's Heartwish (Book 7: Bekka and Jamie – coming soon)
And at least 2 more Heartwishes titles are planned

~<>~

The Drakos Brothers

(releasing summer of 2024)

Small town Contemporary Romance / Romantic Comedy (spice level: scorching-hot and hilarious)

Bold, opinionated Greek men, the Drakos brothers star in this hot, hot, HOT laugh out loud romantic comedy series featuring lots of hunky, delicious Greek men and the women who capture their alpha male hearts. (Can be read as standalones but better appreciated when read in order so you can get to know all the characters.)

Trained by the Greek (Book 1: Jordan and Riley)
Vexed by the Greek (Book 2: Dino and Sophie)
Bossed by the Greek (Book 3: Sebastian and Ardine)
Conned by the Greek (Book 4: Benedict and Angel)
(additional stories for more brothers coming)

~<>~

STANDALONES
Don't Even Think About It (Mindy and Archer)
Laugh-out-loud Romantic Comedy (spice level: scorching-hot and hilarious)
Avowed chocoholic Mindy handles her upside-down life with as much grace and aplomb as possible—by attempting chocolatcide. This steamy, spicy, laugh-out-loud, award-winning romantic comedy novel is brimming with love, snappy banter, sexy inventive scenes that sizzle, and numerous naughty words.

~<>~

MORE SERIES AND STANDALONES
COMING SOON FROM DAISY
Daisy has written close to 100 novels and numerous novellas and short stories over the last few decades. She certainly can't have novels full of pay phones, answering machines, landlines, no email, or the internet, or social media now, can she? Nope, nope, nope. Of course not. So now that she has the rights back to all of her books and stories from her previous publishers, she's been hard at work

rewriting and updating her books for release as an indie author. Revisiting umpteen stories featuring gorgeous, handsome, oh-so-sexy hunks is a tough job, but somebody's gotta do it. So here's a sneak peek at just some of the dozens of titles Daisy's been maniacally, um, I mean, *diligently*, working on (check her website and newsletter for updates!).

~<>~

Visit DaisyDexterDobbs.com[1] for a full, up-to-date listing of Daisy's books. Sign up for Daisy's newsletter and mailing list to get notifications for new book releases, contests, and more.

~<>~

---

1. https://www.daisydexterdobbs.com

About the Author

A born storyteller, Daisy Dexter Dobbs started writing stories at five, satisfying her inner ham by reading them aloud, using a toilet plunger as a microphone. Today, Daisy creates written voyages of the imagination, infused with love, laugh-out-loud comedy, friendships, family and guaranteed happy endings. Some of her books include paranormal and fantasy elements. And some books are scorching HOT on the spice scale.

Having worked at more than 40 different jobs provides Daisy with a ridiculous amount of questionable experience to draw on for her characters. She's been: a ghostwriter for politicians; a library art director; a weight loss counselor; mayor's executive secretary; a Realtor; travel agent; editor; and a butcher's meat wrapper, quitting after she spotted a big eyeball coming toward her on the conveyor.

A Chicago native, Daisy and her husband, now live in the Pacific Northwest. Happily, Daisy no longer feels the need to use a bathroom plunger as a microphone when entertaining.

You can find Daisy here:
Facebook: DaisyDexterDobbs
Instagram: DaisyDexterDobbs
TikTok: @daisydexterdobbs
Amazon: Daisy Dexter Dobbs
Goodreads: daisydexterdobbs
BookBub: Daisy-Dexter-Dobbs
Twitter/X: DaisyDDobbs
Threads: @DaisyDexterDobbs
Pinterest: DaisyDDobbs
Email: DaisyDexterDobbs@gmail.com
Read more at www.DaisyDexterDobbs.com.